BLOOD
REQUIEM

Also by Christopher Husberg

Duskfall
Dark Immolation

BLOOD REQUIEM

THE CHAOS QUEEN QUINTET

CHRISTOPHER HUSBERG

TITAN BOOKS

Blood Requiem
Print edition ISBN: 9781783299195
E-book edition ISBN: 9781783299201

Published by Titan Books
A division of Titan Publishing Group Ltd
144 Southwark Street, London SE1 0UP

First edition: June 2018
10 9 8 7 6 5 4 3 2 1

A CIP catalogue record for this title is available from the British Library.

Printed in the USA.

FOR JASON

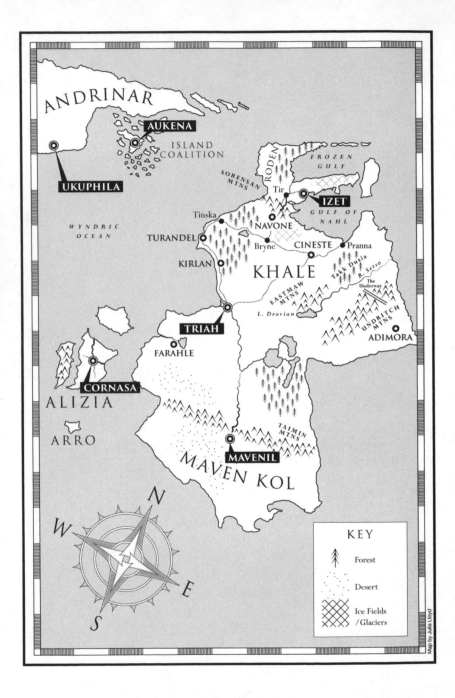

172nd Year of the People's Age, Turandel

ASTRID WOVE IN AND out of the shadows of Turandel's tower-houses silently. It was past midnight, and the Fingers—the five main streets of Turandel—were dark and quiet. Her eyes smoldered, and not just with her normal vampiric green glow.

She was out for vengeance.

Trave waited for her in an alley near Olin Cabral's tower-house, one eye glowing red, the other covered by a crude gray eyepatch. Astrid approached the vampire cautiously. Astrid had not seen Trave since he had helped her escape Cabral's cruelty months before. Despite his help then, she did not trust him. Not after all he had done.

But his proposal of revenge, of taking down Cabral's Fangs and releasing his slaves, was too tempting to pass up. She had been traveling south with the Odenites anyway—the new Church of Canta, as they called themselves now—and had figured she might as well see if Trave meant business.

The moment she saw him in the alleyway, jaw set, his eye glowing an angry red, she knew he did. And, behind his eye, the same obscure emotion she had noticed months ago. Fear, and… something else. She could not quite tell what.

"We're really going to do this, then?" she said without preamble.

"Cabral is not here. It should be easy enough."

Astrid stopped. "What do you mean *Cabral* isn't here? What is the point of this attack if we don't kill Cabral?" She couldn't believe he hadn't told her this. Of course, it'd be difficult to convey such news via messenger—Astrid hadn't exactly been stationary the past few weeks. Still.

"You really think the two of us could take on Cabral? Let alone with all of his Fangs?"

Astrid danced with impatience on the cobbled road. "We *might*," she said, knowing it wasn't true. Cabral had been a vampire longer than Astrid and Trave combined. He was not a simple foe.

Trave grunted. "I'll get us in. The Fangs are probably half-drunk by now."

Astrid followed him into the night.

Trave led the way into Olin Cabral's tower-house, using a jagged iron key to open the immense black double doors.

"Austere as ever, our Cabral," Astrid whispered as she observed the plain stone walls and flooring. Nary a rug, painting, or tapestry to be seen.

"Makes for easy upkeep, if nothing else," Trave said.

Cabral had a habit of accumulating art, only to destroy it, claiming it gave him power. Vampirism in another form.

"He expends more effort to procure the art and destroy it than he would if he simply cared for it," Astrid said. She was about to argue the point further when she heard footsteps approaching.

A young servant girl, fifteen summers at most, walked around the corner. She looked at them both, eyes stopping on Trave, and then she curtsied.

"Master Trave," the girl said. "I hope you found good fortune on your travels."

More than anything, Astrid wanted to reach out to the girl and lift her head, meet her eyes, offer a comforting touch. But Astrid was still a vampire, and the girl would see nothing but pain and peril.

Astrid recognized this one immediately as the same girl who had greeted her when she'd met with Cabral months ago. The girl's low-cut dress left little to the imagination both in terms of the skin and the scars it concealed with varying degrees of success. Raw bite marks and cuts covered rough scabs, which in turn covered multiple scars, some new and pink, others older, crisscrossing the girl's neck and chest.

Hot shame unexpectedly gushed through Astrid's body. Her earlier annoyance at Cabral's absence meant nothing. At least this time, she could do something to help.

"Do not be afraid," Astrid said. She could hardly hold in her anticipation, the breathless feeling of striking back against Cabral, against Astrid's own past. "Gather the rest of the servants. Go somewhere safe. This will be the last night of your captivity."

The young girl stared at her, wide-eyed. Then she shook her head. "I can take you both to the great hall, if you wish."

She must think this a trick. Astrid couldn't blame her; she'd been in this girl's shoes, once, and would have been equally suspicious. She turned to Trave.

"She needs to hear it from you."

Trave looked from Astrid to the servant girl, a sigh rasping through his throat. "I command you, girl. Gather the servants together and go back to your quarters. Wait for us there."

The girl curtsied. "Of course, Master Trave." She took a backwards step, but hesitated.

"*Go,*" Trave rasped.

The girl scampered off down the hallway.

Astrid and Trave climbed the stairs and found themselves in the same dark corridor Astrid remembered from last time, the light from the scattered torches absorbed by the black-painted stone walls and floor.

The moment Astrid walked into the great hall of Cabral's tower-house and saw five pairs of glowing red eyes staring at her, she knew something was wrong.

Had Trave betrayed her after all? Had all of this—his letting her go, luring her back here—been some elaborate game? Only two of Cabral's Fangs had fully transitioned through the curse when she'd last been here months ago. There were five vampires here, and four others in transition—their eyes yellow, their skin pale and clammy. Cabral had been busy, and his followers were growing in number. That could not be a good thing.

"What's the girl doing here, Trave?"

Astrid recognized the speaker as Grendine, a woman who had been in transition when Astrid had last visited Turandel. She was in transition no longer. A full vampire now, her eyes gleamed red in the dim light of the hall.

"I brought her back," Trave rasped, glaring at the Fangs.

"Trave," Astrid whispered, gripping his wrist. She was ready to break it with a twist of her arm, or at least attempt it, and run.

Trave looked down at her. Astrid wished she could read his expression.

"Cabral will be pleased," one of the other vampires said. "He has been worried about her."

"He won't have to worry anymore," Trave rasped. Just as Astrid was about to make a run for it, Trave flashed across the great hall, his glowing red eyes a blur as he collided with the vampire who had just spoken.

"Shit," Astrid muttered, but she sprang into action herself, going straight for Grendine. The woman's glowing red eyes widened, but she reacted quickly, attempting to sidestep. Astrid twisted in the air and crashed into the woman's shoulder, digging her claws into Grendine's arm.

"Trave," one of the other vampires shouted, "what in Oblivion—"

There was a smash, and the speaker was silenced.

"Trave, *did you know?*" Astrid shouted above Grendine's scream. The woman turned on Astrid, claws ready, but Grendine was a new vampire, and thankfully past her bloodlust phase. New vampires always made the mistake of relying on their newfound strength, and forgot how quickly they could actually move. Grendine swung at Astrid with enough force to punch a hole in the stone wall, but Astrid used the claws embedded in Grendine's other arm as leverage and scrambled around to her other side, running along the wall. She twisted Grendine's head around her neck with enough force to make it turn almost full circle.

"Know what?" Trave shouted back, voice hoarse, from across the hall.

"That there would bloody be *five* of them!" A broken neck was never enough to stop a vampire. Grendine was already beginning to regain consciousness, her head slowly twisting back into place.

"We can handle five," Trave said, and when Astrid glanced at him and saw he was taking on three vampires at once, she realized he was probably right. Astrid had learned a great deal about fighting vampires in the three-hundred-plus years she'd been around, but she had nothing on Trave.

Trave wielded two wooden stakes, one in each hand.

Sharpened wood could be far more effective than claws against vampires. While a stake couldn't quite kill a vampire, it could incapacitate it enough to make the killing possible. The three vampires had surrounded Trave, but he moved too quickly for them all, and soon had impaled one of his stakes in a vampire's neck. The vampire spluttered, his movement slowing substantially.

Astrid shivered. While Trave was no longer the monster who had tortured her, he was just as terrifying a fighter as he'd always been.

She turned back to Grendine, who let out a sudden gasp and sat up.

The fifth vampire crept along the wall behind her. She had watched him out of the corner of her eye since she had taken Grendine down. He, too, was clearly new to this. Stealth was good, but it was a terribly human tactic. Speed—at least the type of speed a vampire could summon—was far more effective than stealth.

When Astrid turned on the vampire behind her, plunging her long claws into his neck, the look of surprise on the man's face was palpable.

Astrid flexed the claws on her other hand, then wrapped them around the vampire's neck, plunging the needle-sharp points into his flesh. Vampire flesh was hard, stone-like at night, but another vampire's claws could reliably pierce through.

Now she squeezed, tearing through the vampire's neck, until her hand wrapped around his spine. Astrid gripped the bone with both hands and crushed it. She pulled back, her arms bloody to the elbows, and the vampire's head toppled to the floor.

While vampires could be wounded during the day, they healed quickly. Wooden stakes could incapacitate a vampire, but not kill. Sun and fire could burn a vampire to a senseless, nerveless, but still-conscious husk given enough time. But the only thing that could truly kill a vampire was decapitation.

Grendine stood shakily. Astrid did not give her the time to recover. She leapt from the table onto the woman's shoulders, wrapping her legs around Grendine's neck. She clamped both hands around Grendine's head, gripping her jaw, and *pulled*. It took a moment of effort, one of pure, screaming terror from Grendine, before she tore Grendine's head from her body. Astrid and the head tumbled to the ground.

Trave had staked another vampire, now facing the one who had spoken to him. This one was clearly a veteran. They moved quickly around one another, striking and rapidly retreating, looking for weaknesses.

Astrid was tempted not to interfere. She could let this play out, and then kill whoever emerged victorious. Trave deserved to die. He'd murdered hundreds, perhaps more. He'd been Astrid's personal torturer.

And yet, at least now, he was doing something good. He was helping Astrid, and, more importantly, he was helping the people trapped here in Cabral's tower-house. Trave's actions had to be worth something.

Astrid rushed at the remaining vampire, slamming into him from the side. He turned to her, growling, but Astrid let go and darted away just in time for Trave to leap onto the man with a stake in each hand. One plunged through the man's shoulder, the other through his heart. He struggled on the ground for a moment, before Trave finally showed him the mercy of decapitation. He and Astrid provided the same courtesy to the other two newer vampires Trave had been fighting.

"We need to get the servants out of here," Trave rasped.

Astrid's gaze rested on the fire burning in the hearth at the head of the great hall. The flames mesmerized her, reminding her of a time from long ago, and a promise of a time yet to come. She dreamt she was on a ship, and she dreamt of redemption.

Royal Palace, Mavenil, Maven Kol

King Gainil Destrinar-Kol observed the growing crowd of commoners in the Great Hall, his face grim. Today was an adjudication day, in which the royal family invited the commonfolk of Maven Kol to air their grievances, and receive judgment or counsel. Adjudication day occurred thrice each year, but until recently attendance had been poor. Gainil made it a point to offer obscure and unhelpful advice for expressly that purpose.

Today proved his efforts had been for naught.

Gainil stood, and immediately everyone else in the Great Hall—most of them commoners, hunkered down on the floor—stood with him.

He turned to Barain Seco, his friend and counselor. "Tell them we are convening to discuss the problem from which they apparently all suffer. When you've pacified them, meet me in the Decision Room. Bring your wife."

"Yes, Your Majesty." Barain bowed. He turned to address the crowd of confused commoners, while Gainil swept out of the room.

Moments later, he stood in the Decision Room, at the head of the great square table. A map of Maven Kol was etched onto the surface. The busts of the past kings of Maven Kol looked down on him in silent judgment. A fire burned merrily in the hearth, but even so, and despite his fur cloak, Gainil couldn't stop himself from shivering. It was cold for a spring day in Mavenil.

Captain Fedrick of Gainil's personal guard, the Scarabs, stood at the doorway to the Decision Room. Barain and his wife Jaila entered the room, their daughter Taira trailing behind them. The girl had grown into something quite beautiful; if she wasn't already betrothed to Gainil's son, he'd have thought about courting her himself.

His son, Alain, had also been summoned to the room, and arrived late, as usual. His son's presence was more of a formality. Gainil had all but lost hope that Alain could lead anything, let alone a nation. The boy was too nervous and soft-spoken. Despite being a man of nineteen years, he still seemed a child, afraid of everything.

Gainil only missed one person in the gathering, and that was Lailana, the woman he'd recently begun courting. She was from a minor noble house established on the southern edge of Maven Kol, and a woman of great cunning and beauty. Gainil saw no reason he would not marry her within the year. But Alain would probably see the courtship as an affront to his mother, dead now for sixteen years.

Gainil wiped his brow. Was he sweating? He could swear it had been cold in this room not a moment ago. "Canta's bloody bones, it's good to get out of that room. Now, what in Oblivion are we going to do about this madness everyone is going on about? It seems to be an epidemic."

"The reports continue to increase, Your Majesty," Jaila said. "And we're starting to get verifiable reports from noble families. We can no longer consider this a phenomenon fabricated by the deranged low-born; we must acknowledge its existence among our peers."

Peers. Normally Gainil would criticize such a term in his presence, but he let it go. He wanted to get to the bottom of this.

"Verifiable reports among the nobility? Specify, Lady Jaila."

"The Wastriders sent word of their daughter. She… she is the woman who attempted to take her own life a year ago, but was found just in time."

"Goddess," Gainil muttered. He'd almost forgotten about that. The girl had attempted to hang herself from her bedframe, but the servants found her before she could do the deed. "That was more than a year ago. What does that have to do with the current situation?"

"In addition to her depression significantly worsening," Jaila said, "she has also reportedly manifested some… some interesting side effects."

"Surely not more of this flooding nonsense."

"No," Jaila said slowly, "they say she can… she can manipulate earth and rock, Your Majesty."

Gainil laughed out loud. "Earth and rock? We should employ her in the sandstone quarry. Make some money off the madwoman."

Jaila smiled half-heartedly at the joke, and Barain forced a laugh. Some people didn't know real humor when it slapped them across the face.

"Wastrider is a minor house," Gainil said, waving his hand. "Is that the only report you've received?"

"No, Your Majesty, there have been a few others, more or less the same."

Alain cleared his throat, an irritating tic the lad had developed. Gainil ignored his son. He had no tolerance for silly insecurities.

He was definitely sweating now. If he'd been alone he would

have shed his fur cloak. Why was it so hot? "And none of you have any idea what in Oblivion is happening? What might be causing these incidents?"

Barain shrugged. "I still stand with the mass hallucination theory," he said. "No other reasonable explanation."

Alain cleared his throat again.

"Your Grace," Captain Fedrick said, stepping forward.

"Yes, Fedrick?"

"We have all heard tell of the troubles surrounding the Rodenese throne. But there are… darker, mystical rumors abounding from the same quarters. Rumors about daemons."

"Fedrick, Fedrick. If you're about to suggest these recent incidents are part of some daemonic curse, I might have to find a new captain."

"Of course not, Your Grace. I just wanted to… to make sure you were aware of the situation."

Gainil rolled his eyes. Was there no one in his entire kingdom that could tell him something useful?

He looked over his shoulder. "Would someone put out that bloody fire? It's like a furnace in here." The fire did not look nearly large enough to be causing this much heat.

"Father."

Gainil's eyebrows rose as Alain stepped forward. "Yes, boy? You have something to say?"

"I… I…"

Of course the lad couldn't get it out, whatever it was. "We haven't got all day. Either say your piece or shut up and let the grown-ups talk."

Alain cleared his throat. "I suppose I'm trying to say that it might be worth listening to some of these anecdotes. To entertain the idea that they might be true."

Gainil slammed his fist onto the map table. He was pushing the boy, but at this point he didn't care. If he had one of his supposed anxiety attacks again, so be it. "Alain, my boy, I give you opportunity after opportunity to show your quality, and you throw it away every time. Do you really think these rumors about people manipulating rivers and creeks to change their course, or causing miniature sand tornados, are true? Do you *really* believe that people have that capacity? We live in the real world, boy, not a fable."

"Father, I just—"

"That's the last I hear about it from you, boy. The next time you speak, it had better be something useful or insightful." Alain's eyes had stopped darting around the room, looking from person to person as they often did when he was nervous, and now the lad simply looked straight down at the ground.

"Yes—"

"*Alain!*" Gainil slammed his fist on the table again, and this time Alain looked up at him, met his eyes with a flash of anger. *Good*, Gainil thought. *It's about bloody—*

Gainil blinked. "Are those *sparks* in the air?" he asked. All around the Decision Room, orange and yellow flecks smoldered and crackled in the air.

Then, Alain began to groan.

"Boy, what in Oblivion is wrong with—"

His son's groan became a shout, and then a scream, and Gainil dove behind the table instinctively. Just as he did, a deafening shockwave of fire exploded through the room. The table shook, threatening to tear away from its bolted legs. Fire roared in the room, in tandem with Alain's scream.

Then, all was quiet.

But only for a moment. Slowly, Gainil peeked out from

behind the table, and saw his son lying on the ground, not moving. To one side of him, both Barain and Jaila were *on fire,* screaming, trying to beat the flames from their bodies. Their daughter, too, was alight and screaming, but Fedrick—more or less unscathed, comparatively—smothered the flames with his cloak.

Goddess rising, Gainil thought to himself. Perhaps those rumors were true, after all.

In a time within time, and a place without form, two entities shone in silence. One emitted a deep, burning crimson, the color of fire and the color of blood entwined together. The other's light glowed green, the green of a pine forest in winter and the green of an emerald jewel, multifaceted and shifting. Shadows darker than a moonless, starless sky danced within each of them.

Samann stared at the deep red flame that had once been his eldest brother. He could not think of the last time he had seen Mefiston's face. Millennia, at least. His brother's hair had once been black, his features hard and angular, but Samann could recall nothing beyond that. Not that it mattered. It was a face Samann would never see again, just as he would never again see his own.

"The others are late," Samann said, his voice reverberating through a time within time.

Mefiston said nothing.

The two siblings had never gotten along, but Mefiston could have at least done something more than wait silently, burning. Mefiston already had one of the greatest powers of the Nine; fueled by rage, anger, and warfare, he was physically the most formidable of them all. Samann would gladly take on such powers instead of his own, were he given the chance. He certainly wouldn't be so rude to his brothers, if that were the case.

As Samann and Mefiston waited, their fiery lights slowly took distinct shape. Even in this form, Mefiston stood tall, his frame wide and imposing, contrasting sharply against Samann's wiry build. Around them was nothing, and yet everything at once. Samann had learned to tune out the cacophonous blur, instead focusing on the space immediately around him. A space in which a new, yellow light began to take shape, marred by the same shadows that twisted within Mefiston and Samann himself.

"Iblin," Samann said, greeting his brother. "It's about time."

The yellow light grew larger and larger. Mefiston was huge, but even he was not as massive as Iblin. Of course, while Mefiston was made of muscle, Iblin's size was all in his girth.

"Azael is not yet here?" Iblin asked.

"He'll make us wait. As he always does," Mefiston replied.

Another light appeared, blue this time. Luceraf.

Before they could greet the new arrival, blackness engulfed them. Samann took a deep breath. As much as he hated being around Mefiston, he hated being around Azael even more. He was immune to his siblings' influence, with the exception of Azael's. Whenever Azael was around, Samann could not help but be afraid.

"What's the matter, little brother?" Mefiston laughed, the sound strained.

Samann took satisfaction in the waver of Mefiston's voice. Even the eldest of them could not fully withstand Azael's influence.

"Took you long enough," Iblin whined, his voice high and reedy.

Samann heard Iblin scream, but could see nothing through the darkness. Samann shivered. What had possessed Iblin to speak to Azael in such a way, he could not guess.

Slowly, the blackness faded, and then Azael stood before them. Azael did not emit light like the rest of them, but swallowed it into himself, and the very shadows that writhed and twisted in Samann's green form extended slowly out towards Azael, drawn by his presence.

"Where are our other sisters?" Mefiston asked. "And where is our brother Hade?"

"Hade made his move too early," Azael said. "His avatar was defeated in Alizia."

Mefiston growled. "I *told* the fool he needed to wait."

You'd think the embodiment of death would have more patience, Samann thought. He said nothing, of course. His brothers would never tolerate him criticizing Hade, even if he was right.

"You are sure it was just his avatar that was defeated?" Luceraf asked slowly.

"I am sure," Azael said, his voice hard. "Hade survived. But at least some of the creatures that walk the Sfaera now know our avatars are vulnerable. We need to be careful. We must time our incarnations perfectly going forward."

Azael, not Hade, had been the first of them to lose an avatar. But Samann held his tongue, as he knew his other siblings would. Azael claimed the defeat had been part of his plan, but had yet to share exactly how it benefited them.

"We should act quickly," Mefiston said. "Nadir, too, has claimed an avatar. It cannot be long until she is discovered."

"You know the rules, Mefiston," Azael said. "Hade cannot claim a new avatar until he has regenerated. That will take some time. And in order for us all to take our true forms in the Sfaera, we must first all have avatars."

After that, they would each enter the Sfaera through their respective avatars. The only thing that could stop them at that point was one of their avatars dying.

"But Nadir—"

"Nadir can handle herself. She has always been more subtle than Hade, and far more capable."

"Enough," Luceraf said, her blue light burning brighter. "We did not come here to argue. What of Bazlamit and Estille?"

Luceraf hadn't secured an avatar yet, either, but Samann was not about to point that out. Iblin he could handle. Luceraf was another matter.

"Estille continues her work in Triah," Azael said. "Her avatar is actually *affecting* her populace. I will not distract her from that. And Bazlamit is close to securing her avatar. She has targeted someone of great importance, and could not be called away."

"And the Betrayer?" Mefiston asked.

Silence reigned in a time within time. Only Mefiston would have the courage—or the stupidity—to broach this subject with Azael himself.

"The Betrayer remains bound, though she still has influence. Bazlamit, if she is successful, will have some influence there. Luceraf, you are working in that area as well, are you not?"

"I am," Luceraf said. "I believe I am close."

"Good. Mefiston, you're already infiltrating the Legion. If all goes according to plan, they will be deployed soon. Iblin, you are working in Cornasa?"

"Yes," the huge man said. His light had shaped itself into the monstrously fat figure that Samann had grown accustomed to seeing. While he had vague memories of Mefiston's appearance, he could not recall how Iblin looked before the Betrayal, try as he might.

"And I am moving south. I will soon have an avatar of my own once more."

"How long will it take for Hade to regain his strength?" Luceraf asked. "We each need to have an avatar claimed in order to physically enter the Sfaera."

"Focus on your own work," Azael said. "Hade's regeneration will be complete soon enough. That is why we have this place. In the meantime, it is time we awakened the Outsiders."

Samann perked up at that.

"We can't control them," Iblin warned.

"They'll destroy," Mefiston replied. "That's all we need."

"You have enough of a following?" Samann asked. To bring in Outsiders to the Sfaera, they needed acolytes. You could not have one without the other.

"I have enough to begin," Azael said.

Samann breathed a sigh of relief. At least Azael had answered him. As the youngest, Samann found himself ignored all too often.

He could not doubt Azael, however. The Fear Lord had been the only one of the Nine to have any influence over the Sfaera over the past few millennia. All of the other siblings, Samann included, had been completely cut off after the Betrayal, until now.

"I shall inform my acolytes," Azael said. "I know just where to begin."

Samann could not see Azael's face, only his dark outline, but he could swear his brother was smiling.

PART I

NEVER A RIGHT CHOICE

1

Pranna, northern Khale

As the sun rose on the port side, Winter could finally see Pranna's Big Hill rising up from the gulf, familiar tiny outlines of buildings framed against the brightening sky. The hill was green—the snowmelt and rain had been kind this year—and reminded Winter of the many summers she'd spent sailing, returning to this same scene.

With help from her telenic powers, the ship tacked to starboard. The *Empress Radiant* had been close-hauled all night, but Winter had gotten them through it, and seeing the familiar horizon of her home was worth the exhaustion in her limbs. Winter stood at the ship's wheel while her invisible *tendra* stabilized the boom, took in the sails, and held lines as necessary. The simultaneous burn and chill of *faltira* flowed through her veins. The drug, more commonly known as frostfire, allowed Winter access to her telenic *tendra*—invisible extensions of herself that she could use to interact with any non-living object within range. In this case, almost every part of the *Empress Radiant*. Her traveling companions, Urstadt and Galcc, helped when they could, but Winter found she could pilot the ship by herself quite easily, even through difficult maneuvers. She wished she could show her father the adeptness with which she controlled the ship.

Truth be told, it felt good to use psimancy for something other than violence.

Footsteps creaked on the deck behind her.

"That is your home?" Urstadt asked as she walked up beside Winter.

At the bow of the ship, Galce ran to the port rail just in time to empty his stomach into the waves. The tailor had not taken well to the sea, but it had been his choice to accompany her on the voyage from Izet. He had proven a passable sailor, with some training. And frequent breaks.

If Galce struggled on the water, Urstadt took to it like someone born and raised there. The only conflict had been Urstadt's armor; Winter had practically shouted the chainmail and plate off the former captain of the Izet emperor's guard. Urstadt had finally given in to reason, but Winter had been shocked at how naked Urstadt looked in plain breeches and a long, loose tunic. Urstadt's brown hair whipped around her face in the wind, her skin far more tanned than Winter would have thought beneath all the armor she had worn in Roden.

"That was my home,"Winter responded, looking at Pranna. She was not sure she could call it home any longer. But it was the last place she had felt like a person rather than a weapon. She had returned to feel that again, if it was still possible. She hoped, once she saw *The Swordsmith's Daughter* tied at the docks, once she saw Gord and Darrin and Eranda, that she would feel at home once more.

Her father's boat was not at the docks. Perhaps Gord and the others had taken it out, although if that were the case she'd have hoped to have seen it on her way in. In fact, she'd purposefully navigated directly through *The Swordsmith's Daughter*'s morning route.

She, Urstadt, and Galce walked along the wooden docks

towards the path that led up the Big Hill and into the town. Urstadt had changed back into her armor immediately after disembarking, her rose-gold barbut hanging from a strap at her waist. Galce had changed into a sharp, well-fitting suit— Winter was amazed at the amount of clothing he pulled out of his knapsack—while Winter wore her black, tight-fitting leather. She did not have a *siara*. She had not worn one for almost a year. She thought she had grown used to life without the large wrap of fabric nestled around her neck, but as she approached her old home she began to feel very exposed.

An uneasy feeling grew within her. The excitement she'd felt in returning home shifted into a cold, dark fear.

There was something else, too. Something she'd been putting off thinking about, but could no longer avoid.

She would have to tell Lian's parents what happened to him.

While Igriss and Huro had always been kind enough, Winter had never felt the closeness with them that she felt with Darrin and Eranda, and Gord, and Lian himself for that matter. They spoke little, mostly keeping to themselves even among tiellans, and Lian was their only child.

Winter had no idea what she would say to them now.

"Reminds me of a place I once knew," Galce said. "In Andrinar."

"What village was that?" Winter asked. She had no knowledge of Andrinar, and Galce had been largely silent throughout their journey.

A silence Galce was apparently intent on continuing. Winter did not push the issue.

They crested the Big Hill together, Galce and Urstadt walking on either side of Winter. The town she saw did not look at all like the Pranna she remembered.

It was larger, for one. Pranna had always clustered around one main road for as long as Winter remembered, but now two new roads ran parallel to the old one. Two new roads, and new buildings surrounding them both, along with the Cantic chapel where it had once stood alone on the western edge of Pranna.

Winter reached into the pouch on her belt and pulled out a *faltira* crystal. Cova—Empress Cova, now—had granted her the remaining stash of the dead Emperor Daval's *faltira*, almost two hundred crystals. A fortune. She tried to take them sparingly, every other day or so, but now she could not help herself, even though the high from the ship had only just faded. She swallowed a frost crystal as they turned east, toward the tiellan quarter. Fortunately, the tiellan quarter looked the same as ever—a narrow dirt path leading to a cluster of huts. Winter could see her own home, the hut she had shared with her father her entire life. She wondered who occupied it now.

"Come on," she said, nodding towards the huts. She shivered. *Faltira*'s fire already burned within her. "We're going that way."

Winter recognized a few faces as she walked through the town, but nobody acknowledged her, though there were plenty of people about. There never had been many tiellans in Pranna, and she couldn't see any now. Grind the smith looked away as she passed his workshop. The man had once been a friend to her father, but had severed all contact years ago. A few merchants looked familiar, but they huddled together, engrossed in conversation. She even recognized a Cantic disciple as the very woman who had run away from the chaos at her wedding. The attack at the wedding had forced her new husband, Knot, to flee, and had sparked Winter's own quest to find him. It seemed so long ago now. Winter yearned for the people in Pranna to recognize her, say hello, but she felt differently about the disciple. Winter was glad when the woman turned away, apparently engaged in business with the tanner.

As she approached the tiellan quarter, the silence shocked her. The town of Pranna itself bustled, humming louder than ever. The tiellan quarter was a stark contrast. No noise, no movement. Nothing.

Urstadt and Galce, silent on either side of her, did not help the sensation. Winter wanted them to speak, to say something, but now of all times they chose to remain silent.

Darrin and Eranda's hut was closest, so Winter approached that one first. Ivy crept up one side of the structure, and the door gaped open, the inside dark. Winter poked her head in anyway, knocking on the doorframe, but no one responded.

"Hello?" Winter called out. "Darrin? Eranda?"

The hut was empty. Not just of people, but of furniture as well. Weeds sprouted from the once well-kept dirt floor. Winter remembered filling her pack on the table that was no longer there, after the death of her father. After Knot had left. She could see herself sitting next to Lian in front of the hearth, before they left Pranna together. Lian perhaps still half in love with her, despite her marriage. Now, both Lian and Knot were dead, too.

"No one is here." Winter stated the obvious because she could not take the silence any longer.

"I am sorry, my *garice*," Galce said quietly, "but it seems no one has been here for some time."

Despite her confusion and the hollow feeling expanding in her chest, Winter was grateful that Galce said anything at all. The silence was eating away at her.

She nodded. She knew he was right, but she had not come all this way to give up after one house. "I need to check the other huts. Just in case."

They moved on to Gord's home, and Dent's, and Lian's, all abandoned.

Eventually, she found herself in front of her father's hut. Seawood walls, tiled roof. Simple, but it had protected them from the snow and sun. As Winter reached forth to push the door open, she closed her eyes.

Chaos was there immediately, pure and white as drifted snow.

Winter opened her eyes, breathing heavily. What harm would it do to enter her old home? Perhaps that would help her actually *feel something*. She had come all this way to find her home again, to feel like the person she once was. To shed the trappings of violence she had been unable to escape for the past year. With frost still burning within her, she thought about reaching into the hut with her *tendra*.

Instead, she withdrew her hand.

"We do as Chaos directs," Galce said softly.

Winter looked at Galce sharply. His head was bowed, and he did not meet her eyes. Before Winter could say something, Galce continued.

"I can sense Chaos here, my *garice*. I know nothing of why it comes to you, of what decisions you might face. But I can sense its presence."

Urstadt stood on Winter's other side, dutifully staying out of the conversation. Urstadt had made it clear she did not consider Galce's chaotic religion—and the extent of Winter's involvement in it—any of her business.

"That's all very well," Winter said, after some time, "but

there is nothing for us here." She turned away from her hut, and began walking back to Pranna.

This time, as they walked back through the town, someone recognized her.

"I know you."

Winter turned at the sound of the voice, but her heart sank before she even saw who spoke. The accent was human, not tiellan, and not a voice she recognized.

A man faced her, eyes narrowed.

"You're the tiellan girl that used to live here," he said. He was tall, not quite thirty summers, the hair already receding along his skull.

Another man stepped up next to the one who'd spoken. This one was shorter, with a thick black beard. Nevertheless, both stood much taller than Winter. Humans, with rare exception, were always taller than tiellans. "You're the one that married a human and then left town," the other man said.

The men eyed Galce and Urstadt, standing on either side of Winter.

"She work for you?" one of the men asked.

"On the contrary," Galce said with a smile. "We are her retainers."

Urstadt moved to step between Winter and the two humans, but Winter put her hand on the woman's shoulder.

"I can handle this, Urstadt."

With a nod, Urstadt stepped back to Winter's side. The two men looked at one another. A few others in the street had stopped to watch.

"Where did the other tiellans go?" Winter asked. But the question was superfluous. Two of her *tendra*—her acumenic *tendra*—were already snaking into the minds of these men.

While her telenic *tendra* could only affect non-living objects, her acumenic *tendra* had the opposite limitation. They could interact with other minds, and nothing else. A psimancer could only access one form of *tendra*, but Winter, for some reason, found herself an exception to that rule. There was a third form of psimancy as well—clairvoyance—that allowed a person insight into time itself, but Winter had no control over that particular branch.

"They left," one of them finally said. "And you should, too." *Who does this tiellan think she is?* the man thought.

"No room for tiellans in Pranna anymore," the other man said, eyeing Winter up and down. His thoughts were not so much words, but a feeling. A feeling that reminded Winter of an alley in Cineste, in a moment from another life.

This time, however, Winter had the power.

Winter delved the two men with her *tendra*, and a slew of information flooded Winter's consciousness. Who these men were—Harn Alasta, the tall one, and Breggan Dones, the short one; where they were from—Harn from Cineste, Breggan from Pranna (Winter knew he'd looked familiar); how they'd met—at the local gambling house (Winter wondered when Pranna had built a *gambling house*); who their families were; their political opinions; all the mistakes they'd made and people they'd loved and much more besides.

Winter sifted through it all for the information she sought. She found it in Breggan's mind: the humans had driven the remaining tiellans from Pranna months before. Breggan had no knowledge of where they had gone, but he had heard that the tiellan population in Cineste had been growing recently.

"Cineste," Winter said.

The two men stared at her. Winter's acumenic delving had not taken more than a few seconds. The process was subtle; the two men would not have realized what was happening to them, and likely never would. There were other, more invasive methods of acumency, but Winter had yet to attempt them. These men had been simple to delve—that was not always the case.

Harn, eyes narrowing, took a step forward.

"Best you join them, *elf*," he said softly.

Winter clenched her fist. A small crowd had gathered, watching the confrontation. No one intervened; no one stepped up in her support.

"Be careful, Winter," Urstadt said.

If it had been any other day, Winter might have turned and walked away in that moment. If it had been any other town, Winter might have let it be. But her home was *gone*. Nothing remained in Pranna, not for her. A home ceased to be a home when the people who made it so left.

And worthless people like Harn were the ones who'd chased them out. Harn, whose failings were there to be read for any acumen who cared to do so: a man who beat his wife when he got drunk, and who got drunk all too often. Harn, who had always thought tiellans beneath him. Harn, who years earlier had a crescent-and-cross tattooed onto the inside of his wrist.

Harn the Kamite. Breggan was one, too, though he'd only received his tattoo a few months ago.

To destroy, I must first know love.

The words entered her mind unbidden, unwelcomed. She was through with that, now. She had killed Daval Amok, and now that his daughter had taken his place on the emperor's throne, his ridiculous philosophy had died with him back in Roden.

And yet... she had delved into the minds of these two men,

their lives, everything that made them who they were. What else was love, if not knowing and accepting the faults of others?

Winter frowned. She did not accept the faults of these men. She never would. Instead, she left it up to a power greater than herself. She closed her eyes, seeking Chaos, as Galce had taught her to do, envisioning a perfect sphere. The sphere was black. Chaos had spoken.

Winter opened her eyes, and sent a psionic burst into the minds of both men—a wave of power that pulsed along the two *tendra* that connected her with the men, killing them instantly. Harn and Breggan both collapsed to the ground.

Many in the small group of people who'd gathered around them gasped. A few of the bystanders rushed up to the bodies. People stared at Winter, eyes wide.

She turned, and while Urstadt and Galce reluctantly followed, no one else did.

"Was that necessary?" Urstadt said as they walked away from the town.

"She did as Chaos directed," Galce responded. "Though Chaos is an abstruse master. It has taken me many years to become comfortable with its direction. If I may, my *garice*... I would caution against blindly following Chaos's direction if you can help it. It is best to understand—"

"I've done what I've done, and that's all that matters," Winter said quietly. What Galce said made her uncomfortable; he was the one that had convinced her to trust in Chaos in the first place. Now he spoke of caution?

She had no time for that. Not now.

"Let's go to Cineste."

2

Odenite camp, outside Kirlan, western Khale

"DISCIPLE CINZIA."

Cinzia blinked, then turned to see Elessa standing next to her. She did not know how long her fellow disciple had been whispering her name, but this was clearly not the first attempt to get her attention. Elessa's eyebrows knit downward in a scowl.

"Yes," Cinzia murmured, only slightly ashamed that she had allowed herself to get so distracted during one of Jane's Magnificals. She cleared her throat. "Yes?" she said again, meeting Elessa's eyes.

Magnifical was a word she and Jane had translated from the Codex. It meant something along the lines of "devoutness," as far as Cinzia could tell, and Jane had taken to using the word to describe the daily devotionals she led for the growing crowd of her followers, the Odenites.

"They will not let us pass," Elessa said.

Knot, standing beside Cinzia, leaned over. "Who won't let us pass?"

"It might be best if you see for yourself, Cinzia."

Cinzia and Knot followed Elessa through the crowd.

They had arrived the night before, making camp in the middle of a massive arable field just north of the walled city of Kirlan. The field belonged to a local lord named Alam Derard;

the man was a powerful figure in Kirlan, but had moved his immediate family north to Cinzia's ancestral manor of Harmoth when he had heard of the Odenite movement. A fast convert to the new religion, he had offered his entire open field, and all of his crops and resources, to Odenites for their use. Cinzia was highly uncomfortably with the arrangement; the Odenites would likely bankrupt the Derard house, but Lord Derard himself did not seem to care. He was as devoted a follower of Jane as anyone Cinzia had met.

Now she, Knot, and Elessa stood amongst the crowd of over fifteen hundred Odenites, the sun burning down on all of them. Most of the Odenites were gathered around a large dais at the center of the field. Jane stood on the dais now, speaking to the crowd sprawled before her. A chosen group carried the platform with them as they traveled, assembling it each day in preparation for Jane's Magnificals. Fortunately, Derard's land provided more space than the Odenites needed—for now— but their numbers were growing. When the Goddess Canta had told Jane to move the Odenites south to Triah, their numbers had not yet broken one thousand. But people continued to flock to Jane and the Church of Canta, as if they knew exactly where to go to meet the Prophetess.

They traveled closer to Triah every day. Cinzia felt both a swelling dread and a sense of excitement at seeing the Circle City once more. Navone, her hometown, would always be close to her heart, but Triah was hers—the place she had first dedicated herself to the service of Canta, before she had returned to Navone and discovered her sister's heresy. She hoped that feeling did not change when she returned as a disciple of the Church of Canta rather than as a priestess of the Denomination.

"Don't be discouraged," Elessa said, seeing Cinzia's expression. "Our trek has been more or less uneventful until this point. We were bound to encounter trials sooner or later."

Were we? Cinzia wondered. Of course, Elessa was right. It had taken them over two months to make it this far. But, other than reports from their lookouts that the Beldam's splinter group was traveling shortly behind them, there had been very little to worry about. Canta had provided for them—or that was how Jane framed their survival, anyway. Cinzia supposed there was something to that; whenever the group seemed about to run out of resources, they came across more food, water, and whatever else they needed. Now that they had reached Kirlan, Lord Derard had emerged.

"I suppose you are right," Cinzia finally said with a sigh.

The three of them made their way through the Odenites, who parted easily to make a path.

"Would it be best if we brought your... your daughter with us, Knot?" Elessa asked.

Knot grunted. "Can't say. You're the one won't tell us where we're going or what we're about to see."

Cinzia was glad to see that Elessa would at least speak to Knot. Knot had attacked Elessa during one of his episodes at the Harmoth estate. It had not actually been Knot, but it had been his body, and Elessa had not known the difference at the time. The more Cinzia learned of Knot, the more fascinated she was with him. Knot had woken up in a tiellan town more than two years ago with no memory of who he was or where he came from. He'd eventually discovered that he hadn't actually lost his memory, but had rather been created, somehow, from a psimantic amalgamation of sifts—the condensed essences of other people. Months ago, those individual sifts had begun inadvertently taking control of Knot's body. The episodes had almost destroyed Knot completely—and caused a great deal of trouble otherwise, as some of the sifts were particularly violent—but Knot had thankfully stabilized since the Nazaniin psimancer Wyle had helped heal him. Cinzia was glad to see Elessa had regained some confidence in speaking with Knot.

And Knot's "daughter"—the vampire girl Astrid—was something of a legend among the Odenites. Most still did not know exactly what she was, but the Odenites who had joined them before they left Harmoth had to have some idea. They'd seen what she could do in the battle against the Kamites.

Elessa had accepted the girl's true nature. All of the disciples knew of it; Jane insisted on full transparency amongst their little group. Cinzia thought Jane more than a little hypocritical. Jane, as a prophetess, had a link to Canta, but she only shared the Goddess's communications when she deemed it necessary.

"I don't mean to be evasive, Knot, it's just that—"

"Goddess rising," Cinzia whispered.

The field on which the Odenites mingled met with Kirlan's northern outer wall. The city itself sat on a cliff that overlooked the ocean, its western walls against the edge of the precipice. A wide moat ran along the city's eastern walls, on the other side of which was thick forest. A large gate directly ahead of Cinzia was the only entrance into the city she could see.

All of this was clearly visible from anywhere on Derard's field, but what made her gasp were the Sons of Canta, armor glinting in the sun beneath red and white livery, standing in front of the gate.

Panic rose in Cinzia's chest. "Where are the Prelates?" Jane had ordained the guard force Knot had formed—that now operated under the direction of her brother, Eward—as Prelates a few weeks ago. Cinzia was not sure why; although they had seen the word in the Nine Scriptures, there had been no indication as to what it meant. But Jane seemed sure of the decision.

"There are two contingents just behind us, about sixty soldiers," Knot replied. "There's another on either flank, and two more serving as rearguard."

That made Cinzia feel slightly better. The Prelates had continued training as they traveled, under Knot and Eward's leadership, and Astrid's occasional help. Cinzia felt confident in their abilities.

The Sons of Canta, however, had trained for far longer, and Cinzia had the sneaking suspicion that the soldiers she saw before her were far from the only Sons stationed in Kirlan.

"We'd better talk to them," Cinzia said. "Should we summon more Prelates?"

"Already done," Knot said, signaling to the Prelates closest to them. Five soldiers trotted towards them.

"Only five?" Cinzia asked, wiping her palms on her dress. "Should we not bring more?"

"Don't want to seem too aggressive," Knot said. "Besides, they ain't here to attack us. Not right now, anyway. They're defending the city."

"Defending the city... from us?" Elessa asked, more than a hint of surprise in her voice.

"That'd be my guess."

"Very well," Cinzia said. She was suddenly very conscious of her appearance. She had not been around a group of Sons without her own Cantic robes and Trinacrya since she arrived in Triah for the first time, more than eight years ago. Right now, she wore a simple wool dress, dyed a light shade of red. "We shall see what they want. Let me do the talking, please."

Cinzia began walking towards the gate, Elessa and Knot to either side of her. The five Prelates stepped in time behind them. When they stopped within a few rods of the gate, one of the Sons called out to them.

"Halt! Who are you, and what is your business in Kirlan?"

Cinzia took a step forward and cleared her throat. "My name is Cinzia Oden. I am a…" She hesitated for only the slightest moment. "…a disciple of the Church of Canta. We request safe passage through Kirlan, so we can continue on our way."

The Son did not meet her eyes. "We have been specifically instructed to not let you through the gate, Miss Cinzia. I am sorry."

Miss Cinzia. No longer a priestess.

Cinzia smiled despite herself. "Surely you cannot deny us safe passage," she said, spreading her arms wide. "We are not a small group, obviously, but we are efficient. We would spend very little time in the city itself."

"It is not the city itself we protect, Miss Cinzia."

No, Cinzia realized, *they are protecting Triah, the seminary, and Canta's Fane.*

"But we cannot go around," Cinzia said. "The cliffs block us to the west, and it would be impossible for such a large group to travel through the forest on the east. Kirlan is our only way south."

"I am afraid that is the point, Miss Cinzia. We cannot let you travel any further south than you already have."

"Are you the leader of this section?" Cinzia asked, nodding at the rest of the Sons guarding the gate.

"I am the commander of the battalion that has been stationed in Kirlan."

Cinzia clenched her jaw. The Denomination had sent

a Crucible first, to Navone. Then Nazaniin assassins to Harmoth. And now this, the most mundane of threats that Cinzia had faced in the last year, could be the force that might actually stop them.

And the Denomination had sent an entire *battalion*. At least five hundred Sons of Canta.

"Then *I* am afraid we shall have to set up camp here," Cinzia said, indicating the field behind her, "until your orders change." Cinzia hated to propose such a thing without consulting Lord Derard first, but the truth was she knew exactly what he would say. If the Prophetess required it, he would do it.

The soldier all but shrugged. "Our orders do not prohibit that. You are welcome to do as you wish, Miss Cinzia. Although what the city of Kirlan will think of such a group smothering its front gate, I cannot say."

He kept staring out into nothing, no matter how hard she tried to make him meet her gaze. More than his nonchalance, more than the fact that he was impeding their progress, that gesture threatened to drive Cinzia mad. She knew the protocol for the Sons of Canta: never look a heretic in the eye.

"Very well," Cinzia said. It was all she could do to keep calm. "I daresay this is not the last you will see of me." Without waiting for a response, she turned on her heel and brushed past the Prelates standing behind her. Knot, Elessa, and the Prelates reluctantly followed.

"We need to tell Jane," Elessa said, rushing up to Cinzia's side.

"Of course we do." Cinzia looked up at the sun. "The Magnifical should be over soon. We shall meet her when she finishes."

Perhaps Canta would reveal some insane course of action

43

through Jane. Perhaps Jane had already received a revelation—such a thing would not be untypical. They would need nothing short of a miracle to get through an entire battalion of the Sons of Canta blocking their way. Even if they tried to move through the forest, Cinzia imagined the Sons would be quick to impede their progress. She wondered what force the Denomination had authorized the Sons to use. Given the fact that the Denomination had already sent assassins against the Church of Canta, Cinzia feared the worst.

They reached Jane just as she descended from the dais. Cinzia rushed her last few paces.

Jane smiled. "Cinzia. I was hoping to speak with you, I..." The smile faded from her face. "What is wrong, sister?"

"The Denomination has garrisoned an entire battalion of the Sons of Canta in Kirlan. They will not let us pass."

Jane glanced over Cinzia's shoulder at the city. "They intend to attack us?" she asked.

"I do not think so," Cinzia said. She glanced at Knot.

"If they'd meant to attack us, they'd have done it by now," he said. "Wouldn't have shown themselves. They want to set up a blockade, not a battleground. For now."

"Can we not just go around the city?" Jane asked.

"Not without backtracking," Cinzia said. "The forest is too thick on the eastern side. We would have to go all the way back to Turandel to take a different road."

"That'd add months to our trek," Knot said.

Jane's eyes moved to the Odenites, crowded around the dais.

"We must continue southward," she said quietly. "We must get to Triah in time."

"In time for what?" This was the first Cinzia had heard of any sort of timeline for their travels.

Jane took a deep breath, but did not meet Cinzia's eyes.

Cinzia shook her head. *Transparency.*

Jane opened her mouth to speak, but then stopped, cocking her head to one side.

"We need to get to Triah," Jane said, "but we can make camp here for a time. Lord Derard will accommodate us, I have no doubt."

"He may accommodate us, but he will destroy his house and fortune in the process," Cinzia said.

"What are you two talking about in such hushed tones?"

Cinzia and Jane turned to see Ocrestia, the tiellan disciple, along with the newest disciple anointed, Baetrissa. There were four of them now, and Jane wanted to anoint five more, to match the nine original Disciples of Canta. The process was slow, however. As she explained the situation to the two other disciples, Cinzia wondered whether they would ever find the right women to complete their number.

"Canta will get us through this," Jane said after Cinzia had finished. "She will provide, as She always has."

Cinzia turned to her sister, eyebrows raised. "What do you mean, 'Canta will get us through this'? A moment ago you were afraid we might not make it to Triah in time."

Jane met Cinzia's eyes. "My faith faltered, just for a moment. I am just as human as you are, sister. But now I see the truth of our situation. Canta will aid us. She will make sure we get to where we need to be, when we need to be there."

Cinzia blinked in shock. "Jane, this is a real problem. We cannot just wait for Canta to resolve it for us."

"That ain't what the Prophetess said," Ocrestia interjected. "She's just saying we need to have faith. We should do what we can, but trust that Canta will do the rest."

Jane smiled. "Exactly, Ocrestia."

Cinzia was about to react, when she stopped herself. Had she not just learned the importance of trusting Canta a couple of months ago, at Harmoth? Faith implied a lack of control, and necessitated an act of trust.

"I agree," Elessa said, turning to face Cinzia. "We will do what we can, of course. But we must trust in the Goddess's plan for us. What is the point of all of this otherwise?"

What is the point of all of this? Cinzia could not help but wonder. But part of her suspected she already knew. If she gained nothing out of this but learning to trust in a power greater than herself, was that not worth the struggle?

"Baetrissa, what about you?" Jane asked.

The newly anointed disciple looked at the women around her. "How can my thoughts matter in light of your opinions? You are women of the Goddess."

Ocrestia smiled. "So are you. Your voice matters just as much as ours."

"Every voice matters just as much as ours," Cinzia said.

"Of course. That is what I meant."

"Very well," Baetrissa said hesitantly. "I suppose it doesn't matter much anyway. I agree with you all. I think trusting Canta is the most important thing."

Then all eyes turned to Cinzia.

She sighed. "I am not going to argue against you. And, truth be told, I agree with you, too. Trusting Canta *is* important. But if we discern a way to take action, we need to follow it."

"Of course," Jane said with a smile.

"Are we always going to agree like this?" Baetrissa said after a pause. She was looking at Cinzia, eyebrows knitted together.

Cinzia could not help but laugh. "No," she said, feeling

some of the tension leave her body. The others were right. They would do what they could, but trust that Canta was helping them every step of the way. "I daresay we will not."

"Especially not as our rank grows to its fullness," Jane said. "There are five more disciples yet to be found."

Cinzia turned at the sound of someone clearing their throat behind her. It was Arven, their cleric, and beside her a young man not much older than she. Twenty summers, or thereabouts.

"Can we help you, Arven?" Cinzia asked.

Arven's head bobbed up and down rhythmically as she spoke. "This fellow is a new arrival, and he, well, he is alone, and he just arrived, you see, and because he is alone, we wanted to introduce him to a group that might take him in, perhaps give him a space, offer him food and water. He arrived alone, you see. But, well, he insisted on meeting all of you first."

A smile spread across the man's face as Arven spoke, a smile that sent a chill running up Cinzia's spine.

Jane didn't seem to notice. "It is a pleasure to make your acquaintance, young man. I am Jane. Where have you—"

"I bring a message," he said, his voice steady and firm. Before anyone could respond, the man raised a hand high in the air and continued to speak, this time in a strange tongue. The words struck Cinzia with almost tangible force, and she took a step back.

And realized, at once, that while it was no language she knew, she actually *did* understand what he was saying.

"*My blood for the blood of Aratraxia,*" the young man said, voice rising. "*My blood pays the price of passage, from their realm to ours. My blood for the blood of Aratraxia.*"

Knot darted forward as the man spoke, but too late. The young man brought his hand down—in it he held a dagger, how had Cinzia not noticed?—and drew the blade with a sickening tear across his own throat.

The disciples gasped, backing away from the horrific scene, but Arven froze. The man's body twisted as blood arced out from his neck. Blood sprayed across Arven's face and dress and hair, and the poor girl looked down at herself, silent, as the man fell to the ground.

Knot was already at his side as his body thrashed in the dirt.

"Where did he come from, Arven? Did he say anything to you?"

Arven looked down at Knot, then back at herself, covered in crimson. Blood dripped from her hair, down her forehead, streaked her cheeks like dark tears. The girl did not respond, instead raising her eyes to Cinzia.

"Discip—"

A crack split the air above them, and Cinzia looked up.

Above the man's now-still body, a patch of dark space had appeared, twisting and shimmering. Cinzia's breath caught in her chest.

"Shit." Knot stood, taking Arven by the shoulder, and dragged the girl towards the disciples. "Get everyone as far away from this spot as you can," he growled. He shoved Arven towards Cinzia, and Cinzia wrapped one arm around the young woman's shoulders.

"What is happening?" Cinzia asked. A writhing shadow took shape within the darkness.

"*Get back!*" Knot shouted.

The desperation in his voice galvanized Cinzia into action. She turned, holding Arven close, and led the other disciples away in time to see Astrid rush past her, towards Knot. The girl moved too quickly for Cinzia to ask any questions, and Cinzia had other concerns. Dozens of Odenites stood nearby, gawking.

"Everyone, get back!" Cinzia screamed.

Some of the Odenites turned and ran immediately, while others slowly began to step backwards.

"Help me get them away from here," Cinzia said through gritted teeth to the other disciples. Arven still cringed beneath her arm. Glancing over her shoulder, Cinzia saw the dark twisting shadow topple downward and crash into the earth below. A cloud of dust burst upwards. The dark space above winked out of existence, returning to blue sky.

Then, from the dust, a form rose, and Cinzia could not stop the scream of terror that tore from her throat.

3

As the crowd fled, Knot backed slowly away, keeping his attention on the beast.

He recognized the thing, or at least its general form, as an Outsider—one of the monsters he had fought underneath the imperial dome of Izet, when he had lost his wife, Winter. This one stood three times the height of a human, its body muscled and sinewy beneath slick black skin. It balanced on two thickly muscled hind legs, and its long arms ended in curved claws the size of Knot's arms. Its massive head was oversized for the sinewy neck, with jaws and teeth so large they seemed to weigh the creature down, hunching it over. The creature swerved its head, empty black eyes observing the crowd around it, and dropped its jaw to emit a terrible sound between a roar and a scream.

Questions raced through Knot's mind. The last time he'd seen one of these monsters, Azael had been close. Was he here now? Would more Outsiders follow?

But he had no time to consider them.

"Astrid!" Knot shouted, keeping his eye on the Outsider. The monster took a step forward, and the vibration of it echoed up through Knot's bones.

Why was that girl never around when he—

"I'm here, nomad."

Knot looked down. The girl stood at his side. That was

something, at least. A large hooded cloak shielding her from sunlight. He looked back at the Outsider.

"How are we going to fight this thing?" she asked.

"Was hoping you'd have an idea," Knot said. They continued to back slowly away.

"You think it'll wait 'til nightfall?"

Knot grunted. The last time they'd faced Outsiders, Astrid had been at her strongest, and he'd had access to telesis. What limited ability he had now, after his healing, wouldn't possibly damage the beast before them, and Astrid, while she was still strong, would not be nearly as powerful as she was at night.

"We could ask nicely," Astrid said.

The Outsider roared again, its gaze fixed on Knot and Astrid. Knot heard footsteps behind him, and glanced back to see Eward approaching. The Prelates stood in formation behind him, an unmoving wall amidst the fleeing Odenites.

"Orders?" Eward asked.

"Archers only," Knot said. "Line them up. Fire on the creature whenever you have a clear shot." The Prelates made good footmen, but he had not trained them to handle anything like this. Better that he and Astrid made the front line.

Knot could tell Eward wanted to argue, but the lad raced back to his line. He'd learned not to argue during combat.

The ground trembled as the massive beast rushed towards them.

"Flank it," Knot said to Astrid. "Give the archers space."

Astrid sprinted to the left, cloak billowing behind her, and Knot moved to the right, sword drawn. While Astrid's preferred weapons were her claws, she couldn't extend them in the daytime. Instead she wielded two short swords, one gripped in each hand.

Eward shouted behind them, and a volley of arrows hissed through the air, striking the Outsider's armored skin. Most glanced away, but a few plunged through.

The creature did not scream, and did not falter in its charge. Knot remembered the last time they'd faced Outsiders, and how much damage it had taken to bring one down. A single Outsider had demolished an entire squad of Rodenese Reapers—the emperor's elite soldiers—in moments. If this one got to the Prelates, it would massacre them. He and Astrid had to keep the thing distracted.

The Outsider lunged for Knot first. He dodged a swipe of the monster's massive claw, then rolled out of the way to narrowly escape being trampled by its feet. The Outsider screamed as Astrid leapt atop it, plunging her swords into its back. A high-pitched roar of pain pierced the air, and it bucked her across the field. She rolled to a stop, not moving.

The monster kicked Knot squarely in the chest with one of its feet before he could react. The impact sent him flying backwards, sliding along the grass. Knot gasped, regaining his breath with effort. The Outsider turned, moving in Astrid's direction just as another volley of arrows hailed down on the thing from behind. Knot wasn't sure the arrows had any effect; the creature barely flinched, and continued sauntering towards Astrid, lying still on the grass.

Knot sprinted forward, a growl forming in his chest. The Outsider was almost upon the vampire, raising one leg to stomp down. Knot reached her just in time, sweeping her up and out of the way as the ground shook beneath them. Cradling Astrid in one arm, he turned and thrust his sword through the monster's side. He withdrew the blade quickly, slashing upwards, but the Outsider parried with one monstrous claw and Knot nearly lost his grip on his sword.

Astrid groaned, stirring, but Knot couldn't set her down. She was still disoriented, and she'd be an easy target. Instead, he kept his grip on the girl, dodging swipe after swipe from the Outsider's claws. The monster wasn't slowing down. If Astrid didn't get her senses back soon, they'd both be dead. And being at such close quarters with the monster wasn't helping—the Prelates could not fire without risk of hitting Knot and Astrid.

Knot's muscles strained as he narrowly escaped another slash of the monster's claws. He stabbed up again with his sword, but the monster snaked out of the way. The thing was *fast*, especially for its size. Knot didn't remember the Outsiders he'd fought in Roden being this fast.

He dodged again, then sprinted away as fast as he could, hoping to give Eward's archers a chance to get another volley in. Arrows hissed through the air, thudding into the monster's hide and the grass around it.

"What'd I miss?" Astrid asked.

Knot looked down at her long enough to see her eyes open. "Can you stand?"

The Outsider rushed at them again, and Knot's muscles tensed.

"Give me your sword," Astrid said.

Knot dodged and parried another attack from the Outsider. "I don't think—"

"Those stupid short swords of mine aren't enough, nomad. Give me your sword."

Knot didn't argue further. He let her take the sword, and she shifted in his arms just as the Outsider charged again. Then, the girl kicked off of his chest, springing directly at the charging Outsider, cloak flapping in her wake, a sword as long as she was tall held in both hands. The force of Astrid's leap pushed Knot backwards into the grass.

With a shout, Astrid buried the sword in the creature's torso. Gripping the handle, she swung her feet forward and planted them on either side of the sword. The beast thrashed angrily, trying to smash Astrid against its chest, but the girl was too quick, even in the sunlight. She yanked the sword out of the beast in a flying leap. A spray of blood arced out as Astrid twisted in midair and brought the sword down to sever a flailing monstrous arm. The massive claw fell to the ground in another shower of bright blood.

Knot leapt to his feet. Astrid's frenzied attack on the Outsider had taken only a few seconds. And yet, while the Outsider was clearly enraged at the fact that one claw was no longer attached to its body, it did not seem otherwise deterred.

Knot drew the dagger from his belt, but he knew the weapon would be useless. Then, he saw one of Astrid's short swords nearby on the grass, and sprinted to pick it up.

Another volley of arrows hissed through the air, piercing the Outsider, and this attack finally seemed to affect the thing. It stumbled as the arrows struck, one leg buckling beneath it. But, just as quickly, the monster regained its balance, and turned its attention back to Astrid.

As Knot approached, everything seemed to slow around him. The Outsider slashed at Astrid with its one good claw, both forms moving sluggishly. For the first time, Knot looked into its eyes. Deep, dark pits, unfathomably black. Lifeless and dead. And yet... not entirely so. For a brief moment, Knot thought he saw a flicker in the Outsider's eyes.

If there was one thing Knot had learned to recognize in a look, it was fear.

The monster swiped at the girl again, and Astrid dodged. Her movements were easier, less frantic now that the monster was short a claw. The Outsider stomped again, roaring at Astrid so loudly Knot's ears rang, but the girl was not fazed. She twirled around the monster's next attack, slicing the back of its leg with Knot's sword. The Outsider buckled and fell. Astrid followed immediately, plunging the sword through the thing's skull again and again.

Finally, the Outsider was still.

Knot rushed to Astrid's side, short sword gripped in one fist.

"Dead?"

Astrid, covered in blood, kicked the thing's head, which didn't budge—it was easily twice the size of the girl. She grunted. "That was supposed to be more dramatic." She looked up at Knot. "But yes, I think it's dead."

Knot glanced up, worried he might see the portal still open, shimmering darkly, but he saw nothing.

"Why only one? Why not others, like in Izet?"

Astrid adjusted her hood to cover more of her face. Knot noticed scars there, already fading; she'd been touched by the sun during the fight. "When someone gifts you a horse, nomad, you don't ask after the shape of its teeth."

Knot squatted down to get a better look at the thing. He'd never seen one up close. In Izet, he'd passed out before the battle had ended. Next thing he knew, Astrid was helping him escape, the Outsider bodies buried in rubble behind them.

The Outsider bodies, Reaper bodies, and Lian and Winter, too. All buried somewhere behind them.

Knot shook himself, and took a closer look. The creature's skin was black, so smooth it almost shone in the sunlight. Truth was, now that he was looking closer, there wasn't much more to see. No scars, no marks whatsoever that Knot could discern.

"We need to talk with the disciples," Knot said. He had no idea what they were going to do with the body.

4

Cinzia cautiously approached Knot and Astrid. Jane and the other disciples were rounding up and calming the panicked, scattered crowd of Odenites—in the chaos many had run into the forest, while others had even rushed the Sons of Canta at Kirlan's gate. Fortunately, while the Sons had barred any Odenites from entering, they had kept their word and refrained from seriously harming anyone.

The Odenites, it seemed, would be all right. Cinzia was much more worried about the possibility of this—whatever it was—happening again.

Cinzia eyed the monster's sleek black body, unmoving in the soil, now muddied with blood. "Is it...?"

Knot looked up at her. "Dead. But best keep your distance for now."

Cinzia looked back at where she'd left Arven, in Elessa's care. The young woman had not said a word since the man had killed himself in front of her. Cinzia could not blame her. She, too, was shaken by the whole thing. First the man's violent suicide, and then this monster emerging in the light of noonday, of all things. That it happened in the sunlight made it seem all the worse. Things like Astrid, at least, were not as menacing in the sun. What was different with this creature?

Miraculously, other than a few minor injuries, it seemed

the Odenites had escaped mostly unharmed. Knot, Astrid, and the quick reaction of the guard force had saved them. And yet, despite the relief Cinzia felt at the fact that everyone was still safe, that Astrid and Knot had defeated this monster, another feeling expanded, burning and wild in her chest.

Anger.

"What was that thing?" she asked, keeping her emotions in check with some effort.

Knot and Astrid looked at one another.

"I do not have the patience for you to pretend you do not know."

Knot's jaw was clenched tightly before he answered. "One of the monsters we encountered in Izet. An Outsider—that's what Astrid calls them. Don't know much more than that." He looked pointedly at Astrid. "Do you?"

Astrid shrugged. She had wiped the blood from her face, but messy smears still remained. "There are daemons even daemons fear. This is one of them."

"And yet you defeated it," Cinzia said. "And not even at night. Is that really something to fear?"

Astrid scowled, but Cinzia did not care. Now was not the time to be cryptic.

"Just because we killed one of the things does not mean I don't fear them," Astrid said quietly. "And... I'm less worried about the Outsiders themselves, and far more about what they serve."

"Azael," Cinzia whispered. A voice, deep and rumbling, echoed in her mind.

You will all die screaming, and I will watch, and take pleasure in it.

She remembered Kovac's eyes, leaking iridescent green smoke.

"How is it possible," Cinzia asked through gritted teeth, "that we know so little about him?"

"About who?"

Cinzia turned to see Jane approaching, Ocrestia and Baetrissa trailing behind her.

"Azael, the Fear Lord," Cinzia said.

Astrid coughed. "Not sure saying his name is the greatest idea."

Cinzia wanted to spit. "What difference does it make whether I say his name or not? If he wanted to be here, to kill us, he would." Cinzia wanted to believe what she said was true, but she really had no idea. Was she provoking an unknown force? And yet, at the same time, she could hardly control her anger. Just when she thought they were making progress, they had run into the blockade. And now *this*.

"The Lord of the Nine Daemons?" Jane asked. "Was this his doing?"

Cinzia nodded to Astrid. "She seems to think so."

Astrid raised her hands, palms forward. "Just saying what comes to mind."

"That man who killed himself… he had just arrived in the camp?" Jane asked.

"That is what Arven said." Cinzia hoped the young woman was all right. "But our numbers grow at an unmanageable rate. Arven updates our records daily, but even she cannot keep them updated quickly enough. He may have been with us for some time."

"We need to interrogate Arven," Jane said. "See if we can figure out the identity of this man. See if anyone else in the camp knew him, who he associated with, where he came from."

Cinzia's anger flared. "The man just slit his throat in front of her, Jane. Did you not see Arven's face? Her hair, her hands, her clothes covered in this man's blood? Give the girl a break, for Canta's sake."

"We will give her the time she needs to recover," Jane said. "But we must find the truth."

Cinzia could not argue with that. Her emotions were getting the best of her.

"What connection exists between what the man did to himself, and the daemon that emerged?" Jane wondered.

"We saw the same thing in Izet," Knot said. "Not sure what exactly happened, but there was a connection with the Ceno order." He glanced at Astrid. "And with blood, too."

"It's always blood," the girl muttered.

"Could this happen again?" Jane asked.

"No way to tell," Knot replied. "In Izet, the Tokal-Ceno... he needed both royal blood and tiellan blood. The man who killed himself today was human, and wasn't no king I've ever heard of."

"But only one Outsider appeared today," Astrid said. "In Izet, there were half a dozen at least, not to mention that huge bastard that appeared at the last."

Knot crossed his arms in front of his chest. "And Azael was there, too. Wasn't here today."

"Not that we know of," Cinzia added. She had yet to tell anyone about her encounter with Azael after the Kamite battle. She had killed the man Azael had possessed. He might have been dying anyway, but Cinzia did not know that for a certainty. Just thinking of the event made her feel hot with shame. There was no way she could tell Jane. She wanted to tell Knot, but she had yet to find a good time to do it.

"Is there anything else we can do to protect ourselves from another event like this?" Jane asked.

Knot shrugged. "Getting that information from Arven is a start. Maybe assigning more people to help her. We could train the Prelates in some specific tactics that might help in taking another one of these things down. Other than that, ain't sure what else we can do."

"Then in the meantime, I suppose the rest of us should occupy ourselves with this blockade problem," Jane mused. "Ocrestia, do you—"

"*Jane,*" Cinzia said firmly, interrupting her sister.

Cinzia felt Jane's eyes rest on her, wide and expectant.

"We cannot continue to ignore the problem behind all of this," Cinzia said, voice straining with the effort of keeping herself calm.

Jane let out a heavy sigh. "I believe our best hope of addressing that problem awaits us in Triah."

"I do not agree," Cinzia said.

The others around them were silent. It was the first time any of them had openly expressed such direct dissent against Jane.

Well, it's about bloody time, Cinzia thought. And yet she was surprised to find herself so ardently on the attack. She, too, had experienced Canta's power recently. She had healed her own father. They had nearly finished translating the Codex, too. All things considered, she had witnessed miracles.

But she had witnessed horrors, as well. Horrors they still had no means to understand, let alone deal with.

"We are nearly finished with the translation," Cinzia said. "We need to finish it. See if there is anything in the Codex that can help us with the Nine Daemons, anything other than the scraps we've already found."

"On that, at least, we agree," Jane said.

That was the easier of her two suggestions. "We also continue to ignore the Beldam's splinter group. They've traveled behind us since we left Harmoth, but we've hardly acknowledged them, let alone done anything about them." The Beldam, an eccentric old woman who had once been a prominent member of the Odenites, had nevertheless seemed to have her own agenda— including "getting rid of all the tiellans," as she'd put it—and preached as much to the Odenites. Cinzia had approached the woman with an ultimatum, a deal, that if the Beldam shared what she knew of the Nine Daemons and stopped her campaign against the tiellans, Cinzia and Jane would offer protection from the Nine as best they could. But the Beldam had broken that arrangement, holding secret meetings where she still postured against the tiellans, eventually leading a group of Odenites who agreed with her on that count away from the Church of Canta.

Then, the Beldam had left, taking a few hundred Odenites with her. They had not gone far, however, and had eventually followed the Odenites all the way down Khale's eastern coast, always keeping their distance, but always within sight.

Jane pursed her lips. "We've already tried dealing with the Beldam once, and it did not work."

"Dealing with her, one way or another, can come later," Cinzia said. "Right now, I think we need to work with her. The Beldam broke her part of the deal, but she has still been following us. I would wager she still thinks we can protect her."

"You really want to ally yourself with *her*, of all people?" Ocrestia asked. So far, Ocrestia was the only tiellan appointed as one of Jane's disciples, despite more than a third of the Odenites being tiellan.

Cinzia's heart softened just slightly. "I do not *agree* with her, Ocrestia. But I think she may have knowledge we need.

We need to talk with her. Beyond that, there is no place in this movement for that woman or her philosophies."

Ocrestia said nothing to that, and Cinzia could not tell how her explanation was met.

The Beldam wanted to annihilate Ocrestia's people, yet Cinzia wanted to deal with the Beldam. Cinzia could not imagine how that must make Ocrestia feel. But Cinzia needed to do this. She needed to find out more about the Nine Daemons, and she would go to any lengths to do it. They had other problems, to be sure, and she hoped Jane and the others could do their part to get them through what lay ahead.

But this was what *she* was going to do. This was what she needed to do. No one would convince her otherwise.

5

Cineste, northern Khale

THE FIRST RESPECTABLE INN Winter and her companions found in Cineste was the Wolfanger Inn, which lay near the merchants' quarter of the city. Spring was quickly becoming summer, and she welcomed the late afternoon sun on the streets instead of ice and snow.

The sounds of musical instruments, singing, and loud conversation drifted out to them from inside the inn, but Galce hesitated before entering.

"My *garice*, I am not sure I am comfortable with this plan."

Winter turned to regard him. "This is our best option, Galce. We just need to get settled in, then I'll leave the two of you here with our belongings and find the tiellan inn." She didn't intend to stay there, of course. This would be her base of operations while in Cineste. But if Gord, Darrin, and Eranda were in the city, that was the best place for her to start looking for them.

Galce closed his eyes, and Winter rolled hers. "You've consulted Chaos a dozen times now." An exaggeration, but not by much, if Winter had gotten as good at reading the man as she thought. "Chaos approves. It's your turn to get on board."

"Very well, my *garice*." Galce nodded, and Winter opened the door, allowing both Galce and Urstadt to enter first.

Winter immediately saw why it was called the Wolfanger

Inn: dozens of mounted wolf heads decorated the walls, and wolf pelts covered the floor. She grimaced. She wouldn't have batted an eye at a few pelts or heads, but this was just excessive.

Galce approached the bar, where an innkeeper was pouring ale into a set of mugs on a tray. Winter followed behind him, doing her best to look meek. She drew a few glances, but most humans in the inn apparently still didn't mind a servile tiellan.

"We'll take two rooms," Galce said.

"I'll take two silvers, then," the innkeeper grunted. He didn't look up at Galce until he'd handed the tray of ale mugs to one of his servers. When he saw Winter, the corners of his mouth turned down.

"She a friend of yours?" the innkeeper said, regarding Winter with narrowed eyes.

Galce looked back at Winter.

Bloody stick with the plan.

"Course not," Galce said, turning back to the innkeeper. "She's a servant of mine. The extra room is for her and my guard."

Good. Just as we'd practiced.

The innkeeper nodded. "As it should be," he said. "Two silvers, then."

Galce paid the man, and Winter and her companions were about to walk up the stairs to their rooms when the common room's commotion quickly died down, and the entire inn grew eerily silent.

Winter turned to see a young couple that had just entered the inn. A husband and wife, she suspected. They looked very young, maybe even Winter's age, but they had three children. Two girls stood between them, and a little boy at their feet. Winter could not imagine such a life. To have three children at her age? Such a thing seemed impossible. She had married late, and then her husband had been killed. That had changed much more besides.

The man was human, but the woman, Winter quickly realized, was tiellan, and each of their children bore the pointed ears of the tiellan race—slightly smaller than their mother's, as was the case with most mixed-race children, but prominent all the same. She hadn't even realized the woman was tiellan because she wasn't wearing a *siara*, and her dress was much more stylish than that of a traditional tiellan.

That could have been my life, Winter thought. She had married Knot, a human, in the hope of making her life better than it might have been otherwise. Based on the reaction of the people in this inn, however, Winter began to doubt whether it actually would have made anything better at all.

"Bloody elf-lover," someone in the common room muttered. A few grunts and shouts of agreement followed.

"You aren't welcome here!" someone else shouted.

Winter was about to turn and usher Galce and Urstadt up the steps when the next comment arrested her.

"Look at those mongrels," someone laughed. "Those brats are somewhere between human and tiellan. Probably the worst of both."

Winter turned. They were just *children*, for Canta's sake. But she felt a firm hand on her shoulder.

"You wanted to keep a low profile," Urstadt whispered. "Getting involved here will not help with that."

Winter clenched her jaw, torn between intervening, somehow, and leaving it all behind her. She hadn't come to Cineste for this. But was it really possible for her to stand by while it happened?

Winter closed her eyes, and Chaos shone white in her mind. She swore under her breath. What did Chaos know about this, anyway?

"I... we just want a room," the husband said, stepping in front of his family protectively. "Just arrived here from Triah, and—"

The innkeeper stepped forward. Winter's core tightened; she had no confidence this man would help things, and her instincts were correct.

"We can get you a room, friend," the innkeeper said, spreading his arms wide, "it's your elf wife and mongrel children we can't accommodate. My apologies. You understand, I'm sure."

The husband shook his head, eyes darting around in confusion. Things in Cineste were apparently much worse for tiellans than they were in Triah. Winter noticed a group of human men edging their way towards the family—members of the City Watch, Winter realized—and she clenched her fists.

The poor fool.

The man began to corral his family towards the door. "We'll just find somewhere else to—"

The violence came more suddenly than Winter would have expected. Two of the armored men grabbed the husband, one of them bringing his gauntleted fist into the man's gut. The wife screamed, reaching out for her children, but four other City Watchmen converged on the family, and forced the woman and her children out the door.

"Where are you taking them?" the husband screamed, then gasped as the watchmen punched him in the gut again.

Winter jammed her hand into her *faltira* pouch and took a crystal. Urstadt's grip on her shoulder tightened, but Winter didn't care. Urstadt would not control her. She closed her eyes, saw that Chaos was still white, and opened them again. Chaos didn't bloody control her, either.

"Stay here,"Winter said to Urstadt and Galce.

She charged out of the inn after the watchmen that had taken the rest of the family, frost warming her veins.

It didn't take her long to catch up to them. She made quick work of the four watchmen, each of them dying with a look of surprise on his face as his own weapon turned on him.

Winter approached the tiellan woman and her children. The young ones were sobbing while the woman tried to shield their eyes from the murdered men that had only recently taken them away roughly from their father.

"Come with me," Winter said, "I can get you somewhere safe." Or as safe as a tiellan could be in Cineste, she imagined.

The woman stared at Winter, eyes wide. "Who are you?" she asked.

Winter shrugged. "Doesn't matter. But I suggest following me. If more watchmen catch you around those bodies, things'll get much worse for all of you."

"What about my husband?" the woman asked.

Winter said nothing in response. She couldn't guarantee anything on that front.

Fortunately, the woman gathered her children around her, and followed Winter to the tiellan quarter. Unfortunately, the one place in Cineste Winter knew tiellans would be just so happened to be the last place on the Sfaera she wanted to go.

The woman and her children followed Winter to the Black Eye Inn, near the center of the tiellan quarter. The same inn she and Lian had visited when they were searching for Knot, after he'd run away in the wake of their disrupted wedding. At the time she'd been so caught up in her quest that she hadn't even noticed the inn's name, but now that she stood in front of it, a large faded sign drew her eyes.

Her mind had been occupied by other things back then. A shiver crept up her spine.

The fault doesn't lie with you, she remembered Kali saying. *End of story.*

Winter believed that, now. But that did not take away the memory of the man who had pulled her out of this place—of Lian knocked unconscious, of the tiellans in the bar who had pretended not to see what was happening. The memory of his rough hands on her, of her helplessness. She'd been rescued by a human, of all people, by Nash, her first mentor in psimancy. She wished she had not asked Galce and Urstadt to stay behind. Almost immediately, she ridiculed herself for such a desire. Why did she need their help? She had *faltira*. What had happened to her here, in a nearby alley, would never happen to her again.

"Is that where you're taking us?" the tiellan woman beside her asked.

"Yes," Winter said. Fortunately, the children were no longer sobbing. The empty way they stared at nothing made Winter think they were anything but calm. She folded her arms tightly, trying to think of something other than the terrible things that might have happened to these four had she not intervened.

And the terrible things that, in all likelihood, might still happen to them in a place like Cineste.

Winter pulled her eyes away from the family and looked around. Here in the tiellan quarter, Winter saw traditionally dressed tiellans for the first time in nearly a year. Her unusual attire had already drawn some questioning glances. The tiellan women wore floor-length dresses and the traditional *siaras*—

wide, thick scarves wrapped around the shoulders and neck; the men sported loose-fitting trousers and long-sleeved shirts, along with their wide-brimmed *araifs*. Winter could recall, at the edge of her memory, a time when she had found such sights comforting. Their effect was different now. Winter had not worn a *siara* since she had crept through the Blood Gate of Navone with Knot, Lian, and the others. She no longer cared to wear one, let alone the hot, oppressive dresses that were traditional among tiellan women. Instead she wore the dark leather outfit Galce had tailored for her in Izet. Sleek, form-fitting, utilitarian. Very different from the garb of any other tiellan woman Winter had seen in Cineste. Her hair didn't help, either; she'd woven both sides of her raven-black hair against her skull in tight braids that snaked behind her ears, while she'd made the braids and twists at the crown of her head looser and more voluminous. All of the weaves opened up at the back of her head, falling down past her shoulders in untied locks. Tiellan hairstyles were never so intricate.

Her discomfort stemmed from more than appearance, however. As much as she disagreed with some of their traditions, most tiellans she had known were good folk. Kind, trying to do right by those around them. Winter had no idea what she qualified as at the moment, but "good folk" did not seem high on the potential list.

Taking a deep breath, Winter steeled herself. She was glad she still felt frost in her veins. Recently she'd been taking one every other day, even though she rarely needed to use her telenic powers. But if she didn't take *faltira*, she just did not feel like herself. The drug did not burn or freeze her the way it used to; now, she felt only the slightest warmth, the hint of a chill.

"Come on," Winter said, and led the family into the inn.

Her first order of business was to see the tiellan family off. She grabbed one of the servers as she walked in, and nodded toward the woman and her children.

"They're not in good shape. They need help. You'll see that they get it."

The server, an older woman, looked from Winter to the tiellan woman and her children. Her face creased with empathy, but not surprise. Helping tiellans in need must be something she did often, lately.

Winter did not look back at the family as she walked away and further into the common room. The inside of the Black Eye Inn looked just as familiar as the outside, although Winter had only seen it at night, in the middle of winter; the light of the setting sun made for an odd change. She recognized immediately the round table where she, desperately searching for Knot, had approached the human nobleman. How naive she had been, then.

And there, a few paces away, was the table at which she had sat with Lian.

Winter did not allow her gaze to linger. Instead, she walked straight to the bar, asking after the innkeeper.

"That'd be me, darlin'," the tiellan man behind the counter responded. "What can I do for ya?"

"I'm looking for—"

"Winter?"

Winter turned at the sound of the voice behind her. A deep bass voice, one she recognized immediately.

"Gord?"

The huge tiellan man rushed forward immediately, wrapping his arms around her, and the two of them embraced in silence for what felt like a very long time. How light she felt in his arms—he lifted her like he had when she was a child. But soon, the weight of how much she had changed crashed down on her. She resisted the urge to squirm; as uncomfortable as she felt, she wasn't willing to let this moment go.

When Gord released her, tears were streaming down his cheeks and into his beard. Gord was of an age with her father, but his shoulders were still broad, his arms thick with muscles. Last she'd seen him, he'd been gravely injured after the Ceno monks had attacked her wedding party. She smiled to see him looking so strong now.

"Goddess rising, girl." Gord placed his heavy hands on Winter's shoulders. "Where have you been all this time? Is Lian with you? And Knot?"

The mention of the two men opened a chasm in Winter's belly she had almost forgotten was there. She ought to cry at this moment, at having to tell Gord that they'd both been killed. She should feel sadness. But, beneath the dull burn of frost, she didn't feel anything at all. She only shook her head.

"Oh, Winter." Gord embraced her once more, but he must have sensed her stiffness this time, as he released her much more quickly. "My apologies if I'm bein' overbearing," he said, his voice husky. "It's just… I thought I'd never see you again."

"I am happy to have found you," Winter said. She meant it. As awkward as she felt, she *wanted* to be accepted by Gord, to return to whatever semblance of life she could muster.

But she could not stop one hand from straying to the *faltira* pouch at her waist.

"I looked for you in Pranna," Winter said, finally able to muster her thoughts. "Why did you leave?"

"Had to, child. Things in Pranna… life in that town ain't what it once was. Goddess rising, it ain't been that way in a good long while."

"Did anyone else come with you?" She inquired after all of her friends from home, of course, but again fear rose in her as she thought about informing Lian's parents of his death.

"Well, all of us that remained left together, of course. Eranda and Darrin and their little ones are here. I can take you to them, if you like."

"Please," Winter said.

Winter found it difficult to navigate the contrasting joy, fear, and shame of the next few hours. Darrin and Eranda, and their children, Sena, Lelanda, and Tohn, received Winter with tears of happiness into their small living quarters, a tiny basement area in the tiellan quarter of Cineste. Tears of pain followed, when Winter told them that Lian and Knot had both been killed. She refrained from details, for now—how to even begin to explain her journey to these people, Winter could not fathom.

Igriss and Huro were nowhere to be seen. When Winter asked after them, Gord lowered his head.

"They didn't last long, after you and Lian left," he said sadly. Winter's gut tightened. "Humans?" she asked. "Did they...?"

Gord's eyes stared out into nothing. "No. No, for once humans had nothing to do with it. After they'd discovered Lian had left with you, they just... they wasted away. Both passed within a year of you being gone."

Guilt pierced Winter's chest. Lian's parents had not been particularly young; her father had once told her they had married late, and even then had great difficulty bearing children. Lian was the only baby Igriss had carried that survived leaving the womb. Nevertheless, she did not remember them being particularly weak or frail at the time of her wedding to Knot. She could only imagine what the couple had gone through when they found out Lian had chased after her—a woman already married to another man.

And now they, like their son, were gone.

As Winter spoke with Gord, Darrin, and Eranda, her sense of dissociation increased. Where her friends were welcoming and loving, Winter felt only an aching emptiness. She attempted to return their affection, and by the Goddess, *wanted* to connect with them, but as the effects of *faltira* faded from her blood, she felt nothing strong enough to hold a candle to its fire—muted though it had become—let alone replace it.

She had hoped to rediscover herself by returning to Pranna, and that hope had remained at the thought of seeing her friends again. But, now that she was here, the hope itself seemed foolish. Even before her wedding, before she'd ever met Knot, she'd always felt a part of her was missing, different. It was no use rediscovering a person that was already broken to begin with.

Despite her disappointment, Winter did feel some happiness at seeing her friends again. Tohn and Lelanda had both grown so much that Winter hardly recognized them, and Sena was now a woman of sixteen summers. Winter could remember thinking what a beautiful couple Darrin and Eranda made, both with long hair and smooth, refined features, and while that beauty remained, the past months had clearly taken a toll. Their faces were gaunt, ashen, and creased.

Winter coasted through the conversation, like her father's boat would skim over calm waters in summertime.

What did you expect from this reunion?

Something more than this.

Winter was contemplating leaving, and perhaps never returning, when something Gord said caught her attention.

"Did you say Druids?" Winter asked.

Gord nodded solemnly. The conversation had turned to the state of affairs for tiellans in Cineste.

"Lian spoke of the Druids," Winter said, almost involuntarily. "He told me he'd been coming to meetings in Cineste. Trying to bring back the Age of Marvels or something." Winter had thought his words crazy at the time, about how the tiellans should be returned to their former glory, how tiellans lived in harmony with the Elder Gods and with Canta and how things could be that way again. She had scoffed at such things.

You'll understand, one day, he'd said. *You'll understand why this is so important.*

Gord grunted. "Always suspected that boy had a rebellious streak in him," he said. "Lian was quiet, but he had a strength to him, too. Never could stand for the injustice done to us."

"Do you both... do you both attend their meetings?" Winter asked.

Darrin looked down at the dirt floor, silent. Instead, Eranda spoke up.

"Aye," she said. "I do, with Gord, on occasion. We've yet to convince Darrin of their... importance."

"Can't leave our children by themselves," Darrin mumbled.

"Sena is more than old enough to tend them for a few hours, love. That ain't what's keeping you from them." Eranda glanced at Winter. "But this ain't the time or place for such arguments. We can talk of something else, Winter, if it throws you off. If this is somethin' that Lian—"

"No," Winter said quickly, surprised at her own insistence. "Please, I'd like to hear more about the meetings. I'd like to attend one, if that's all right."

Eranda's eyes widened. "I don't think that'd be a problem at all," she said. "You'd be welcome among them, I'm sure of it."

Winter was as surprised as Eranda. But, considering how lost she felt around the people who'd helped raise her, perhaps she sought acceptance in something greater.

She had to belong somewhere.

Gord coughed. "Might want to find yourself a *siara*, though, child. Best be respectful of such things at these meetings."

"*Gord*," Eranda whispered. It was considered bad form for a tiellan man to ask about a woman's *siara*, and similarly taboo for a woman to ask about a man's *araif*.

"It's all right," Winter said. "I'll think about it, Gord, but the *siara* never did anything for me before. I can't imagine it would now if I were to put one on."

The silence that greeted her told Winter how shocking her statement was to her rediscovered friends. She did not mind. She was done following rules just because of tradition.

"You will take me, then?" Winter asked.

Gord still seemed reluctant, but Eranda smiled. "Of course, Winter. We will take you to one of the meetings."

"Good," Winter said.

After they had shared a meal together—a meager thing prepared by Darrin and Eranda, but savory and filling—Winter was about to say her goodbyes when Eranda pulled her aside.

"You have a place to stay?" Eranda asked.

Winter nodded.

"You're welcome here anytime."

"Of course," Winter responded, attempting a smile. "Thank you, Eranda."

"Are you all right, Winter?" Eranda's dark blue eyes looked into Winter so deeply that she was afraid Eranda might see, somehow, everything she was trying to hide.

Winter looked away. "I'm fine, Eranda. Things have been difficult, but…"

Eranda embraced her, and Winter was surprised to feel the woman crying softly against her.

"I'm so sorry," Eranda said, whispering as she wept. "I am so sorry for what you've gone through, for all you must have had to do to survive. I am so sorry we could not have helped you more."

Winter patted Eranda's back softly, wanting desperately to comfort the woman but feeling completely inadequate. What could she say? What could she possibly do to help this woman? Eranda's feelings were faulty, that much was clear. Nothing *Eranda* could have done would have changed anything about Winter's life over the past year. Why Eranda felt badly for this, she could not say. But that did not change the fact that she wanted to stop Eranda's tears, to take away her pain.

Eranda still felt her wounds deeply, while Winter's own pain had become so dull she hardly noticed it anymore. Perhaps, somehow, Winter could do something to help Eranda. It was something she would consider.

"There's something I want to give you," Eranda said, disappearing into the other room.

Winter heard laughter, and turned to see Gord, Darrin, and Sena playing a game with the younger children, Lelanda and Tohn. Bridge Over, the game was called. Winter could remember playing it with Lian, Gord, and her father when she was very young.

Eranda came back out, a cloth held tightly in her hands. When Winter recognized the thing, she froze.

It was the swaddling cloth she had received during her Doting, the day of her wedding.

Eranda extended the cloth, draped over her hands, to Winter. "You left this with us, when you and Lian went after Knot. I know it wasn't practical to take with you, but I kept it, in case you ever returned. In case you ever..."

In case I ever needed it. She could not imagine having a child in this world. With Knot, there was a part of her that had thought it might one day be a possibility. She had even dreamt such a thing, a vividly real dream, when Kali had first administered *faltira* to her. But those days were gone. A great dread welled up within her at the thought of even touching the swaddling cloth. She wanted to reach out and take it, just to be polite, but she could not. A consuming fear stopped her, as if she no longer had control of herself.

Eranda, after a moment, must have realized Winter could not take the cloth. Quickly she lowered it, tucking it under one arm. "It was presumptuous of me to offer it, after everything you have gone through. I should've waited."

"It's all right," Winter said softly, tearing her eyes away from the pale swaddling cloth to meet Eranda's eyes once more.

Eranda nodded, ever so slightly.

"I need to go." Winter made for the door. She turned back to look at each of them, these people from her past, who had shown her such kindness. Kindness she did not deserve. "I will see each of you again soon."

"Winter," Eranda said, catching her eye once more. "I will keep it for you. Until you are ready."

The woman drifts in the Void, sometimes slowly, ripples of color circling outward at each step, sometimes levitating, sinking within herself and into the blackness of the great expanse around her.

In the Void, the woman has realized, everything is peaceful. "Peaceful" is perhaps not the right word, but the feeling comes as close as the woman can imagine to peace, short of death. The woman senses Kali's presence nearby, as she always does, but ignores her former teacher. Kali is always close, but has not approached since Chaos dictated the woman attack Kali with her newly discovered acumenic *tendra*. The woman senses other presences as well, nearby and very far away, but none of them are of any import. None of them could bring back what the woman has lost.

One of these presences is close. Something large, imposing, a force the woman has never encountered before, neither in the Void nor out of it. The presence looms, a bright red light that slowly forms in front of the woman.

The woman scowls, halting her slow drift. The red starlight coalesces into a man, bigger than any she has ever seen, all muscle and sinew and unadulterated power. His face is indistinct, like Kali's shifting visage, but where Kali's features shift, merge, and transform between different faces, this figure's visage is blank, a smooth blur where eyes, nose, and mouth should be.

Nevertheless, the form speaks to her, its voice hardened and sharp.

"Hello, Winter."

The woman steps back, light rippling away from her.

"My name is Mefiston," the form says.

The woman is not familiar with the name. And yet the way she feels, the sensation of anger welling up within her, resonates. She has felt it before, but not like this. She has felt fear like this before, but not anger.

"You are one of the Nine."

"The Nine," Mefiston echoes, laughing. The laugh is soft, gentle, in sharp contrast to the steely edge of his speech. "A peculiar moniker. Confusing. There were Nine Disciples, once, and they wrote Nine Scriptures. Nine Marvels of the Sfaera, and Nine Ages in Eternity. And, before there was one Goddess, there were Nine."

Mefiston has now formed enough that his footsteps, too, ripple in the Void, though his face remains shrouded. She realizes, if she were to see him in the Sfaera, he would be the biggest man she has ever seen. Not just in height, but in girth as well, formed of muscle and sinew, with no excess to speak of.

"You are Wrath," the woman says.

"I am Wrath."

"And you serve Azael?"

A bright flash of red emanates from the form, and the woman takes another step back.

"I serve no one," Mefiston says, and the woman cannot be sure but she thinks the form grows larger as he says it.

"You are associates, then."

"Azael does not concern us," Mefiston says. "I am here to discuss something else with you."

"And what is that?"

"Your ascendancy."

The woman must be cautious. She speaks to one of the Nine Daemons, to a lieutenant of Azael—the woman knows this to be the case, whatever Mefiston himself says—and that act alone puts her in great danger.

But the woman has cared little for her own well-being for some time. She sees no reason to begin again now.

"I see I will have to explain further. I would like you to be my avatar, Winter. I would like to invest in you my power, and for you to be my mouthpiece on the Sfaera."

"Why don't you just go there yourself?"

Mefiston paces, now, light rippling back and forth from him, extending out into the blackness. "I will, eventually. But gaining an avatar is part of that process."

"That did not work out so well for your master."

"*He is not*—" Mefiston stops, another flash of red light bursting outward. The Daemon's huge frame is still for a moment, before he finally speaks again. "He is not my master."

It seems to the woman that such vehement denial belies underlying truth, but she says nothing about it.

"You want me to be for you what Daval was for Azael?"

A low growl emanates from Mefiston's frame, but he eventually responds. "Yes. That is what I want."

She laughs, letting the sound ring through the Void. When it fades, she looks at Mefiston, jaw set.

"Are you done?"

A third flash bursts forth from Mefiston's frame, and for a moment the woman anticipates conflict, and a thrill rushes through her, blended with anger, anticipation, and fear.

Instead Mefiston, too, laughs; the same soft, fluttering laugh she heard from him earlier.

"Very well, girl. I figured it was worth the asking. I will not force myself upon you, but the day will come when you'll wish you'd accepted my offer."

"Forgive me," the woman says, "if I choose not to believe a word you say. And please, take my words to heart."

Then the woman winks out of the Void, and feels herself rushing back to her body in the Sfaera.

6

Odenite camp, outside Kirlan

"KNOT, I WISH TO speak with you."

Knot turned to see Cinzia. He had been absorbed in watching the maneuvers of the guard force. They had found a space in the fallow land that stretched out before Kirlan's walls, away from the general hubbub of the Odenite camp. He signaled to Eward, indicating the lad should take control of the training exercises.

"At your service," he said. The Outsider's attack a few days before had shaken Cinzia more than most. She kept insisting on discovering more about the Nine Daemons, but didn't seem to have much to go on. Knot sympathized with her—she wasn't wrong, they *needed* more information—but it was useless to spin a wheel that didn't touch the ground. They had other problems, ones they could actually do something about, that needed addressing first.

"Walk with me, please," Cinzia said, and began moving away from the training Prelates.

Knot fell in beside her. It was a warm day, the sky cloudless above as the sun arced into the evening.

"Astrid has not returned?" Cinzia asked, voicing his thoughts.

"Not yet."

She had left on her little spying mission late the previous night. This was not the first time the girl had taken her time on such a task, but worry clouded Knot's emotions anyway.

Cinzia cleared her throat. "I must admit, I…"

Knot glanced at Cinzia, waiting for her to finish, but she didn't.

"You what?"

"I believe I misjudged her," Cinzia said. "I still do not understand how or why she is what she is, but… it was wrong of me to assume."

Knot grunted. "Ain't me you need to say that to, I reckon." There was a long line of people who needed to make that kind of apology to Astrid, and Knot was one of them. But it only did good if they actually said it to *her*.

They walked in silence for a few moments. Knot enjoyed Cinzia's company, whether they were speaking or not. The woman had a calming effect on him. Made him feel more himself.

As they fell out of earshot of the others, Cinzia spoke again. "I'd like you to be my Goddessguard, Knot."

Knot continued walking in stride with her. "Didn't think having a new Goddessguard was something you'd take an interest in, all things considered."

"What do you mean by that?"

Knot cleared his throat. Kovac, Cinzia's previous Goddessguard, was a sensitive subject for her. "I mean a few different things," he said slowly. "You cared for Kovac. What happened to him must've been rough on you, to put it lightly."

Cinzia nodded, but did not respond otherwise.

Knot continued. "And now… you're no longer a priestess, last I checked, and only the ministry in the Denomination have Goddessguards. Unless Jane has revealed something different?"

"Unless we uncovered something different in our translation, you mean?"

"Sure," he said. "That, too."

"The text says nothing about Goddessguards, for or against. Neither has Jane. And, honestly, I do not care. I think it is something I need."

Knot raised an eyebrow. "Something you need, or something you want?"

Cinzia sighed. "Need, want. I can hardly tell the difference anymore. I need someone I can confide in. Someone who will be on my side."

"I've got to be your Goddessguard to do those things for you?"

"No." Cinzia frowned. "That... that is not what I meant. My relationship with Kovac was important to me. Right now, I question many things. I feel better about a lot of things, too—my relationship with Canta, and my faith, but... but I still wonder about Jane. She should be the closest person in the world to me, and yet I feel we grow further and further apart every day."

"That can't be easy for you." He meant it. Truth was, he felt the same thing happening between himself and Astrid. There was something between them, some invisible wedge that drove them apart, no matter what either said or did. "And that's why you want me to be your Goddessguard?" he asked.

"And to protect me, of course. And Jane, and the other disciples."

"I already protect you," Knot said. He was already willing to do all she asked. Why did she need the label to go with it?

"I think it might be good for me, Knot. For both of us."

Knot let out a deep breath. Beside him, Cinzia stopped. They'd reached the edge of the forest, sparse undergrowth sprouting before them.

"I'm grateful for our friendship, and I'll protect you," Knot said, "but I don't think I need to be your Goddessguard."

Cinzia looked down, and for a moment didn't say anything. Finally, she met his eyes. "I understand," she said, with a slight nod.

"Do you?"

Cinzia shrugged. "It is not something I wish to impose on you, or anyone, for that matter. Kovac chose to be my Goddessguard, after I asked him. I would never have it any other way with you. If you choose not to do it, I cannot hold that against you."

"There's more to it," Knot said. "I've been a lot better since the *cotir* healed me."

"You have. As much as I hate them for what they did to us, in a way I'll always be grateful. They made sure you could stay with us. Permanently."

Knot understood the sentiment. The Nazaniin *cotir* that had healed him of his fits—Wyle, Cymbre, and Jendry—had also hidden their ulterior objective to assassinate Jane. Jane and Cinzia had defeated them, but the duplicity still stung. Even more so when Jane had insisted they let the *cotir* go. She had reasoned that the Nazaniin would no longer cause problems for the Odenites, and while Jane had a suspiciously good track record when it came to such statements, Knot hated the idea of Wyle, Cymbre, and Jendry wandering the Sfaera as they pleased.

Nevertheless, here Knot was, more stable than he'd ever been. He hadn't experienced a single episode since Wyle had guided him through the stabilization process.

"There's more to it," Knot repeated. "Other people taking over my body ain't a worry of mine anymore, but that's given me time to think about other things." He hesitated. He had yet to say this out loud to anyone. He might once have told Astrid, but the gulf between them felt unbridgeable at times. But he wanted to express it now. With Cinzia, it felt... it felt right. "I'm nobody, Cinzia," Knot finally said.

"Knot, that is not true, you are—"

"Don't mean it in a derisive way, darlin'. Just in a factual way. I'm just... no one. I didn't lose my memories; I just don't have any. I don't have parents. I don't have ancestors. I'm in a stolen body, and it was never mine to begin with."

"But you have done so much good."

"Ain't sure good and bad has much to do with this," Knot said. *It's about identity,* he wanted to say.

"And you worry that if you say yes to being my Goddessguard, you might not discover who you are?"

"That's about right," Knot said, surprised at how astute Cinzia's observation truly was.

"I think I can understand that," Cinzia said. "If you ever do find yourself..."

"I'd be privileged to serve as your Goddessguard," Knot said, and realized he meant it.

"I would be privileged to have you. But you should not feel any pressure from me," she added quickly. "I do not need a Goddessguard. I can do what I need to do on my own. I just thought..." Cinzia trailed off, and Knot did not know what else to say.

So he turned back to the camp. "We should get back," he said. "It's growing dark, and I have business to attend to." He needed to find out where Astrid was, and whether she'd discovered anything about the garrison in Kirlan.

"As do I," Cinzia said, her jaw set. Knot almost asked what business that might be, but refrained. They walked back to the camp together, in silence.

7

Kirlan

UNDER COVER OF NIGHT, Astrid slipped into the city of Kirlan. Her claws, sharp and strong enough to dig into stone, allowed her to scramble up the walls. She waited just below the ramparts, clinging to cracks in the mortar and rock, and strained her ears. A pair of Sons walked by, patrolling the walkway overhead. The fact the Sons of Canta had taken guard duty of the city upon themselves did not bode well. They must be serious about keeping the Odenites out of Kirlan.

After the Sons passed, Astrid dug her claws in and leveraged herself just enough to flip silently up onto the walkway. As soon as she landed, she felt a familiar, faint tugging sensation in the back of her mind.

"Shit," she whispered. Someone voking her, now, of all times.

Astrid retrieved one of the voidstones from her pocket—she knew exactly which one she needed—and placed her thumb on the rune inscribed upon it.

"Yes?" Astrid whispered. To her left, the guards she'd heard pass by were out of earshot. To her right, the walkway was empty. Glancing at the city below her, she saw a dark alley separating the wall from a quiet, unassuming-looking building.

"You are taking too long." The Black Matron's voice was cracked with age. And Astrid had to obey it. She had to, at all costs.

Astrid leapt down from the rampart, raising a small cloud of dust as she landed in the alley. She checked to see if anyone else was close enough to hear her before she responded.

"We've run into a problem. From *your* end, by the way. A contingent of the Sons of Canta have garrisoned themselves in Kirlan, blocking our progress. We cannot continue to Triah until we find a way around them."

"The false prophetess and her followers have been barred from continuing their journey," the Black Matron said, "but I see no reason why you and your charge cannot leave their company and follow the orders we've given you."

"Things are not that simple," Astrid said.

"Redemption is always that simple, child. You either do as your Goddess commands and find absolution, or you do not, and pay the price in blood."

Canta's bones, it's always blood.

"Where are you now, child?"

"I'm with the Odenites," Astrid whispered. "Trying to keep a low profile." She swept down the alley, cloak billowing behind her.

"I see. How soon can you get away from them?"

Astrid cringed inwardly. She'd wanted absolution, wanted it more than anything she'd ever known, until the price of her absolution became Knot. Now, she was not sure about anything.

"I cannot arouse suspicion—"

"Suspicion be damned. You're never going to return to those people; you should not care whether they suspect anything of you. When you're gone, you'll be gone forever."

Astrid had nothing to say to that. Instead, she moved quickly through the streets of Kirlan. Her original intent in coming here had been to scout the Sons' garrison. The longer the Black Matron kept her occupied, the less chance she had of achieving her goal.

"You are not answering me, little girl. Should I take this to mean you are going to forego any chance you may have at absolution?"

Astrid stopped running.

Shit. Shit, shit, shit.

"No," she breathed. "Please."

"Then fall into line."

Was that an echo Astrid heard?

"You don't want me to send someone along to help you in your task, do you?"

Astrid looked around. She was right—every word the Black Matron said had a ringing echo, as if…

Astrid sprang forward, realizing she had to run, but a woman stepped out of the street in front of her, a sprig of nightsbane pinned to her white and red cloak. Just being in close proximity to nightsbane significantly weakened vampires of any type. Astrid's strength began to drain immediately. If the nightsbane were to touch her, the weakness would turn quickly into excruciating pain.

Astrid skidded to a stop and turned, only to find another white-and-red-cloaked woman had appeared behind her, also wearing nightsbane.

"Please," Astrid said.

And then she saw *her*. Another woman, older, robes almost completely crimson, only trimmed by white. A thin face, with high cheekbones and wrinkled skin around sunken eyes.

In a flash, Astrid suddenly saw herself alone in a small shack, sitting on a chair in the middle of the space. There was a single door, in front of her. Closed. Astrid gripped the chair on which she sat so tightly her fingers cramped in pain. Her breaths were quick and ragged, her heart pounding violently in her ears. *She was coming. She* would be here. Astrid didn't know when, but it had to be soon.

"Come with us, child," the Black Matron said.

Astrid had no choice but to follow.

They brought her to a Cantic chapel, and dragged her into a large side room. Compared to the ornate painted grandeur of the chapel itself, this chamber's plainness was glaring. A table ran along one side of the room, with two mismatched chairs nearby. A row of cupboards lined another wall, and that was all the room had to offer.

The last time the Black Matron had been angry with her, she'd been tortured by a priestess in Izet. Astrid wanted to vomit just thinking of the nightsbane water that woman had poured all over her, burning her, choking her, killing her over and over again.

And yet, Astrid was no stranger to torture. If it was torture she faced, she could get through it.

"Sister Arene taught you a lesson in Izet," the Black Matron said, as if reading her thoughts, her gaunt eyes lingering on Astrid, "but it seems that lesson did not stick. You have been obstinate since you joined paths with Lathe, or Knot, or whatever he calls himself lately. Obstinacy is not an attribute we appreciate in servants, child."

"What do you want with him?"

"Our business is our own."

"If I knew, it'd be easier to—"

The Black Matron slammed her fist down onto the table with such force that Astrid heard the wood crack beneath her hand. No woman of her age should be able to do such a thing.

"Redemption does not require knowledge, girl. Only obedience. When will you comprehend this lesson?"

"Give me more time—"

"Did you give your family more time before you slaughtered them?" the Black Matron asked.

Astrid froze. She herself did not remember anything about her family, her life before she was turned. Nothing more than a single hollow, meaningless, horrifying memory. It was impossible for the Black Matron to know anything.

"My family died hundreds of years ago," Astrid said. "You couldn't possibly know what happened to them."

"But you do," the Black Matron said. "And because you do, so do I."

"You couldn't, not unless you're..."

Astrid stumbled backwards, crashing into the cupboards behind her. The Black Matron was an acumen.

"Yes," the woman said, her eyes dark. "And I can tell you every detail of how you killed your family. I can tell you exactly what you did, how *you* tortured *them*. I can tell you about every victim of yours, the innocent and the guilty, given enough time. I can tell you exactly what you need redemption from, little girl."

Flashes of things Astrid once knew, of friends and acquaintances and actions, crackled through her. This had happened before, she realized. The Black Matron had leveraged this against her before. And because she was an acumen, she had simply forced Astrid to forget.

Astrid cowered against the wall as the Black Matron closed in on her. She was truly helpless.

"Believe me, child. The list is long."

* * *

Astrid did not know how long she stayed in the Black Matron's custody. The nightsbane made her senses dull and groggy, and the Black Matron's words... Astrid could not believe them. And, at the same time, she had no choice but to believe them.

The sky was dark when they released her, but the moon had waned. They'd kept her an entire day, then. She felt, on her way through the streets of Kirlan, that she ought to be limping. It was an odd sensation. They had not harmed her physically, other than keeping her in close proximity to nightsbane. Astrid did not remember what the Black Matron had shown her. The details of her past, especially before she was turned, were still unclear to her.

But she could remember the pain.

Questions crept across her mind, but Astrid could barely acknowledge them. Why had the Black Matron come herself? What did they want with Knot? How had they found her? One of their number must be a voyant, she decided.

And had the Black Matron been telling Astrid the truth?

The Black Matron had promised her redemption. If that meant escaping the pain she felt from all she had done, it was something she had to consider.

8

Cineste, northern Khale

DUSK HAD FALLEN, BATHING the streets of Cineste in cool, gray-violet light, as Gord and Eranda led Winter to a tall, unassuming building at the border of the tiellan and merchant sectors of the city, not far from the Wolfanger Inn. A tiellan man stood at the doorway, short but thickly muscled, and eyed Winter uneasily. She could almost see him squirm, trying not to look at her bare neck, the clothing she wore that he must surely find strange, if not outright offensive. The man's gaze shifted to Gord. "She's with you?"

"Aye, Talian, she's with us," Gord said.

"Very well then," Talian said, glancing again at Winter's neck and then quickly away. "Ain't gonna turn any tiellan away. Need all the support we can get."

Talian stepped aside, allowing Gord, Winter, and Eranda to enter. Darrin had stayed home with the children, while Galce and Urstadt had stayed at the inn they shared with Winter. Winter wanted to introduce them to her old friends, but it was not yet time. She wasn't ready.

Inside was a wide room, full of tiellans. The space was larger than Winter would have expected. A few long tables had been pushed entirely to one side of the room near a set of stairs leading to a second level, leaving the other side relatively open. A small wooden platform opposite the door through which they'd entered stood at the front of the large open space. Tiellan bodies milled together in front of the platform, chattering together. Winter noticed more than one tiellan staring at her unusual appearance.

"How many come to these meetings?" Winter asked. She could not think of the last time she saw so many of her people gathered together.

"More than a hundred," Gord said. "This serves as the headquarters for the movement, but it is just one of the many meeting places in Cineste, these days. Some of the Druids estimate over one thousand tiellans have joined the movement."

"They really call themselves Druids?" Winter asked. The term seemed so… archaic.

Before Gord could respond, a handful of tiellans approached the platform, and the crowd cheered. Winter inspected the group carefully: three men, two of them quite old, climbed onto the platform ahead of two women. Each of the men wore an *araif*, pulled slightly back on their heads to let the light shine onto their eyes. This wasn't unusual—it was considered impolite to shade one's eyes indoors.

"Are they elders?" Winter asked, leaning towards Gord. Elders were the cultural leaders of the tiellans; ages ago, they had held real power, but now the name was nothing more than a formality. Too often, they and their female counterparts, the matriarchs, had seemed a superfluous, outdated remnant of a lost past to Winter.

"The two older are, but not the younger. The younger is Ghian Fauz." Gord said the name as if Winter should recognize it, but the man meant nothing to her. He was older than Winter, but not by much, and handsome, with silver hair cut short above a round, handsome face and long, sinewy limbs.

"Goddess, is that Matriarch Esra?" Winter asked, her eyes widening. The older of the two women—though both had clearly waxed long in age—looked very familiar. Long, auburn hair streaked with gray. Firm, smooth features. And the way she carried herself... Very few tiellans moved as confidently as Matriarch Esra, her back always straight, shoulders square, neck long and proud even beneath her *siara*.

"Aye," Gord responded quietly. "Was wonderin' if you'd recognize her."

Matriarch Esra had lived in Pranna for years, when Winter was young. But she left before Winter had seen her fifteenth summer.

"So the Druids are just... elders and matriarchs?" Winter asked.

Gord grunted. "Not exactly. Ghian is the true leader of the Druids. When the elders and matriarchs started to see the popularity of the Druid movement, they attached themselves to it."

"And Ghian just... allowed this?"

"Ghian believes the Druids must unite tiellans," Gord said. "He wants to include all who are willing."

Or, she thought, *he knows how to stay in power.*

That thought brought a frown to her face. It sounded very much like something Daval would say. Surely she had left all of that behind, in Roden.

Esra stepped forward, hands raised, and the crowd quieted.

"My brothers and sisters," she said, her voice firm and strong. "Welcome. We like to see so many of you. Our numbers continue to grow. A welcome to those of you who are new here."

Winter could not be sure, but she thought Esra met eyes

with her when she said that. Winter could not pretend she was surprised; she stood out in the crowd. She wondered if Esra had recognized her as Bahc's daughter, or simply as a newcomer.

A round of gentle applause and muted cheers greeted Esra's welcome. She lowered her hands, and the crowd quieted once more.

"Tensions keep risin' between humans and tiellans. We've received word of more atrocities, and our people keep bendin' their backs beneath the hand of human persecution. Many of you know of the long walk of Sazar Mekeen."

The crowd murmured at the mention of that name, though it was another that meant nothing to Winter. She glanced at Gord.

"A tiellan man from Farahle City in southern Khale," he whispered. "Physician's assistant who eventually became a physician himself."

Winter's eyebrows raised. Tiellans never became full physicians. That was a human's job.

"He saved many lives, human and tiellan," Gord continued, "but was, of course, unable to save everyone. A few human patients of his perished, and then the humans turned on him. Put him through a farce of a trial, and then made him walk Farahle's streets, naked and beaten, stripped of honor, until they finally executed him."

Winter stared forward, eyes unfocused. How could such a thing have happened? What could possibly possess the humans to hate a tiellan man so much—a tiellan man who had helped them, no less?

At the head of the crowd, Esra continued speaking. "Here in Cineste, we've had our own Sazar Mekeen. Jemmen Kantrel was beaten to death in the street just last week."

The crowd's murmurs transformed to shouts, and, looking around, Winter saw the anger on the faces around her. Gord's face was red as he shook his fist in the air. Eranda, on Winter's other side, was quiet, her jaw set.

Goddess... Beaten to death in the street? What has happened since I've been gone?

"And we've just got word of a massive attack on the west coast," Esra continued. "A mob of Kamites—more than one hundred, if the rumors tell it true—attacked and slaughtered dozens of our people near the town of Tinska just a few weeks ago. An attack of such a blatant and malicious nature ain't occurred yet in Cineste, but I fear it's only an omen of what's to come."

An *attack*. Winter could hardly believe it. There had been nothing like this, not since the King Who Gave Up His Crown.

"Make no mistake, brothers and sisters," Esra continued, "things'll only get worse before they get better. We *must* band together. Show our strength. And we have strength. I know it."

Winter's hand strayed to the pouch at her belt as the crowd murmured in agreement. On either side of her, Gord and Eranda were nodding.

She was not sure what to think of any of this. The persecutions, murders, and attacks might have horrified the girl Winter had been in Pranna. But the woman she was now looked at them differently. Tragic, to be sure, but no worse than some of what she had seen—some of what she had *done*—in the past year of her life.

Which, perhaps, was all the more reason to help these people.

Esra pursed her lips. "I've said enough. Here's a man who needs no introduction." She looked behind her at Ghian Fauz.

"Although I do wish you'd let me say a bit more every once in a while. Some of the newcomers ain't heard all you've done for your people, Ghian."

Winter could not tell if the matriarch's words were sarcastic or genuine. A low murmur of polite laughter rippled through the crowd. They, at least, read it as praise.

"Suppose they'll find out, one way or another. Brothers and sisters, I give you Ghian Fauz."

Ghian stepped forward to take her place. "Thank you, Matriarch Esra," he said, smiling at her. He removed his *araif*.

Winter tensed, looking around her. Had he removed it because of her? But the rest of the crowd did not seem put off by the gesture. Was this something he did frequently?

And yet, as Ghian began to speak, Winter felt his eyes rest on her. He looked right at her, it seemed, almost *through* her. He spoke with confidence, his voice assured, his words clear and concise. He, like Winter and her father, did not speak with the typical tiellan drawl, and immediately Winter felt a sense of kinship with him, something she had longed for since she'd reunited with Gord, Eranda, and Darrin but had not yet found.

She turned, suddenly, looking at the door behind her. She'd thought she heard voices outside, but as she strained her ears, she sensed nothing out of the ordinary. The guard was probably still posted outside the door; maybe it was a short exchange with someone in passing.

"Make no mistake," Ghian said. His accent was that of an educated human. "A war is coming. We cannot avoid it. We cannot stop it. We will have to fight for our families, our way of life, and our very lives."

Winter blinked. A war. Between humans and *tiellans*?

"We have already begun preparations for that war: we are

learning to fight, to defend ourselves. Many already participate in our Ranger training programs. I encourage the rest of you men to begin as well. We are stronger when we are together, and when we fight at our full strength, there is nothing on this Sfaera that can stop us."

Ranger training programs? Tiellan Rangers had been the great warriors of the Age of Marvels, the militaristic counterpart to the mystical Druids, but they were warriors of legend. It seemed a bit pretentious to use the name. And he'd invited only men to be "Rangers," something that made Winter bristle.

She flinched as three loud, sharp knocks rang through the large meeting space. Everyone turned to look at the door. Winter instinctively slipped a frost crystal into her mouth.

The door burst open, and Talian, the short, stout man who'd been guarding the door from the outside, tumbled into the room. From her position close to the door, Winter could clearly see the blood on Talian's face. He groaned, writhing on the floor.

A dozen humans strode into the room, armed with cudgels, clubs, and rods. As *faltira* took effect in her veins, Winter was suddenly acutely aware of the vulnerability of the tiellans around her. None of them were armed, at least as far as Winter could tell, and despite the fact that they outnumbered the humans almost ten to one, they shrank back towards the platform.

Almost before she was aware of it, Winter extended one of her *tendra* before her, snaking towards the club held by the human closest to her. But, before her *tendron* made contact, she stopped herself. She knew nothing of the Druids, nothing of their true goals or motivation. She had only just arrived in Cineste, only just reunited with Gord, Eranda, and Darrin. She had sought them out to let go of all she had done in Roden and

Navone. Despite that not going as well as she would have liked, she hesitated.

Slowly, her *tendron* retracted, and she closed her eyes. There, Chaos awaited, smooth and pearl-white. It was not her time to intervene.

"What do we have here?" one of the humans asked, swinging his club with a flick of his wrist.

"An elf orgy, by the looks of things," another said. A few of them chuckled, but most of the men were straight-faced. Angry.

"Can I help you folk?" Ghian stepped down from the platform and walked through the parted crowd towards the humans. Ghian did not seem a coward. That much was in his favor, at least.

A human stepped forward. "You can shut this shit down."

"We're within our rights to meet here," Ghian responded, walking up to the man. Ghian was of decent size for a tiellan, about the same height as the man he faced. They looked at each other eye to eye.

"Your rights don't concern me. What does is the safety of those I care about."

Ghian smiled. "We do not mean any harm to you, and certainly not to those in your care."

Winter scoffed. Had Ghian not just been advocating war with the humans? How did that not invite harm towards them?

"Your 'training programs' tell a different story," the man said.

Ghian's smile faded.

A lanky man laughed. "What, didn't think we knew what you people were up to? Trying to train yourselves to fight against us? Take everything that's ours and claim it for your own?"

The man facing Ghian raised a fist, and the lanky man closed his mouth. "I have nothing against any of you personally," he said, looking around the room. "But I will protect my family. And I'll cross any line to do that." He dropped his club and snapped forward in a smooth movement, twisting Ghian around and wrapping one arm around his head. In the other, he brandished a thin-bladed dagger.

The tiellans gasped, stepping back, and once again Winter instinctively activated her *tendra*. She could stop this. She had the power to do it. She could show Gord, Eranda, and the Druids her power.

And, at the same time, show them the monster she had become.

Again, she consulted Chaos. The sphere remained solid in her mind, unfalteringly white. Winter forced herself to relax. She had no part in what was about to happen.

"Any one of you tries to leave, any one of you even *moves*, and your leader dies," the human leader shouted. He nodded to his fellows, who stalked slowly forward.

"We're going to make examples out of a few of you," he said. "The rest of you should consider yourselves lucky. You will go home to your families tonight."

Winter, Gord, and Eranda stepped back, away from the advancing humans with the rest of the crowd. Winter's chest was tight, constricted, but she felt no fear for herself. She would be all right, whatever happened. But the feeling was there, all the same.

"Each of you choose one," the leader said to the men advancing on the tiellans. "Choose one, bring them up here with us. We'll do it in front of everyone."

Tiellans screamed, clinging to one another, but the humans

tore them away one by one, forcing them to the front of the room near the door, compelling them to kneel.

"Take men or women, young or old, it doesn't matter," the man said. "This lesson is for all."

Winter, Eranda, and Gord huddled together, Gord wrapping his arms around both Winter and Eranda in a vain attempt to protect them. Now, twelve tiellans knelt before twelve humans, not including Ghian and the human leader who threatened him, near the doorway into the building. People wept, but none of the tiellans moved to stop what was being done to them.

They are weak, Winter realized. Centuries of captivity had done this to her people. Even after emancipation, decades of persecution and derision and hatred had made them soft, brittle. They knew nothing but submission.

"Now," the human leader began, but before he could continue, one of the kneeling tiellans, a young man, turned on his captor and lunged. He took the human to the ground, but as quickly as he did the human standing directly beside them swung his club down on the young man's head with a sickening *crack*. The young tiellan buckled to the ground. The club swung again, this time with more of a crunch than a crack. It swung again, and again, until the tiellan's body was a bloodied mess on the floor.

All around Winter, the other tiellans were hysterical, weeping and crying, but they seemed frozen in place, as Winter herself felt frozen, too. She shed no tears, made no sound, but the constriction in her chest had magnified, and her arms and legs felt very heavy. The one tiellan among them that had the courage to stand up to the humans had been slaughtered.

What hope was there for the Druids?

"It's unfortunate he chose to do that," the leader said,

looking back into the tiellan crowd. "Because now that one doesn't count. Rudd, go find another."

The tiellans began screaming again as, silently, the man who'd been tackled walked forward, glaring into the tiellan crowd with hooded eyes. He stopped directly in front of Winter.

Winter, oddly, wanted to laugh. Let this man take her. Let him see what she would do to him.

But when he reached out he did not grasp Winter. Instead, he dragged Eranda with him to the front of the room, forcing her to kneel down next to the sickening remains of the young tiellan man they'd already killed.

A host of emotions burst inside of Winter. Anger at the helpless tiellans around her. Frustration at her inability to feel at home with Darrin, Eranda, and Gord, and fear that such a thing would never be possible again. Shame, knowing that what kept her from those she loved was what she herself had done. The person she had become.

She had come home in an attempt to let go of her past, to give up being a weapon. But she'd been wrong. More than anything, these people—her friends, her family, her people— *needed* a weapon.

Winter stepped forward. "You should have chosen me," she said.

This time, Winter did not consult Chaos. She did not hesitate, and reached out with thirteen *tendra*, one for each human in the room. Her first plucked the thin dagger out of the hands of the human leader. The man stared at his hand in shock. Her other *tendra* yanked the weapons away from the other humans, sending the clubs and cudgels and rods clattering, then lifted each human up by their clothes, and the building shook with the force of thirteen men slamming against the walls.

"You think you have the power here," Winter said. She heard Gord whisper her name, but ignored him. She was a monster, and he would have to grow used to it. She walked right up to the ringleader of the humans. "You're wrong."

She stabbed the man's own dagger through his neck, in one side and out the other. He fell to the floor with a gurgle, blood spouting from the wounds as he choked.

Then, keeping the other humans pinned to the wall, Winter did the same thing to each of them. The act was simple, pushing the dagger in with one *tendron*, pulling it out with another, until each of the men was dying or dead. Then she dropped them all to the floor at once.

Silently, Winter approached Eranda, helping the woman to her feet. They turned to face the other tiellans. Her people stared at her, wide-eyed, shocked, frozen. No one said anything, not Gord or Eranda or anyone.

Winter did not care whether they said anything or not. It would not change what had happened, or what was about to.

"They will not be the last," Winter said. She glanced at Ghian. "You said a war was coming. It's already here. You have multiple meetings like this that occur in the city?"

Ghian only stared at her.

Winter resisted the urge to roll her eyes. "I'm told you do. You need to band together. No more meeting separately. No more secrecy. Declare yourselves, make yourselves a force to be reckoned with. They will come after you now, there's no stopping that. You need to be prepared."

"Who are you?" Ghian rasped, finally rising to his feet. He looked around at the bodies slumped against the wall. "How did you..." He glanced up at her, eyes wide. "Are you a goddess?"

This time, Winter could not stop herself from laughing. *I'm a daemon,* she wanted to say. *But to you, what is the difference?*

"Danica Winter Cordier."

Winter turned at the sound of Matriarch Esra's voice. No one else here could possibly pronounce her name in that tone.

"Hello, Matriarch. I wasn't sure you would recognize me."

Esra approached, meeting Winter face to face. "I didn't, not 'til just now. You... you've got your mother in you."

She had heard that before, time and time again.

Gord had put his arm around Eranda's shoulders. "Winter, we have much to discuss, you and me. But I fear you're right. We ain't got much time. Need to band together, as you said." He hesitated, and in his eyes Winter suddenly saw a host of emotions she could hardly begin to understand. Fear. Pain. Horror. Love. "Will you stay with us?" he asked.

Winter looked around, at Eranda and Gord and Matriarch Esra, then at Ghian and the matriarchs and elders and other tiellans in the room. She looked at the bodies, the men she'd killed.

She did not belong here, just as she did not belong in Izet, or Pranna, or anywhere. But she *wanted* to belong here, and that hint of connection she'd felt with Ghian, through his speech and the removal of his *araif*, kept her here. Her desire to protect her old friends kept her here. She was a weapon, but she was the weapon her people needed.

"I will," Winter said, touching Gord's arm. "I will, for now."

9

North of Kirlan

WHILE KNOT'S REFUSAL TO accept the position of Goddessguard had hurt, Cinzia understood why he had refused. She could not imagine what it would be like, to be without family, without home or background or identity.

But it meant that she would have to do what she had planned next on her own.

Cinzia wrapped her cloak—an old, thinning brown thing she'd borrowed from her father—around her shoulders as she made her way through the Odenite tents. The sun had set, and it was getting dark. Cinzia lifted her lantern, checking the candle within. Plenty of wax and wick to light her way.

When she got to the edge of the clearing, she entered the forest. The location she sought was northeast of their own camp, not a mile away.

She was going to see the Beldam.

Their scouts—they had scouts now, which was something Cinzia had never considered, but Knot insisted was essential with a group this size, facing such opposition—kept vigilance over the Beldam's group at all times. While the Beldam and the Odenites who had defected with her had not expressed any outright hostility towards them, their intentions were still unclear, and any attempts to make contact and discern those intentions had been rebuffed.

But perhaps if Cinzia went herself, alone, the Beldam would listen. Unless they could finish the Codex translation soon—and that was unlikely—the Beldam was the only person she could think of who might have more information about the Nine Daemons, and about the Outsider that had attacked them the other day.

As Cinzia moved through the forest, dusk became darkness, the shadows of the trees grew until they encompassed everything, and Cinzia shivered despite the relative warmth of the night. She was alone in a dark, unfamiliar forest; she had not anticipated the fear that would creep along behind her.

Sooner than Cinzia expected, she began to hear voices carrying faintly through the trees. Lights flickered ahead. She stumbled on roots, and twigs caught in her hair despite her lantern, but she finally came upon a clearing, at the center of which was a small pond.

Dozens of tents were packed into the clearing, and four or five large fires burned between them, each one surrounded by people. She ought to know these people, she thought. Not long ago they were Odenites, though the number of Jane's followers had always been such that she had found it difficult to pick out more than a few individuals from the crowd. And the people in this clearing had chosen to follow the Beldam rather than Jane—rejecting their Prophetess almost as soon as they'd found her.

For them, tiellans had no place in the new Church of Canta.

Cinzia swallowed hard and pushed those thoughts down. She was not here to debate that issue. She was here for one reason only.

Cinzia walked slowly into the camp, looking for any indication of where the Beldam might be. She approached one of the fires cautiously. Around the fire, people drank and sang and chatted with one another. Other than the conspicuous absence of any tiellans, it looked exactly like one of the fires in the Odenite camp.

It did not take long for her to draw attention. One person glanced at her, then two, and soon everyone around the campfire she approached was staring at her in silence.

They would not have forgotten her, of course: Jane's sister, the first disciple.

"What do you want?" someone finally asked.

"I am looking for the Beldam," Cinzia said, straightening her shoulders. "I need to speak with her."

"Of course you do," someone muttered, their voice not quite low enough to be shielded by the crackle of the fire.

"Where can I find her?" Cinzia asked. She did not believe any of these people would actually hurt her, but they clearly did not think much of her waltzing into their camp.

"In her tent, near the fire at the center of camp," a woman said, nodding her head in that direction.

"Thank you." Cinzia heard whispering as she walked away, but was grateful she could not make out specifics. She was not sure she wanted to know what the Beldam's followers thought of her.

The Beldam's tent was not difficult to recognize. As Cinzia approached the larger fire at the center of camp, she saw one tent in particular that stood taller than the others, doors wide open. She drew more stares as she approached the tent, but she did not care. She blew out the candle of her lantern before she set it down.

Through the open tent flaps, she spotted the Beldam sitting on a large wooden chair, furs lining the ground beneath her feet. She looked even more thin and wiry than the last time Cinzia had seen her.

"It seems you have upgraded your living conditions since leaving us," Cinzia remarked. The furs, the chair upon which she sat, the quality of the tent, were all a bit much.

"Hello, Priestess Cinzia. It is good to see you again."

Cinzia inclined her head, but before she could respond the Beldam continued.

"I have only done what my followers have requested of me," the Beldam said with a smile. "They insisted I live in comfort. I could not disagree with them; I am growing old, after all."

"Your followers?" Cinzia asked, raising one eyebrow.

The Beldam's smile faltered just slightly.

"Madam, is this woman bothering you?" Two men, both tall and strong, approached the tent on either side of Cinzia.

This woman? These men knew perfectly well who she was. Her scouts had reported no signs of the Beldam's group becoming larger. But she said nothing. With the men on either side of her, she quite suddenly felt very small and alone. This was exactly why she had hoped to bring Knot, and now she regretted not simply asking him to come, even if he had refused her request to be her Goddessguard.

"No, of course not," the Beldam said, her smile once again wide and unbending. "Leave us, why don't you? I imagine we have a thing or two to discuss."

"Very well." They walked away together, although Cinzia could not imagine they went far.

"Some of the people in the camp have taken it upon themselves to protect me," the Beldam said, watching the two men go. "They insist upon it, though I think there is very little from which *they* could actually protect me."

"You still fear the Nine Daemons," Cinzia said. She wanted to get to the crux of their conversation as quickly as possible.

"Of course I do," the Beldam snapped. "As should you."

"That is why I have come," Cinzia said. "I wish to speak to you of them."

The Beldam laughed, a halting cackle. "You had your chance at that," she said, "when I was still in your camp."

"I did not, actually." Cinzia took a slow breath. She would not back down. She had the high ground here, and she would not allow this woman to twist the situation into something it was not. "You promised to share what you knew of the Nine, and you did not. Instead, you began holding your anti-tiellan meetings in secret. You absconded with hundreds of Jane's followers before we even had a chance to speak again."

"Jane's followers?" The Beldam sat back in her chair. "I thought they were Canta's."

"Jane speaks for Canta," Cinzia said. "Those who follow her follow the Goddess." The dissonance between the words she spoke and her lack of conviction in them struck Cinzia with tangible force. The Beldam was right to criticize her for the slip.

"You don't really believe that, my dear," the Beldam said with a smile. "You cannot hide your doubt from me."

"My doubts are not part of our current discussion, Beldam. I thank you to let them lie."

The Beldam pressed her lips together, but then nodded, once.

"The meetings I held were not in violation of our agreement. You said yourself that I could speak whatever I wish when I'm alone. That was all I did, Priestess."

"But you shared nothing of the Nine Daemons with us," Cinzia said.

"You never sought after me to ask."

So you left the very protection you sought from us in the first place? Cinzia wanted to say. *That was your solution?*

Instead, she took another breath. "I am here to ask you now," she said.

The Beldam hesitated, and for a moment Cinzia had hope that the woman might actually cooperate. Then, the Beldam frowned. "If you came here to talk about the Nine Daemons, you will only meet disappointment, my dear. That ship has sailed for us."

Cinzia clenched her jaw. She would not get angry. There was no need for that.

"The more time passes before we do something about them, the more power they accrue. Is that not true?"

The Beldam's frown faded, her eyes boring holes into Cinzia. "Their gathering power is not something we can halt," she said evenly. "I have accepted that, and so should you."

"One of their emissaries appeared in our camp a few days ago."

The Beldam leaned forward. "One of their emissaries?"

"An Outsider," Cinzia said. "If that word means anything to you. We were fortunate to deal with it quickly. If we had not been prepared, it could have killed dozens."

The Beldam leaned forward. "What did it look like? Did you see it yourself? How large was it?"

Cinzia stood a bit taller. "I can tell you. I could even show you the body, if you wish. But we need to have a frank conversation about this."

The Beldam's eyes narrowed, and she sat back in her chair.

At least that isn't a no, Cinzia thought.

"Goddess rising," the Beldam whispered. "It really is happening, then."

"Of course it's happening," Cinzia snapped. "If you had any real knowledge, you would understand that."

The Beldam waved a hand. "Knowledge does not equate with understanding."

Cinzia stalked forward, and before she was aware of her actions, she grabbed the Beldam by the collar, thrusting her face into the old woman's. "You *will* tell me what you know, before I—"

Someone yanked Cinzia backwards, sending her sprawling into the dirt outside the tent. Cinzia coughed, looking up to see one of the men who had approached earlier. Despite the fear swelling beneath her, she felt an overwhelming anger raging on the surface.

She stumbled to her feet, ignoring the man, and looked back at the Beldam. "Come with me," she pleaded. "See for your—"

A stinging blow connected with one side of her face.

Cinzia blinked, looking up in shock at the man who had struck her. Her vision was blurry, the man's face out of focus. "Why would you—"

The man's fist came down again, and Cinzia collapsed to the ground, her vision fading in and out of blackness. She breathed in the dust, felt the dirt beneath her fingertips, and then there was a sharp pain in her abdomen. Had the man *kicked* her?

A part of her wondered where Canta was in this moment. Where was the power she had felt, protecting Jane from assassins? But another part of her knew better. If she was not receiving that power now, it must be for a reason.

But Goddess, this *hurt*.

Another kick thudded into her belly.

"That's enough," the Beldam said, but as she said it Cinzia felt another kick crunch into her ribs.

"I said that's *enough*, Simmon. You'll stop this instant."

Cinzia heard a muttered response, and the kicks stopped. The moment they did, pain exploded in Cinzia's belly. She curled up, moaning.

"Goddess rising, you idiots are more trouble than you're worth. Help her up, for Canta's sake."

Arms slid beneath Cinzia's shoulders roughly, yanking her to her feet. She doubled over and another burst of pain cramped through her abdomen.

"Why?" Cinzia managed, the question coming out in a rush of air.

"What kind of world do you think you live in?" the Beldam asked. She had not moved from that wretched wooden chair this entire time. "What did you expect from this encounter? To be treated like a noble? A priestess? What?"

Cinzia's gut, her face, her whole body hurt too much to reply.

"There is no room in the Sfaera for fairness, Priestess Cinzia. Freedom, true love, redemption—all take up far too much space to be allowed. They are fictional concepts, twisted from a reality that hasn't existed since the Age of Marvels. Constructed by historians, writers, storytellers, so we could escape the mundane world for moments at a time. That's all they are."

Finally, the Beldam stood, her legs quivering as one of the men rushed forward to steady her. Goddess, the woman was frailer now than she had been only months before.

"There is no fairness, no freedom, nothing of the sort," the Beldam continued. She took an old, gnarled cane from the man who had steadied her, and shooed him away. "There is only truth and the inevitable pain that follows. The *truth* is that the

Nine Daemons have been plotting to re-enter the Sfaera for thousands of years. The *truth* is that their success was always inevitable. The *truth*, Priestess Cinzia, is that we don't stand a chance against them. And now, the pain will follow."

Between gasps, between the waves of unbearable fear she felt, between spikes of pain, Cinzia raised her eyes to glare at the Beldam.

"If you..." Cinzia stopped to cough violently. "If you care about... truth..." Cinzia rasped. The pain still pulsed through her, but she was regaining her composure. "...then tell it to me. I am willing to take the pain that comes with it."

The Beldam looked at Cinzia for a few moments, then the wide smile returned to her face. "Come visit me again, Priestess Cinzia," she said, waving her away. "I enjoy our time together. And yes, if it is truth you are after... perhaps, next time, we will have a real conversation." The old woman nodded, and the two men on either side of Cinzia dragged her away. Somewhere in the darkness of the forest, they released her, and let her lie.

10

Knot saw Astrid approach from afar. She walked slowly, hood pulled low over her face. It was almost morning, just an hour or so before dawn, and Knot had been up all night waiting for her. He clenched his jaw. The girl seemed fine, and that only fueled Knot's anger, but that was nothing compared to the relief he felt at seeing her again.

"'Bout time you came back," he said as she approached.

She said nothing, instead walking right past him into their tent.

Knot frowned. Astrid had mood swings; that was not abnormal. Whether because of the age that had trapped her or the fact that she was a vampire or something else altogether, he couldn't begin to guess, but it didn't matter. He'd grown used to it, and to her.

But he knew immediately this was different.

The way she slunk past him without a glance, without even a sarcastic remark. The way her shoulders slumped as she shuffled along contrasted with her normally alert, nimble pace.

Knot ducked his head as he followed her into the tent.

"What's wrong?" he asked.

She did not respond. Instead, she curled up on her cot with her back to him, her cloak pulled over her face.

Knot's sense of unease sank deeper. He could feel its weight pushing inward, against itself. He cleared his throat. He'd never been good at comforting people. Course, he hadn't had much opportunity in the two years he'd been alive, but still. Based on all the skills the sifts within him provided, comforting someone in pain would have been one of them.

Perhaps this is something no one is ever good at, Knot realized. *Something no one can ever do right.* He sat on his cot, opposite hers, staring at her back. Then he reached across the small divide between them, and placed a hand on her shoulder. He could think of nothing to say.

They remained that way for some time, until the rising sun peeked over the eastern horizon, filtering into the tent.

From the movement outside, Knot became aware of someone waiting hesitantly at the entrance.

"Knot?"

Knot sighed. It was Arven, the eccentric genius who'd taken charge of camp logistics and record keeping. She had recovered, more or less, from the trauma of the man killing himself to bring in the Outsider, and had recently volunteered to go back to work.

"Another time, Arven."

"But—"

"*Another time.*"

Silence for a moment from outside the tent. "Of course." Her footsteps rushed away.

Arven fled just as quickly from Knot's mind as Astrid turned slowly in her cot to look at him.

"You're needed."

Knot frowned. "Maybe," he said slowly. "But I won't go anywhere unless you tell me to."

Astrid did not respond, so Knot stayed.

They remained that way for a time, Astrid lying on her cot, Knot sitting across from her. Finally, Astrid spoke.

"I must tell you something."

"Anything you like," Knot said.

Astrid sat up, hair tousled and hanging over her face. She removed her hood, tucked her hair behind her ears, and looked into his eyes. The moment she met his gaze, Knot knew he would not like what she was about to say. He decided that didn't matter. If Astrid needed to tell him something, let her tell him. They would deal with the consequences afterwards.

"I've been lying to you," she said.

The words actually did hurt him, like a dagger that pierced through skin and tissue and into something much deeper. But Knot didn't respond, not yet. He could tell there was more to come. Best to let her get it all out first.

"Since I first met you, I've been lying," she said. "Our meeting was not chance. My following you was not arbitrary. You suspected as much at first, and I refused to acknowledge it. But you were right. I was tasked to find you, follow you, and eventually lead you back to Triah."

Knot stared at her, dumbfounded. The strangeness of their first encounter—she had saved him from two Nazaniin operatives—and the mystery behind her following him, had made him extremely suspicious of the girl. And while he had never forgotten the unusual start to their friendship, it had faded from his mind the more time they spent together. He hardly thought of it anymore.

But now it mattered. "You made me think it was my fault. You blamed it on my own memory problems."

Astrid lowered her head. "I was wrong to lie to you. I was following orders at first, but then you and I connected; I found something in you that I thought I'd lost. I started shirking my orders, prolonging the time between contacting them, but... but I could only do that for so long."

"'Them'? Who are you working for?"

"The Denomination," Astrid said, without hesitation. "They *own* me, Knot. I take orders from a woman who calls herself the Black Matron."

The Black Matron. Had he heard that title before? It sounded familiar.

"I haven't led a good life," Astrid said, no longer meeting Knot's eyes. Instead, she looked to the tent entrance. "Humans, you live such short lives, I almost can't blame you if you don't accomplish anything good. You never have the time for it. A few mistakes and you're in deep enough to never climb out. But me... I've had time, Knot. I've had time, and none of it has been well spent."

"And your time with me? Hasn't that been well spent?" Knot did not know why he was trying to defend Astrid, from *herself* of all things, but he felt the compulsion to do it.

"Not when I've been lying to you the entire time."

"Why, then? How do they own you?"

"They offered me redemption. They can save me, help me clear away the shitstorm that has been my life. I *want* that, Knot. I'm still not sure what they want with you, I can't imagine it's anything good, but... I'm trapped. I've been trapped for a long time, and I don't know what to do."

Knot took a deep breath. The immensity of Astrid's confession washed over him, like wave upon wave crashing into a rocky beach.

"I have more to tell you," Astrid said, "but... I think that can wait. Until you are ready."

Knot hardly heard her. Empathy washed over him, and he was surprised how easy it was to hold on to it and let his other emotions go. His conversation with Cinzia had made him think about what he wanted to be. He did not want to be angry. He did not want to be sorrowful. He did not want to hurt, either, but he suspected there was no stopping that.

Knot could not imagine keeping something like this from Astrid for so long. He could not imagine his affection for her being marred for so long, so invasively. It would be truly miserable. As much as it hurt him to hear these words, to hear that she had betrayed him, it...

It hurt even more to think what it must have done to her.

"That must have been incredibly difficult," Knot said quietly.

With a sob, Astrid leapt forward and threw her arms around him.

Knot did not return the embrace at first. He'd meant what he said. That did not mean he was ready to forgive her, and that did not mean they could ever go back to the way things were.

But perhaps they might. It all came down to one question.

What kind of person did he want to be?

Slowly, he wrapped his arms around the girl's shaking frame. He held her tightly, until her tears ceased, and the sun had risen high.

Knot followed Arven through the Odenite tents. The woman had finally gotten a hold of him, having tried and tried numerous times, but Knot had spent the entire morning and afternoon with Astrid. Now, with Astrid resting in their tent, Knot figured he finally had a moment to see what Arven had wanted to speak to him about.

Turns out she hadn't wanted to speak to him about anything.

Instead, she led him to Cinzia and Jane's tent, where she indicated he should enter. This tent was larger than most. Before they'd left Harmoth, a group of Odenites had volunteered to make tents for those who did not have them, including Jane, Cinzia, and their family.

When he entered, the crowd inside surprised him. Cinzia's parents, Ehram and Pascia, were both there, along with the triplets, Wina, Lana, and Soffrena.

And there, on one of the cots, lay Cinzia.

Knot moved quickly to her side, and as he did so he saw the bruises on her face, her puffed-up lower lip. One eye was swollen shut.

"What happened?"

"I am all right, Knot," Cinzia said. She sounded far better than she looked.

"You are not all right," Pascia retorted. "She could barely walk, Knot. Our people found her crawling out of the forest on her hands and knees. In there all night, she was, in the dark."

"Who did this to you?" Knot demanded.

"Later," Cinzia said. "But… I think I've made progress." She looked around at her family. "Please, leave us for a moment. I need to speak with him alone."

Pascia began to protest, but Ehram put his arm around her and the fight seemed to go out of her. Ehram looked to his daughter. "Are you sure, Cinzia?"

"Of course, Father."

"We'll be just outside if you need us."

When they had gone, Cinzia looked back up at Knot, her one good eye bright. "I think we will soon know more about the Nine."

Knot couldn't help but laugh.

"Knot, what is wrong with you?"

"You're lying here, looking like that, and the reason you've called me to see you is some bullshit about the Nine Daemons?" Knot laughed harder. He realized most of his mirth came from the fact that she was still alive. He could not bear to lose two people close to him in so short an amount of time.

You haven't lost Astrid, he told himself. He wished that was something he could believe fully.

"*Knot.*"

"I'm sorry," he said, wiping a tear from his cheek. He placed a hand on Cinzia's. "Glad you're all right, that's all."

Cinzia relaxed back into her pillow. "Well, so am I," she muttered.

"I'm so sorry this happened to you." Then, suddenly, he remembered. "You asked me to be your Goddessguard," he said quietly. "Was this... was this why?"

Cinzia looked away. "This is not your fault, Knot. I did something stupid, and only I deserve the blame. I am lucky to be alive, actually. But... but I would ask you, even if you will not be my Goddessguard... I would like you to accompany me next time."

"Of course." Knot realized as he said it that something in him had changed. Because of Astrid? Because of how Cinzia looked now? He wasn't sure. "I'll be your Goddessguard," he added. "I can do that for you. I can do that, and find myself at the same time. I'm sorry I couldn't before."

"You do not need to be sorry. But... if you truly feel that you could be my Goddessguard, I... I would like that very much."

"I would, too."

Cinzia smiled. "That is some good news, then."

The decision felt surprisingly good. Funny how something

that felt wrong only days ago could feel so right now.

"You won't tell me where you went? What you did?" Knot asked.

Cinzia took a deep breath. "I suppose there is no harm in it, especially if you will accompany me there next time. I went to see the Beldam, Knot. I went to ask her about the Nine Daemons."

"The Goddess-damned Beldam. Of course. You asked her about the Nine, and she did this to you."

Cinzia rolled her eyes. "The *Beldam* did not do this to me, Knot. I am not *that* helpless. She had guards, two men... they did this."

Knot clenched his jaw. If he ever met these men, he would kill them where they stood.

"I do not think the Beldam wanted them to do this to me; they did it on their own. She stopped them, and she agreed to speak with me. Will you come with me when I return?"

"Are you sure that is what you want?" Knot asked. To go back into the lair where she was so recently hurt seemed pure madness.

"I *know* it is. It is not for me. It is for the good of us all. It is what I must do. Will you come with me?"

"Of course I will."

"Thank you."

Cinzia smiled up at him, then shifted in her cot, and fell asleep in moments.

PART II

FROM FIRE, BY FIRE

11

Cineste

WINTER LOOKED FROM GALCE to Urstadt. "You both are ready?" she asked.

"Are you?" Urstadt asked.

Galce smiled. "I am ready for whatever Chaos would have me do."

Winter ignored Urstadt's question—of course she was ready—and led them up to the same building where she'd attended her first Druid meeting, and she'd ended up killing a dozen humans.

It was time for Galce and Urstadt to meet the Druids.

The same short, stout man—Talian, Gord had called him—stood outside the entrance, his face still healing from bruises and cuts. Good on him for taking up his post once more. A lesser person might've refused, given the beating he took last time. The man's eyes widened as he recognized Winter. She could not tell whether he was happy to see her, frightened, suspicious, or all of the above. The tiellans had been difficult to read. She could not pretend she'd done them a favor; dealing with thirteen dead humans could not have made their lives any easier.

While Talian's reaction to Winter was ambiguous, his opinion of Urstadt and Galce was clear as his eyes narrowed when he saw them behind her.

"No humans."

"They're with me,"Winter said.

"Don't matter. No humans allowed."

"You let a dozen humans in a few days ago, and you're lucky I intervened then."Winter flinched internally at her own words; she was being far too harsh on the man.

Galce placed a hand on Winter's shoulder. "It's all right, my *garice*."

Winter ignored him and glared at Talian. "Stand aside."

Unhappily, the guard obeyed, and Winter, Urstadt, and Galce entered the Druid headquarters.

Inside, tiellans bustled back and forth, scribes prepared messages for the other factions, couriers strode purposefully in and out of the room, and the tables that had been clumped together along one edge of the room during the meeting had been spread out across the floor, maps and documents of every size sprawled across them.

Urstadt drew stares from almost everyone in the room. Taller than most human men, she stood almost an entire head over average tiellans. Add to that her ornate armor, plated with rose gold, and she was impossible to miss in any crowd. Galce, short and portly, would have been more difficult to notice had he not been in the company of Urstadt and Winter.

The only tiellans too occupied to have noticed them walk in were Ghian and the matriarchs and elders Winter recognized from the meeting she had attended—they were speaking in quiet but emphatic tones as she approached. Ghian and one of the tiellan elders seemed to control the conversation.

"You are certain the City Watch is investigating?" Ghian asked. He once again had removed his *araif*, and stood tall with squared shoulders as he spoke with the others, his hand on the shoulder of the elder closest to him. Ghian had clearly regained his air of calm despite the recent attack.

"They are beyond investigating," the elder said. "They know what happened. They know the humans were killed by tiellans, during a tiellan meeting, and they intend to make us pay for it."

Winter felt a stab of guilt. She had killed the men; she had never intended for the Druids to be blamed for what she had done. But the alternative would have been worse. Tiellans would be dead instead of humans. *Eranda* would be dead.

The tiellans had needed a weapon, and Winter had stepped into that role.

"And you trust your contact in the Watch's leadership?" Ghian asked.

"I do," the elder said. "He's one of the few humans left whose word I trust."

Ghian ran a hand through his hair and let out a long breath. He looked around, finally noticing for the first time the silence from the rest of the room as the other tiellans stared in awe at Urstadt. His eyes met Winter's.

"Back to work, all of you." Ghian said it loudly, but with a smile on his face as he looked around at the other tiellans. Immediately, the room returned to the chaotic bustle that had greeted Winter when she first walked in.

Ghian's smile broadened, which made it seem all the more fake to her. He reached both arms out, perhaps to place them on her shoulders—or even embrace her—but Winter stopped him.

"Do not touch me," she said. She liked that he removed his *araif* on occasion, and that he spoke like she did, but the fact that he thought he could be so friendly with her was a mark against him.

Ghian backed off. "I am sorry. I did not mean to offend." He seemed sincerely apologetic, at least, and that was something. Then again, he'd also witnessed Winter murder a dozen people at once, which might have something to do with his penitence. Come to think of it, she was surprised he'd had the balls to approach her in the first place.

Ghian held out his hand, this time. "We have not been properly introduced. I am Ghian Fauz."

Winter returned his gaze steadily, but did not grip his hand. "Winter."

"It's a pleasure to meet you, Miss Winter—"

"Just Winter."

"Of course. Winter. The pleasure is mine."

"Hate to interrupt," the elder who had been conversing with Ghian said, his voice gruff, "but she's brought humans here. They can't be allowed to stay."

"This is Urstadt, and Galce," Winter said. "They are my advisors. They are with me."

"It's all right, Elder Pendir." Ghian's gaze shifted to Urstadt and Galce before returning to Winter. "Surely they could at least wait outside?"

Winter did not back down. "They go where I go. If you want me here, you must get used to them as well."

A few of the elders and matriarchs whispered quietly to one another, but Ghian apparently did not need to consult them to make a decision. His smile returned, and he spread his arms.

"We will put our trust in you, Winter."

Winter broke eye contact. She did not want their trust, but she couldn't say as much.

Now that the commotion from the rest of the tiellans had resumed, the same elder—the one Ghian had called Pendir—spoke again.

"The City Watch have already been hard on us," he said. "With human deaths at our feet…" His eyes shifted to Winter, but he looked away quickly. "I fear the worst."

"I've seen their brutality," Winter said, "and I've only been here a few days." She described the scene she'd witnessed in the Wolfanger Inn—the way the City Watch, without the slightest provocation, had stepped in and violently separated a mixed family.

"Such things are not uncommon, lately," Ghian said, his face grim. "Humans known to be in mixed-race relationships, at the wrong place and wrong time, are severely beaten, usually by the City Watch itself. Some have even been killed."

"What of the tiellans?" Winter asked. "And the children?"

"In the best of circumstances, they show up days later in the tiellan quarter, beaten within an inch of their lives. In the worst, they've been raped, too, or some of them don't show up at all."

Winter looked around her in disbelief. "How can you tolerate such abuse?"

"What could we possibly do to stop it?" Pendir asked in return.

"One thing is clear," Ghian said. "A conflict with the City Watch is inevitable. We need to be prepared."

"And the best way to do that is to negotiate with them," Pendir said, "to make an arrangement."

"We need to *leave*," Matriarch Esra said. "There's nothing left for us here."

"We aren't ready for that," Ghian said, "not yet."

"The City Watch ain't gonna wait for us to be ready," Esra said.

Pendir waved a hand at the Matriarch Esra. "Where would we go, Esra?"

Esra had no response for that.

Galce, apparently, did.

"What about Adimora?" he asked.

Everyone in the circle, including Winter, turned to stare at Galce. He and Urstadt had both been standing slightly behind Winter, not even part of the circle, really.

As Winter looked at Galce, she had the strangest sensation. It felt like the slightest tremor echoing up her spine, but slowly, one vertebra at a time. Winter closed her eyes, and Chaos was there, black as the sea under a moonless sky.

Chaos wanted them to go to Adimora. Galce had known it somehow, sensed it, and made the decision to propose the idea, even though he was one of the only humans in a completely tiellan group.

Pendir frowned at Galce. "What do you know of Adimora?"

"Not much, to be honest," Galce said, smiling calmly at the tiellans around him. "I have only heard tell of a city on the eastern plains, beyond civilization. A city of tiellans."

Adimora. Winter had heard it spoken of, but rarely with any seriousness. It was more legend than anything else; some claimed it was only a tiny settlement, others a massive hidden city, past the Eastmaw Mountains and beyond where any roads led.

Pendir scoffed. "This human knows nothing. Shouldn't even be here."

"And yet he speaks wisdom," Esra said. "Adimora might be our salvation."

The more the idea persisted in Winter's mind, the more she agreed with the logic behind it. Tiellans were always in the minority. Whether in cities or in the country, they were too scattered and spread out to stand up to even the slightest human persecution. But on the eastern plains—in Adimora, if it was real—tiellans were the overwhelming majority. They certainly led lives very different from those of the tiellans in the west, but that might not be a bad thing.

If they could band together, they could become something powerful.

"Adimora is barely a city," Pendir said. "Uncivilized. Savage."

Esra wagged her finger in Pendir's face. "You can hardly call the way we live now in Cineste anything different. The idea ain't my favorite, either, but it is necessary." She looked to Ghian. "If we truly want to unite *all* tiellan people, we must treat with the clans eventually. Better sooner rather than later."

All eyes turned to Ghian. The man took a moment, staring off into nothing, and the others waited. While Winter had suspected it before, this made it clear that he had the final say for this movement. Normally, if the matriarchs and elders made a decision, the entire population over which they presided accepted it, but the same power dynamic seemed to exist between the elders and Ghian.

"I had hoped to wait to reveal this," Ghian said slowly, "but the truth is I have been planning to take us to Adimora eventually for some time, now."

The elders and matriarchs looked at one another, eyes wide, exchanging whispers. Ghian silenced them with a raised hand.

"Matriarch Esra is correct. If our goal as Druids is truly to unite our people—all our people—then we need to contact the eastern clans."

Winter found herself nodding. She cared less about Chaos directing this decision, as Galce would have put it, and far more about it simply being *right*. If this movement was going to continue, it needed to attract more tiellans. They needed to find a gathering place, where they could unite.

"But we cannot abandon Cineste yet," Ghian said.

Winter shut her eyes, out of frustration more than anything, but she found Chaos waiting for her, black as a moonless night.

"Why can't we?" Winter asked. "Matriarch Esra is right. There is nothing for us here. You yourself said it was part of your plan all along."

"There are almost ten thousand tiellans in Cineste," Ghian argued. "Most of the tiellans here can barely scrape enough food together as it is. We cannot possibly lead an exodus of that magnitude out of the city successfully, let alone travel such a distance. Not yet. But, given time, given the right preparation, we could."

"Then we don't take everyone," Winter said. "We take the Druids. We take those most at risk. We lead the way for others to follow."

Many of the elders and matriarchs around her were beginning to nod their heads. Only Pendir still seemed opposed.

Ghian kept his calm well enough, but Winter noticed the way his eyes darted from face to face rapidly. He was worried. "We'll be leaving the rest of our people here, at risk," he said. "They will pay for our mistakes."

"I think it's clear any tiellan in Cineste is at risk," Winter said. "And, if we make it public that the *Druids* are leaving— the tiellan faction causing all the trouble—we might placate, at least to some extent, the City Watch's grudge."

Ghian shook his head. "We simply aren't ready. We—"

"Know when to admit defeat, lad," Pendir said. "You're our leader. We respect you, we like your stubbornness. But even I can see this woman has a point. If it might help our people here, we should leave."

Ghian stared at Winter, a frown creasing his face. Finally, he nodded. "If you all think it is best, I will concede. But we must leave some behind, to direct others to Adimora…"

As Ghian and the others continued to discuss logistics, Winter closed her eyes, a question forming in her mind and an idea brewing in her head. Chaos responded, its form snowy white.

She turned, and took Galce aside for a moment.

"I want you to remain here, in Cineste," Winter said.

Galce's eyes widened. "My *garice*, I left Roden to accompany *you*. What would you possibly have me do here that—"

"The only order is Chaos," Winter said, knowing it would prompt Galce to consult Chaos himself. If he did, and then agreed with her, there might be something to this Chaos credence after all. If he didn't, she had good reason to be wary of it.

Galce closed his eyes, and almost immediately Winter felt the same gradual, trembling sensation roll up her spine.

When Galce opened his eyes again, he was frowning. "I do as Chaos directs," he said, "always."

"And what does that mean?" Winter asked. She needed him to be clear.

"I will remain here."

Winter mulled that over. She'd half hoped he would refuse, if only to have more of an excuse to doubt this Chaos business.

"What would you have me do?" Galce asked.

"Ingratiate yourself among the tiellans as best you can," Winter said, though her mind was elsewhere. It had taken her father dying for her to finally be free of Canta. What would it take for her to break free of Chaos?

Winter refocused on Galce. "Monitor the tiellan situation here," she continued, "and help the tiellans wherever possible.

For those interested, send them onward to Adimora. We will send emissaries back as soon as we can with more details about the journey."

Galce inclined his head. "As you say, my *garice*. The only order is Chaos."

12

Odenite camp, outside Kirlan

ASTRID WAS GENERALLY IMPRESSED with the progress Eward's Prelates had made. She and Knot had just finished a double round of training with them: one round skirmishing against each other, the next practicing maneuvers against potential threats—Outsiders. The former had gone well; against a typical armed force, Astrid thought the Prelates would be able to hold their own. The latter was a different story.

Without much knowledge of Outsiders, it was difficult to formulate a specific strategy, so they focused on teamwork and adaptation, mutable plans and formations, and changing combat styles mid-battle.

"I thought that went well," Knot said. "Better than the first session we did a few days ago, at least."

"Oh yes, nomad, that was great. Now the Prelates will look vaguely organized when an Outsider rips them to shreds."

"Give them some credit." Knot wiped sweat from his brow. "They did well against the first one." They were walking away together from the fallow section of the field Eward had claimed for the Prelates. The day was cloudy—such days were rare this far south, to Astrid's chagrin—and behind the clouds, the sun must be nearing the horizon. She could feel the night approaching.

"Only because we held the front line," Astrid said. She had glimpsed panic in the Prelates' eyes when they faced the

Outsider. They were good men, but being a good man didn't mean shit when you faced a daemon on the battlefield.

Knot sighed. "It's good you're bein' a realist about it. I'm being positive to encourage them, but…"

Despite Knot's validation, Astrid suddenly felt guilty for casting aspersions on the Prelates. "We handled one Outsider already," Astrid said. "We can do it again, and the Prelates will continue to learn."

Knot didn't say anything to that, and they walked in silence for a few moments.

Astrid cast thoughts of Outsiders and the Prelates aside. It was time for a long-overdue conversation.

"There's a reason I don't remember much past a hundred years ago," Astrid said.

"Always figured there was."

Astrid glared at Knot. "Doesn't mean you have to be rude about it," Astrid muttered. She took a deep breath. What she was about to tell Knot, she had never told anyone else before. Not willingly.

"The Denomination found me forty-seven years ago," Astrid said. "I… I thought they would kill me, at first."

"How did they capture you? A group of Sons? Goddessguards?"

"Priestesses," Astrid said. "That's all they were, really. But they had nightsbane. And they were psimancers."

"Was psimancy even around then?"

"People had just begun to manifest the abilities, but it was extremely rare, and all very confusing from what I remember. It didn't take long for the Nazaniin to get a hold on most of them, of course, although the Denomination kept a few to themselves."

"And they captured you?"

"Imprisoned me. Tortured me. But then, they… they began to show me kindness." Astrid shook her head. "Kindness is not the right word. They became less hostile, that's all it was. At the time I was practically feral, Knot. Because of what I'd done—"

"What *had* you done?"

"I'm getting to it, if you'd shut your mouth for more than a minute."

Knot, graciously, shut his mouth.

Astrid continued. "I can still remember those first days, when the torture stopped. I remember how confused I was, I remember almost being *angry* that it had stopped. It was what I deserved. There was a small part of me that wanted it, another part that expected it, and a much larger part that simply could not understand why they would stop. For a while, I thought that leaving me to sit alone with my guilt was just their new form of torture. And I knew, almost immediately, that it would break me. I could not last long. So I begged for it to stop. Or, I guess, I begged them to *start* again. To torture me, to kill me, to do anything to get me away from myself.

"Eventually, they made me an offer. They said they could take away my memories. In return, they wanted me to… to take assignments from them."

"Assignments?"

"They wanted me to kill. Intimidate. Destroy evidence. Silence witnesses. Sometimes even within the Denomination itself. You'd be surprised at the places a little girl can get into and out of unnoticed. It was easy for me.

"In return, they took my memories."

"An acumen did that?" Knot asked.

Astrid nodded. "She obliterated specific parts of my

memories, the ones I hated the most. The things I never wanted to relive again."

"And it worked?"

"For a while." Astrid stopped. "No, that's not true. It didn't work at all. From the beginning, something was wrong. I didn't remember what had happened, she'd done that part right, but... but the feelings were still there. The guilt, the shame, the fear, the hatred. All of it was still there, only it was worse, now, because I had no memories to associate with them. Nothing to attach those feelings to, so they were just... they were just there, constantly, all the time.

"That's when the priestesses began to talk to me about redemption. They told me how taking my memories was only a temporary fix, that if I wanted any real peace, I needed to work toward absolution."

"And they told you that was something they would help you get? You, a vampire?"

Astrid shrugged. "I wanted to believe it. I couldn't die, not of my own hand, but I couldn't live anymore, either. So I did what they asked me to do, because they promised me an end to it all."

"And doing what they asked, taking these assignments, eventually led you to me."

"Yes," Astrid said quietly. She still had no idea how Knot had done what he did a few days ago, when she first told him. The act of simply attempting to understand meant more to Astrid than anything anyone had ever done for her. She did not need all her memories to be sure of that.

But things were not the same between them. They might never be. She hated it but at the same time, she was grateful. At least now, from here on out, she could live the truth.

"That's why you don't remember anything," Knot said. "And now your memories are gone? You'll never get them back?"

Astrid shivered. "The Black Matron placed them in a voidstone." She pulled the stone out of her pocket, holding it up for Knot to see. The stone was a shining black, polished and smooth, with a blood-red rune carved into the surface.

Knot reached out, almost touching the thing, and for a moment Astrid wanted him to, wanted him to take it from her and never give it back. Instead, he stopped just before he made contact with the stone.

She put the voidstone back into her pocket. "On occasion… twice, actually… the Black Matron has used my memories against me, as another form of torture. At one time I just wanted to be done with the Denomination. They talked about redemption for decades, but I never saw anything from it, and then, after one assignment, I just… I just stopped going back. Eventually I found my way to Turandel—that's where Cabral made me a slave, for a time. After I escaped Cabral, the Denomination somehow caught up with me, torturing me with my own memories. I didn't leave their service again, not for another twenty years or so. Not until…"

"Not until you met me."

Astrid nodded. "Not until I met you."

"You said they tortured you with your own memories twice. Once after Turandel, and the second time…"

"It was three days ago."

Silence, then. A silence that could fill an ocean, that could expand beyond the Sfaera and the Void and Oblivion itself, a silence of infinite parts that was both deafening and toneless all at once.

"Are you all right?"

Astrid wanted to laugh at that question, but she wanted to cry as well, so instead she said nothing at all. Not for a while. She was grateful for Knot's patience, as they stood out in the night air together.

"No," she said, after some time. "I don't think I am. Is that all right?"

"Yes," Knot said, then coughed, clearing his throat, and Astrid wasn't sure but she thought she heard his voice break, just for a moment, in the growing dark. "Yes," he said again. "That's fine."

They continued walking, once again in silence, but the silence this time was not of infinite parts. It could not fill an ocean, or the Void, or anything of the sort. Instead, it was just enough to fill the space between them, comfortably, warmly, and easily.

"Astrid?" Knot asked, when they got to their tent.

"Yes?"

"I am a psimancer. My powers are all but gone, but I can still summon, on occasion, very small *tendra*. Enough to use a voidstone."

"What else is new, nomad?"

"Would you let me see your memories? The ones stored on that stone?"

Astrid recoiled. "Why in Oblivion would you want to do that?"

"Things are different between us, now. I wonder if it would help me understand you better."

"*Understand* me better? I'm not the girl I've been in the past, Knot. I'm not who I once was."

"We're always who we are," Knot said.

"These memories aren't pleasant, nomad. You don't want to see them, trust me." She leapt onto her cot. This conversation was clearly ridiculous. Knot didn't know what he was asking.

"I do want to see them," Knot said quietly. "But if you don't want me to, I understand. Sometimes it helps to share my experiences with others. Even when they're horrific, and I want them to go away, to never think of them again. Shedding light on a thing helps kill the shame. The guilt."

Astrid snorted. She wanted to argue the point, but what Knot said made a certain kind of sense to her. Perhaps sharing some of what had happened to her might help.

Finally, she sighed. "All right. If you really want to, that's fine. But don't expect me to go through them with you. I'm back to not remembering anything, and I'd like to keep it that way."

"You said that was worse."

Astrid frowned. "It is, but... it's complicated."

"All right then."

"All right."

"I'd best get some rest."

"Best you should."

Astrid closed her eyes, hearing Knot slip into his cot. Soon, his breathing evened out, and she was alone with her thoughts.

13

Cineste

ALMOST A THOUSAND TIELLANS gathered in the streets of the tiellan quarter of Cineste as the Druids prepared to leave—nowhere near the majority of tiellans in the city. Winter did not like leaving so many behind, but she hoped this exodus would set a precedent. She hoped soon many others would follow.

Some of the elders and matriarchs had already begun leading tiellans out of the city, while Winter, Ghian, and Matriarch Esra remained to lead the main group. Gord, Darrin, and Eranda waited nearby with the children, but Winter had yet to speak to them. She was not sure what to say to Gord and Eranda. They hadn't told Darrin the details of how the men at the Druid meeting had died, and that somehow made it worse. They clearly weren't interested in discussing what had happened, let alone hearing what Winter had gone through to bring her to that point.

Winter stood in the middle of a crossroads near the Wolfanger Inn with Galce and Urstadt. Urstadt wore full armor, including her wicked-looking barbut, rose gold to match her armor but fashioned in the shape of a gaping horned skull. She carried her glaive as well, and a short sword at her waist. Urstadt was dressed for battle, on the chance that the humans might resist the tiellan exodus. Other tiellans, mostly those who had been training as Rangers, were armed as well, although they were doing their best not to appear as a military force. They were trying to leave the city, not threaten it.

Winter carried her pack, as well as the pouch attached to her belt, both full of *faltira*. If something happened, she would be prepared this time.

Throughout the morning, the Cinestean City Watch had hovered over the tiellan quarter. Winter could see a brace of them now, spears in hand, at the end of one street.

Winter walked up to Ghian. "How many of those you've trained are with us?"

"About a hundred and fifty," he said. "But... but they are not soldiers, Winter."

They might need to be, soon enough.

Ghian gave a brief, inspiring speech, about how the tiellans had been friends of nature before, and would become so again, and how this was their opportunity to make that happen. He could still work a crowd, even when he internally opposed the decision to leave. The Druids, packed together in the streets around the crossroads, received it well; Winter observed hope on most of their faces, although caution and fear were equally prevalent.

Winter's hand crept toward the pouch at her belt, and she willed it to stop. She did not want to take frost now, only for the high to expire when she actually needed it. She could wait. She could do that much, at least.

When Ghian finished his speech, he took his place at the front of the tiellan crowd. Winter stood to his left, Matriarch Esra on his right. Urstadt remained directly behind Winter, with the other Pranna tiellans a few paces back in the crowd. Winter couldn't help but wonder what the tiellans thought of her—a young tiellan woman most of them had never heard of, without a *siara*, suddenly walking next to their Druid leader.

She could hazard a guess that, in short enough time, they would all know exactly who she was.

Winter could not say why, but she expected more than what happened next. Ghian simply started walking, Winter and Esra followed, and the rest of the tiellan crowd began to move behind them.

They marched quietly at first. Winter caught a few whispers, and the cries and shouts of children along the way. Winter felt, for the briefest moment, that the silence suspended her and all the tiellans around her. She felt a connection with her people, a singularity of purpose, as they moved together through the city. Perhaps she was not so different from them after all.

The more they walked, the more people began to talk behind her, and soon the tiellan crowd was abuzz with conversation, and the sacredness of the silent moment departed. The Cinesteans they passed along the way stopped to stare at the strange exodus. News traveled faster than the tiellan crowd, and soon both humans and tiellans lined the streets, cautiously hanging back, interspersed with groups of City Watchmen. She could not help but notice the rarity with which she saw members of the City Watch. She would have thought there would be more of them, monitoring the tiellan march.

Looking up, Winter saw other people leaning out of windows, staring with open curiosity at the anomaly before them. She wondered what the tiellans who remained thought of the Druids leaving the city. The Druids had attempted to get word out, convincing others to leave with them, but the response had been reluctant at best.

The elders had chosen the Tiellan Gate as their departure point. It stood perhaps twice the height of a man and consisted of a single large wooden door. The door itself led to a tunnel through the outer wall, inside of which multiple iron portcullises could be lowered. The tunnel opened into a large field of gradual rolling hills on the southeastern side of Cineste. Winter and Ghian were the first in the procession to walk through. Funneling a thousand tiellans through the Tiellan Gate would be a logistical nightmare, and Winter wished she'd argued more strongly against it.

The sun greeted them as they emerged from the tunnel onto a grassy incline. Almost immediately, Winter noticed a large group in the distance at the crest of another low hill.

Urstadt stepped up beside Winter. "Who are those people ahead of us?"

Winter hesitated. "I think they're the previous groups that left the city," she said. "They should be waiting for us."

"I am not sure that is accurate," Urstadt said slowly.

"No," Winter said, squinting at the group. A hard knot of fear was forming in her chest. "I'm not sure it is, either."

The group was farther away than she'd thought, and packed together tightly. As Winter led the march up the incline, she got a better view of the hills around them. Scattered across the rolling hills between herself and the group ahead were hundreds of dark forms, barely smudges against the yellowish-green of the fields. Some alone, others clumped together, all of them still and unmoving.

Bodies.

Winter swore. She could make out many riders on horseback in the group ahead of them. Tiellans who owned horses in Cineste were few and far between.

"That's the City Watch," Winter said. The hard knot in her chest grew as it sank and filled her gut.

"And those are the tiellans the elders and matriarchs led out before us," Ghian said softly, looking out at the corpses on the rolling fields. Then he swore sharply, turning on Winter. "I *told* you we should not have left yet. We were not ready." He pointed his finger in Winter's face. "Their blood is on *your* hands."

What Ghian said was true. She should have known something was wrong when she saw so few of the City Watch actually monitoring their march through the streets of Cineste. She should not have allowed the others to lead groups ahead of the main Druid body. There were many things she should have done, and had not.

She packed the guilt, fear, and anger away for a later time. Instead, she reached into her pouch, but stopped herself. She needed to save her powers for the imminent battle.

"We need to break through their force," she said, her mind racing. "The future of our group, of this movement—Goddess, of our entire bloody *race*—rests on what we do next. If we don't make it through, or if we take heavy casualties, the Druid movement will be crushed beyond repair. But if we can break them, we keep hope alive." *And ourselves as well.*

Ghian, his eyes wide with fear, nodded. He looked back at the tiellan mass behind him, still pouring out of the Tiellan Gate. "Rangers!" he shouted. "Into formation at the head of the crowd, immediately!" Armed tiellans began pushing their way forward.

Then, he turned to Winter. "I am a spiritual leader," he said. His voice trembled, but he met her eyes unwaveringly. "I am not a general. You've gotten us into this, and I need you to get us out of it."

"Yes." The moment she said it, the lead ball in her stomach vaporized. This time, she did not need to consult Chaos. She knew exactly what she needed to do.

Be a weapon.

And with that thought, Winter was surprised at the swelling purpose she felt within herself. That moment of belonging, of suspended purpose she had felt in the city as they walked in silence, returned. Even as a little girl she had never felt she belonged among her people. She had never felt she belonged anywhere, to be fair, but least of all with other tiellans. Even when her father was alive, even when she was growing up, she'd always felt out of place. Without purpose.

But now... now she felt something different.

She had value. She could not remember the last time she had felt as though she had something to contribute.

"Should we treat with them?" Ghian asked.

"Look around, Ghian. They did not treat with those we sent before us. They will not treat with us. Our only option is to fight our way out of this." Winter observed the armed tiellans, lining up directly behind them.

"Are any of your Rangers at the end of the column?" Winter asked. When Ghian didn't respond, she grabbed him by the arm.

"*Ghian.* Have you set up a rearguard?"

"I... no. No, I haven't."

"Do it."

"It will split our forces," Ghian said. He stared at the City Watch, eyes wide.

Winter looked to Urstadt, who nodded at her. "We need a rearguard," she said. "We cannot risk an unprotected attack."

Ghian's voice was monotone. "But we'll need all the Rangers in our front ranks to deal with the Watch."

Winter grabbed Ghian by the shoulders, forcing him to look at her.

"You asked me to lead, Ghian. Let me lead."

Ghian's face was pale, but he nodded. "Yes, you're right."

Winter released him. "Take a fifth of the Rangers to the back of the crowd," she said. "Lead the rearguard. We need someone there to take charge. Leave Urstadt and myself to lead the vanguard."

"All right," Ghian said. He began to walk away, but turned to look at her.

"What if the Rangers in the vanguard aren't enough?" he asked.

"Then you have me," Winter said.

This, surprisingly, seemed to calm Ghian down somewhat. "Yes," he said. "Of course."

As he walked away, Winter called after him. "Tell the Rangers who you're leaving in command. Make sure they know who to follow."

Ghian took a deep breath, then addressed the Rangers.

"My friends," he said, his voice steady. His nervousness and doubt all but disappeared as he addressed the crowd. "Many of you recognize Winter Cordier. I have appointed her as your commander. She, and her guard captain Urstadt—that's the tall one in the armor—will lead you in the coming battle. You are better off in their hands than mine, for the time being. I will take some of you behind our friends and family to act as a rearguard.

"We do not know what awaits us, but we need to protect our people. That is what matters. You will follow every order Winter and Urstadt give as if it were my own. They will lead us to victory. First Ranger company, with me." Ghian signaled, and a group of Rangers peeled away, following Ghian to the back of the column.

The tiellan crowd, having now seen the force awaiting them and the bodies scattering the hills, was beginning to panic. Another problem that needed solving.

Winter looked back to the City Watch, still stationary at the crest of the hill. They hadn't charged, which Winter counted as a blessing. The tiellans were so disorganized coming out of the city, the Watch could have slaughtered most of them before they knew what was happening. This way, her people at least stood a chance.

And Winter had *faltira*. She could use that to help, but the force ahead was large. A few hundred at least. She could not take them all.

She noticed, out of the corner of her eye, the elders and matriarchs grouped in conversation.

Winter turned to Urstadt. "Keep the Rangers in line," she said. "I need to see what this is about."

Before Urstadt could respond, Winter walked quickly over to the cluster of old tiellans speaking with one another.

"We need to keep the elders and matriarchs safe above all else," Pendir was saying. "Otherwise we are all lost. We should slip away."

Winter grabbed Pendir by the collar, and threw him to the ground with as much force as she could muster. "Like Oblivion you will."

Pendir fell into the dust with a squeal. Winter turned to the others.

"I need each of you to walk through the crowd behind us. Calm these people. Say soothing words. Keep them together."

Esra regarded Winter with pursed lips. A few of the elders scoffed, but Winter didn't care. If they didn't want to do it, she would *make* them. She met Esra's eyes.

"Will you do this?"

"Esra, who is this girl to order us around?"

"We'll do as she says," Esra said, turning to her peers. "Come. We'll keep our people together. We can be the strength they need."

Winter nodded to Esra in appreciation, and the group began to move back into the tiellan crowd. Hopefully, they would do something to calm the people. As Esra passed, she whispered to Winter, "I hope you know what you're doing."

Winter found herself hoping the same thing.

When she returned to Urstadt, the woman had organized the Rangers into three ranks of about forty tiellans each. Winter looked over them, and was not encouraged by what she saw. Tiellan men and women of all ages formed lines, brandishing whatever weapons they apparently could scrape together: daggers, staffs, clubs, even a few pitchforks here and there. They looked strong enough as a collective, but as Winter looked into their wide eyes, saw white knuckles gripping their weapons, she knew they were afraid.

The Rangers after which they were named—the elite tiellan warriors of the Age of Marvels—could famously use any weapon on the battlefield, from bow to sword to spear to axe and beyond, were experts in battle strategy, and when they fought together, fought as one. Winter imagined Rangers as warriors like Knot, or Urstadt—not the rabble she saw before her.

But they would have to do. They were all bound together, now. And whether Winter cared to admit it or not, she had pressed the tiellan hand in Cineste. She had all but forced them into this exodus by killing the humans at the Druid meeting. She would not abandon them now.

"Do you think we stand a chance against them?" Winter asked Urstadt.

Urstadt's eyes were unreadable. "With us, yes," she said.

"I'll take *faltira* at some point during the battle," Winter said.

"I expected as much."

"If I do, I'll need to concentrate on what I'm doing. You will have full leadership of the Rangers." Not that Winter would have much input anyway—she was no soldier—but it needed to be said.

"I can do that, Winter."

Winter nodded. "Good." Then, she turned to the Rangers.

"We are going to march on the force ahead of us," she said loudly. "They stand between us and freedom, the first real freedom we will ever know. They will not let us pass without a fight. They have enslaved us, oppressed us, and persecuted us, simply for being who we are. From this moment forward, we will no longer accept that.

"They outnumber us. They are better armed, better trained, and they may be bigger and stronger than us. But they are human. They bleed, and die, just as all humans do. And like all humans, they wear their power on the outside.

"You are *tiellans*. You may not look like you can stand up to them, but you can. Your power comes from within. Some of you saw what I did to those men who attacked us. That is only the first hint of what we can do. Remember that you are *tiellans*!"

To Winter's surprise, she actually elicited a cheer from the Rangers, and many of the tiellans behind them as well. Her eyes settled on one Ranger in particular, not unlike Lian as she remembered him. Thin, sinewy, handsome, with a smolder in his eyes.

"You," Winter said, pointing at the man. "With me."

The man looked surprised for a moment, but followed orders and walked quickly up to Winter's side. He carried a staff in one hand, and a long dagger in his belt. The sight of his weapons in contrast with their opposition—armored in leather and chainmail, with swords, spears, and shields—made Winter flinch inwardly. She was under no illusions. She was the weapon that would make or break this battle for the tiellans. She was powerful, but she had never faced so many at once. And she had to be careful; she did not want to cause tiellan casualties.

"What can I do for you, ma'am?" the man asked.

"What is your name, Ranger?"

"Selldor."

"Are you fast?"

Selldor hesitated. "I am," he said, "but I can also fight—"

"Then you'll do both," Winter said. "You'll carry my and Urstadt's orders to the other Rangers, running up and down the line. Your duty is more important than any other, do you understand me?"

Selldor bowed his head. "I do, Commander."

"Good. Stay close."

Winter turned, and led the march forward.

"That was an effective speech," Urstadt said beside her.

"More effective than I thought it would be." Winter squinted at the force ahead. "Can you tell how many there are?"

"More than three hundred," Urstadt said. "Not more than four."

Winter swore under her breath. More than twice their numbers; perhaps more than triple, since they'd sent Ghian's force back. Winter and Urstadt's Rangers were considerably ahead of the rest of the tiellan group; they did not want civilian casualties in the battle, but they had to keep them close to their defenders. Winter hoped it was a balance they could maintain.

"Some of you are afraid," Winter shouted over her shoulder as they marched. "That is all right. Take that fear, and use it. This battle is for our freedom. It is to show who we *are*, as a people."

Winter thrust her fist into the air. "It is to show our power!"

They had reached the base of the low hill on which the City Watch was stationed. Fortunately, the slope was gradual, but even Winter knew enough to see the advantage it gave the Watch.

For a moment, panic threatened her. The hard lump of fear had returned, settling in her gut. Everything was happening so quickly. She needed more time to think, to plan. Instead, she reached into her pouch, and—finally—slipped a frost crystal into her mouth.

It was time to act.

"You'll lead the charge," she told Urstadt. She took deep breaths, felt the effects of frost on her skin and in her veins. "I'll be of no use on our front line, but I think I can take out theirs."

"Yes, Winter."

Winter nodded. There was only one thing left to do.

"*Charge!*" The word grated from Winter's lips, and Urstadt took off up the hill, glaive extended, the Rangers running behind her.

At the same time, Winter extended her telenic *tendra*. Dozens of them snaked out of her, each seeking one of the City Watch soldiers at the top of the hill. She focused on their front line first, although exactly how many that was, she was not sure. The men had taken a defensive formation, each holding a large rectangular shield out in front of them, forming a solid wall through the cracks of which jutted dozens of spear-points.

Winter seized the shields out of the hands of each of the men, and turned them on their owners. She saw a few surprised looks, mouths agape and eyes wide, staring at the shields levitating before them. Then Winter smashed each shield back down into the face of its owner.

Using her *tendra* was not difficult, nor was snatching the shields from the stationary soldiers. Her *tendra* were far stronger than a normal human arm or grip. What *was* difficult, however, was splitting her attention so many ways. Fortunately, as she focused on one *tendron*, then *two*, then a dozen, the others seemed to instinctively follow suit.

The front line of City Watchmen screamed as a wall of their own shields crushed them into the ground.

Winter threw the shields into the rear ranks of the City Watch just as the Rangers crested the hill, trampling over the cowering first rank and smashing into the unsuspecting second rank of watchmen.

She needed a better vantage point to keep controlling the battle, so she sprinted up the hill behind the Rangers, her *tendra* already seeking new targets.

Tendra were strange things. The telenic variety could interact with inanimate objects and inanimate objects only; they could not touch or move any living thing. Acumenic *tendra* were the opposite; they had no effect on inanimate objects, but could penetrate the minds of living things. Winter had to be careful as she used her telenic *tendra*; she had to interact with the objects around the humans she fought against. That meant lifting men by their armor and clothing, or swiping the weapons from their hands.

When she reached the hilltop, her *tendra* immediately went for the watchmen on horseback, currently splitting to either side of the tiellans, aiming for a flank attack. More than four dozen *tendra* twisted away from Winter, each snatching a lance or sword from the Watch's cavalry. Once again, Winter turned the soldiers' own weapons against them. She knew each strike wasn't completely effective—some barely penetrated chain, others glanced away and slid into thin air, and still others simply got lost as Winter tried to manage so many *tendra* at once. But her onslaught worked; the Watch's cavalry formations crumbled before her eyes.

Hope cracked upwards through the hard lump of fear in Winter's gut. With another burst of energy, Winter sent as many *tendra* as she could muster into the second wave of cavalry, knocking them all from their horses. Men fell to the ground as horses panicked, some trampling the men who'd been riding them not seconds before.

Now, at least, the ground was even. Winter swiped the few watchmen that remained on horseback with her *tendra* easily. Hopefully Urstadt could manage the Rangers through the rest of the battle.

Urstadt planted her feet and thrust her glaive up into the ribs of an oncoming watchman. The man screamed, spattering Urstadt with blood, and at the last second Urstadt twisted out of the way, yanking her glaive with her. The man collapsed to one side, writhing in pain.

Urstadt rammed her glaive into the man's chest, then turned to take stock of the battle.

Winter had decimated the entire force's cavalry. Urstadt could not imagine how the girl had done it. She had seen Winter's powers, watched personally as Winter killed Lord Hirman Luce in the middle of a Ruling Council meeting, and as the girl had fought her former lord, Daval Amok—a man imbued with the power of a Daemon—and won.

But Urstadt had never seen anything like this.

Winter flattened wave after wave of the watchmen. The attacks weren't always efficient, and never elegant, but they were consistent and inescapable as the tide. Virtually all that remained of the City Watch was a portion of their infantry and unhorsed cavalry.

More than two hundred watchmen remained, but that was significantly better than the odds had been only moments ago.

"Hold the line!" Urstadt shouted at the tiellan men around her. In the distance, she heard Selldor repeating the order, running up and down the line to spread the word.

These tiellans were beginners, some too old and others too young, all wholly unfamiliar with the business of killing. But they rallied to her nonetheless, and so far had not given any ground to the City Watch. Urstadt knew the power a strong leader could grant her soldiers, and fought like Oblivion to provide that for the tiellans.

Another human soldier charged the tiellan fighting next to Urstadt, but she thrust her glaive up into the man's face before he closed the gap. The man slumped into her weapon, gray matter seeping down the blade and onto the pole. Urstadt did not have time to wipe the gore before advancing, shoulder to shoulder with the tiellans next to her, on what remained of the City Watch line.

Tiellan after tiellan around Urstadt fell to the City Watch blades, but the training these men had undertaken had not been for nothing. If the soldiers penetrated their front line too deeply, or got around enough to flank or surround, the Rangers would have a much more difficult time of things. The left tiellan flank had given the City Watch a few rods at the beginning of the battle, but now held its own, and the right flank had actually gained ground, as the center, led by Urstadt, was now doing.

For now, they were doing enough.

Urstadt dodged the spear thrust of an oncoming soldier. She knocked the weapon aside and charged forward, ramming her blade into the man's gut. She stepped back, parrying another attack, twisting around to kick another watchman in the back who'd been fighting the tiellan man next to Urstadt. The watchman fell and the tiellan man pounced, stabbing downward with a spear.

Something whirred above Urstadt's head, and another oncoming watchman fell, impaled by a javelin. The weapon had moved with far too much force to have been thrown by a man.

Urstadt looked over her shoulder and caught a glance of Winter, standing still about a dozen paces behind the front line. The girl needed to do something soon to tip the battle in their favor.

As if in response to Urstadt's thoughts, suddenly a huge group of City Watch soldiers—at least four dozen; Urstadt could not count them quickly enough—rose quickly into the air, squirming and screaming, limbs flailing. There was a moment's hesitation where the entire battlefield paused, looking up, watching the men writhe as they rose into the air. They moved so high so quickly that they were barely visible when Winter finally dropped them. The men fell, screaming, back to the ground. She must have shifted their position, as most of them fell behind the City Watch's force. A horrible plethora of sound followed; a crunch here, a smack there, a crash in the distance, with screams of terrified men overarching it all. A knot in Urstadt's stomach tightened. She had never enjoyed heights, and did not envy the fate of these men.

When all the bodies had fallen, the watchmen turned back to the Rangers. A few of them raised their weapons, faces pale, but then the call came out from behind them.

"Retreat!"

Immediately, the watchmen turned and ran, fleeing the battlefield, leaving the Rangers amongst the dead.

A ragged cheer rose from the Rangers as the Cinestean City Watch retreated.

"We should go after them!" one of the tiellans shouted, looking back at Winter. "Make sure they never forget what happened here!"

A few other tiellan voices rose in affirmation, but for the most part, the Rangers were silent. Pale faces, weapons held in trembling hands or dropped to the ground completely, and the stink of shit on the battlefield told Winter all she needed to know. A few of the tiellans collapsed, sobbing, the moment the watchmen began their retreat.

"Hold your ground," Winter shouted, her voice hoarse. They were in no shape to chase after the watchmen.

"Hold your ground," she repeated, more softly.

She was in no position to pursue the watchmen.

It had been a very long time since she had accessed that much power via frost. She felt the chill indicating the drug's waning effect, and while she could take another crystal, it would not be a good idea. Kali had told her that taking too much *faltira* could burn out a psimancer's power. Winter had already risked that once, in Izet—the last time she had used this much power, and more—but, in the moment, she'd thought it was her only option.

That was not the case today. In fact, if anything, Winter wanted to live if only to take more frost, to use more power, another day.

Urstadt approached, splattered with red, glaive bloody and dripping. The warrior looked like something out of legend, or nightmare; Winter could not decide which. Looking down at herself, Winter appeared no different than when the battle began. No blood on her clothes, her hands, anywhere near her at all.

"What are your orders?" Urstadt asked.

You should give the orders, Winter wanted to say. Exhaustion threatened to overwhelm her. But, instead, Winter took a deep breath before responding. "We take all the weapons and armor we can from the fallen," she said, looking out over the field. The dead and dying were numerous; they might be able to provide better weaponry for the entire Ranger force that remained. Goddess knew such a thing was needed. "Round up any remaining horses we can find, too. I have a feeling we'll need them in the future."

"As do I." Urstadt nodded, and Winter felt a thrill that the woman approved of her orders.

"I'll inform the Druids of our victory," Winter said. "And then, we will move west. To Adimora."

14

Odenite camp, outside Kirlan

CINZIA LOOKED DOWN AT the pages of the Codex of Elwene, open on her lap. She took a moment to marvel at them, at the crimson shimmer that danced across the thin metal pages, at the characters that were incomprehensible to her until she looked at them as a whole.

It had been too long since Jane and Cinzia had sat down together to work on their translation. They were nearly through the book now, just beginning the last section of the Codex, the words of Elwene—a coda that followed the Nine Scriptures already translated, and the only part of the text not written by one of Canta's original Nine Disciples.

"She lived *before* Canta?" Jane asked, turning to look at Cinzia. Cinzia sat cross-legged on her cot in their tent, while Jane sat at the small writing desk they had brought with them, with paper, quill, and ink at hand.

"She says she lived during the Age of Marvels, but that makes no sense. She also says she compiled the writings of the other Disciples, even abridged some of them. But Canta was not born physically into the Sfaera until the middle of the Age of Reification, and she did not call her Disciples until she was twenty-two years old."

"Perhaps Elwene lived a very long life," Jane suggested. "Long enough to abridge the Disciples' writings."

Cinzia laughed softly. "You have forgotten your history lessons, Jane." Cinzia could not blame her. She probably would have as well, if they had not been reiterated time and time again during her time at the seminary. "The Age of Reification was one thousand and one years long, and Canta was born in the exact middle of that age, in the Zeroth Year. That means the Age of Marvels ended five hundred years before Canta was born, before she called her Disciples. Elwene would have been more than *five hundred years old* when she assembled the Codex."

Jane stood up. Her head nearly touched the roof of their tent, despite it being one of the larger tents in the camp.

"Canta has given us unusual powers at times," Jane said. "Healing, strength, inhuman reflexes. Perhaps she empowered Elwene to live an abnormally long life." She didn't hide the skepticism in her voice.

"Strength, inhuman reflexes, abnormally long life," Cinzia mused with a slight smile. "Perhaps Elwene was a vampire."

She had made the suggestion in jest, but Jane did not seem to take it that way.

"Canta's ways can be peculiar," Jane said, nodding. "It would not be the first time Canta used such methods."

Cinzia's eyebrows shot up. "It would not be the first time Canta used a *vampire*? What are you talking about, Jane?"

"It was your suggestion," Jane said defensively. "Do you have a better one?"

"Perhaps. There is a theory." Cinzia ran her hand along the metal pages of the open Codex—she loved the feel of the cool metal on her fingers; it never felt warm, no matter the temperature or how long she had been holding it. "A few in the Ministry believe the Disciples spoke in allegory."

Jane looked at Cinzia flatly, her eyes hooded. "Cinzi, *I* know the Disciples spoke in parables. That is not news."

"I don't mean that they just used parables on occasion; I mean these few believe the Disciples spoke entirely in allegory, that perhaps most of what they wrote is fiction."

"They believe the Codex isn't *true*?" Jane asked, her voice rising.

Cinzia shrugged. "I found this particular theory the least interesting of the many we discussed in the seminary. But it may be relevant here. Maybe Elwene's words are not true in the literal sense, but true in… in another sense."

"How can her words be true if they are not literal?" Jane asked.

Cinzia thought about it for a moment, trying to remember what some of the priestesses who espoused this theory had told her. "It is just like an allegory, Jane, but on a larger scale. An allegory is a fiction meant to illustrate a moral."

"But at a certain point the fiction overpowers the lesson; a moral cannot be conveyed through deception."

"Really?" Cinzia asked. "Are allegories not, at their most basic level, a lie? Something that did not really occur?"

"When you frame an allegory *as an allegory*, it is clear that the story being told is fictional. But when you frame an allegory *as truth*, that is deception, Cinzia."

"Even if the deception teaches a truth?" Cinzia asked. "Even if the deception makes us better?"

"A deception cannot make people better."

"We might disagree in that respect," Cinzia said.

Jane now stood beside the cot, looking down at her. Cinzia could not be sure, but she almost sensed a hint of anger in Jane's voice. Cinzia felt bad thinking it, but she enjoyed hearing the twinge of frustration. Jane had been so calm, unflappable, for so long now, it was good to see her falter.

It was good to see her act human again.

Cinzia wondered whether Jane was not getting slightly defensive at this topic. Jane had worked miracles; she could not deny that. Cinzia had worked miracles herself. But the nature of Jane's claims still echoed discordantly to Cinzia; she was not sure, after all this time, that her sister actually communicated with the Goddess.

Was Jane's anger an indication that she actually did *not*? But that didn't make sense. If Jane's story was a deception, would she not embrace this narrative—that deceptions could still teach truth?

"Cinzia, are you listening to me?"

Cinzia blinked, and her eyes refocused on Jane.

"I... I am sorry, sister. I lost myself for a moment."

"Clearly. Did you hear anything I said?"

"You said a deception cannot make people better."

"And then you disagreed with me. And then I explained myself further. You remember none of that?"

"No, Jane, I am so sorry. I have had much on my mind, lately." That much was true, at least. Between the Sons of Canta's blockade, Cinzia's effort to find out more information about the Nine Daemons, and her own physical recovery from the injuries she had sustained at her encounter with the Beldam, Cinzia had felt distracted of late.

Jane sighed, and sat down on her cot, opposite Cinzia. She slumped back, leaning on her elbows. "It is all right, sister. I understand. Sometimes I wonder what in the Sfaera we have gotten ourselves into."

We have gotten ourselves *into?* Between the two of them there seemed one clear culprit that had led them all into trouble, and it was not Cinzia. But she could not see a point in arguing. Instead, she turned back to Elwene.

"Elwene spoke of truth in what we've just translated," Cinzia said. "She said some will not recognize the truthfulness of her words. She spoke of finding the truth *behind* the meaning. Surely those words are significant."

"If she were trying to tell us something, would she not simply write it for us? What is the point in veiling it within allegory and language?"

A thought entered Cinzia's mind, a memory of something Jane had once said. "After Navone, after the false revelation I experienced, you said something about Canta. You said she had been blocked, somehow."

Jane nodded slowly. "I did say that."

"Could the same thing have happened with Elwene? Could something have blocked her from writing down exactly what it was she needed to say, so instead she was forced to speak in allegory?"

Jane was silent for a moment. "That might actually make sense."

Cinzia was about to respond when she noticed the sun falling below the horizon. Cinzia sat up immediately. She was supposed to meet Knot.

"I am sorry, sister, I must go."

"But we've just begun to make progress—"

"I am sorry." Cinzia grabbed her cloak and swept out of the tent.

Knot waited for her at the edge of camp.

"Did you find anything helpful in the translation?" he asked. "Anything about the Nine Daemons?"

"Unfortunately we did not." They started walking together,

into the woods. Cinzia felt apprehensive at making this journey once more, but she reminded herself that she had Knot at her side this time. She would be all right. "We've just begun translating the Words of Elwene—that's the section by the woman who claims to have compiled the entire book—but... her words are curious, so far.

"She claims to have lived during the Age of Marvels, for one. Of course that does not make one whit of sense. If that were true, it would mean she was abridging the records of women who lived five hundred years after her. The primary records that remain from the Age of Marvels are so few, we know very little. Legends are all we have, really..." Cinzia trailed off. She glanced at Knot, and felt her cheeks color.

"I am sorry," she said. "I just start rambling, sometimes."

"Can't say I mind," Knot said.

Cinzia could not help but smile at that. "Thank you for coming with me."

"Should've told me the last time you went to see this woman. I could've prevented what happened to you."

"I made that mistake in anger," she said. "Anger at my sister, anger at what had happened, anger at our own ignorance. I suffered the consequences of that mistake."

"Didn't mean it in a way to offend you. You're free to make choices, and I damn well don't want to get in the way of that. Just don't like the idea of anyone hurting you."

Cinzia could understand that. She felt that way herself, of course.

"Think you'll learn anything useful from this woman?" Knot asked.

"I think it is worth the effort."

* * *

Perhaps, after all, it was not worth the effort.

Their meeting with the Beldam passed without more violence, but it hardly seemed helpful. The older woman had been open, at least, and that was something, but she had not said anything Cinzia did not already know.

The Nine Daemons each had a vice or pain that fueled them: fear, wrath, death, enmity, greed, lust, insanity, deception, envy.

They were either family or an adopted family of a sort.

Azael was their leader, for some reason.

There were nine of them.

Canta's bloody bones, perhaps this was a useless pursuit. If the Beldam hardly knew more about the Nine Daemons than Cinzia did, what was the point of meeting with her?

She and Knot stalked through the forest, now dark but for the torches they each carried, in silence. Surely he would notice her not saying anything. He would think she was angry.

"I am not angry," Cinzia said.

"That's good," Knot said.

"Just because I am not talking does not mean I am angry."

"I don't mind silence. Can be a good thing once in a while."

Cinzia blinked. Of course he did not mind the silence. He was *Knot*, for crying out loud. Why was she suddenly acting so strangely around him? Now that she had actually said something, called attention to the silence, he would *surely* think it was odd. Should she say something about *that* now? Or would that only make things worse?

Goddess, why was everything so complicated?

Knot stopped. Cinzia stopped with him.

"What is it?" she whispered.

Knot held a finger to his lips, looking around slowly. After a moment, he leaned close to her, whispering, "You hear that?"

Cinzia listened, straining her ears. She heard nothing.

Her eyes widened. She heard nothing *at all*. No creaking branches, chirping crickets, wind, nothing. Now that she noticed it, the silence rushed into her ears, filling them with its emptiness.

"What—"

Before them, a bright blue light sliced through the darkness, as if a blade had cut an opening in the night air in front of Cinzia, and now the night bled blue light and iridescent smoke.

Slowly, the light expanded until it seemed to encompass everything, and it grew so bright it almost became white. Then, gradually, it faded.

But now, everything was different. Cinzia still stood in the forest—or *a* forest, of some kind—but the trees were shadows of what she knew, gray and ethereal, shimmering in the weird blue-gray light that enveloped everything.

Cinzia glanced to her left, where Knot had been walking. He was not there. She felt a moment of panic, but before it bubbled up from her chest, she heard a voice. Female, low, and inviting.

"Welcome, my daughter. I am glad I have found you."

Cinzia blinked, shielding her eyes as a form took shape before her, coalescing from the bright blue light.

"You are not Canta," Cinzia said immediately. The feeling radiated from her bones, deep within her. She could still recall that moment on the rooftop in Izet; she had felt love from the Goddess of late, as well as comfort and serenity.

She felt none of those things now.

"No need to mention *her*, darling. I would never expect you to think I was such an outcast."

An outcast? Canta?

"You are one of the Nine Daemons," Cinzia said. The form had finally taken shape before her, and Cinzia found herself face to face with the most beautiful woman she had ever seen. Smooth, unblemished skin glowed with a faint blue light, and the woman's eyes glowed a blue even brighter—Cinzia raised an arm in front of her face to shield herself from their brilliance. The woman's hair, also tinged with blue, flowed in waves over her shoulders and back. Her arms, long and elegant, extended outward, greeting Cinzia, but though her fingers were slender, they ended in sharp claws. Cinzia was envious of the woman's beauty, until she saw the claws. A sharp end to something so beautiful. She could not help but imagine a deep blue rose, accented by sharp thorns.

"Of course I am," the figure said. "The question is, do you know which one?"

Cinzia almost laughed. She felt afraid, to be sure, but the irony was not lost on her, either. She had been so desperate for information about these beings, and here one was, standing before her.

"Are you going to make me guess?"

The woman frowned. "Not if you don't want to, although I am disappointed you wouldn't at least try."

When Cinzia did not respond, the woman sighed. "Very well. I am Luceraf."

"Enmity," Cinzia whispered.

Luceraf stared at Cinzia, eyes cold despite the bright light emanating from them. "Enmity," she said, spitting the word out of her mouth. "Is that all anyone can ever think when they hear my name?"

"Is there anything else to be thought?" Cinzia asked.

Luceraf held Cinzia with her cold gaze for another few

moments. Panic slowly began to rise in Cinzia's chest. Was she making a mistake, speaking so flippantly with a Daemon? If Luceraf wanted Cinzia dead, Cinzia would end up dead, of that she had no doubt. If Luceraf wanted something else, however…

Suddenly Luceraf threw back her head and laughed, the sound echoing in the dreary gray forest.

"No," she said, after the laughter had subsided, although Cinzia could swear she could still hear it echoing all around them. "No, I suppose there is not. Not after so much time has passed. Not after my legacy has been tainted, diluted to what is only a small part of me."

"So you do not embody enmity?" Cinzia asked, endeavoring to keep the hint of hope from her voice. If she was truly in the presence of one of the Nine, there was no reason not to try to get a bit of information from the Daemon.

"What does that even mean, to *embody* something?" Luceraf mused. And she was musing, clearly. The woman turned and actually began pacing before Cinzia.

"Of course I know what it means *technically*, but what does it mean when said in reference to an actual person? Can any concept truly be diminished to a single paradigm? Is thought not more complicated? Are people not always more than the parts that make them?"

"People, perhaps," Cinzia said. "But you are a Daemon."

Luceraf laughed again, but there was no humor to the sound this time. Luceraf's chin fell as the chuckle leaked from her.

"Is that what I am?" she asked softly, in a moment that reminded Cinzia of Astrid. But, just as quickly as the vulnerability showed itself, it was gone, and Luceraf glared at Cinzia once more with hard, glowing blue eyes.

"What I am does not concern you," the Daemon said. "But

I am sure you have other questions for me."

Cinzia stared at Luceraf, blinking. "Why have you come to me? Why now?" The bizarreness of the situation overwhelmed her.

"And where is Knot?" she added, embarrassed she had not asked the question already.

She also wanted to ask why Luceraf had not killed her yet, but there did not seem to be much point in bringing that up if the Daemon herself did not care to discuss it.

"Not here. When I return you to the Sfaera, he will be waiting for you."

Cinzia felt a rush of relief, not only that Knot was all right, but that she would—supposedly, if Luceraf could remotely be trusted—be returned to the Sfaera.

"I have come to you, specifically," Luceraf continued, "because I think you are a person of great import in many coming conflicts—and you desire more knowledge about us. I wanted to introduce myself to you."

"Can I trust you?" Cinzia asked. She might as well at least try to establish that early, although no matter Luceraf's response, the issue was still highly problematic.

"I think you already know the answer to that."

"If I cannot trust you, what is the point of speaking with you?"

"I have nothing to lose in sharing information."

"And you have everything to gain?"

"I have... something to gain, yes."

"And what is that?"

Luceraf frowned. "I am giving you an opportunity to satiate your curiosity, Cinzia. Are you going to accept my information or not?"

"Where do you come from?"

Luceraf closed her eyes, winking out what Cinzia now realized was the source of most of the light in wherever she was. The strange gray forest around her darkened for a moment, illuminated only by the faint blue of Luceraf's skin and hair, until she opened her eyes once more.

"I am from separate worlds, before they were separate," she said. "Before the sundering."

"The sundering?" Cinzia asked.

"An event you will not recognize, of course. But perhaps the most important event in all of history."

"I never heard anything about a sundering in the Denomination."

"Even if they knew about it, they would not say anything. It goes against their entire dogma."

"What *was* the sundering?" Cinzia asked.

"It was a war, and a great battle between gods. The biverse was never the same afterwards."

"The what?"

"Never mind. You need to ask different questions, Cinzia. I could not possibly explain everything about the sundering in the few moments we have left."

Cinzia scoffed. The few moments they had left? But she could not pass up the opportunity for more information. This was what she had been seeking, was it not?

"How old are you?" she asked.

"Many thousands of years," Luceraf said.

"Are you a goddess?"

"Yes… and no."

"Can you be killed?"

"Any living thing can be killed."

"Can *you?*"

Luceraf smiled. "Time is up, Cinzia. I will come to you again, but you must understand that you cannot tell anyone about our meeting. I will keep it a secret on my end, but you must also keep it a secret on yours. Your sister would never understand. Neither would Knot. If you want me to come to you again, you must keep this from them."

Before Cinzia could respond, she felt a rush around her, and the whole gray world around her seemed to expand, then contract, and then she was back in the forest, surrounded by darkness.

"Cinzia? Did you hear what I said?"

Cinzia looked at Knot standing next to her, and for the briefest moment wanted to tell him everything about Luceraf. She did not want to have to lie to anyone, least of all him.

But she did not tell him. She could not, not when she was so close to finally getting the information she had sought for so long.

"I... How long was I gone?" Cinzia asked.

"Gone? What're you talking about?" Knot frowned at her. The torch he held crackled faintly.

"The silence is gone," she said suddenly. She could hear the rustle of trees, and all the other noises of night that she had never realized could be so comforting.

"Aye," Knot muttered. "Already said that, but aye."

"I am sorry, Knot. I am all right, now. Shall we make our way back to camp?"

Knot nodded, once, and then led the way through the forest, Cinzia walking close by his side.

15

KNOT KNEW CINZIA WAS hiding something, but he did not want to press the woman. She would tell him if, and when, she was ready. Just as he would tell her what had happened to him, if he could ever understand it.

When Cinzia had frozen, her eyes locked on something ahead, Knot had been conscious of *something* happening to him as well. His vision had darkened at the edges, and he'd felt himself being pulled back, deep into himself. It felt very much like the moments in which he'd experienced episodes months ago, before Wyle had healed him.

Perhaps even Wyle's efforts had only offered him a temporary fix. But, at the same time, he did not think that was the case. He *did* feel stable now, and had since Wyle helped him, in a way that he had not since he'd awoken in Pranna. But he had felt the sensation nonetheless, and while it had not amounted to anything, the memory of it made the hairs on his neck and arms stand on end.

And the fact that something had clearly happened to Cinzia, too, made him wonder.

But he couldn't tell her anything, not yet. He hardly had anything to tell her, anyway. A sensation? What did that mean? No use in bringing something up that had no meaning to begin with.

If it happened again, he'd tell her.

16

House of Aldermen, Triah

RICCAN CARRIERI WALKED THROUGH the large double doors and into the assembly chamber of the House of Aldermen. Gold trim adorned the doors and frame, both decorated with carvings of the first assembly that had taken place after the abdication of the King Who Gave Up His Crown.

He walked down a long corridor that led to a dais, upon which rested a circular table at the center of the room. Granite platforms rose upward and outward from the stage in concentric tiered circles. To Carrieri's surprise, the nine chairs around the center table were occupied. This was a full, not a qualified, assembly.

Two councils comprised the governing body of Khale. The first, and most important, was the People's Parliament, consisting of representatives from Triah and all of the provinces of Khale. The tiered platforms around the center table consisted of ninety-nine seats, occupied by nobles, merchants, and citizens alike, one for each member of the People's Parliament.

A qualified assembly required only the presence of two-thirds of the People's Parliament; the status of the meeting was upgraded to full when the Minor Council joined them. Carrieri recognized the eight members of the Minor Council seated around the table.

Traditionally, the Minor Council consisted of three seats

reserved for the Triunity of the Denomination: the Oracle, the Holy Examiner, and the First Priestess, all present today. The Venerato and Authoritar of the Citadel occupied two more seats, while elected Triahn nobles occupied two others. The last seat of the Minor Council belonged to the Consular, elected from the People's Parliament, who acted as head of both the Parliament and Minor Council.

That, of course, left one seat at the table. Today, that seat was meant for Riccan Carrieri, elected Grand Marshal of the Khalic armed forces.

The People's Parliament was in full argumentative flow as Carrieri made the long walk across the marbled floor towards the round table at the center of the room. As he mounted the stage and took his seat, he looked around at the tiered platforms, rising up above the table at which he sat. Senators stood on the various tiers, shouting at one another, dressed in the traditional Khalic political *togar*—long, flowing violet robes, draped over one shoulder.

Carrieri curled his lip. This was why he hated assemblies.

The Consular's hammer cracked against the table, echoing over the shouts in the room. Her clear, confident voice followed.

"Order! I call this assembly to order!"

Carrieri glanced at Karina Vestri, elected Consular. The shouting voices quieted almost immediately, and for a brief moment a hollow feeling sucked at Carrieri's chest. There was a time when he'd felt pride at Karina's ability to call the most powerful people in the world to order. There'd been a time when she would have caught his eye, given him the slightest of smiles.

"We welcome Grand Marshal Riccan Carrieri to the full assembly," the Consular continued, not meeting Carrieri's eyes, "by our request. Thank you for coming, Grand Marshal."

Carrieri inclined his head. "I live to serve the great nation of Khale," he said, taking his seat at the table.

"I call for an immediate vote to action!" one of the senators shouted from the platforms. A dozen or so other voices murmured in consent.

A vote to action. There were only two reasons to call a vote to action during a full assembly. One was to evict a sitting senator or councilperson, but if that had been the case Carrieri could not imagine why he would have been invited to this meeting.

The other, of course, was a declaration of war.

Roden could not possibly have attacked without Carrieri hearing about it. There had been rumors of the neighboring country gathering troops, but Carrieri had not heard of any movement, not yet. Unless, somehow, Roden's maneuvers had slipped past his spies. Such a thing was not likely.

The Consular glared up at the platforms in the general direction from which the voice had come. "You are out of order, Senator Nalo. The assembly will receive a full briefing before we make any such motion."

Carrieri heard soft grumbling from the platforms, but no formal dissent.

"Venerato Lothgarde, do you have the intelligence report?" the Consular asked, turning to a bald man about Carrieri's age—forty-five summers—with spectacles and a trimmed circle beard. Kosarin Lothgarde, the Venerato of the Citadel. Carrieri also knew him as the head of the Triad, the ruling body of the Nazaniin assassins.

Lothgarde nodded. "Authoritar Aqilla will give the report, madam."

All eyes turned to Sirana Aqilla, who stood up from her

seat next to Lothgarde and walked around to a set of steps that led onto the table. Whenever someone addressed the entirety of the House of Councils, they stood upon the grand table.

"Human–tiellan tension has reached a tipping point in Cineste," Aqilla said. Her eyes were sharp and alert, her fiery red hair tied back in a loose bun. Carrieri dismissed many in the Parliament, and in the Minor Council itself, as incompetent or mildly stupid. Neither Aqilla nor Lothgarde fell into that category.

"A tiellan force of almost a thousand left the city of Cineste yesterday. As near as we can tell, each of these tiellans called the city their home. This movement stems from a group of tiellans within the city who call themselves the Druids."

Murmurs filled the hall. While some seemed to have heard the news already, it was clearly the first word of it for others.

It was certainly the first time for Carrieri.

He envied the Nazaniin information network. He had tried time and time again to convince them to open their communication channels to him, but the group was maddeningly obstinate. They hoarded information like the dragons of legend hoarded gold.

A gathering tiellan force, named after the most powerful mortal beings in history, was something Carrieri would have liked to hear about earlier. Between this and the Odenite Church moving south, rumored to be almost fifteen hundred strong, the historians might as well already start calling this the Age of Exodus.

"The Cinestean City Watch met these Druids outside the city gates, slaughtering two hundred tiellans."

"Canta's bones," Carrieri whispered under his breath. He knew Drille Garastoni, the magistrate of Cineste, by reputation, and he could not imagine a worse man to handle human–tiellan relations. Garastoni was a Kamite sympathizer, advocating the re-enslavement of all tiellans.

"A small group of tiellans retaliated," Aqilla continued. "If my sources are correct, that force crushed the City Watch in a skirmish just outside the city walls."

With a collective gasp, the House of Councils erupted into chatter.

Carrieri raised his hand. As the assembly's guest, he had in theory as much governing power as the Consular. This was foreign territory, or at least it felt that way to him, and he had to be cautious.

Fortunately, the Consular lent him her aid, even if she still refused to meet his eyes. She slammed her gavel on the table sharply, three times, and the prattle quieted.

"Grand Marshal Carrieri, you have a comment?" she asked.

"Some questions," Carrieri said. "How large were the forces that engaged in this skirmish? What were the casualties?"

"My sources estimate the City Watch fielded just over four hundred soldiers," Aqilla said. "The tiellan numbers are less clear. Roughly a thousand left the city, but the force that engaged the City Watch seemed to have consisted of just over a hundred fighters. Casualties were minimal for the tiellans, but catastrophic for the City Watch. They lost nearly two hundred men and almost a hundred horses, either killed or taken by the tiellans."

Stunned silence permeated the hall.

Carrieri blinked. City Watchmen had never made particularly strong soldiers, but they were at least trained in battle. While tiellans were technically allowed to join the army, only a small portion of them actually did, and all of those were billeted in Triah.

"My source tells me the tiellans fought fiercely, but they

were obviously green," Aqilla said. "The City Watch should have crushed them. But it appears the tiellans had a psimancer." Aqilla paused, clearing her throat. "Probably more than one, if the reports are correct. Countless weapons flying through the air, dozens of bodies."

Carrieri frowned amidst further murmuring of the senators around him. Aqilla was hiding something. He would need to find out what.

"Where have these tiellans gone?" Carrieri asked. "They left Cineste, defeated the guard force the magistrate so foolishly placed in their way... now what are they doing?"

"They have moved east," Aqilla said.

"They're going to recruit the clans!" a senator shouted. "We need to stop them before they gather more power!"

The Consular's gavel cracked against the table. "Order!" Karina shouted. She looked up at Aqilla. "Do you have anything else for us, Authoritar?"

"I do not, Madam Consular."

"Thank you. You may be seated."

Aqilla stepped down from the table and took her seat next to Lothgarde. Carrieri watched Lothgarde lean over to Aqilla and whisper something in her ear. The two were definitely hiding something—but chances were, at any given point in time, the Venerato and Authoritar were hiding a great many things at once. Carrieri would speak to them afterwards to discover whether this was actually of any importance.

"We will now hear proposals on this topic," Karina said. She glared up at the senators. "We will *not* entertain any calls to action. Not yet. We will hear knowledgeable suggestions from those closely related to the incidents outside of Cineste, and that is all."

Silence reigned for a moment. For all the anger and frustration the senators had shown, they were remarkably reluctant to offer any real solutions. Finally, one of them spoke up. Carrieri recognized Griggan Dai, a representative of the combined towns of northern Khale outside of Cineste.

"I propose we do nothing," Senator Dai said. He was immediately met by scoffs and hisses, but he continued over them, to his credit. "Nobody has spoken to the intentions of these tiellans," he continued. "Perhaps they wanted to leave peacefully, and the City Watch stopped them. They might not cause any more trouble. We should track them, stay informed, but that is all."

Carrieri pursed his lips. Another senator was already responding, arguing that the tiellans couldn't possibly have anything in mind other than human destruction, but Karina shut that line of argument down quickly, as Carrieri suspected she would.

Carrieri met eyes with Senator Dai. Dai was a tiellan sympathizer; promoting an option that would protect them was not a surprising move. While Carrieri himself was no tiellan sympathizer, he would always side with reason. The idiot magistrate of Cineste had overreacted; it would do Khale no good if the senators overreacted too, provoking the tiellan group further.

"We need to send Carrieri," one of the senators shouted. Carrieri looked up, scowling. He hated having to sit down at this damned table. He could never tell who was bloody speaking on the tiers around him.

"Carrieri will crush them," another senator agreed.

Carrieri rolled his eyes. "What good would it do to crush a movement of one thousand tiellans?" he asked. "Must each of you be reminded that they were the ones first attacked in Cineste? The loss of lives was Magistrate Garastoni's fault, and no one else's."

"We do not know they wouldn't have attacked otherwise," another senator said.

Carrieri clenched his jaw. For the first time since he'd entered the assembly chamber, Karina Vestri met his eyes. They both raised a single eyebrow at one another, a glance they had exchanged dozens of times before.

Senators can be such astounding morons.

Carrieri looked away quickly, as did Karina. He had glanced at her more out of habit than anything else. Such things died long, slow deaths.

"They're preparing to take revenge on us," another senator said.

Bloody Oblivion. With a burst of energy, Carrieri stood and leapt onto the table, bypassing the stairs opposite him.

"*Enough*," he roared. The senators quieted immediately, thank the Goddess. Carrieri turned slowly, speaking to all of the senators in the room. "You act like children who cannot fathom anything beyond yourselves."

Silence met him. Carrieri reveled in it. It had been too long since he'd berated the fools that governed his nation. And, since they had invited him to the full assembly as their guest, he had full rights to do so.

"If you want to send *me* north to take care of your tiellan situation, you will have to order me to do it, with the power of full assembly. No other action would make me abandon reason to go after whatever shadows frighten you.

"Surely you are all aware of the threat of Roden. The empire is more unstable than ever now, and more unpredictable. They have been amassing power and could move against us at any moment. Do you truly want me to abandon Triah to waste time on a threat that is not even a threat?"

Carrieri paused as he looked around him, at each raised platform.

"My whole life has been committed to Khale, to protecting us from danger, but particularly against our greatest rival, Roden. I will not abandon that post now. Not unless you force me to do so. Will you force me?"

"Do we have any forces in the north?" a senator finally asked. Carrieri turned, craning his head to see the woman who had spoken. He did not recognize her—she must be newly elected.

"The Steel Regiment is the closest force. They are already in the area to keep the peace in the Eastmaw Mountains." The mountain villages had been at each other's throats recently, as they tended to be every decade or so. Carrieri had sent Publio Kyfer and his Steel Regiment to the area weeks ago—mainly because Carrieri could not stand Kyfer's presence in Triah any longer. There were already rumors that Kyfer was in the running to replace Carrieri whenever he stepped down, or was killed, and Carrieri could not abide the idea that such a fool would succeed him.

"We could send them after these tiellans," the senator said. "An entire regiment would make quick work of them."

"It would," Carrieri said slowly. The Steel Regiment consisted of roughly three thousand soldiers, as well as a Nazaniin *cotir* of their own. Even if the tiellans had a dozen psimancers, they could not hope to stand against such a force.

The biggest problem, in Carrieri's opinion, would be Publio Kyfer. But he could not express such a sentiment here, where Kyfer had a strong following.

"Then we should send the Steel Regiment," the senator continued. "Grand Marshal Carrieri can stay here where it is safe, and we will take care of the tiellan problem once and for all."

Carrieri bristled. *Where it is safe.* He kept his breathing even, however. One did not become the Grand Marshal of all Khalic forces by rising to meaningless provocations.

"I do not think this Cinestean force is the extent of your 'tiellan problem,'" Carrieri said. "The Steel Regiment would likely quell this group, but such a drastic action could provoke the tiellans to greater anger. We might face full rebellion throughout our nation."

"Better to quell them now," the senator said, "than to wait and watch this threat grow beyond our power."

Carrieri and the senator held one another's eyes for a moment. The woman was younger than Carrieri had first thought, certainly younger than he, with voluminous black hair and a cold, calculated gaze.

"Is that a proposal, Senator Tristani?" Karina asked.

The woman, Senator Tristani, looked around at her fellow senators, then nodded slowly. "Yes," she said. "I propose we order the Steel Regiment to attack the tiellan force in the north, annihilating them. We must deal with our problems quickly and decisively."

Someone swiftly seconded the proposal, accompanied by many other murmurs of agreement.

Karina struck the table with her gavel. "We have a proposal before us, then. Is there any discussion on the proposal?"

Carrieri stayed standing on the table, watching the senators discuss the issue. Many were for the proposal exactly as Tristani had said it, but others seemed more hesitant. In the end, thankfully, a hybrid approach passed. A message would be sent up to Publio Kyfer through his Nazaniin *cotir*, informing him of his orders to track and gain intelligence on the tiellan movement. If the tiellans threatened the lives or well-being of any Khalic citizens—or any *humans*, as Carrieri understood it—Kyfer would engage. Because only a regiment was involved, and because the opposing force was very small, no call to action was needed. But the action the assembly had decided upon, and the message it would send to the tiellans, was clear enough.

Karina closed the assembly, and Riccan Carrieri strode out of the House of Aldermen. The Parliament could have come up with a worse solution, but this one was far from the best.

Outside the large double doors, Carrieri waited in the grand hallway that encircled the assembly chamber. After a few moments, he glimpsed the Venerato and Authoritar walking silently together away from the chamber.

Carrieri caught up with them, falling in beside Kosarin Lothgarde.

"Grand Marshal Carrieri," Lothgarde said, inclining his head as they walked.

"You are keeping something from the Parliament," Carrieri said. "What is it?"

Aqilla glanced at him. "We made a full report, Grand Marshal."

Lothgarde still stared straight forward.

"I don't care what you keep from the Parliament," Carrieri said. "They are paranoid fools. But I do care what you keep from me. My duty is to protect you as much as them."

"Grand Marshal," Aqilla said, "I'm afraid I must insist—"

"Grand Marshal Carrieri is right," Lothgarde interrupted. "We should tell him, Sirana. But not here." He looked at Carrieri for the first time since they'd begun the conversation. "Come with us."

They crossed the great Center Circle of Triah, and Lothgarde and Aqilla led Carrieri, predictably, to the Citadel.

The Citadel, considered the most prestigious school in the whole of the Sfaera, was actually a palace that had once belonged to the kings and queens of Khale. But, one hundred and seventy-odd years ago, when the king gave up his crown, everything had changed. The royal palace became the Citadel, and today many said the Citadel ruled the nation—and in some ways, the Sfaera—more effectively than the Khalic monarchs ever had.

The Citadel, Canta's Fane, and the House of Aldermen made three points of a triangle that spanned across the Center Circle of Triah, forming a Trinacrya, the famous circle-and-triangle symbol of the goddess Canta and her Denomination. Carrieri had always thought the symbol a bit much; the Denomination already had enough say in political and military decisions, and the Trinacrya in Triah's Center Circle only made that fact more obvious.

They brought him through the large doors of the Citadel into an antechamber. Lothgarde and Aqilla looked as one at a group of students lounging in the room, who fled immediately. The Venerato and Authoritar turned to face Carrieri. Apparently, just being inside the Citadel and relatively alone was all the privacy they needed. It was a huge room for such a private conversation. The arched ceiling of the antechamber was twice Carrieri's height, the wooden supports of the arch covered in precious metals etched with pictures and symbols of just about anything he could imagine, and some things he couldn't. A large fresco covered one wall and most of the ceiling, while paintings and a tapestry draped the others. The Citadel was known for its art collection; Carrieri recognized the tapestry as Andrinarian, the figures woven with delicate ease, contrasting with harsh, clashing colors. The paintings were from Maven Kol, and the fresco of course was Khalic.

"What are you keeping from the Parliament?" Carrieri demanded. While either of them could work their psimantic magics on him at any moment—Carrieri had seen it happen— he was confident they would not. Carrieri's position was important enough—and he was damn good enough at what he did—that they would not attempt any move against him. Not now.

Whether or not they would in the future, of course, remained to be seen.

Aqilla looked to Lothgarde, clearly uncertain.

Lothgarde inclined his head towards her. "Tell him."

Aqilla frowned, but turned to face Carrieri. "There was just one psimancer with the tiellan force," Aqilla said. "A young woman."

"Just one?" How could one psimancer turn the tide of a battle against hundreds of soldiers? "And a tiellan? I thought tiellans could not access psimancy." While Carrieri did not much care for psimancy, he could not afford to be ignorant of it. Much of his education had come from these two people.

"We... we may have been wrong about that," Aqilla said.

"You *may* have?" Carrieri raised an eyebrow.

"Psimancy is still a relatively new science," Aqilla said defensively. "We assumed, after a few decades without encountering a single tiellan psimancer, that they simply could not access the Void."

"But this woman can?"

"We have had dealings with her in the past that suggest she can."

Carrieri thought about this. A tiellan psimancer. If the Nazaniin were wrong about this, what else did they not know?

"You said there were dozens of people being thrown about by psimancers at the battle." Carrieri looked slowly from Lothgarde to Aqilla. He'd seen what a powerful telenic could do—Oblivion, he'd seen what *Aqilla herself* could do—and she came nowhere near such power. "How could one woman do all that?"

"She is special," Lothgarde said. "That's about all we can say about her at the moment."

"You won't tell me anything else?"

"We don't *know* anything else, Riccan."

Carrieri frowned at Lothgarde. "If she is truly special, as you claim, is she the only tiellan psimancer? Or if this tiellan movement actually does grow into something greater, are we going to have to worry about more?" When they didn't answer, he asked, "Rune has nothing to say about this?"

Both Lothgarde and Aqilla were silent for a moment. Carrieri's eyes narrowed just slightly. Rune was always the more reclusive member of the Triad, but Carrieri had never seen them both react so strangely at just the mention of Rune's name.

"Not at the moment," Aqilla said, after a pause that seemed to take entirely too long.

"Very well. Is that all you're willing to tell me?"

He noticed the twitch of a smile at the corner of Lothgarde's mouth. "Yes, Riccan. For now, that is all we are willing to tell you."

Carrieri took a deep breath. "Very well. I'll be seeing the both of you."

He left without a backward glance.

17

Eastern plains of Khale

ARROW NOCKED, WINTER SUCKED in her breath and took aim. The bow had a decent draw, though it was nothing like the bow she'd once made for herself in Pranna. She missed that weapon; the curve of the wood, the strength of the draw were aspects of perfection she had worked on through countless iterations of the same object until she finally got it right.

With an exhalation, Winter loosed the arrow. Fifty rods ahead of her, a single bison within a herd of dozens flinched. In response, the entire herd took off in a gallop away from Winter's position in the grass and the small creek around which they'd crowded. The ground trembled beneath her; there were at least a hundred bison in the herd. She watched as the animals receded into the distance.

Two bison lagged behind the rest, however, and eventually both toppled to the ground, one face-first and the other crumpling to the side, each sliding to a stop in the grass.

Winter stood, squinting in the sunlight.

"Well shot," Urstadt said as she stood next to her.

Winter thanked Urstadt. She liked being the recipient of the warrior captain's praise, perhaps because it came so rarely. Urstadt had been the first to admit she was no hunter—she only accompanied Winter for her protection—but Winter valued the woman's judgment just the same.

And the truth was, it felt good to go hunting again. She had considered felling the bison with *faltira*, but the decision to find a bow and actually go *hunting* had been surprisingly easy. This was one thing for which she had never needed *faltira* to augment her abilities. It was something she had worked at for many years in order to become proficient.

Winter began walking towards the kill when she heard a shout in the distance behind her. She turned to see Selldor walking excitedly towards them, three horses in tow.

"That was incredible," he said. "How did you get two at once? I only saw you fire one arrow."

"The arrow went through the first and pierced the second," Winter said. "But that's only the first part of the process. We still have to field dress the kills before we take them back to camp."

"Please, Winter, that is no task for a commander. We are not far from camp; I can come back with other tiellans who would be willing to dress the animals and bring them back."

Winter pressed her lips together. Truth was, she hated butchering her kills. Tiellans never had much of an option—humans could hire servants for the task—but her father had always taught her that it was important to dress any animal she killed herself. Now that she thought about it, she could not remember any compelling reason behind her father's counsel, but it was something she'd absorbed without questioning. It just felt right.

Then again, there were two large kills here. More people, and more horses, would only help.

"Bring more men and horses and meet us there," Winter said, nodding in the direction of the fallen bison. "Urstadt and I will get started."

About half an hour later, Winter, Urstadt, Selldor, and three other tiellans rode back to camp with the bison carcasses distributed among a few extra horses.

Windswept grassy plains surrounded her, and had for the past two days of travel. The vastness almost frightened her. No forests, hardly any hills. To the southeast she could make out the Undritch Mountains clearly, their peaks still white with snow. But even the massive mountain range did little to ground her in the plains. There was nothing out here between her and the sky. She felt as if she might fall upwards, her feet leaving the ground to tumble endlessly towards the open, cloudless expanse above. Winter had never seen land so... flat.

Two weeks had passed since the battle at Cineste's Tiellan Gate. Now that the Rangers had horses, armor, and better weapons, they could both scout the land around them with relative ease, and make quick hunting and watering trips to provide for the main tiellan camp. The tiellans who had left Cineste had fortunately gathered a fair amount of food and supplies for the journey, but it was important to supplement and grow that reserve whenever possible. The plains, thankfully, did not lack either food or water, so far. Long-horned antelope and bison ranged the grassy land freely, and there had been many streams and creeks along the tiellan path so far. Winter counted them fortunate; she was conscious of the strain that such a large group of travelers placed on the land around them, and hoped the fortune followed them until they reached Adimora.

Now that the Rangers had horses, armor, and real weapons, they had the beginnings of a real army. During the day Winter rode with about seventy men, while the rest stayed under Ghian's command with the main group. One of her first orders of business after taking command of the Rangers had been to open up the training courses that Ghian still ran—now under tight supervision from Urstadt—to tiellan women as well as men. Eranda had even begun training, hoping to one day ride with Winter—and Gord, who had joined up with the Rangers recently despite his age—into battle. The idea made Winter uncomfortable, but she could not very well tell Eranda no.

The order had gone over well enough; the Rangers seemed content to let Winter take charge despite the fact that she was a woman and they were a company of men, and allowing more women into their army seemed the logical next step. She imagined some of them were less than comfortable with the idea, but Urstadt was one of the greatest warriors Winter had ever seen, and if her men could not acknowledge that and consequently make themselves comfortable fighting alongside tiellan women, she had no use for them anyway.

While Winter hardly knew what to do with the new responsibility, and understood that she was really nothing more than Urstadt's mouthpiece, she could not deny the sense of purpose the position gave her. For too long she had drifted, aimless—even before she had met Knot. For now, at least she had a clear role, unearned though it might be. Urstadt had made it clear she had no intention of taking command herself—the tiellans would not accept a human as a leader anyway—but Winter was learning a great deal from her. Perhaps, one day, she might actually grow into this role.

They had yet to cross the Undritch Mountains, let alone arrive at Adimora. After leaving Cineste their course turned southeast, passing through the forest of Takk Dusia just north of the Eastmaw Mountains. The massive Undritch range, running parallel to the smaller Eastmaws, split the eastern planes in half, and Adimora was supposed to be on the easternmost side of the mountains. It was because of the mountains that the tiellan clans hereabouts had very little contact with other people, let alone other tiellans. Winter had only met two tiellan clansmen herself, and then only briefly, as they passed through Pranna when she was a girl. She could remember her excitement at seeing them; the two men had worn their wide-brimmed *araifs*, of course, but the brims were wider than any Winter had ever seen, and pulled down low over their eyes. Their leather clothing had been encrusted with dust, and each carried a variety of weapons she had never seen before. They looked so exotic, so dangerous. She was looking forward to meeting more of them.

Other than a few distant riders on horseback, however, they had seen no one on the plains. The riders they had seen had kept their distance, watching from afar, then riding off to who knew where. Always one at a time, their outlines distinct on the horizon. They could be tiellan tribesmen, or human nomads. Winter had no way to be sure.

This was a world Winter had never known, had never imagined, and being here made her oddly happy—despite the maddening flatness of it all. As much as the daytime sky on the plains made Winter uneasy, she loved the nights. The millions of stars stretching out above her as she lay on her bedroll were far more comforting than the blue emptiness that gaped above her during the day. She had slept well last night, and was glad the sun was now close to setting.

When they returned to camp, Urstadt approached her after they'd dismounted and made sure their horses were taken care of. "Are you ready for your training?" Somehow, the woman had already procured two swords, and was holding one in each hand.

"We've only just returned," Winter said. The tiellan camp occupied the crest of a low ridge, along one side of which a small river ran through a gulch.

"A fight is never convenient," Urstadt said. Winter was starting to regret her request that Urstadt teach her to fight. Urstadt did not seem to think Winter was making very remarkable progress, as she monopolized every spare moment with more training.

Urstadt stabbed one of the swords into the ground, twirling the other as she walked a few paces away. She had shed her plate armor—reluctantly—while traveling on the plains in favor of boiled leather. The grasslands grew quite hot during the day, and it was almost summer. Winter's own black leather was becoming uncomfortable on the hotter days.

Winter grasped the hilt of the sword buried in the ground, hefting it in one hand. The sword was not heavy, but it wasn't light, either. "You're sure I can't train with a lighter sword?"

Urstadt scoffed. "We will train with all types of weapons, but always a standard sword first. This is the weapon you are most likely to use on a battlefield, should you lose your own."

Winter did not argue; she did not yet have a specific sword to call her own, but she had been through this with Urstadt before. The weapon seemed particularly heavy today. Wasn't she supposed to be getting stronger?

The hilt was made to be held with one hand, and the leather-wrapped metal fit Winter's grip well enough. She gave the blade an experimental twirl; Urstadt did not always give her the same blade, and this was not one that Winter remembered using. On the pommel she recognized the cresting sun of Cineste; this, like most of the other swords she had used, had belonged to a Cinestean watchman.

"Take a defensive stance," Urstadt said. "Your choice."

Winter obliged, lifting her sword, holding her free hand

out before her, and placing the majority of her weight on her back foot. *Bu-tine* stance, a versatile defensive beginning but not particularly strong, according to Urstadt. Winter felt comfortable with it for now. There seemed to be a sort of hierarchy of stances when it came to swordplay that Winter did not understand yet. Hopefully, in time, it would be something she would pick up.

Winter blinked. She was *tired*. A full day of traveling, followed by a hunt, had wiped her energy. Usually a dose of frost helped with that, but now wasn't the time to give in to that urge.

"Now, defend yourself." Urstadt attacked. Winter parried one strike, then another, and then Urstadt's sword-point found her throat.

"Good," Urstadt said. "Again."

"How was that good?" Winter asked. "You would have killed me in seconds."

"I've been training my entire life," Urstadt said. "If I couldn't kill you in seconds I wouldn't be good at what I do. Again."

Winter took the *bu-tine* stance again, despite Urstadt having cautioned her in the past about using the same stance over and over. Winter just wanted to get comfortable with one, then she would move on to others.

Urstadt came at her again, and this time Winter could only parry one attack before Urstadt's sword came singing towards her face. Winter flinched, but of course Urstadt stopped the sword a few fingers away from Winter's cheek, the blade quivering. Winter could not fathom how the woman had such control over a blade. She felt clumsy, shaky, her sword never quite doing what she wanted it to do.

"Not so good," Urstadt said. "You lost control early. You moved with your arms when you should have moved with your feet."

"Swordplay requires too much legwork." Urstadt had gone over step after step with her before she had even picked up a sword, saying that every swing, every parry, needed to begin from the toes and move upwards. Winter understood that concept now, more or less, but it was difficult to put into practice when a woman twice her size and a hundred times her skill bore down on her.

"Again," Urstadt said.

They sparred time and time again, enough for Winter to work up a solid sweat as the sun set, and for a small crowd of Rangers to draw around them. A few tiellans always took interest in her training sessions with Urstadt. She supposed just watching Urstadt helped them in their own training, run by Urstadt at separate times of the day, and in groups. But Winter herself was clearly terrible with the sword; she usually only lasted two or three strokes against Urstadt, sometimes up to five or six if she was lucky.

After a particularly long bout—Winter wasn't sure whether she lasted six or seven strokes this time; if the latter, it would be a record for her—Winter thrust the sword into the ground and took a deep breath.

"You're learning," Urstadt said.

"Thanks for stating the obvious," Winter gasped. Urstadt hardly seemed winded.

"I do not think it is obvious," Urstadt said. "Some do not learn, especially when they are older."

Winter raised one eyebrow. "Older?"

"You are no longer a youth," Urstadt said, as if that explained it.

"I've seen only twenty-two summers."

The sun had now set completely. The night was dark, and the stars were out. Urstadt tossed her a waterskin, and Winter took a long, gulping drink gratefully.

"Once you have mastered the basics," Urstadt said, "you should begin to practice fighting while using telesis."

Winter lowered the waterskin. She had not thought of *faltira* since beginning the training session. That seemed a good thing. "What do you know about fighting while using telesis?"

"Nothing," Urstadt responded. "But it is a skill you cannot neglect to develop."

True enough, Winter thought.

"Commander Winter!"

Winter made a face as she turned to face the oncoming Ranger. She hated the title the Rangers had given her, and they did not seem interested in alternative suggestions. It sounded ridiculous. "Commander Urstadt" rolled off the tongue, had a certain ring to it. "Commander Winter" was as clunky and awkward to say as Winter felt she was at the job.

The Ranger was just a few years Winter's senior. "Riders in the distance," he said.

"More than one?"

"Many more," the Ranger said. "We can't quite make out an exact count yet, but… dozens, at least."

Winter's heart pounded more quickly. They had not seen so many before.

"To arms," she said. "Don't form up yet. They may not want to fight us. But be ready."

Winter looked to Urstadt. This would be their first encounter with the tiellan clans. Winter needed to make sure it went well, one way or another.

* * *

In moments, Winter was mounted, Urstadt on the steed next to her, watching the riders approach in the distance. Selldor waited on his horse on Winter's other side. He had become her de facto lieutenant-of-choice. While his military prowess did not seem any greater than Winter's, he did appear loyal, and he was certainly angry. That was an emotion Winter could channel.

Her seventy Rangers formed up behind them, mounted and armed with spears and swords. A few of them had bows, but they had very little experience using the weapons from horseback—nothing like the fabled riding archers of the tiellan clans.

Four ranks of about a dozen riders each approached. Tiellans, certainly. Winter recognized the long brown leather coats and wide-brimmed hats. It was said that, among the clans, even female tiellans wore the wide-brimmed *araifs*. The riders were now close enough for Winter to see the truth behind that claim. A good portion of the approaching riders were women, and all were heavily armed. Another reason for Ghian and the Druids to consider enlisting women into the Rangers.

Each rider carried a bow and arrows, a short throwing spear or two, and long curved swords.

Winter's Rangers outnumbered the clan riders, but from all Winter had heard, the clans spent as much time warring with one another as they did doing just about anything else; every clan rider was a warrior in his or her own right. Winter's Rangers had seen one victory in battle, but they were still green. As was Winter herself. She had her psimancy, of course, but if they could win the support of the clans without a battle, all the better.

A group of five riders broke off as the others slowed to a stop. The five continued forward, towards Winter, Urstadt, and

Selldor. Winter took a frost crystal from the pouch at her belt. Better to be safe.

"May we all be blessed," one of the clan riders said, a man, as the five neared Winter.

Winter inclined her head, unsure what to say. "Good day to you all," she finally decided, painfully aware of how stupid she sounded. Like she was greeting a group of nobles on the street in Cineste.

The five riders exchanged glances with one another. Clearly Winter had not given the expected response.

"Under the sun and moon," one of the riders said slowly.

The five riders did not remain still. Their horses trotted to and fro, sometimes in circles, and every once in a while one of them would move at a gallop for a moment, only to slow and return to the group.

"We are wondering why you have come to the great plains," another rider said, this one a woman, her wide-brimmed *araif* pulled low over her face, long brown hair protruding beneath.

"My name is Winter. Behind me are a group of Rangers from Cineste." She felt the dull fire of *faltira* beginning to take effect within her.

All five of the clan riders burst into hearty laughter at the mention of Rangers. Winter frowned. Perhaps she should not have used the word. She tried to ignore the laughter, and continued. "We have traveled east to escape the human persecution in Khale, and to seek the help of the tiellan clans."

It took a moment for the riders' laughter to die, but when it did, they fell quiet for a moment, their horses fidgeting and trotting distractedly. Winter wondered how they could stand it; if her horse were so restless, she would hardly be able to focus on anything else.

"You say you have come escaping the humans," another rider said, "but you are in the company of one. Why did you bring what you are trying to escape?"

Winter glanced at Urstadt, who remained stone-faced next to her.

"Urstadt is different," Winter said, very aware of how lame her explanation sounded. "She is my friend, and she is loyal. She has sworn to serve me."

A few of the riders murmured at that, but Winter could not make out anything specific they said.

"Many hundreds travel behind you," another said. "They are yours?" There did not seem to be a specific commander, at least not among these five. It was a strange dynamic; there seemed to be no order in which they spoke, and it mimicked the controlled chaos of their restless horses.

"We are part of the same group, yes."

"And are they also Rangers?" Another round of laughter from the clan riders accompanied the question.

"Some of them, yes." Winter could feel her face turning red. She tried to keep her breathing even. It would do no good to get angry, just as it would do her no good to be embarrassed in front of these people. What was said was said.

"And you command this army?" asked another rider.

"I do," Winter said.

"And you wish to challenge us for control of this area?"

"No," Winter said emphatically, "not at all. We desire your help."

A few of the riders once again exchanged curious glances.

"You desire our help, but do not wish to challenge our power?" The brown-haired rider asked the question as if the two concepts were intertwined.

Winter glanced at Urstadt, but the woman did not return her gaze. She stared at the clan riders intently.

"We see that she does not understand our ways," one of them said.

"Then we must teach her," another responded.

More quickly than Winter could have imagined, the brown-haired rider drew her bow and had an arrow nocked and aimed at Winter.

A *tendron* burst forth from Winter, latching onto the bow, and Winter shifted the arrow's trajectory just in time for the arrow to fire at an awkward angle, thudding lightly into the grass.

The other riders turned to look at the woman who had fired the arrow, their eyes wide in surprise. Then, they turned back to Winter, and suddenly five tiellan warriors at once were nocking arrows aimed directly for her.

Winter was ready this time, and sent *tendra* out to each one, plucking the bows from the hands of each rider. She kept one eye on the clan ranks in the distance, about fifty rods away, but the riders remained relatively still, watching the exchange. Winter dropped her reins and raised both hands, telling Urstadt and Selldor to give her space. They obliged, reining their horses back a few strides.

The five riders reacted quickly, reaching for spears, but Winter was ahead of them. She'd already taken each of the spears, and with one quick strike slammed the butt end of them into the faces of their respective riders. A couple fell from their horses, but they were on their feet quickly. All of them drew their swords.

Goddess, they're just going to keep coming. She had to be more emphatic. The clanfolk had said she did not understand their ways. That much was true. But they did not have to teach her.

She would make them understand hers.

She stabbed one of the spears into the neck of the brown-haired woman. She fell, gurgling.

"I will accept your surrender whenever you wish to offer it," Winter said loudly, her voice hard.

The clan riders looked at one another, but continued advancing on Winter, three on horseback, one on foot, all with swords drawn.

Winter attempted to drive another spear through the neck of another rider, but the man parried the thrust with his sword. He didn't see the other spear Winter had raised behind him. Winter stabbed the weapon into his side, and he fell from his horse, groaning.

"No more of you have to fall," Winter said.

The three remaining tiellans continued advancing, faces grim.

Winter took the swords from the dead riders with two of her *tendra*, and attacked the tiellans still on horseback simultaneously. They parried and fought their invisible foes, but as Winter added more *tendra* and weapons to the dance, both fell quickly. Now only one clanswoman remained, on foot.

"Submit to me, and this will end," Winter said, looking down at the woman.

Slowly, the woman lowered her sword, and looked up to meet Winter's gaze. Winter saw dark black eyes staring up at her from beneath the woman's *araif*, eyes that looked very much like her own. The fabric of her *siara* was light, almost transparent. The woman took a step towards Winter, and both Selldor and Urstadt flinched, but restrained themselves. They both knew by now that Winter could handle herself.

The warrior took her sword in both hands, placing the flat of the blade in her palms as she raised it to Winter.

"You have defeated my four chiefs," the woman said. "I submit myself, and my army, to your power."

Goddess rising, you could have done that from the beginning.

"Thank you," Winter said. "Are you a chief? What is your name?"

"I am Rorie, of the Black Hills clan." The woman's eyes narrowed in confusion. "And you are my chief now, Winter."

18

Kirlan

THE NIGHT WAS DARK and the moon new as Astrid moved through the shadows of Kirlan. The bumbling, emaciated man she'd recruited to help her, however, was significantly hindering her usual stealth.

"Is it much farther?" the man asked as he stumbled around a corner, more or less tracing Astrid's footsteps.

"You can't possibly have somewhere to be." Astrid didn't look back at the man. She was annoyed at even having to bring him along, but he was necessary. She'd found him in an alley, more alert than most but still completely desperate. When she'd tossed him a silver coin, promising more if he followed her for an hour or so and did as she said, he immediately stood and began walking after her. She'd woven a glamour for herself, so the man did not see her claws, fangs, or the color of her eyes. She hoped there would be no need for those.

"Just keep close and keep quiet," Astrid said. "We're almost there."

It was late, past midnight, and the streets were all but empty, especially in the residential area of the city. Tower-houses rose above her, but she slipped through the alleys between them. Astrid did not know the city well, but she had been in this area once before. She knew exactly where she was going.

The Cantic chapel where the Black Matron had taken her.

Astrid crept past dark windows and closed doors, the man trailing behind her, until she saw one side of the carved stone chapel ahead.

Kirlan was home to three Cantic chapels. The largest was close to the city center, while another was located near the tiellan quarter. This one, the one Astrid sought, was in the middle of the residential quarter, where most nobles, high-earning merchants, and government officials made their home.

The residential area consisted of three long parallel roads, and the Cantic chapel sat in the center of them, cutting the middle road into two segments. Though tall, the chapel did not reach the height of many of the tower-houses in the area, some of them five or six stories high. Such houses were common in central and southern Khale, whereas manor houses and castle keeps were still the norm in the north.

Astrid stood on tiptoes, barely able to get her eyes to the very bottom of the stained-glass window. The place was empty and dark. That was good.

She relaxed back onto her heels, and then moved away, the man staying close and blissfully silent. When she had crept around the entire perimeter of the building, keeping as close to the chapel wall as she could, she began to think that her idea might not have been all that bright.

Then she felt it. A sickness, gently churning her insides at first, growing slowly stronger as she moved.

Nightsbane.

She was near the northeast corner. The main entrance to the chapel was on the west face of the building, but there was a smaller private door on the northern wall. Astrid made her way around to the smaller door, looking in each window she came across hesitantly. The green glow of her eyes was a nuisance;

if there was someone inside, they surely would have seen her peeking in by now.

But Astrid had seen no movement, and that was enough for her. The priestesses must all be in their quarters tonight. No one up burning the holy oil.

Astrid broke the lock on the side door with a quick twist of her wrist.

The thin man behind her made a low groaning sound. "I... I don't think you're supposed to do that."

Astrid looked back at him. "If you want more silver, stay here and wait for me. Soon, your job will be over."

When the man nodded, Astrid gently pushed the door open and walked inside.

Moonlight filtered faintly through the stained glass into an otherwise dark hall. Astrid's eyes provided the brightest source of light by far, illuminating the decorative carvings and paintings wherever she looked. In one corner of the chapel was a sculpture of Canta herself, her long, back-length hair sweeping out behind her, as she reached upwards for something, a look of concentration or pleading on her face. Rare to see such a sculpture at all, really. While the Denomination did not forbid depictions of Canta, they were certainly uncommon. Most statues and paintings focused on the Nine Disciples and their works after Canta's death.

Against her better judgment, she found herself walking towards the statue of the Goddess. It was not quite life-size— Canta was maybe Astrid's height in the depiction—but the Goddess stood on a pedestal that rose roughly to Astrid's waist. The sculpture was carved from marble, but unlike many of the worn statues Astrid had seen in chapels and cathedrals, this one looked pristine.

Slowly, Astrid reached across the pedestal to the foot of the statue. She did not know what she expected; no flash of light, no voice from the Praeclara, but she did hope for something. As her fingertips brushed against Canta's feet, Astrid felt only the cool touch of marble.

Astrid looked over her shoulder, scanning the chapel to be sure she was alone. Satisfied, she turned back to the sculpture, two fingertips still gently touching the Goddess's foot.

"Don't know if you can hear me," Astrid whispered, looking up into Canta's face, "or if you're even there at all..."

She hesitated. She had not expected to say anything, and she was suddenly unsure of what else to say. She stood there for a moment, the marble perpetually cool against her fingers, which had no heat of their own to offer.

"I need your help, I guess," Astrid said after a moment. "Things aren't good, and..."

The Black Matron is just using me, for one. Knot will probably never forgive me, even if he says he does. I don't know if I'm worth forgiving, anyway. I just...

"I need your help," Astrid said again. That was, she realized, all she was prepared to say.

Then, the chapel around her shifted.

Slowly, she realized, she was once again standing on the bow of a ship.

Calling it a ship would work, she figured. It seemed slightly too large to be called a boat, despite Astrid once again being the only person on the vessel. It was the same ship as the strange vision she'd had before. Its sails swelled, full of wind, driving the ship forwards, once again in the direction of a bright sunrise. Astrid looked over her shoulder. Behind her, the sky was still dark and full of faintly twinkling stars. The night sky in her wake faded into the blue-gray-violet of daybreak directly above her, which in turn warmed into the rosy orange hues straight ahead as the sun broke the horizon. The ocean was so still that it offered an almost perfect reflection of the sky above. Black water behind, blue-purple water to either side, and gleaming pink and orange water before her.

The gentle heat of the rising sun's rays washed over her face. Just like before, there was no fear. The sun did not burn her; instead, it made her whole. In an instant, all the darkness was gone, and a bright golden light ignited across the sky and sea around her.

The ship took an unbidden turn into a great fjord, tall cliffs rising on either side of the still water. Once again, Astrid knew exactly where she was going. The word rang in her mind like the tolling of a great bell. *Home.*

She was going home.

Then, her surroundings shifted again, and Astrid found herself standing in the chapel in Kirlan once more.

"Was that… you?" Astrid asked the statue before her. "What does it mean?"

No feelings, no thoughts or voices or otherwise, came in response.

"Why a ship?" Astrid asked. "And where am I going?" *Or where was I going?* For all she knew, it was a memory.

The empty chapel responded in silence.

Astrid sighed. She retracted her hand, and turned. She had come here for a reason, after all.

Slowly, she approached the northeast corner of the chapel. This building, like most chapels, consisted of a large central hall, leading into a warren of smaller rooms and offices. A few rooms occupied the northeast corner of the building. Based on what Astrid had felt, the nightsbane would be in one of them.

She approached one door, and broke the lock on it easily. Slowly, the door creaked inward, and Astrid peeked inside.

A desk, some bookshelves, a few chairs. Nothing more. She felt only the slightest hint of sickness from nightsbane—the herb couldn't be in this room. There was no other exit in the small office, either, so Astrid closed the door behind her and tried the other one.

Astrid began to feel the effects of nightsbane before she even broke the lock.

She pushed the door open and looked inside, trying to ignore the churning, burning sensation in her gut as it began to spread through the rest of her body. She took one step into the room and the pain intensified, blossoming in her skull. Astrid clutched her head, looking around the room in a squint.

She recognized the place immediately, even through the pain. The room was simple, with a table along one wall and two mismatched chairs nearby. A row of cupboards lined another wall, and that was about it. This was the room the Black Matron had taken her to before, where Astrid had been tortured with her own memories.

The nightsbane must be in one of the cupboards.

Quickly, she stepped back out, backing away, gasping in deep, heavy breaths.

When she'd regained her composure, Astrid walked back out of the chapel. She looked around outside, and finally saw the emaciated man she'd dragged along with her.

"Come with me," she said, motioning for him to follow. "*Quickly*," she added. His saunter was not nearly quick enough. Of course, that was the price she paid when this was the kind of help she sought.

She led the man into the chapel, toward the room with the nightsbane.

"In there," Astrid said, pointing to the room. "In the cupboards, there is an herb. Make sure you get it all, then bring it out to me."

"That's it?" the man asked, craning his neck to look into the room. "That's all you want from me?"

"That's all I want," Astrid said, "and then the silver is yours."

The man glanced at Astrid, his eyes hollow, then shrugged and walked into the plain room.

Astrid stood at the doorway watching him, making sure he checked every cupboard, even ordering him to look in the corners of the room and under the table. Sure enough, in one of the cupboards he found a large bunch of nightsbane, the small white flowers standing out against the darkness.

"Bring all of it outside," Astrid repeated, stepping out of the chapel as the man followed at a distance behind her.

When they'd reached the street, Astrid turned. The man continued walking towards her, but she raised her hands.

"Stop right there," she said. "Do not come closer to me."

The man stopped, clearly confused. Astrid didn't care.

"I gave you flint and tinder," Astrid said. "Take it out, and burn the herb."

"This is the strangest request I've ever—"

"*Just do it*," Astrid growled, and for a moment let the glamour she'd woven for the man dissipate. Instead of an innocent, well-dressed girl, he would glimpse what she really was. Her claws, her teeth, her wild hair and glowing eyes.

The man's eyes widened, and he took out the flint and tinder and began striking them together. Sparks showered down on the nightsbane.

The convenient thing about nightsbane, of course, was that it was a dry flower. Even shortly after being cut, it was not a difficult thing to burn. It caught fire almost immediately.

Astrid watched it smolder. Slowly, she stepped forward. Step after step she took towards the small fire on the cobbled road, but she felt nothing.

No sickness. No pain.

She ordered the man to stamp out the fire, which he did. Then, Astrid held her hand out. In it, she held a half-dozen silver coins. She had no illusions about what the man would use it for, but she did not much care. He had made his choices. He had done what she had asked, and that was all that mattered.

"Thank you." His eyes shone as he looked at the money.

Astrid turned her back on the man. She entered the chapel one more time and approached the room where the Black Matron had tortured her. No sickness, no pain. She nodded to herself. That was good.

She glanced at the statue of Canta once more before she left the chapel. She wasn't sure why she'd thought the look depicted on the Goddess's face had been pleading or concentration. The look on the sculpture's face was one of fulfillment; the hand that reached upwards was closed, as if Canta had finally grasped whatever it was She sought. Astrid was surprised she had not noticed it before. Darkness cast strange shadows on things, sometimes.

Astrid made her way back out of the city to the Odenite camp. The Black Matron would have other sources of nightsbane, to be sure, but at least Astrid had made progress. She had struck back.

It would not be the last time.

19

Eastmaw Mountains, Khale

WHEN THE SOLDIER'S SCREAMS faded to whimpers, Publio Kyfer knew it was time to talk.

Not that the man could really be called a soldier. A good soldier would always stand tall, back straight, chin up, even after a flogging. Kyfer had never cowered the way this man did, curling into a ball as the chains that had kept his arms spread apart between two posts were unlocked, blubbering like a baby. A flogging bloody *hurt*—that was the point, of course—and it drained a man, too, but it was nothing to sob over. Kyfer had been flogged, and taken wounds a dozen times worse, and had yet to shed a single tear over it.

"Bring him to me," Kyfer said. His soldiers—*real* soldiers—lifted the man by the arms and half dragged, half carried him to where Kyfer stood a few rods away.

The faint smell of smoke on the air still stung Kyfer's eyes. Around him were the smoking remains of what had once been a thriving village. It was a shame to lay waste to a part of Khale's economy, however small, but such actions were necessary when the village willingly housed traitors to the republic.

Kyfer's soldiers threw the man at his feet in a cloud of dust. Dirt already caked the man's bloodied back, and mud and sweat covered his face. The man groaned, and Kyfer rolled his eyes.

Kyfer crouched down, bringing his face closer to the man's

level. He almost reared back at the overwhelming smell of shit, sweat, and blood, but pushed through it.

"Are you ready to talk?"

The man looked up at Kyfer, and the beginning of another sob escaped his lips before he caught himself, choking it down.

"I... I told you I was willing to talk..."

"That was halfway through the beating," Kyfer said impatiently. "I could not very well curtail your punishment just because you changed your mind after it had begun. Actions have consequences, my friend. We can never escape consequences."

The man whimpered again as Kyfer stood. "Tell me what you know about the remaining rebels, and your punishment can end."

The man looked up at Kyfer, saliva slowly leaking down his chin, dripping to the dust in long, viscous strands.

Disgusting.

"A cave," he rasped, head bobbing. "A cave on the southern side of the mountain, near the peak. They'll be holed up there... waiting for you to leave."

"You are sure?" Kyfer asked.

The man's head bobbed more quickly.

"And can you take us there yourself?"

"No... need. The cave is easy to find. A path leads up the face of the mountain, and there is a hidden fork... you'll know it by the *rihnemin*..."

"Very well. Thank you for your honesty, my friend."

"Please," the man said, reaching up to Kyfer. "Help me. I have a family—"

Kyfer raised one knee and brought his heel down onto the man's face with such force that blood splattered in all directions in the dirt. He groaned something unintelligible, so Kyfer slammed his heel twice more into the man's face.

"Be grateful," Kyfer told the corpse. "If you'd lied to me, your death would not have been nearly so painless."

He had, of course, received the same information this man had just given him from several other villagers. Some had told him freely, others had taken some persuasion, just as this man had. But so many voices confirming the same thing was good news; they were likely to root out the rest of the rebels within the day, and perhaps Kyfer would finally receive some well-deserved recognition.

"General Kyfer."

Kyfer turned to see his telenic, Genio, with forearm extended forward and bent across his chest in the Khalic salute. While Genio was one of the Nazaniin, he was also conscripted into the Khalic army, and took orders from Kyfer. Through Genio and the other two in his Nazaniin *cotir*, Kyfer could communicate instantly with his superiors in Triah. The price he paid for the convenience was that all such communication passed through Nazaniin operatives—who might, in some cases, be more loyal to the Citadel than to the House of Aldermen.

Kyfer returned Genio's salute, then walked over to a patch of grass and began wiping the heel of his boot.

"What is it, Nazaniin?"

"Grand Marshal Carrieri wishes to speak with you."

Shit. It wasn't a request. Carrieri never made requests.

"Very well." Satisfied his boot was clean enough, Kyfer nodded. "Lead the way."

They walked through the charred remains of the village, towards the clearing in the mountain forest where most of the Steel Regiment had made camp. They were in the middle of the Eastmaw Mountains, south of Cineste. Kyfer was grateful for the mountain assignment; summer had all but arrived, and the cool air made him feel at home.

"I assume the Grand Marshal did not tell you what this was about?"

"No," Genio said, shaking his head. Genio was a short man, but tough and stout. Not a man Kyfer would fancy fighting against, telesis or no.

"Of course he didn't," Kyfer muttered. He could not imagine it would be something good. He and the Grand Marshal did not have the greatest of relationships. Carrieri had actively fought Kyfer's promotion to general. It had only gone through with the help of the Parliament.

Genio led Kyfer to the Nazaniin tent. Kyfer ducked through the entrance to find his other two Nazaniin, Ila and Pruse, lounging within.

"Let's get this over with," Kyfer said.

"He's here." Ila was the acumen, and she was not looking at Kyfer. Her eyes were glazed over, and she stared out at nothing.

Shit. Whatever this was, it was important enough to keep the Grand Marshal of all of Khale waiting to speak with Kyfer. He was suddenly very glad he had not resisted Genio's summons.

"General Kyfer," Ila said, although she was not looking *at* Kyfer but rather *past* him, "this is Grand Marshal Carrieri."

Kyfer saluted immediately, even though Carrieri could not see him. Only psimancers could communicate through the Void, and neither he nor Carrieri were psimancers. So they had to communicate through respective spokespeople, two Nazaniin acting as translators, more or less. The acumen on the other end, whoever it was, could see Kyfer, and he or she would be doing exactly what Kyfer did, copying his body language and speech patterns as accurately as possible to ensure communication was as clear as possible. Ila, on Kyfer's end, would in turn mimic Carrieri's every move. Kyfer had long gotten over the strangeness of seeing Ila—a short woman, even shorter than Genio, and as petite as they came—act with the authority and power of Riccan Carrieri. Ila pulled it off rather well, all things considered.

"Grand Marshal," Kyfer said, relaxing when Ila saluted in return, "to what do I owe the pleasure of this conversation?"

"Do not patronize me, General. We both know how little we enjoy one another's company. I have orders for you, and these come directly from the Parliament."

Kyfer tried to keep his face still—many acumens even mimicked facial expressions—but could not stop his eyes from widening just a bit. Kyfer was used to taking orders from Carrieri, but even then they usually came through one of the other generals.

Orders from the Parliament were another matter entirely.

"I live to serve the will of the people," Kyfer said.

"A large group of tiellans have left the city of Cineste," Ila said, speaking for Carrieri. "A thousand, maybe more. On their way out of the city..."

Here Ila hesitated, and Kyfer wondered whether the hesitation was some hiccup in the communication process through the Void, or something on Carrieri's part. Communicating through the Goddess-damned Nazaniin was incredibly frustrating.

"On their way out of the city," Ila continued, "they encountered a cohort of the Cinestean City Watch. The tiellans demolished that force, and are now making their way east, towards the plains."

Kyfer tried not to seem surprised by the information. Tiellan–human relations were bad and getting worse, but he had not expected something so drastic.

"Your orders are to move the Steel Regiment north."

Kyfer felt a rush.

"Monitor the tiellans. Send us intelligence. We will send you further orders when we have discerned more about the situation."

As quickly as the rush came, it subsided. "If they have destroyed one cohort, they surely could do worse to other groups, other towns and cities…"

"You are not to engage them," Ila said. Clearly, Carrieri understood Kyfer's implication. "Not unless they put the lives of other Khalic citizens in danger. Is that understood, Kyfer?"

"Yes," Kyfer said, although his mind was already working on engineering a way to make that happen. If he waited for the tiellans to do something on their own, he might wait a lifetime. But if he could add another victory to his imminent one in Eastmaw, he'd return to Triah a hero. "I understand."

"Good. Monitor them. Trail them. But do not engage. That is all, General. Until we meet again."

"Until we meet again," Kyfer muttered. By the time they met again, it would be on equal footing, if Kyfer had anything to say about it.

20

Odenite camp, outside Kirlan

KNOT HELD ASTRID'S VOIDSTONE, running one thumb across the rune, blood-red and jagged, etched into the rock.

It's always blood, he could hear her say.

He reconsidered what he was about to do, and not for the first time. Thought it might help him forgive her. Might help him *help* her. But these memories had tortured Astrid for centuries. Did he really want to uncover them?

Knot took a deep breath, and extended a *tendron* into the voidstone. His remaining *tendra* were small in number, two or three at the most, and incredibly weak. But he could access them nonetheless, and this seemed about the only thing they might be good for.

As soon as his *tendron* made contact, Knot felt the stone open up to him. Not physically; it remained between his thumb and forefinger, solid and unyielding, but at the same time Knot felt the shell of it open, and while he had not returned to the Void since Wyle put him there to stabilize his sifts—as a telenic he could not access the Void himself—he felt the residue of it, could almost see the tiny star-lights shining around him. The voidstone he held in his hand was almost one of these lights, but not quite. It blinked in and out of darkness. Knot focused on the shadow of it, until the voidstone's light expanded into dozens of smaller, multicolored lights. Knot was not sure whether the light representing the voidstone expanded, or he moved *into* it. The latter seemed more likely, despite the fact that he knew, deep down, he was still just sitting on his cot, in his tent, in the Odenite camp, holding a stone in his hands.

Stood to reason that each of these lights represented a memory Astrid had lost. The fact that there were dozens of them made him wonder exactly how many things she had done that she wanted to forget. There was no semblance of order among the memories, no way to intuit when it was from or what occurred in it.

"Might as well start with the closest one," Knot said to himself, and with another *tendron*—his first was still connected to the voidstone itself—he dove into the closest memory.

Knot watched as Astrid walked through the darkest forest he had ever seen, her green eyes glowing brightly. She moved with purpose but not secrecy. Before Knot's eyes, Astrid's appearance shifted. Her claws and fangs disappeared, and the glow of her eyes faded until it was hardly noticeable at all, even in the dark forest. Her clothing looked nicer, her hair well kempt and tied neatly behind her head. She had told him she could use something called a glamour to change her appearance at night, but he had never actually seen her do it.

Soon, she came upon a group of four men, heavily armed, conversing together.

"You've brought them?" Astrid asked.

The four men stared at Astrid for a moment, and then three of them burst out laughing. The fourth stared at Astrid, eyes narrow.

"This some kind of joke?" one of the laughing men asked.

Astrid held up a large purse, jingling it before her. "No joke. I have your payment. Where are they?"

The laughing men sobered at the sight of the coin purse, and one of them pointed at it. "That real money, girl?"

"Either way, we've struck a vein of luck today, boys. I say we take what she has, add her to the package, and sell it to the next bidder."

Two of the other men nodded, while the serious one stayed quiet.

"I recommend you take the money," Astrid said. "It'll go better for you."

The same three men chuckled again, but each drew their weapons and started to fan out around Astrid.

"I think we should listen to her," the serious man said, hanging back. His sword remained in its sheath.

"Don't be a fool, Hedro," one of the others said. "We've got money just asking to be taken, right in front of us. We both know we can't afford to pass it up."

The men closed in on Astrid, but she did not give any ground. One of the men lunged forward, reaching for the coin purse, but Astrid whipped the purse away while simultaneously slapping the man hard on the face. He stumbled away at the force of the blow.

The other two men laughed, and Knot pitied them. They had no idea what was about to happen.

"You just got knocked around by a little girl," one of the men laughed. "I can't wait to tell everyone what happened to..."

The man's voice trailed off as Astrid's glamour faded. Fingers formed into claws, teeth into fangs, and her eyes began to glow the eerie bright green color Knot had grown so used to.

"I tried to give you a chance," Astrid said, "but you had to be greedy."

She leapt onto the man who'd just spoken, her claws tearing

into his chest. A bright spurt of blood arced through the night.

She moved, a band of green light against the darkness, and slammed into the man she'd slapped, crushing him into a large tree. Bone snapped, wood cracked, and Astrid, now covered in blood, turned on the third man. He looked at her, eyes wide, his entire body trembling.

"Please—"

Astrid ripped the man's arm off with a scream so horrific Knot could not tell whether it was Astrid's, the man's, or a combination of both. She did not stop there, but proceeded to tear the man limb from limb until he lay in pieces on the blood-soaked ground.

Only Hedro, the serious man, remained, his face white as he stared at Astrid in the darkness.

"Where are they?" Astrid asked again.

Hedro swallowed, hands raised. "I'll get them," he said, retreating slowly into the forest.

Looking up, Knot realized why everything seemed so dark here. The tree trunks and leaves were all dark grays, browns, and blacks. Blackbarks. This must be the dark forest, Takk Dusia. Above, the leaves and branches were so thick they almost seemed to weave together, creating an unbroken canopy above. Not even starlight streamed through.

Hedro emerged, chains clanking behind him. Four children, all more or less Astrid's age—or the age she looked, anyway—trudged behind him. Gaunt faces looked up at Astrid with horror.

"Can't imagine they'll make much of a meal," Hedro said.

Knot's stomach churned. This could not be what it seemed.

"They aren't for me," Astrid replied. She walked around the chained children. Was she... inspecting them? The children cringed away from Astrid as she approached. Knot didn't blame them; between her glowing green eyes, claws, and the fact that she was covered in blood, Astrid was a fearsome sight.

"They're for my employer."

Knot wondered who that could be. Cabral? Another vampire Astrid had served as thrall? He did not know when this took place.

"We aren't *for* anybody," one of the children, a little boy with black hair and black eyes, said defiantly.

"That's Jidri," Hedro muttered. "The other three'll do as you ask, but he'll give you some trouble."

"He won't give me trouble," Astrid said, glaring at the little boy. The boy, cowed, stepped back in line.

Hedro shivered visibly, and then tossed the chain toward Astrid.

"I don't need payment—"

Astrid threw him the coin purse. It landed at his feet.

"There's more where that came from, if you can find more where these came from," Astrid said, nodding at the children. "Now leave, before I change my mind."

Without another word, Hedro scooped up the purse and sprinted away from Astrid like a deer that had just spotted a hunter.

"Follow me," she said, grabbing the chain. The children, eyes wide and shaking, had no choice but to obey.

As the image faded into blackness, Knot detached his *tendron* from the voidstone. He was back in his tent, in the Odenite camp, alone.

Knot's stomach still squirmed at the violence he had just witnessed. The men might have been trafficking children, but

Knot wouldn't wish their fate on anyone. And the children... Astrid had been leading them somewhere. To some*one*, and it hadn't sounded good. Knot didn't think he'd wish the fate of those children on anyone, either.

A scream in the distance, loud enough to be in the camp, interrupted his thoughts. He swore, slipping the voidstone into the most secure place he could think of—a small hidden pocket sewn into the inside of his trousers—and rushed outside to see what had happened.

21

Undritch Mountains

It was midmorning as Winter and the Rangers traversed the foothills of the Undritch Mountains. She was with the Third and Fourth Ranger companies—the same two companies that had been serving as the vanguard for the greater Druid host—all of whom had stood with her in the battle outside Cineste.

Rorie—the chief of the Black Hills clan—and a few dozen of her riders accompanied them, too. Rorie had pledged herself to Winter, and had promised to take her—and all of the Druids—over the Undritch Mountains and on to Adimora. Winter rode with Rorie, Urstadt, and Selldor.

"I never thought I'd see mountains taller than the Sorensans," Urstadt said quietly.

Winter followed Urstadt's gaze upward.

"On clear summer days in Pranna," she said, "my father would show me the King's Crown."

Urstadt looked at Winter quizzically.

"One of the Undritch Mountains," Winter said. "He told me it was the tallest peak in the Sfaera. Seeing its snowy outline on a clear summer day all the way from Pranna made that claim difficult to dispute." And seeing the mountains stretched before her now, each one seemingly taller than the last, only increased her awe.

"Which one is the King's Crown?" Urstadt asked. "They are

all so tall, I can hardly tell them apart."

"Not the King's Crown," Rorie said. "That's the human name for the peak. To tiellans here, it's Eritravistaya. The King of Now and All." She pointed at a distant group of peaks that stood even taller than the others. "There," she said. "Lucky it's a clear day; usually he's draped in cloud cover."

"If these are the tallest mountains in the Sfaera," Selldor said, "how are we supposed to cross them?"

"Ain't gonna cross," Rorie said. "We're gonna go through."

Winter and Urstadt exchanged a glance. The idea of "going through" was news to her, but if it meant they didn't have to traverse a mountain pass, she was all for it. She and Ghian had already discussed the possibility of leaving some of the Druids in a camp on this side of the mountains if the trail became too difficult. She wanted to avoid that option at all costs.

Winter turned to Rorie. "You've seen who travels with us. Women, children, older folk. Could they go through as well?"

"Aye, Commander," Rorie said. "They'll make it through just fine. We'll go through close by; won't even go near Eritravistaya. The northernmost mountains ain't as tall as the rest, and the weather's more agreeable here than it is by the tallest peaks. If we move now, the majority of your group can make it through to the other side before nightfall."

Slowly, Winter reached an acumenic *tendron* into Rorie's mind. She'd done this before, but wanted to try again just to be sure. Winter welcomed Rorie's devotion, but she had her suspicions. But as Winter explored the woman's mind, she found no hint of deceit. Rorie intended to lead them safely through the mountains.

"Very well," Winter said. "Lead the way."

* * *

Winter and her Rangers followed Rorie through the Black Hills—the foothills were Rorie's home, from whence her clan claimed its name—and eventually down towards the mouth of a small cave.

"This is it?" Winter asked, eyeing the grotto entrance. Hardly more than a crack in the mountainside, it reached up about twice Winter's standing height, and was roughly three rods wide at its base.

"It'll be something of a bottleneck for your people," Rorie said, "but once we're through the entrance, the cave opens up. There's plenty of room in the Underway, Commander."

"The Underway? No tiellan name?"

"Not all things are about us, Commander." Rorie winked. "Most, but not all."

Winter dismounted. It would be easier to lead her horse through the entrance than ride. "Do many people know of the Underway?"

"Only the tiellan clans, Commander, and a few human nomads." Rorie glanced at Urstadt.

"But surely other humans have discovered it," Winter said.

Rorie shrugged. "Of course they have. But they pay it no mind. Humans, so far, have no interest in the plains east of the Undritch Mountains. They are too busy with their stone cities in the west."

Winter handed her horse's reins to Selldor, and walked slowly toward the cave. "We'll need torches," she said. "Lots of them."

"You won't have to worry about torches," Rorie said.

Winter looked back to see Rorie with a crooked smile on her face.

"See for yourself, Commander."

"Winter, I do not think you should go in alone," Urstadt said.

Winter turned back around to face the cave entrance. "It's all right, Urstadt," she said. "I'll be fine."

She walked through the rift, her eyes widening as they adjusted to the sudden darkness. When she had her bearings, Winter found herself in a small, craggy corridor. Bright yellow daylight lit the cave from behind her, but Winter was surprised to see that was not the only source of light in the cave. Ahead of her the chamber angled to the left, and bright blue light emanated from wherever the passage led.

Hesitantly, Winter walked towards the blue light. She followed the tilt of the chamber, moving around a corner, and then stopped in shock.

A tunnel extended before her, straight as an arrow shaft and carved almost perfectly in the shape of a semi-circle, with the floor forming the flat side and the walls and ceiling arching high above.

The thing was *massive*. Fifty people could easily fit comfortably, side by side, across the width of the tunnel, and the ceiling arched many times Winter's own height. She doubted she would even be able to make out the ceiling, if it weren't for the most striking aspect of the tunnel, and the source of the blue light: hundreds, maybe thousands, of carved, glowing blue runes. The tunnel reminded Winter of some kind of reverse *rihnemin*; instead of a great stone structure, this was a hole carved out of stone; but the runes seemed the same.

Winter heard footsteps and voices, and turned to see Urstadt and Rorie entering the huge tunnel behind her. Urstadt stopped short, staring at the glowing blue runes all around them, while Rorie simply smiled her crooked smile.

"This... this is incredible," Winter whispered. The tunnel extended into the depths of the mountain, farther than she could see. "When... How..." She was utterly lost for words.

"It's said the Druids of ancient times carved it," Rorie said. "No one knows exactly how long it's been around. The blue lights, though, are recent. You used to have to carry torches through this tunnel, as you said, but less than a year ago the runes began to emit their own blue light. It's remained like this ever since."

Less than a year ago. Winter wondered what could have triggered it. The events in Roden—Azael's presence and the reappearance of the Nine Daemons—stood at the top of her list.

"It is beautiful," Urstadt said, her voice reverent.

Winter, eyes wide, could still only take it in. She felt a pang of sadness that her father, Lian, Knot—and even Galce, though he at least was still alive—were not here to see it with her. Such beauty deserved to be shared.

At least she could share it with the rest of her people.

"Get the other tiellans moving through here," Winter said, coughing to clear her throat. "We still have a fair journey ahead of us."

Rorie's smile grew wider. "Aye, Commander. I'll send word, and we'll get moving through the Underway immediately."

Winter nodded, already looking back at the glowing blue runes.

She was entering a different world, indeed.

Rorie was right; the tiellans made it through the mystical tunnel in good time, and just over a week later were approaching Adimora.

"We are close." Rorie of the Black Hills clan looked out at the twilight-immersed plains.

"How close?" Winter asked. She saw nothing before her but more grassland. The plains on this side of the Undritch Mountains were the same as the ones to the west, as far as Winter could tell.

"You are a few dozen steps away, at most."

Winter spurred her horse forward. It was a strong mare, mottled gray and black, that reminded her very much of another mare that had briefly been hers, Nynessa. She looked back at Rorie, but her face was indiscernible in the darkness beneath her *araif*.

"Just over that rise."

Winter pushed her mare forward, cautiously. She had thought about naming the animal, but decided against it. Nynessa had died quickly, defending Winter against an ambush on the lonely road between Brynne and Navone. She did not want to get attached again.

As she crested the small hill, she saw three things. The first was a *rihnemin*, larger than any Winter had ever seen, jutting upwards from the ground. *Rihnemin* were large standing stones, usually only slightly taller than a person. This one was the size of a cathedral. Even from this distance, Winter could discern runes carved into the stone, just like the ones she had seen in the Underway. These, however, did not glow. *Rihnemin* dated back to the Age of Marvels, and stood as monuments to the tiellan culture and power from that time.

The second thing that caught Winter's eye was the city of Adimora—and city was, indeed, a poor term for it. In almost a perfect circle surrounding the *rihnemin*, the grass was clear, but outside of a certain distance ramshackle houses and other buildings surrounded the stone. A few dozen, certainly no more than one hundred. No walls or towers or defensive structures whatsoever. Winter had to admit, the city—the town, really—disappointed her.

What did not disappoint was the third thing Winter saw: a dark crack in the land that separated Winter from Adimora, splitting the grass and the plain and plunging into darkness.

"What is that?"

"The Ravine of Adimora," Rorie responded. A few other tiellans had crested the hill behind them, and Winter heard gasps of surprise. The ravine was truly a shocking sight—like a crack of black lightning that split the very Sfaera in two.

"And this," Winter said, indicating the disorganized town below her, "is Adimora?"

Rorie laughed. "Yes and no. I will show you the rest of the city once you and your people have settled in."

Winter looked back at the houses sprawling away from the *rihnemin*. "How do we cross the ravine?"

"The ravine does not extend forever. We will show your people the best way to cross." Rorie signaled back at a few of her followers, who rode off to do as asked.

"You want us to camp around the houses already there?"

"Undoubtedly some of your force will have to do so," Rorie said, "but many of you should be able to find shelter in those homes."

Winter blinked. "You mean what we see here isn't even *full*? How can you call this a city? I'd eat a dragon eel if there were more than two hundred people down there."

"Above ground, there're far fewer than that, usually," Rorie said.

"And... below ground?"

Rorie smiled. "Many more."

"So you're telling me the city of Adimora is…" Winter dismounted, and walked closer to the ravine. The closer she moved, the blacker the inside of the thing looked.

She turned back to face Rorie. "You're telling me it's down *there*."

"Of course. Get your people settled, Commander. I'll head below and get the lay of things. Once that's taken care of, I'll come for you. Any luck, you'll challenge the Cracked Spear this very night."

Winter stopped. "The what?"

"The Cracked Spear. That's why you're here, ain't it?"

Winter knew nothing about a cracked spear. "I seek the aid of the tiellan clans. That's why I'm here."

"Right," Rorie said, nodding. "So you'll be challengin' the Cracked Spear, then."

Clearly this all made sense to Rorie.

Winter had come all this way; she would not balk now. If she could bring the tiellan clans to their cause, they would be one step closer to uniting all tiellans.

She was not whole. She did not belong. But if she could make that happen for someone else—for all tiellans—she would do it.

"Very well," Winter said. "Send for me when you are ready."

Later that day, the rest of the Druid caravan arrived at Adimora. Winter accompanied Darrin, Eranda, and their children to secure them one of the huts that encircled the *rihnemin*. The structures here were certainly no worse than the humble tiellan huts of Pranna, and when they found a suitable residence— Darrin and Eranda would have been content with the first hut they came across, but Winter insisted they find one closer to the *rihnemin*—it was actually larger than any home the family had ever had. This one had two separate bedrooms, as well as a living space, and even some rudimentary furniture.

"Thanks to you, Winter," Eranda said. Darrin had taken the children to the other room, putting them to bed early after a long day of traveling. Winter could hear him singing a soft lullaby through the thin walls. "I can't believe all you've done for us. Your return is truly a gift."

Winter looked at Eranda, unsure what she meant. "I've hardly done anything for you, Eranda. I… I've done what I can, but—"

"Apologies, I did not mean for me, or my family specifically. I meant for the Druids, and for us as tiellans."

"I only do what Ghian and the other Druids ask me to do."

"Might be you doing the asking, one day."

The evening was warm and still light, and the sun shone through an open window as it set, bathing the room in rustic light. "What do you mean?" Winter asked.

"The Druids didn't really accomplish much 'til you arrived, Winter. They helped the tiellans, yes, but at a snail's pace."

"You didn't seem this grateful after I killed the humans at the Druid meeting," Winter said. She could still remember the fear with which Eranda and Gord had looked at her after that.

Eranda closed her eyes. "Wasn't right of me to judge you like that," she said. "I was scared of what'd happened, but… but you saved my life, Winter. I have you and you alone to thank for that, and I'm grateful to you. I'm sorry I didn't say it to you before."

Winter felt frozen as she faced Eranda in the dark room. "You're welcome," she muttered, unsure of what else to say.

Eranda nodded, and continued. "The exodus, this journey we've made, was more than I expected, I ain't afraid to admit it. But I believe it's been a good thing. Many of us want change for our people. You came, and suddenly things *did* change."

Winter laughed quietly. She did not want to wake the children in the other room, but she was also glad the conversation had moved on from her saving Eranda's life. "You put too much faith in me. I do not dictate the will of the people, Eranda."

"But you *could*."

"You cannot be serious," Winter said. Most tiellans still had no idea who she was, where she came from. How she could have any influence whatsoever over them was incomprehensible.

And yet, she had *faltira*. She had telesis, and acumency. She had Urstadt, and she had Galce, even if he was still in Cineste.

And, really, she had nothing to lose.

"Tiellans used to have monarchs, you know," Eranda said.

Of course she knew. Tiellan kings and queens had ruled the Sfaera for ages. Only after the Age of Marvels did they decline in power.

"We could have monarchs again."

"Goddess, you sound like Lian."

Eranda sucked in a breath at the name. "You bring him up so rarely."

"I never know what to say about him."

Darrin sang in the room next to them, and outside the hut the low buzz of hundreds of tiellans finding their own accommodation, or setting up tents, blended with the sounds of the approaching night.

"How do I sound like Lian?" Eranda asked, after a time.

Winter thought about saying goodbye and leaving before

the conversation progressed any further. She did not want to talk about this now. She did not want to talk about this ever. And yet, she could not stop herself.

"He spoke of the Age of Marvels while we traveled together. He said the tiellans could become what we once were. It just… you sounded like him just now, that's all."

"He was the first of us to hitch himself to the Druids," Eranda said. "After all this time, I'm glad he did."

"You knew he was involved with the Druids? For how long?" When Lian told Winter of his involvement with the faction in Cineste—what seemed like ages ago—it was the first Winter had heard of it.

"At least a year before you left," Eranda said. "More'n a year, in fact; it was before Knot arrived."

Before Knot arrived. A time before time.

"He'd be proud to see what you've become," Eranda said. "He'd be proud to see you leadin' your people."

Just like that, the crushing shame of everything Winter had done came crashing down on her. Winter had only discovered her telenic *tendra* when she had found Knot, about to be executed, in Navone's Circle Square. She'd flailed about with her newfound power like an infant, slaughtering dozens of people—innocent and guilty alike. She had faced Daemons and Outsiders in Izet, only to then join Roden's new emperor, Daval, doing his bidding simply because he had offered her *faltira*.

Eranda did not know what Winter was capable of.

Lian *had* known. And Lian had not lived long enough to see her do anything good with her power.

Would Winter?

She shook her head, breathing in quickly through her nose.

Her eyes were beginning to sting, but she would not cry. Not now. Not ever again.

"He'd want you to become the queen," Eranda said.

Winter laughed again, this time more to stop herself from weeping than from anything else. She cleared her throat, getting a hold of herself. Enough talk of Lian. There was a reason she hated talking about him, about Knot, about her father.

She did not need any more shame than she already had.

"I could not be a queen," Winter scoffed. She, the daughter of Bahc the fisherman from Pranna, a queen. More than ridiculous. And yet, the question was not whether Winter thought she *could* be a queen. As silly as the idea seemed, it was certainly possible. She had *faltira*, after all, and she could do just about anything with that.

The question in her mind was whether or not she *should*. Less of a question, really, than a powerful feeling that she *shouldn't*.

"The tiellans would follow you. *I* would follow you."

"I may have saved your life in Cineste," Winter said, "but it bothered you. Gord, too."

"I am sure there is an explanation—"

"Not a good one."

"We all make mistakes, Winter. That don't change who we are."

"I know," Winter said. "But some of us are not more than our mistakes."

22

Eastern Plains, near Takk Dusia

PEERING THROUGH HIS SPYGLASS, Kyfer watched as a group of tiellans streamed out of the woods in the afternoon sun. When he'd received multiple reports of tiellan refugees fleeing from Cineste, following in the footsteps of the first Druid group to leave the city, an idea had begun to form in his head of how to expedite his management of the tiellan problem. The Steel Regiment had been monitoring the eastern edge of the Takk Dusia, the dark forest, for the past few days, waiting for the right moment. Most tiellan groups that came through the forest consisted of a few dozen refugees, but the crowd that continued to pour out of the forest now was far larger—over a hundred tiellans so far, and counting.

Kyfer lowered his spyglass, adrenaline flowing through him. He turned to Razzo, who stood next to him. "This is it. Form up three of our cavalry companies. Any three will do. We just need five hundred or so troops to make this look realistic."

Razzo squinted at the tiellans. "Sir... these look like families, not fighters. Are you sure—"

"I gave you an order, Captain. Form up the regiment."

Razzo saluted. "Yes, sir." He barked orders to two nearby legionaries, who mounted their horses. Kyfer and Razzo followed suit.

"If we don't do this," Kyfer said, annoyed that he felt he had to explain himself at all, "it could take weeks, perhaps months before we have real cause to quash this little tiellan rebellion. No telling what they might do between now and then, how much their force might grow, or who they might recruit. Best to nip the bud of this rebellion straight away."

"I understand, General."

"The first group of tiellans attacked the Cinestean City Watch when they left the city. It stands to reason this group will attack us."

"Yes, General."

Kyfer glared at Razzo. Usually his second was more animated than this. He didn't know what had gotten into the man.

They rode their horses back to the Steel Regiment's position, directly south of Takk Dusia and a few hills away from where the tiellans were emerging from the forest. Kyfer ordered his three designated companies—roughly five hundred cavalry—to ride as close to the tiellan position as they could while still remaining hidden, and to await his signal. Then, he and Razzo and a squad of fifteen other riders took off to meet with the tiellans directly.

The tiellan refugees huddled together in one huge mass as soon as they saw Kyfer and his squad crest the hill closest to them. *Goddess*, Kyfer thought to himself, *this is going to be too easy.*

Kyfer led his squad around to the front of the tiellan group, blocking them from progressing forward. He held his fist up, ordering his riders to stop where they were.

The tiellans looked up at Kyfer and his riders, clearly unsure.

Finally, after some whispering among a group of tiellans at

the front of the crowd, one elf man stepped forward.

"Will… will you help us?" the elf asked. "We don't have much food, almost no supplies. We weren't *ready* for this journey. Ain't got nothing to our names, left everything we had in Cineste. All we want is to move on, as quickly as possible, to find our people. If you could offer us any help at all, we'd be in your debt."

Kyfer did not respond, and neither did his men. He'd ordered them to remain completely silent.

"What… what do you want?" the elf asked.

Kyfer and his men did not move, or say a word.

The elf looked cautiously over his shoulder, signaling behind him.

Kyfer's grip tightened on one of his sword hilts, but the man had only signaled for some of his group to start moving around Kyfer's squad. Kyfer raised a hand at the tiellans on the move, and the legionaries on his flank moved their horses to cut them off.

The tiellan spokesman began to walk backward, horror dawning on his face. Satisfaction rose in Kyfer's chest at the sight.

"We just want to pass peacefully," the elf man said, his voice rising in pitch. "We are not warriors. We have no intention of harming you, or anyone. We just want to find our people." He signaled again, and more tiellans began walking, some of them running, toward the other flank of Kyfer's squad. Kyfer responded by pointing in that direction, and his riders repositioned themselves to cut the tiellans off again.

If you find your people, you'll make them that much stronger, Kyfer thought. *More will follow. I will not allow it.* But he remained silent.

The tiellan hastily conferred with several people behind him. He shook his head frantically, pointing at Kyfer and his squad, but after a moment he walked hesitantly forward once more.

"If... if you do not let us pass, we'll resort to violence," the man said. "We are desperate. There are more of us than there are of you. We'll overwhelm you eventually. Please, if you value your lives, *let us pass.*"

Kyfer said nothing, but this time he smiled, and dismounted. He wore full plate armor, and it clanked as he dismounted. The tiellans had very few weapons at all among them, and the man who spoke for them had none. Kyfer walked towards the man, and tossed him the extra sword he carried at his side. Kyfer's own sword remained sheathed.

The man looked down at the sword, then up at Kyfer. He reached down for the blade, picking it up, and Kyfer held his arms out wide, the smile still on his face.

He was close. It was almost time.

Then, with a shout, the elf charged him. The man was clearly a stranger to a blade; he held the longsword in an awkward two-handed grip, one fist clenched over the other, and slashed at Kyfer as he approached.

Kyfer leaned to the side, but deliberately timed his movement to allow the man's strike to just barely glance off his armor, then kicked the man in the back as he stumbled past. The tiellan fell to the ground, and quickly rolled over to face Kyfer.

"You just attacked an officer of the Khalic Legion," Kyfer said, loud enough for his voice to echo. "That is an affront we will not tolerate."

The tiellan was now frantically backing away from him,

but Kyfer caught up to him easily, smashing his armored boot into his face. Blood exploded from the tiellan's nose, and Kyfer leaned forward to punch him with his gauntleted fist. Once, twice, and a third time, and then the man lay still.

"*Now!*" Kyfer shouted, and immediately the ground began to rumble. To his left, his three cavalry companies crested the hill, riding at full tilt toward the small tiellan crowd.

The tiellans had already begun to cry and scream when they saw Kyfer beat their spokesman, but now they lapsed into full panic.

Kyfer grinned as he mounted his horse and charged the tiellan force himself, finally drawing his sword. The tiellans did not all have to worry; some of them would survive. He needed some to make it back to wherever the rest of them were hiding, so he could draw out their main fighting force. There would be survivors.

But, for now, Kyfer reveled in the slaughter.

23

Odenite camp, outside Kirlan

I HAVE TRANSCRIBED THESE words for an express purpose. Part of this purpose I understand, and part of it I do not. I do know that, when these words shall be read in their entirety, it will be to help fight against the Nine.

And here I must say a few words about the Nine, for their presence on the Sfaera will one day be unleashed, and they shall threaten all that is good and virtuous.

Cinzia's heart beat in her chest like the clapping of thunder. This was it. She was finally going to learn something significant about the Nine Daemons, she could feel it.

"Cinzi, why have you stopped?"

Cinzia looked up from the pages of the Codex and met her sister's eyes. She was surprised to find her own stinging with the sharp threat of tears.

"I… I feel that we have needed this information for so long, and now that we are finally about to get it…"

"You feel grateful?" Jane asked.

Cinzia blinked. She would not have put it exactly that way. Gratitude was part of it.

"And doubt," Cinzia said softly. "We cannot be sure the information Elwene will give to us will even be useful. Honestly, not much of what we have read has been applicable to our situation. With a few exceptions."

"Not yet," Jane said. "As for what she is about to say… should we translate it, and decide whether it is useful or not afterwards?"

Cinzia nodded. "Of course, sister." Then, she looked back down at the shifting, shimmering characters carved into the metal page.

The Nine were once people, as normal as I, or you who will one day read what I now write.

They lived, and died, and lived again, but now they are imprisoned. While they cannot reach us, the day will come when their influence will be felt upon the Sfaera once more.

The Nine warp the reality around them, twisting humans and tiellans into darker versions of themselves, even when not physically present. With this dark corruption comes power, and power appeals to many. This manner of power will only destroy, and there is no escape from it.

The Nine choose willing avatars from among those who walk the Sfaera to do their bidding. They endow their avatars with immeasurable power, and their avatars spread their influence. When one of the Nine has chosen a mortal as an avatar, that Daemon will begin to communicate with the mortal. From such offers, turn away; any communication with one of the Nine is an abomination, and all those who interact in any way with the Nine are lost, and do not walk in the light.

An avatar is powerful, but he or she can be stopped. Decapitation is said to have worked, but this is often difficult, as the bond with a Daemon physically enhances the avatar. The avatar grows stronger than any human, with skin like stone or steel. An avatar may not fully be under the control of one of the Nine, and might be swayed to break the hold the Daemon has upon him or her. But this is only a theory, and has never been known to happen.

Avatars do the will of the Nine, and they usher in a new era, a new destruction.

Beware the day, should all Nine claim avatars on the Sfaera, for on that day they will have the power to take physical form once more. On that day, hope will die, and darkness will reign.

"What is it, sister?"

Cinzia looked up. "That is the end of the passage."

"Very well. Shall we keep going? Or did you want to discuss what you just read?"

Cinzia did not want to do either. The information about the Nine Daemons intrigued her, it was exactly the information she had been looking for, but one paragraph stood out to her in particular.

When one of the Nine has chosen a mortal as an avatar, that Daemon will begin to communicate with the mortal. From such offers, turn away; any communication with one of the Nine is an abomination, and all those who interact in any way with the Nine are lost, and do not walk in the light.

Luceraf had communicated with her. Did that mean that she wanted Cinzia as her avatar?

Did that mean Cinzia was lost?

"Cinzia, are you all right?"

"I... I believe I might need a break, Jane."

Cinzia felt her sister's eyes on her for a moment, when suddenly the hairs on Cinzia's arm stood on end. A horrifying scream outside their tent made them both start.

Cinzia and Jane rushed out into the evening, trying to locate the source of the screams. They seemed to be coming from the center of the Odenite camp, not far from their tent, but other than the outline of a gathering crowd, Cinzia could not make out much. The sun had already set, darkness had fallen, and stars twinkled above.

Cinzia froze, grabbing Jane's arm, when she finally saw what all the screaming was about.

In the middle of the camp, three bodies surrounded the central bonfire. Each had their throat cut, blood flowing out onto the grass. Above each body, suspended in the air, were three dark, shimmering portals. Strange, twisted forms emerged from the portals. The ground shook beneath her as the forms landed, still solidifying from their primordial liquid state. The shapes mesmerized the crowd.

"Jane, find Knot and Astrid." Jane could not be here when the forms took shape.

"What about you?"

"I need to get the people away from here." She did not wait for her sister to respond, but instead turned and moved through the growing crowd towards the center of camp.

"Everyone get back!" Cinzia shouted. "Away from the fire, away from the Outsiders! Get as far away as you can!"

Cinzia's voice galvanized the Odenites into action. Immediately the crowd pressed back. People turned and ran, others backed away. Each Outsider now stood on monstrous hind legs, deep black eyes looking out at the crowd for the first time.

Before Cinzia could do anything else, before she could say another word, one of the monsters leapt a seemingly impossible distance, seven or eight times the length of its own body, and landed amidst the fleeing crowd, crushing people and tents beneath its huge clawed feet. The monster roared, a horrific screech with a deep, rumbling undertone, and Cinzia clapped her hands over her ears at the sound. Even through her hands, she heard another roar and more screams behind her. She turned to see the other two Outsiders charging into the fleeing crowd. One of the beasts twisted its long neck downwards to clamp its massive jaws around a fleeing Odenite. The other whipped its tail around, crashing through tents and the large bonfire at the center of camp, sending sparks flying onto the group of tents and fleeing Odenites in its path. Immediately, the tents caught fire, as did some of the Odenites.

Her stomach churned. Cinzia willed herself not to vomit. Instead, she pleaded with her Goddess. *You have imbued me with your power before. There is no better time than now to do it again.*

And yet Cinzia felt nothing as she rushed forward. Her muscles moved slowly, achingly, and she felt no sense of strength or speed as she had before, when saving her sister from assassins, or when battling Wyle's *cotir*.

Any communication with one of the Nine is an abomination, and all those who interact in any way with the Nine are lost.

She was unworthy. The Goddess could not, or would not, communicate with Cinzia now that she had spoken to one of the Nine Daemons.

She could only watch in horror as the Outsiders laid into the panicked Odenites, and blood and carnage erupted into the once peaceful night.

* * *

Astrid had been at the edge of camp when she'd first heard the screams, and by the time she reached the center, the Outsiders were already wreaking havoc among the unprotected Odenites.

Fortunately, it was night, and these Outsiders would face a very different vampire.

A tumult of emotions clamored within her as she sprinted forward, her entire frame faster and stronger, affected by the power that overcame her at night. Her hands were claws, her teeth long fangs, and her eyes glowed green. She focused on the closest Outsider, roaring near the central bonfire as it stomped forward, looking for prey. She did not have Knot's sword, but she could make do with her claws. They were sharper and stronger than any blade.

And Astrid was angry. She was angry at the Odenites for being so helpless. She was angry at whoever caused more Outsiders to attack their camp. She was angry at Cinzia and especially at Jane for forming this stupid movement to begin with, for attracting evil the way they did. And, most of all, she blamed herself. She had not been here when these people needed her. She had not been here to protect them.

But she would bloody well make up for that now.

Astrid leapt into the air and landed on the creature's back. The thing roared, but Astrid held on tightly, her claws digging into its thick hide. She scrambled forward and wrapped her legs around its neck, slashing wildly with her claws. Hot blood burst outward, spraying her face and arms, but she raked at the beast for as long as she could until the Outsider reached one of its own huge claws upwards, dislodging her from her already precarious position.

Astrid rolled, but the Outsider's clawed foot stomped

down onto her leg. She heard her own bones snap, and she screamed in pain.

Astrid could not stop. If she stopped, she would die, and if she died, so would all of the people around her. There were two more Outsiders, and Knot and Eward's warriors could not possibly hope to fight two of them.

She was their only hope.

The Outsider lifted its clawed foot again, ready to crush Astrid under it, but she rolled away just in time. She leapt up, placing weight tentatively on the leg that had been smashed, but knew immediately it was useless. The bone was shattered. That would take some time for even her to heal, a few days at least.

She would have to make do with what she had.

The monster's claw swiped towards her, and Astrid let herself be taken by it, the force of the impact dizzying and sending waves of pain shooting through her injured leg.

The Outsider raised Astrid upward towards its gaping maw. Hot breath rushed down onto her, but Astrid smelled nothing. No rotting flesh. Nothing at all. Just uncomfortable heat.

And, of course, the fear of being snapped in half by the thing's jagged teeth.

Astrid gripped one of the larger fangs on the Outsider's lower jaw. She braced herself, pushing with all her might, barely stopping the thing from shoving her into its mouth.

The beast shook her in frustration, but she held onto its fang. Finally, the beast let go of her, but Astrid kept her grip on the fang and lifted her feet up to brace against the monster's jaw. Pain shot through her crushed leg, but her good leg held strong, and Astrid pulled with every bit of strength she had.

With a sickening crack, the Outsider's fang broke off in her hands, and Astrid tumbled to the ground.

The monster roared in pain, but Astrid did not waste time. She lifted herself onto all fours, finding it easier to crawl than to walk, and picked up the fang lying next to her. Then, she scrambled to the side where the creature's nearest foot was planted on the ground, and slammed the thing's own fang into its ankle again and again, warm blood gushing from the wounds.

The creature buckled, tottering for a moment, and Astrid scrambled away just in time for the creature to topple to the ground behind her. She crawled towards its head as quickly as she could—the beast was already trying to push itself back up onto its feet—and wrapped her hands around two more fangs as the Outsider tried to stand. She used all of her enhanced strength to keep it from standing. The monster growled down at her, its dead, black eyes gaping, but Astrid held firm.

With a mighty twist, she yanked the thing back to the ground, almost flipping it over. The earth shook, but Astrid did not stop. She kept her grip on the Outsider's fangs and *pulled*, bracing her legs against the ground. She fell to one knee, her left leg screaming in pain, the muscles tearing. Astrid pulled through it. The Outsider roared, the sound rushing over Astrid like a hurricane.

Then the resistance ceased. Astrid fell backwards onto the ground, and the jaw came with her. The Outsider's roar faded into a low groan.

Astrid threw the jaw off of her to see the creature writhing on the ground.

"Shit," she breathed.

Her leg screamed in pain, but she had to be sure. A short distance away, she saw the loose fang. She crawled to it, and then made her way to the monster's head. Its writhing had calmed, now, but it still twitched every few seconds. Astrid made her way to the bloody remains of its head, where one eye stared upwards, blackness into blackness. She raised the fang and drove it down into the creature's eye.

The twitching stopped.

Astrid still heard screams and roaring. There were still two Outsiders. She took a deep breath. The night was not over.

"Again!"

The few Prelates Knot had managed to gather fired another volley of arrows into the Outsider they faced. The thing roared, but was otherwise unfazed. The arrows wouldn't be enough, but at least they were distracting the beast from attacking more Odenites.

Knot had rushed to the center of the camp in time to see three Outsiders drop from three separate dark rips in the air. Fortunately, he'd spotted Eward quickly, whom he'd ordered to find some spears. Arrows would not be enough to take this thing down, and getting close enough to use swords would be all but impossible for Eward's soldiers.

"Knot!"

Knot turned to see Eward running towards him, a bundle of spears in both hands, and half a dozen more soldiers with him, each also carrying as many spears as they could manage. They dropped the weapons at Knot's feet.

"Grab a spear," Knot said to Eward and the soldiers who approached him. He turned to the archers, and pulled seven from their rank, telling them each to grab spears as well. That left ten archers; Knot deliberately left the most skilled. That should be enough to cause a distraction when he needed one.

"Form up around me," Knot said to his spearmen. "We charge as one. Get one of your spears stuck in that thing's hide—and pull it out, too, if you can. Cause more damage that way. If we lose momentum, we retreat to get new spears while the archers provide cover fire. Then, we charge again."

Around him, the Prelates nodded. All of them were afraid. None of them expressed doubt in his orders.

He hoped this would work.

He hefted the spear he'd chosen—a wooden shaft longer than he was tall, with a wicked-looking steel barb on one end. Around them, the injured moaned, and panicked Odenites fled in all directions, screaming. His vision was limited to the dozen fires in the camp, and the center fire, which had spread to a few of the nearby tents, burned more brightly. Everything he saw alternated between shadow and flickering orange light. Knot heard another Outsider roar in the distance, the sound reverberating in his chest.

He waited for the roar to subside, then he let out his own. "Charge!"

He rushed forward, Eward and the others with him, all of them shouting. The Outsider turned to face them, and did not hesitate to press its own attack. A massive black claw slammed into their line, knocking a few of the soldiers aside. But the rest of them charged forward, Knot in the lead, and he thrust his spear up into the monster's ribcage. When he felt the point penetrate the creature's hide, he yanked it out, but the barb broke from the shaft, still embedded in the Outsider.

Cheap Goddess-damned spear.

A few of the others managed to stab their weapons into the Outsider, and one or two even ripped them out as well. But the monster had already lifted one screaming Prelate up with its claw, raising the woman towards its gaping jaw. There was nothing Knot could do for her now. Another soldier, a young man, lay screaming on the ground, one or both of his legs injured in the charge. Knot knelt and was about to pick up the man, when Eward was there.

"I'll take this side," Eward said, sliding under the injured man's left arm.

Knot immediately took the other, following suit on the right.

"Archers!" Knot shouted, and immediately a volley of arrows whipped above them and into the Outsider.

He ordered the retreat as he and Eward made their way back, the injured lad between them.

The archers continued firing volley after volley at the Outsider, but the beast had turned its head to them now, and Knot swore the thing was looking directly at him.

"Time for one more charge. Spears!"

He and the remaining soldiers each grabbed spears from the pile. Knot grabbed two for himself, hefting one in each hand.

With a roar, the Outsider rushed towards them.

Goddess, he wished he knew where Astrid was right now.

"Charge!" he shouted, leading the soldiers once more. Almost immediately they met with the Outsider, and Knot muscled one spear into the thing's leg, but didn't have time to pull it out before he had to maneuver away to avoid getting trampled. Some of Eward's soldiers were not so quick, and fell amidst screams and moans.

Knot immediately turned, lifting his other spear. His archers had managed to get one more volley off, but the Outsider was already among them, swiping with its massive claws. A half-dozen spears and more than two dozen arrows protruded from its hide. Blood poured from multiple open wounds, dripping to the ground. A *lot* of blood, Knot realized. The grass was slick with the substance. And Knot was surprised the thing hadn't—

The Outsider took one more swipe, this time connecting with Eward, sending the man flying, and then collapsed to the ground with a crash that shook the dirt beneath Knot's feet.

Knot rushed forward and slammed his spear into the Outsider's skull. The shaft broke as the spear blade pierced skin, but glanced off the thick bone.

Knot cursed, but before he could turn to look for another spear, a Prelate handed him one of the pair she carried. He thrust the spear into the beast's eye, while she stabbed her own through its throat.

Then the Outsider was still.

Knot took a moment to breathe, the air moving raggedly through his lungs.

"Regroup!" he shouted to the remaining soldiers, many of whom lay injured on the ground. He saw only one other Outsider, towards the edge of camp, wreaking havoc among unprotected Odenites. He could barely see the other's massive form, lying still near the center of camp.

Perhaps the girl had come through, after all. Knot could not imagine anyone else taking down the beast at the center of camp.

"Gather the wounded. Find Eward if you can. We need to stop the last Outsider."

They had perhaps a dozen spears left, and as many soldiers, unless they could pick up more on their way to the final Outsider.

Knot did not know whether they could defeat it, but they would sure as Oblivion try.

Cinzia could not believe the carnage around her. People

screamed, the wounded moaned, the dead lay silent in the grass. Blood everywhere.

She had tried to help the Odenites flee, and many of them had, but many had died, too. She had sent Jane away, but for all she knew Jane was dead. Or her parents, or her brothers and sisters. Looking back, she saw two Outsiders were down, which gave her a spark of hope. Perhaps Knot and Astrid were working together to kill them. But now a roar from ahead caught her attention. The third beast prowled not a dozen paces from where she stood. The sun began to rise, bathing the thing in soft light.

Cinzia had been encouraging people to flee, but now she began to make her way towards the Outsider. She did not know why she was moving towards the beast. She was unworthy of Canta's power, and had none of her own. There was nothing to stop it from devouring her completely. The light grew stronger behind Cinzia, and suddenly she realized something.

The Outsiders had been attacking them for what seemed like an eternity, and yet it could not have been long. Certainly not past midnight. The sun could not possibly be rising yet.

And as the light behind her grew in power, Cinzia saw it was not the pink, rosy tones of a sunrise. It was white, and pure, and harsh.

Cinzia turned to see the light moving towards her, growing so bright she had to shield her eyes. Had the Goddess returned to the Sfaera to help them in their hour of need? But, almost as quickly, she remembered her battle against Wyle and the Nazaniin *cotir*, and the light she had seen then. The light that had come from her sister.

"Jane!" Cinzia shouted. As the light drew closer, Cinzia could make out a figure within it, from which all the light emanated. Squinting through shielded eyes, she saw that it was, indeed, her sister.

Jane walked right past Cinzia, the light going with her, and moved directly towards the Outsider. Slowly, she raised her arm.

A beam of white light, brighter than the sun at noonday, brighter than anything Cinzia could imagine, shot from Jane's palm and collided with the Outsider.

The beast screamed, writhing, and the stench of burning flesh filled the air.

The beam grew in circumference, until it engulfed the Outsider completely. The beast roared, its skin searing, and then Cinzia lost sight of it in the brightness.

The light winked out.

For a moment, Cinzia thought the light had blinded her. All she saw was darkness, no matter where she looked. But, slowly, her eyes began to readjust. She noticed the orange glow of a bonfire in the distance, first, and then shadows, and then those shadows gained texture and color.

She turned around, disoriented, until she discerned Jane, collapsed on the ground. Cinzia rushed to her side. She could not see the Outsider anywhere.

"Jane?"

Her sister appeared unharmed, but was not moving. Cinzia bent down, placing her ear at her sister's mouth. The faintest draw of breath.

As Cinzia sat back up, her sister's eyes opened.

"Jane," Cinzia said again, half sobbing. "Are you all right?"

"I... I am fine," she said. "Just... weak. The Outsider?"

"Gone," Cinzia said, looking up. "The light must have caused it to flee; I do not know where it went..."

Then, Cinzia saw the ash that caked the ground where the Outsider had been when Jane had confronted it. Ash at least a hand's thickness. She had not noticed it before, because her vision had been adjusting, and the ash was as black as the night around her. But now she saw it clearly.

"You killed it," Cinzia said, hardly believing what she said—hardly believing what she had *seen*.

"With Canta's power," Jane said, attempting to sit up.

Cinzia helped her. Slowly, Jane looked around.

"The other two Outsiders?" she asked.

"Dead, I think."

"Knot and Astrid?"

"I... I do not know."

Jane gripped Cinzia's hand tightly. "Help me stand. We must find them. We must help the wounded."

"You can barely sit up," Cinzia said, nevertheless returning her sister's grip. "Please, rest here. I will go find the others."

"We can help."

Cinzia turned to see Ocrestia, Elessa and Baetrissa standing behind her. She felt the slightest release within her. "Goddess, you are all safe. I am so glad."

Jane attempted to stand again, but Cinzia gently restrained her. "You need to rest, sister." She turned to the other disciples. "Elessa, stay with Jane. Help her. Ocrestia and Baetrissa, come with me."

Cinzia stood up as Elessa took her place at Jane's side.

"We need to help everyone else."

24

Adimora

IT WAS DARK BY the time Rorie came for Winter.

"Come on, Commander," she said, "the Cracked Spear is waitin' for you."

Winter peered cautiously into the darkness of the gorge. "How exactly are we getting down?"

"There are a few ways," Rorie said. "We'll be taking the stairs tonight. It's the best way to get an understanding for the city."

"I don't see any—"

Rorie leapt from the cliffside before Winter could finish her sentence.

Winter rushed forward. "*Rorie,*" she called into the darkness, somewhere between a shout and a whisper. "*Rorie, where are you?*"

"It ain't far, Commander," Rorie said from below.

"Light a bloody torch," Winter said. "I'm not jumping into darkness."

Rorie laughed, but there was a sound of flint striking tinder, followed by a few sparks, and then a torch lit up a small pocket of the chasm beneath Winter.

"Where's your faith, Commander?" Rorie asked, her smile illuminated by the flame. She stood on a ledge two or three rods below the edge of the cliff.

"Dead," Winter said.

"Canta's bloody bones, you sure know how to kill a mood. Are you coming down, or not?"

Winter hesitated. She did not love the idea of leaping down onto that ledge; one misstep and she'd plunge into a seemingly limitless darkness.

But Rorie thought of her as a leader, now. She wanted the Cracked Spear to see her that way, too. She could not show fear.

So Winter jumped.

She landed with a small stumble, and Rorie stabilized her, gripping Winter's upper arm.

"There we are. Now, for the stairs."

It took a moment for Winter to see them, plunging diagonally downward from the ledge on which she stood, cut into the side of the cliff face itself. Rorie began to walk down, torch in hand, and Winter followed. There was no handrail or safety hold of any kind, and one stumble in the wrong direction would send Winter plummeting.

"Are we going all the way to the bottom?" Winter asked, her hand trailing along the rough rock to her left.

"No," Rorie said, "not the bottom. Only a few among us have ever descended that low."

"Have you?"

Rorie shook her head. "No. A few members of the Cracked Spear are all I know who have done it."

"The Cracked Spear. Tell me more about them."

"They lead the clans, as much as the clans have ever been led," Rorie said. "A council of chieftains—Keepers, we call them."

"And who leads the Cracked Spear? Who leads the Keepers?"

Rorie was silent for a moment. The only sounds Winter

heard were their own footsteps echoing in the chasm, and the soft crackle of Rorie's torch.

"No one ever has," Rorie said. "They counsel, and they often disagree, sometimes so greatly that they war amongst themselves. But they do not have a leader."

Winter considered that. It made her wonder once again what she was doing here, and what she expected to accomplish by meeting with these people.

"Any advice for when I meet them?" Winter asked.

Rorie shrugged. "State your case. Nothing more, nothing less. If they think you worthy, they'll grant you whatever you request of them. If they don't..."

"They'll kill me?" Winter guessed.

Rorie turned to look at Winter, eyes wide. "No, Commander." The playful lilt of her speech that Winter had grown used to was gone. "That ain't how the Cracked Spear operates. They'll not kill one of their own, not in an official meeting."

"But I'm not one of their own."

"You're tiellan. And you're a chieftain now, or a commander, at least. That's good enough." Rorie turned and continued walking down the steps.

Winter followed. She couldn't help but think that Rorie sounded uncertain. And, as they walked again in relative silence, Winter began to hear other sounds. Voices. Shouting, talking, even singing.

"Is that...?"

Again Rorie stopped in front of her, but as Winter looked ahead, she saw the steps ended. Rorie flashed a smile, her playful demeanor returning as she ducked into a tunnel in the rock that Winter had not even noticed in the darkness.

Winter followed Rorie through the tunnel. The woman's torch illuminated the rock around them, brown and gray bathed in an orange glow. The tunnel was barely wide enough for them to walk side by side, the ceiling perhaps a rod above Winter's head. At the other end of the tunnel towards which Winter walked, she saw a faint light. It looked to Winter for all the world like light pouring through a keyhole from a well-lit room into a completely dark one.

The sounds grew in volume as she walked through the tunnel towards the light. She could almost make out conversations, now, people shouting good-naturedly, and one song that stood out to her, the words unintelligible in the cacophony of sounds, but the melody familiar.

The keyhole light grew larger and larger until Winter and Rorie approached it, and then passed through.

Winter blinked as bright lights greeted her and her eyes adjusted enough to take in the massive cavern before her.

A space at least the size of Ocrestia's cathedral in Cineste greeted her; she could barely see the top of the cavern in some places, despite the bright lighting. Pillars of rock where the ceiling had grown to meet the floor spaced the cavern, most with strings of what looked like lanterns hanging from them, illuminating their surroundings in perpetual twilight.

Streets and buildings lined the huge cave, as if a section of any city Winter had known had been lifted and crammed inside; merchants lined the streets, shops opened to customers, and more besides. In the middle of it all, Winter saw a gargantuan column, much larger than the other pillars in the cavern, rising upward. As she looked more closely, she realized it was more than a column of rock.

This was a *rihnemin*.

Runes covered the face of the huge monolith. Winter half-expected them to glow like the Underway beneath the Undritch Mountains, but these remained dull scratchings.

"This is Adimora," Winter whispered.

"Aye," Rorie said, "this is Adimora."

"An entire city underground."

"This is just the main cavern. Other homes and structures have been built into the surrounding rock. More tunnels, smaller caverns."

"How many people live here?" Winter asked.

Rorie laughed. "That number changes all the time. Difficult to be sure at any given point; most of the clans still roam the plains, after all. But most of us come home for a spell every now and then, too. At any given time, there are at least five thousand tiellans living underground here. Sometimes, that number can as much as double. And once every few years, when we hold a festival, that number increases much more. This is our home, after all."

Our home. "Are there any humans here?"

"Your friend Urstadt is the first to set foot above Adimora in years. If she were to be allowed underground, she would be the first human down here in centuries."

Thousands of tiellans, all in one place. No humans. Winter could hardly fathom the thought, but the slightest hint of warmth blossomed in her chest. It was not much, but it was perhaps the most significant sense of belonging she had felt in a long, long time.

"Do humans even know about this place?" Winter asked as she followed Rorie through the streets of the underground settlement. Tiellans moved back and forth around them, and Winter caught wisps of conversation that sounded surprisingly mundane. Haggling over the price of onions. Asking after a friend's child who had been sick. An argument about something called a... tree-box?

"Did *you* know about it?" Rorie asked, one eyebrow raised.

"No," Winter said. "Not like this, anyway. I knew there was a tiellan settlement out here, but..."

"We like to keep it that way," Rorie said. "Even our own kind don't know the extent of our settlement here, as you can see."

"But if humans were to find out? Wouldn't they feel threatened?"

"Maybe. But that ain't our business, until they come knocking. That's assuming they realize there is more to the place than what you saw above ground."

"And what if they did?" While the underground city fascinated Winter, she could not imagine it was easy to defend. "The path you led me down was treacherous, but an army could force their way through it."

"Don't know what you don't see," Rorie said. "Arrow slits and other defenses lined the stairway we walked down. Murder holes in the ceiling of the tunnel. And that stairway ain't the only entrance into Adimora; it ain't even the main entrance. Others exist, all of 'em secret, all of 'em defendable, some of 'em capable of allowing many through at once. Adimora ain't an easy city to get into, or to leave. It's designed that way on purpose."

Winter nodded, Rorie's phrase ringing in her ears.

Adimora ain't an easy city to get into, or to leave.

Rorie led Winter through the main cavern, down bustling underground streets, between homes and businesses, until they reached the *rihnemin* at the center. The stone had to be at least ten rods in diameter; six Winters could have fit head to toe along the base.

Winter stared at the runes engraved on the huge stone. Tentatively, she reached out one palm and placed it on the *rihnemin*'s smooth, cold surface. As she did so, a memory caught in her mind: Lian, while they had traveled together, had approached each *rihnemin* they'd crossed, had reverently placed his hand on each one.

She wondered what Lian would think of her now. There was no way in Oblivion he'd have approved of what she'd done in Roden, but she liked to think he might cautiously encourage her actions now. He'd already been connected with the Druids, after all, and now here she was, fighting alongside them.

A sudden emptiness overtook her, an ache that echoed throughout the walls of her heart. She still missed him.

"You coming?" Rorie asked.

"More stairs?" Winter asked, eyeing the steps that spiraled downward around the *rihnemin*, atop which Rorie stood.

"To speak with the Cracked Spear, we must go down." Rorie disappeared down the staircase. Winter quickly followed.

As she walked, she allowed her fingers to trail along the *rihnemin*'s surface, feeling the carved texture of the stone.

"This is the largest *rihnemin* I've ever seen." *Rihnemin* were always a single piece of stone. The smallest Winter had seen was slightly smaller than a person, oblong and not quite two rods in length. Others had been much larger, some the size of houses.

This one was incredible.

As Winter thought about it, she began to realize the large cavern would be roughly beneath the abandoned village on the surface near the gorge, and at the center of that village was a *rihnemin*, protruding from the ground and jutting high into the air. If that *rihnemin* started there, and sank deep down into the earth…

"This is the same *rihnemin* from the surface?" Winter asked.

"It is," Rorie said, "and ain't no surprise this one's the largest you've ever seen. It's the largest in existence."

"How do you know?" The largest *rihnemin* in existence. It had to be at least five hundred rods tall, if not more.

Rorie shrugged. "How do we know the sun'll rise in the morning? How do we know all will one day die? Some things we just know, Commander. Some rumors say one of the most powerful tiellans from the Age of Marvels carved this from an entire mountain, and moved it here, to Adimora."

"And moved it down the Underway?" Winter asked. She did not think even a stone shaft of this size could fill the Underway, however.

Rorie shrugged. "No one knows for certain."

It made Winter think. If she used every *tendra* she could, concentrating all her power, she *might* be able to lift a stone of this size. But to rip it out of the ground, or carve it from a mountain, and carry it that distance… she could not fathom that kind of power.

She had not used telesis to the full extent of her powers since that night under the imperial dome in Izet, when Azael had appeared and she, Knot, and Astrid had been attacked by Outsiders. In truth, it was becoming more and more difficult to determine what her limits actually were. That night under the dome, she'd taken more *faltira* than any person had a right to take at one time. According to Kali, she should have died by taking so many, or at least burned herself out. Instead, shortly after she woke in the aftermath of that battle, she'd been able to access not only telesis, but acumency as well. Winter could not be sure whether her access to acumency had somehow been caused by her *faltira* overdose, but it seemed likely.

"Who was this tiellan?" Winter asked. "The one who was said to have moved the *rihnemin?*"

"Same person the city's named after, of course. Adimora."

Adimora. The name, quite suddenly, sounded familiar. Something she had heard before…

"We're here," Rorie said, after a moment. They'd reached the bottom of the stairs, which ended anticlimactically by colliding with a plain dirt floor and what Winter had to assume was the actual base of the massive *rihnemin.*

"This is where the Cracked Spear meets?" Winter asked. She could not imagine the most powerful elders of the tiellan clans meeting in such a place. It seemed absurd.

Rorie laughed. "No, Commander. Come, follow me."

"Anything else I should know about the Cracked Spear before I meet them?" Winter asked. Rorie had given her a brief rundown earlier.

"The Keepers can be fickle," Rorie said. "Best approach is to be flexible, willing to bend in whatever direction they tend to be leaning."

That was not Winter's style, but she did not want to ruin this meeting. Then again, she did not want to waste time, either.

Rorie led her to an unadorned door, and the rugged wood, cracked and split and aged, echoed hollowly throughout the lower chamber as Rorie knocked. Five times. The door opened, and Winter and Rorie entered.

The austere nature of the chamber did not impress Winter. The most arresting aspect was a strange table that stood at its center. The table, like the door, was made of simple, aging wood, but it was shaped like a triangle, each side equal. Along two sides of the table sat a group of tiellan men, long ears protruding from beneath wide-brimmed *araifs*, their wrinkled, scarred faces glaring at Winter with hooded eyelids. The third side of the table, empty of either people or chairs, faced the doorway through which Winter and Rorie had entered.

Rorie had neglected to mention they would *all* be men. Winter had assumed, because the tiellan clans allowed women to fight with them—and Rorie, at least, had led forces in battle—that this Cracked Spear would have women in it, too. Apparently she had been wrong.

"Rorie, was it?" one of the old men said.

"Yes, Keeper," Rorie said, bowing.

"Very well. Thank you for bringing this... woman down to meet us. You may leave."

Winter's eyes widened slightly as she glanced back at Rorie. *You brought me down here just to leave me alone with these men?*

Rorie clearly caught the meaning behind Winter's glance. She bowed again to the men of the Cracked Spear. "By your wisdom, Keepers, Winter ain't aware of our cultures and customs. If it please you, I'd stay with her to help."

"It doesn't please us," the same Keeper said, voice firm. "Leave us, Rorie."

Rorie shrugged apologetically. "I'll be just outside," she whispered to Winter.

Then, Winter was alone with the Cracked Spear.

Winter frowned. She did not like what she saw of them so far. What made these men think they could treat Rorie that way? Winter walked to the side of the table without chairs, and stood at the edge's center. She kept her shoulders square, her neck long. She had dealt with Nazaniin assassins. She had confronted lords and emperors. She would not be intimidated by these men.

"May we all be blessed," one of the Keepers said.

Winter opened her mouth, but one of the other Keepers beat her to it. "Under the sun and moon," he said.

Winter frowned. So much for using one of the only pieces of clan culture she'd learned.

"Who is this that has been brought before us?" another Keeper asked. It was the same who had bid Rorie leave. He wore his *araif* at an angle, shadowing one eye in darkness. The other that peeked out from beneath the brim was bright green and alert, contrasting with his other weary, worn features. His face was rough and creased. He wore simple, dust-covered clothing, all leather in varying shades of brown. He wore no weapon. In fact, as Winter scanned the room, she saw no weapons at all.

Winter opened her mouth, about to answer the man's question, but again she was cut off before she began. Another Keeper spoke in response to the first, though neither met Winter's eyes.

"This is Danica Winter Cordier, daughter of Bahc Cordier and Effara Daggerkind." This Keeper was younger than the first who had spoken, and sat at the other corner of the table, nearest the side where Winter stood. He was younger, but not young; probably a few years her father's senior when he had died. His face was smoother, tanned, and his *araif* worn high on his head, revealing both eyes—jet black, just like Winter's.

Winter blinked. How did they already know who she was?

"She recently journeyed to Roden, though what she did there is unclear. Rumors say she allied herself with some of the nobility in Izet, and was involved in the deaths of both late emperors, but we cannot be certain."

"Wait, how do you—"

"And what is she doing here? What does she want with us?"

"She led a tiellan force out of Cineste, defeating a contingent of the City Watch outside the gates. Some say she has come with her tiellans—they call themselves Druids, after the old ones—seeking shelter. Others say she has come to recruit us to her cause."

"I can answer all of these questions if you'd only let me—"

"Do you think she has anything to do with the prophecy?" the first Keeper asked.

This question, for whatever reason, brought silence to the room.

Winter looked at each of the Keepers. None of them met her eyes. She had had enough of this, and she had certainly had enough of prophecies.

"Why have you brought me here if you do not intend to speak with me?" she asked.

"I do not know whether she has anything to do with the prophecy," one of the other Keepers said. "But perhaps the Spearholder knows."

Slowly, all eyes around the table turned to the third point of the triangle, the one directly opposite the edge where Winter stood. A man, neither the oldest nor the youngest, sat there, very much like the others—a wide-brimmed *araif*, dusty leather clothing. Long hair fell freely down to his shoulders.

Winter suppressed an urge to take a frost crystal from the pouch at her belt, or to use acumency to discern the thoughts of these men. These were her people, after all. She did not want her first impression on them to be one of violence.

You've already made that impression, a voice echoed in her mind, *when you killed the chiefs that stood by Rorie. All these people will understand is violence. It is their language. Speak it to them.*

Winter's hand twitched, though she had not brought a physical weapon. It would be simple, however, to take a crystal and reach out a *tendron* to one of these men, to make an example of him...

"Let the woman speak," the Spearholder said.

A few of the other Keepers grumbled something along the lines of that not being the tradition.

Winter had two choices. She could keep her head down and bide her time until an opportunity presented itself, or she could go on the offensive.

Canta knew, she found the latter option more appealing. Violence was her language, too, whether she liked it or not. She was a weapon, above all else. But when she closed her eyes, the Chaos sphere was a pure, reluctant white. No violence this time, then. She would have to try something different.

Winter bowed her head. "By your wisdom, Keepers," she said, taking note from the way Rorie had addressed them before they'd sent her out, "I am a newcomer to Adimora and to your culture, and I do not mean to presume, but... what is the point of calling me in if you are not willing to speak directly to me? I can answer the questions you've asked one another, if you would allow it."

More grumbles from the Keepers. The Spearholder, however, stared directly at Winter, a frown on his face. He was the only one of the men at the table, Winter realized, who would meet her eyes. She wondered whether that was an internal choice or dictated by some strange culture of the Cracked Spear.

"Go ahead, Winter," the Spearholder finally said.

There it was. This was her chance. Winter started walking, moving around the table. If they would not meet her eyes of their own accord, she would force them to do it.

"You're right about who I am and where I've travelled," Winter said. "I don't know how you know it, but you're right. I come from Pranna. My father was killed there, and I left."

She moved slowly to face the first man who had spoken, the older man with his *araif* covering one eye. Winter put one hand on the table, leaning in close. She could smell the dust on him, the aged leather. "I left, and eventually found myself a prisoner in Roden. I did dark things there, and I saw far darker. What you've heard is partly correct—I killed one emperor. The other was killed by something much worse than me." She made her voice hard as she spoke.

She straightened and continued along the table, her side brushing against the backs of the Keepers seated around it. Her shoulder brushed against an *araif*, knocking it from the man's head to reveal a balding spot amidst a mess of wiry white hair. The old man grumbled something incoherent, then bent to pick up his hat. Winter reached it before he did, and swung the rim around one of her fists as she continued walking.

"I left Roden, hoping to find what remained of my family and friends in Pranna. They had left, because the humans there had driven them out. When I found them in Cineste, the persecution still followed them. So I led them out of the city, and crushed the City Watch that tried to stop us."

Winter continued slowly around the table, passing the Spearholder at the head corner. All eyes in the room were on her, now. The man whose *araif* she had taken glared at her, a frown wrinkling his face. Winter did not care. If this was what it took for these fools to notice her, so be it.

"And now here I am," Winter said. The Keepers had asked what she wanted, and now that she had their attention, she would bloody well tell them. "I want, first of all, food and shelter for the Druids—my friends, who I have brought to your city." Rorie had assured her that her people would find enough food by hunting and fishing the surrounding area, but Winter wanted to be sure. The Druids were mostly city folk, after all. Not all of them had experience hunting and fishing.

"But more importantly," she said, "I want justice for the tiellan race." She thought of Lian, and his hope and optimism. She thought of the empty tiellan huts in Pranna, and of the boy lying broken and bleeding on the floor at the Druid meeting in Cineste—how Eranda would have been next. She forced herself to remember that night in Cineste, the snowy ground cold and melting through the clothing on her back, the human heavy on top of her.

"I want you to help me fight back. We've been emancipated for almost two centuries, but we have not been free. You sit here, on the eastern plains, and you fight amongst yourselves, you squabble, but you do nothing for your brothers and sisters who suffer in the west."

Winter made her way back to the empty side of the table. She threw the *araif* she'd been holding into the middle of the triangle, where it sat crumpled and untouched.

Eranda's words echoed in Winter's head. *The tiellans would follow you. I would follow you.*

"I want your armies," Winter said. She looked directly at the Spearholder. "I want your assistance in finding justice for our people, in carving a place for us in the Sfaera."

A few of the Keepers scoffed.

"We cannot simply *give* you our armies," one of them said. "We hardly get along with one another, let alone you, an outsider."

"I am *not* an outsider," Winter said harshly. "I am one of you."

"But—"

"This is not a request," Winter said. "This is a demand. You left out something from my history. Something you surely know. I met with a half-dozen chiefs on the plains, a few days ago. They refused me. Now Rorie, the woman you sent away a moment ago, is the only survivor. She recognized the right decision, and I've rewarded her for it. The same rule applies to each of you. Join me now, and I'll reward you for that decision. Not only that, but I'll lead our forces to victory."

Winter's hand strayed to the frost at her belt. With some effort, she stopped herself from taking a crystal.

"If you don't join me now, there will be consequences. I will kill you, first of all. It will be quick, relatively painless, but, well, you'll definitely be dead. I'll take whatever forces you command as my prisoners. You'll forfeit their lives, as well."

"If that is your ultimatum," one of the Keepers said quietly, "how are you any different from the worst of the humans?"

Winter shrugged. "Maybe I'm not." She stepped away from the table, and leaned her back against the door to the chamber. The only door, as far as she could tell, that led in or out of the room.

"You have a quarter of an hour to make your decision," she said. She closed her eyes again, and this time Chaos loomed black and impenetrable in her mind.

25

Odenite camp, outside Kirlan

KNOT WANDERED THROUGH THE camp searching for the last of his injured soldiers, stunned by the blinding display of light. The third Outsider was gone. None remained. The threat had passed, for now, and yet Knot still felt a twisting feeling in his gut. Something was not right.

The column of burning light that had destroyed the last Outsider must have been called up by Jane, or perhaps Cinzia. Knot had never seen anything like it. He remembered the shining white light Jane had displayed when the *cotir* had attacked them at Harmoth, but this had been different. Far brighter. Far more focused. The beam lit up the night brighter than the sun ever could.

It had destroyed a Goddess-damned Outsider, for Canta's sake.

He found Eward in pain with what was likely a broken arm, but otherwise unharmed. After making sure Eward and the other injured soldiers were being cared for, Knot made his way towards the center of camp, where the first Outsider had fallen, surely at Astrid's hand.

The center bonfire still burned brightly, and a group of charred tents nearby hurled smoke upwards.

Lying in the grass was the dead Outsider.

Knot circled the thing grimly. The Outsider he and Eward's

soldiers had taken down sported dozens of wounds. This one, on the other hand, showed almost no injuries at all. The Outsider's hide was smooth blackness. A few deep gouges marked the thing's neck. Astrid's claws, surely. Then, Knot walked around the thing and saw its head. Or what was left of it, anyway.

The lower jaw had been completely torn from the skull. It now lay a few rods away from the beast, the grass beneath soaked in blood. One of the creature's own fangs, longer than Knot's sword, had been jammed into a big black eye.

"She killed it by herself."

Knot turned to see Cavil, Ocrestia's husband.

"You saw it?" Knot asked.

"It was…" Cavil looked down. "…horrifying. But Astrid killed it, on her own."

"Is she—"

"She's all right, she's all right," Cavil said quickly. "Guess I should've led with that. Leg looked a bit messed up, but she limped off that way." He pointed in the direction of where the final Outsider had been obliterated by the beam of light, on the southern edge of camp, closest to the city.

Knot looked at the Outsider's body, and couldn't help but chuckle. His girl had done this. It was odd to be proud of her for killing an Outsider on her own, but there was no mistaking the feeling that swelled in his chest.

He looked to Cavil. "You all right?"

Cavil shrugged. "Ain't dead, if that's what you mean."

Knot grunted.

"Go find her," Cavil said. "She was looking for you."

"Thank you," Knot said.

It took him a few moments to get to the edge of the camp. So many injured Odenites. He saw Ocrestia and the new disciple, Baetrissa, leading a small group administering to the injured. He had yet to glimpse Cinzia or Jane. They would have to wait until after he found Astrid.

As Knot approached the southern edge of camp, the twisting feeling in his gut intensified. He looked around, trying to discern what might cause the sensation. At the edge of camp, he noticed a carriage.

The Odenites had many horses among them, and a few wagons. But the people had given up any carriages they had to make the trek south. Jane had insisted on it.

A woman in the red and white robes of a matron walked around the carriage. Astrid's words came to mind, about who she worked for. Who *owned* her, as she put it.

A specific faction of the Denomination, led by someone who calls herself the Black Matron.

A low growl began deep in Knot's throat. He picked up speed, moving towards the carriage. He did not see Astrid anywhere. But the carriage had bars on the windows, a strong lock on the door. Its passengers were not meant to ride in comfort; they were meant to ride to prison.

"Stop!" Knot shouted, breaking into a sprint.

The woman in robes looked back at him, then rushed to the front of the carriage. A Goddessguard and a half-dozen Sons of Canta were with her. They all leapt onto the carriage, and the Goddessguard snapped the reins. The carriage began moving south, towards Kirlan.

Knot swore. He would not catch them on foot. He looked back at the camp and saw a group of horses, saddled up, tied to a set of posts hammered into the ground. They would have to do.

He ran back to the horses. The first animal shied away at his touch.

"Easy," Knot coaxed. The animal looked strong, certainly the strongest of the group tied here.

The horse sidestepped, then cocked its head in Knot's direction.

Good enough. Knot made sure the girth was tightened, then untied the horse.

"I know I'm a stranger," Knot said, his voice low and calm, "but I need you to trust me right now. Can you do that?"

The horse stamped a hoof.

Knot took that as a yes. He pulled himself into the saddle, and urged the animal forward. The horse fought him at first, reluctant to leave its companions, but eventually gave in, picking up speed as Knot chased after the carriage, already fading into the night.

He had gained ground on the carriage, but the city walls already loomed over them. The gate was open, despite the late hour. The Black Matron must have arranged for the Sons of Canta to keep it open for her.

Could she have arranged for more than that? The Black Matron's timing, arriving at the camp right after the Outsiders attacked, could surely not be a coincidence.

Doubt cracked through his resolve as he rode after them. Had these people even taken Astrid? But what else could they have been there to do? A matron, showing up at a time like this, shortly after Astrid had revealed what she had done, was too much.

Astrid had to be with them. Knot knew it in his gut.

Twenty rods out from the carriage, now. He was a single rider on a single horse, easily able to outpace the two horses ahead, weighed down by their load. He could just about make out one of the Sons sitting on the bench at the back of the carriage. The darkness made it difficult to tell, but Knot thought he saw a crossbow.

A bolt whispering past his ear confirmed that theory.

Knot clenched his jaw. He was getting close. Ten rods.

The Son with the crossbow took aim, and Knot shifted at the last moment as another bolt split the air where he'd been a moment before. He regained his balance, and kicked his horse forward.

"Come on, boy," he said. Wasn't sure whether the horse was male or female, now that he thought about it. Didn't matter. "Just a little farther."

Five rods.

The carriage slowed as it approached the gate, but Knot did not slow his own horse. Instead, gripping the reins, he climbed to his feet, balancing on his horse's back, and then leapt forward. His momentum, along with the slowing carriage, caused him to crash right into the Son with the crossbow. The carriage continued to move through the city gate as Knot slammed his fist into the Son's jaw. Knot ripped the weapon from the man's hands, then threw him from the carriage. He pointed the crossbow at one of the other Sons standing from the bench, and fired a bolt directly into the man's belly. Knot tossed the crossbow aside and kicked the man off the carriage. The remaining Son on the back bench drew a dagger, stabbing at Knot, but Knot deflected the attack and rammed his palm up into the man's chin, following through with an elbow to the man's face. Out cold, the Son toppled from the still-moving carriage.

The Goddessguard, the matron, and another Son sat on a raised bench at the front, their heads just visible above the top of the carriage. The Son and matron looked back at him, while the Goddessguard kept his eyes on the road. They were through the gate, now, and moving into the city. More quickly than they should be, even at this late hour.

Knot peeked through the bars into the carriage. Sure enough, he saw Astrid there, eyes wide, body frozen. There had to be nightsbane in the carriage. Either that, or Astrid had been right about the matron she served being an acumen. A powerful acumen could incapacitate even a vampire.

"You cannot save her," the woman said, craning her neck to look back at Knot. "She belongs to us."

Knot didn't respond. Instead, he leapt onto the roof of the carriage and made his way forward. The carriage barreled through the empty streets of Kirlan, rattling over cobbled and dirt streets alike. Knot had to be sure where he placed each step.

The Son stood, turning to face Knot, and drew his sword. That was a mistake on the Son's part; there was not much space to swing a sword between them. The Son took an awkward defensive stance balanced on the bench as Knot approached. Glancing ahead, Knot saw the road shift from cobbles to dirt, and waited until the carriage careened over the change in terrain to lunge forward.

The Son swung his sword in defense, but between swinging the sword and the change of terrain beneath him, he lost balance, and it was easy to give the man the extra push he needed to topple off.

"Stop," the matron said. The Goddessguard reined in the horses.

"Leave the girl with me," Knot said.

"You still care about her, after what she did to you?" The matron raised one eyebrow. She was older than Knot had first thought, her face wrinkled and hair white under the hooded robe.

"Ain't your business," Knot said. Before the Goddessguard could turn, Knot propelled himself forward on his hands, ramming his feet into the back of the Goddessguard. The man fell from the carriage and crashed to the ground, his armor clanging.

"Get off the carriage," Knot said, stepping up to the bench.

"You wouldn't banish an old woman from—"

Knot pushed the matron and she fell, her robes flapping around her. Knot did not wait to see her response. Instead, he shook the reins, urging the horses forward.

"After him!" he heard the matron yell behind him.

Knot looked back, and swore. A group of Sons on horseback turned the corner. They would easily catch him, the same way he'd caught the carriage in the first place.

The horses picked up speed. Fortunately, the streets of Kirlan were not wide, and it would be difficult for the Sons to come up alongside him.

Knot glanced into the cage. "Astrid!"

The girl did not respond.

Knot gritted his teeth. He could have at least gotten a Goddess-damned key from the matron before he'd pushed her off the carriage.

The Sons gained ground on them, closing the distance quickly. Knot heard a thump, and looked back to see one of the Sons already on the carriage.

Knot guided the horses around a sharp corner, feeling the wheels on one side of the carriage lift from the ground as they turned. Fortunately, they lifted just enough to knock the Son who'd just leapt onto the carriage onto the dirt road with a yell and a cloud of dust.

The carriage barreled down a narrow road with homes on

the right side, the city wall on the left—and this particular road seemed to run the entire length of the east wall.

Two more thumps. Knot glanced back to see two more Sons had leapt onto the carriage. Two more on horseback closed in behind them. He urged the horses on, biding his time. He glanced back again; the two Sons had progressed forward enough that they'd almost reached him, and two more were close enough to make the leap onto the carriage.

Knot took another corner, sharply, but the two Sons remained despite the wild turn. Ahead, the road was straight for a while yet. Then two more Sons leapt onto the carriage, and Knot made a snap decision.

He guided the horses even closer to the wall on his left. He stood up, preparing himself, then leapt from the carriage bench, running along the wall as the carriage moved past him. He pushed off the wall just in time to slam into the two Sons at the front of the carriage. One fell to the road in another cloud of dust, while the other barely held on.

Knot stamped his foot down hard on the man's hand. He screamed, then let go as Knot punched him in the face.

The two remaining Sons on the carriage turned to face him, eyes wide, but Knot didn't wait for their surprise to process. Knot moved on one of the Sons, whipping the dagger from the man's own belt and stabbing it into his neck. While he fell, Knot turned on the other Son, dodging a blow from the man's fist, and then ramming the dagger into his belly. The blade pierced chainmail, and another kick sent the man flying from the carriage.

Knot looked behind him. There were no more horses, no more Sons, other than the few writhing in the dust in the distance. The carriage slowed almost to a stop, but Knot wasn't ready for that. He leapt forward onto the bench once more and urged the horses forward.

He looked back into the carriage, saw Astrid was now face down on the floor. The jolting around must have knocked her down.

"Hey," he said. "Astrid."

No response. He still saw no nightsbane in the carriage; Astrid's state had to be a result of the Black Matron's acumency. Knot cursed. If he could get her far enough away, the matron's hold would diminish. It was the only way he knew to break the hold she had on Astrid.

He spurred the horses onward, racking his brain for a solution. There was no way they'd be able to get out of the northern gate; it was under the constant guard of the Sons of Canta. He might be able to get out on the southern side, but that meant he'd be cut off from the Odenite camp, and that still didn't solve the problem of getting Astrid out of this bloody carriage. The thing was too bulky; it only slowed them down. He—

His horses spooked as a half-dozen more riders charged at them from a street that ran perpendicular to theirs. The carriage shot past the opening just in time.

"Shit."

He looked behind him, and sure enough another dozen riders at least were coming up behind him, Goddessguards among them.

"Why can it never be easy?" he muttered to himself as he tried to regain control of the horses. But between the exhausting ride and their recent spook, it all seemed to be too much for them. They barreled forward at full speed, heedless of Knot's attempts to steer.

The horses widened the gap between them and the approaching Sons, at least, but it would not end well. Another sharp turn rapidly approached ahead; apparently Knot had ridden the entire length of the wall, and the wall turned sharply to the west about two hundred rods in front of him. The road took a slight downhill turn here, too, which did not help their unsafe speed.

Knot would not regain control of the horses. Not in time. Even if he could, there was no way he'd be able to outrun his pursuers.

He looked back into the carriage, then forward at the wall ahead of them. One hundred rods.

He reached for the knife he'd taken from the Son on the carriage, and leapt forward onto one of the panicked horses. He cut the reins for both horses, then the tug line that attached the other horse to the carriage. The horse bolted, leaving Knot and the carriage behind. Finally, he cut the tug line attached to his own horse, which did the same. Fifty rods. The horse sped off, although the carriage was rolling so fast, now, that the horse could barely outrun it. Knot leaned forward, stroking the beast's neck, and then guided the horse sharply right. It leapt into an alley, as the carriage rumbled past. Moments later, he heard a monstrous crash.

Knot patted the horse's neck, whispering soothing sounds. Fortunately, the horse already seemed to be calming. He rode out of the alley and towards the crash site. As he had hoped, the carriage was in ruins. The pursuing Sons were close, now, one hundred rods out themselves, but they, too, were now slowing. They had cornered their prey.

Astrid lay on the ground, her body trapped beneath the roof of the carriage, which had completely detached from the rest of the body. Knot dismounted, keeping hold of the horse's severed reins. With one movement born of desperation and adrenaline, he threw the carriage roof off of Astrid. He lifted the girl, placing her on the horse. He secured her there as best he could, tying her on with what was left of the horse's reins, and then slapped the animal on the rump, sending it running off into the city. Hopefully, the horse would take her far enough away that she'd regain consciousness and escape before the Sons found her.

Knot turned to face the oncoming horsemen. For now, he had to make sure he gave her that time.

To his surprise, all of his pursuers stopped, surrounding him. None of them broke off to go after the horse that carried Astrid.

Had they not seen him place the girl on the horse and send her away?

"Any of you going to say anything?" Knot asked, as the Sons and Goddessguards circled him. Fifteen Sons. Four Goddessguards. All on horseback. The odds were not in his favor.

"I suppose I will take that honor."

The men on horseback parted, making way for a woman. A woman clad in the white and red robes of a Cantic matron.

"Canta's bloody bones," Knot muttered. "Didn't I push you off of that carriage?"

It was the same woman, there was no denying that. The wrinkled skin, white hair, now fully revealed with her hood down. The same blazing, intelligent eyes.

"You did," the woman said, frowning. "I've seen almost eighty summers, you know. That's bad form no matter who you ask."

"You telling me you didn't deserve it?"

The woman burst out laughing, bending over, clutching her stomach. She went on for a good minute. Knot kept a straight face. He hadn't been joking.

"You might've lost the girl," Knot said. "I'd like to say I'm sorry about that, but..."

The Black Matron waved a hand in the air. "Oh, I'm not worried. That girl always turns up, even when she doesn't want to be found, somehow. Besides, she was never our final target."

Knot blinked.

The woman chuckled again. "Oh, you'll have to excuse me. It's just that we've pursued you for so long. You cannot know how good it feels to finally have caught you, and yet here you are making jokes."

Astrid had told him they were using her to get to him. That was exactly what they'd done here.

"How long have you been after me? Were you after Lathe, too?"

The matron shook her head. "We never had much interest in Lathe, my dear. But when you became... well, *you*, my superiors took a sudden interest."

"And your superiors are?" Knot was surprised at how calm he felt. He had no way out, not now. That was all right. Astrid had made it out, and somehow, despite her betrayal, despite her lying to him, knowing that she was safe was enough.

"Oh, you'll find that out soon enough. Very soon, in fact."

"Forgive me if I'm not impressed."

The woman's smile faded. She sighed. "Our conversation ends here." She signaled to the men around her. "Take him."

26

Odenite camp, outside Kirlan

ASTRID LET CINZIA LEAD her to the tent she shared with Jane, where the disciples regularly met. Cinzia had to slow her pace so Astrid could keep up as she limped along. She had returned to camp, barely conscious, on a horse that morning, but her leg would still take another day or so to fully heal. Broken bones always took longer to heal than cuts and piercings.

Astrid clenched her jaw. She was rarely present for the disciples' meetings, unless Knot was, too, and that was usually fine with Astrid. She didn't care much to participate in whatever in Oblivion they were talking about, anyway.

But now Knot was gone, and they needed to get him back.

Jane, Ocrestia, Elessa, and Baetrissa waited for them. Astrid thought it was a bit silly that each of Jane's disciples had been named after one of Canta's original Disciples. Seemed more than a bit contrived.

"Welcome, Astrid," Jane said. "Cinzia, I am glad you found her."

Everyone was still exhausted from the battle with the Outsiders the previous night. Jane and her priestesses wore rumpled clothing, their hair disheveled.

"Do you have an update on the dead and wounded?" Jane asked.

"Ain't good," Ocrestia said quietly. "Death toll's up to thirty-one. The wounded almost double that. We healed as much as we could last night, but… but we are not experienced with Canta's power. We could only do so much."

"I am sure you did what you could," Jane said, placing a hand on Ocrestia's shoulder. The gesture seemed oddly fake to Astrid. But she was in a pretty terrible mood.

"What about Eward's Prelates?" Jane asked. "How many of them were lost?"

"Five," Ocrestia said. "And more wounded. Still have a strong force, though, over one hundred volunteers."

"By Canta's grace," one of the other disciples whispered. Astrid wasn't sure which one, and she didn't much care.

"We need to make sure this does not happen again," Cinzia said. "We cannot take another attack."

"We must address the toll this has taken on the Odenites," Jane said. "I will give a speech. The more opposition we face, the clearer the importance of our movement becomes. What we do here matters. I will emphasize that."

Astrid rolled her eyes. Normally, she liked Jane, but this all seemed too much. Especially when there were other matters that needed to be dealt with.

"What about Knot?" Astrid asked.

"What about him?" Jane asked.

Astrid looked at Cinzia. "She doesn't *know?*"

"I have not had time to tell her," Cinzia said. "You barely came to me yourself."

Astrid sighed. Made sense, actually, but she didn't have the patience for apologies. "Knot has been captured. We need to get him back, as soon as possible, before… before they do something bad to him."

Jane shook her head, bewildered. "Captured? Astrid, what

are you talking about? Who would capture Knot? I thought the Nazaniin had been dealt with."

Astrid snorted. If Jane thought the Nazaniin had been dealt with, she was more naive than Astrid had thought. "Not the Nazaniin. The Denomination."

"*What?*" Cinzia looked at Astrid sharply.

Astrid cleared her throat. No sense in hiding anything now. She'd come clean with Knot, and that was what mattered. These women did not.

"Long before I met any of you, a faction of the Denomination coerced me into working for them. I tried to break free of them, because they were using me to get to Knot, and I did not like that."

"A faction within the Denomination would never employ a vampire," Cinzia said quietly. "Unless…"

"It's the Cult," Astrid said. "Led by a woman who calls herself the Black Matron."

"Canta rising," Cinzia whispered.

"Cinzia? What is the Cult?"

Cinzia stared off, wide-eyed, into nothing. "A dark tale girls at the seminary tell one another. But even as a priestess, I heard… rumors…"

"Rumors of what?"

"Of women in the Denomination who serve a darker purpose," Cinzia said.

"A darker purpose?" Ocrestia asked.

"I did not know it at the time," Cinzia said, "but I can only assume they serve the Fear Lord, Azael, master of the Nine Daemons."

"But how can they profess to serve Canta, and yet ally themselves with the Fear Lord?" Elessa asked. "It cannot be possible."

Astrid barked a laugh. "If you're still putting limits on what is and isn't possible, you're a bloody slow learner."

Ocrestia chuckled.

"They must have used me to get to Knot," Astrid said. "I was ambushed after the Outsider attack last night, and the next thing I knew, I woke up barely conscious on a horse in the city." While she'd destroyed the Black Matron's nightsbane, she hadn't been immune to her acumency, and in the chaos the Black Matron had surprised Astrid easily, incapacitating her.

Astrid looked at Ocrestia. "Your husband, Cavil, said Knot went after me last night. The only explanation is that they used me as bait. Apparently, it worked.

"If you ask me, the Black Matron orchestrated the Outsider attack. They want Knot, and they'd do just about anything to get him." She glanced at Cinzia. "Them serving the Fear Lord doesn't sound that far off, either."

"They would do that?" Jane asked. "Cause all of that destruction, just to get to one man?"

"I think they would," Astrid said.

Jane took a deep breath, while the other disciples were silent. Finally, Jane spoke.

"We need to figure out a way past Kirlan," she said, "and continue our trek south. That is Canta's will."

Astrid blinked.

"Jane," Cinzia said quickly, "we cannot just leave Knot to his fate."

"We can if it is Canta's will," Jane said. She looked at her sister. "Remember Navone? Canta's will was for me to turn myself in, Cinzia. We *both* thought I would die. But I did not, and here we are. Canta has a plan for Knot, and if it requires him to live, he will."

"*If?*" Astrid growled.

"Jane, dozens of people died in Navone," Cinzia said slowly. "That action was not without consequences. Collateral damage. If we can do something to help…"

"Knot has protected you," Astrid said, unable to keep the edge from her voice, "helped you, all of this time. You would just abandon him?"

"We are not abandoning him if we leave him in Canta's care," Jane said. "There is no better help."

"If you lose him, you lose me," Astrid said. "And the next time an Outsider attacks, nobody will be around to save you." She turned and left the tent without another word.

Astrid limped away, every step a reminder of her own inadequacy. The fact that she couldn't run, could hardly walk away from those heartless women fast enough, made her want to scream. Made her want to murder someone.

"Astrid!" Cinzia caught up with her easily.

"Get away from me," Astrid muttered.

"I want to help you," Cinzia said. "And Knot."

"Your bloody sister doesn't feel that way."

"My sister… my sister can be a bitch."

Astrid stopped, turning to face Cinzia. She raised one eyebrow.

"What?" Cinzia asked. "She can be. Sometimes."

Astrid snorted, shaking her head. She couldn't stop the slightest smile from creasing her cheek, despite everything that was going on. Had to take the pleasures of life as they came to her, after all.

"Knot is my Goddessguard," Cinzia said. "I am going to help him. I do not care what my sister says."

Astrid wrinkled her forehead. "What do you mean he's your Goddessguard? I thought you weren't a priestess anymore."

"I am not," Cinzia said slowly. "He... he did not tell you?"

"Haven't been talking much, he and I. Not since I told him about my association with the Denomination."

Astrid sat down on one of the many makeshift chairs that scattered the camp, near the coals of a dying fire.

Cinzia hesitated, then sat next to her. "I am sure you hurt him," she said quietly. "It could not have been easy for him to hear you had been working to betray him."

"I *know* that. But I've been trying to avoid the bloody Denomination since Izet. Since—"

"What changed?" Cinzia asked.

Astrid shrugged. What *had* changed? What made her want to help Knot more than she wanted redemption for herself?

She knew the truth. She'd known it all along, since her first moments with him. "I like being around him. I feel safe. Like I'm a part of something."

"Like you are part of a family?"

Astrid snorted. "I wouldn't know the first thing about a family. Been without one for so long, I might as well never have had one at all. I certainly don't remember anything about mine."

"Family is not about what we remember, or where we are," Cinzia said. "It is only about how we feel."

Astrid kicked her legs against the stump on which she sat. "He didn't even get mad at me when I told him. I wish he had, but he just... he said he could not imagine how *difficult* it would have been for me, that idiot bastard..."

Astrid turned away from Cinzia, and raised a sleeve to her cheek.

"Because he must feel the same way about you," Cinzia said,

wrapping her arm around Astrid's shoulder.

Despite the simplicity of the gesture, Astrid felt immensely grateful for it. Cinzia's touch sent a wave of warmth through her. They sat that way for some time, until Cinzia finally broke the silence.

"Do you think you can find him?" she asked.

Astrid shrugged. "I can't leave you. I can't leave the Odenites. Not when attacks like last night might happen again." Not because *she* cared all that much. It was what Knot would have wanted.

"You can check back on us every few days," Cinzia said. "Keep training Eward and the Prelates when you do. But otherwise... You heard Jane, Astrid. She has no intention of going after Knot, but someone has to."

"I hate admitting you're right," Astrid said, "but at the same time, I'm glad you are."

"If it were one of us, Knot wouldn't rest until he found us."

"All right, all right." Astrid slipped out from under Cinzia's arm. "You've made your point."

When their eyes met, Astrid was surprised to see Cinzia was smiling. "Go after him, Astrid. Bring him back to us."

27

Flatlands, northwest of the Undritch Mountains

WINTER WALKED THE FIELDS in the early morning with Urstadt, Selldor, and Rorie of the Black Hills clan. When she'd received word of the massacre of tiellan refugees at the hand of the Steel Regiment, she'd immediately mobilized her forces back through the Underway to confront the Khalic soldiers. Now almost eighteen hundred strong with the addition of the Cracked Spear's riders and a few hundred new Ranger recruits from the Druids, the force made for the beginnings of a true army.

Her men had set up camp at the edge of the Undritch foothills, overlooking the wide Eastmaw Valley—the sprawl of land between the Eastmaw and Undritch Mountains. A narrow but surprisingly deep river ran along the base of the foothills— the Setso, according to Rorie. The Steel Regiment waited for them on the other side of the Setso; the Khalic soldiers had already engaged her scouts in a few minor skirmishes.

Winter starkly refused to treat with the Steel Regiment. They had massacred over one hundred tiellan refugees, completely unprovoked. Nothing they could say would stop her from destroying them, utterly and completely. She didn't care if she had to slaughter the entire regiment herself.

"What will you do with the Cracked Spear prisoners?" Rorie asked. When Winter had confronted the Cracked Spear

Keepers, a few had resisted. She'd leveraged her power with the Keepers who had joined her to take the riders of those who resisted prisoner, and had brought them here today with a plan in mind.

Winter shivered. The sun had not yet risen, and the sky in the distance had only begun to turn from black to deep, dark blue. For a morning approaching the summer months, it was cold. She pulled her dark cloak more tightly around her.

"I have a plan for them," Winter said. It was based very much on what she had learned of the clan culture, so she hoped it would work.

Rorie nodded. That, for now, seemed to be enough of a response for her. Winter was not sure the effect her plan would have, but she would soon find out. With any luck, it would not only inspire her soldiers on the battlefield today, but also win over some of the Cracked Spear Keepers that had abstained from supporting her.

Another chill reverberated through her, and she realized the tremble came as much from nerves as it did from cold. The battle of Cineste had been an impromptu event, unlike this confrontation with the Steel Regiment. This would be her first intentional attempt at directing a battle, and eighteen hundred tiellans were relying on her. She was lucky to have Urstadt and Selldor's counsel.

Her scouts informed her last night that the Steel Regiment had finally begun maneuvering for a conflict, moving its entire force directly opposite Winter's camp, across the river. Thanks to the tiellan clan riders, more than half of her force was cavalry, but the Steel Regiment still had the numbers: almost three thousand soldiers, trained and battle-hardened, if Winter's scouts were correct.

Which was why Winter now found herself observing the potential battlefield in the early hours of the morning, looking for any possible advantage.

"Shouldn't we cross the river now?" Winter asked.

"No," Urstadt said. "We should make them cross to us. I have heard of this Publio Kyfer who commands the Steel Regiment. He is aggressive, and hungry for glory. He will take the shortest, easiest route to us, and will assume his numbers and brute force will be enough to win the battle."

"If they truly want to engage us," Winter added, "they will cross. And if they do not, all the better for us."

"We should advance to where the river is shallowest," Urstadt said. She looked to Rorie. "Do you know where that is?"

"Aye," Rorie said. "That stretch south of us should do well enough."

"Don't we want them to cross at the deepest part of the river?" Winter asked.

Rorie shook her head. "We might *want* them to, but they'll know where it ain't possible. The Setso runs deep. The Legion will just look for the shallowest place to cross, anyway."

"If we are not there to meet them, they will flank us," Urstadt said. "We want to dictate the grounds for this battle. We want to meet them just as they come out of the river."

Winter pointed to the place Rorie had indicated, where the River Setso straightened out, and the land grew flatter. "There, then. We advance our forces to the river."

"Allow some space," Urstadt said. "We want the option to attack them while crossing, or to allow them room to form up on our side, with the river at their backs."

"Between a rock and a wet place," Rorie said with a smirk.

"Very well." Winter observed the land. "That copse there." She pointed at a long, narrow outcropping of trees, on a hill to the north of their chosen battleground. "Could we hide some of our forces there? Have them wait until the Legion crosses the river, then attack their flank?"

Winter watched Urstadt, who remained silent for a moment, looking at the long, narrow grove.

"Not sure splitting our forces is a good idea, Commander," Rorie said. "We should stand together."

Urstadt narrowed her eyes. "Rorie is correct, but sometimes the unexpected is just the thing to turn the tide of a battle. How many Rangers were you thinking of hiding, Winter?"

"Not many," Winter said. "A few hundred at most."

Slowly, Urstadt nodded. "That might be effective."

Winter resisted another shiver. "I don't think *might* is the term I want to hear when talking about a battle."

Urstadt chuckled dryly. "Might is the *only* term you'll hear when talking about a battle. Best get used to it."

Winter's mind continued to work. "If we flank them from the north," she said, "we could hide more forces on the south, too. Take them from three sides, with the river at their back."

This time, Urstadt shook her head. "A river hastens down and away from the mountain, avoiding what is strong. So should we. Surrounding a larger force rarely ends well."

"I thought surrounding an enemy was a good thing."

"Not always. There is an ancient proverb: 'When ten to one, surround your enemy. When five to one, attack him head on. When double his strength, split him in half. When equally matched, find the high ground. When weaker, know your escape. And when completely unequal, avoid him at all costs.'"

A cold wind rushed past them, sending strands of Winter's

hair across her face. She would have to be sure to redo her braid before the battle. "Sounds like a bunch of oddly specific rules for warfare."

"Ain't nothing more important in warfare than rules," Rorie said. Then, she smiled. "'Til suddenly there is."

"It is important to be familiar with the rules," Urstadt said, "so that we know when to break them. There are exceptions to every rule, but they arise in specific application."

Winter nodded. The sky was now a deep, dark blue, and the ground around her was more clear. She envisioned her forces where they had planned them, imagined them fighting the Steel Regiment, and winning.

"Selldor, Rorie. Each of you will select ten of your best soldiers. They will, in turn, select ten of their best. You will take them to the grove I indicated earlier, and hide them in the trees. Wait there for my signal. Do it immediately." She turned to Urstadt. "Let's go back. We make sure our Rangers are well-fed and well-clothed. The morning is chilly, and we do not want them going into battle cold. Then, we form up where we've indicated, and wait for the Legion to meet us."

Publio Kyfer had only just sat down to breakfast when his second-in-command, Razzo, approached him.

"The tiellan forces have already formed up." Razzo cut an imposing figure, a full head taller than Kyfer himself, and Kyfer was not small. Where Kyfer was clean-shaven and impeccably trimmed, Razzo's full beard reached his chest, and his long brown hair was tied back.

Kyfer had just taken a sip of mulled wine, and at this news almost spat it out all over the table his servants had just set up for him.

"They've already formed up?"

"Yes, General."

If the tiellans were out this early, his troops could match them. Carrieri's criticism still stung, but if he wrapped this up quickly, he would justify his means with the tiellans' end.

Kyfer stood. "Form ranks," he said. He took another sip of his mulled wine; it was a cold morning for late spring, and the warm liquid felt good coursing down his throat. Just the right form of courage. "We ride out to meet them immediately."

"Sir, perhaps it is best we allow our men to finish eating. Many of them have just barely risen from their beds, and the pre-battle festivities went long, last night. I think—"

"Razzo."

"Yes, General?"

"Do I look like a Goddess-damned brothel keeper?"

"No, General."

"Then our soldiers don't need to sleep in. They don't need their Goddess-damned breakfast. They can fight anytime, anywhere. They're professionals, are they not?"

"Yes they are, General."

"Then form them up."

Razzo saluted. "Yes, General."

It took the better part of an hour, but finally, as the sun rose in the east, the Steel Regiment moved out towards the River Setso.

Kyfer rode out in front of his men. The horrors of battle were just as terrible for him as they were for anyone, but if there was one thing Kyfer reveled in, it was giving the speech beforehand. He loved inspiring his troops to do exactly as he commanded.

"Countrymen!" Kyfer shouted, as he rode his horse out along the riverbank. "I see before me the greatest warriors in all Khale. We are the Steel Regiment, and enemies fear our name."

A cheer rose from the regiment.

"We have experienced victory after victory over the past five years, and never known defeat. I am happy to say that today will not end that streak." To say that they had never known defeat was arguable at best, but in the moment Kyfer didn't care. Neither would his men.

Kyfer looked out across the river at the assembled tiellan forces. Curiously, he could see fighting among them—some kind of spectacle, it seemed. Dozens of pairs of soldiers fought one-on-one, while the rest looked on. Kyfer scoffed. "We stand before a force that barely deserves to be called an army. They are inexperienced. Disorganized. They fight among themselves even as we speak."

Many of his men chuckled at this. A force that was divided against itself had already lost. Cleaning them up would be easy.

"Not only that," Kyfer continued, "they are also tiellans. They were our slaves for centuries, because they have always been weaker than us. They were given inferior forms, inferior skills, and inferior intellects. That has not changed. I am tempted to say that our assured victory today is not even ours to claim, but that of simple biology. An army of lambs could never stand up to a pack of lions, no matter how great in number. And we have the numbers today. There is no advantage that we do not have. There is no scenario in which we will not be victorious!"

This time his soldiers let out a louder cheer, banging weapons on shields and stamping their feet on the ground. Kyfer nodded. This would be his defining moment. He would put down the tiellan rebellion as it began, and finally be recognized as he deserved.

Tiellans would die today.

* * *

Winter rode her black mare to the front of her army. Tiellans from east and west, coexisting. Fighting together as Rangers— even those drafted from the Cracked Spear now answered to that title.

"Lead the prisoners out to the front," Winter commanded.

A Ranger relayed the order. Across the river, the Steel Regiment was just beginning to move into position. Winter still had time for her plan for the prisoners.

Urstadt was beside her, along with Nardo, the younger Cracked Spear member, who had tanned, smooth skin. He was one of the Keepers that had immediately sworn fealty to her. Selldor and Rorie had already hidden their force away in the grove.

The sword she wore at her side was simple, something Urstadt claimed was "better than average quality," forged of folded steel and with good balance. Winter had practiced with the weapon a few times, and felt a certain familiarity with it.

Far more comforting than the sword, however, was the pouch of *faltira* hanging from her belt, and the larger knapsack of the stuff tied to her mare. She had taken a crystal early that morning, before scouting the field, but had refrained from taking another. She needed to be ready to take one the moment the battle began, and perhaps more as the battle progressed. A frost crystal generally lasted between a quarter of an hour and half an hour, but unlike the skirmish with the Cinestean City Watch, this fight would certainly extend beyond that.

The Cracked Spear prisoners were assembled before the river, with her army behind them, still gathered around their fires to ward off the morning chill, per Winter's orders. Winter spurred her mare between the two groups.

Winter shouted, addressing the prisoners. "I have gathered you here to make you an offer."

· The prisoners' horses, weapons, and armor had already been taken from them, and they looked up at her with suspicion in their eyes. Winter did not mind. With any luck, half of them would soon look at her with respect. The other half would be dead.

"Who among you will take up arms against one of your fellow prisoners?" she asked.

Some of the prisoners shifted uncomfortably. Behind her, Winter's army was silent. They would want to know what was happening here, too, and for good reason. It would affect them as well.

"Any prisoner willing to fight another of their number to the death, who emerges victorious, will be granted a horse, weapons, and armor. That person will be given leave to return home, immediately. Any prisoner not willing to accept this ultimatum will remain our captive."

Murmurs rippled through the army behind her. The prisoners before her remained silent for a moment, some looking at her, others looking at one another.

This was the moment where Rorie's intelligence would be proven. She had emphasized to Winter the value the clans placed on strength.

Then, one prisoner, an older man knotted with muscle, stepped forward. "I will accept this offer," he said.

Another, down the line, stepped forward as well. "As will I."

Soon, dozens of Winter's prisoners were stepping forward, ready to accept the offer.

Winter nodded. She motioned for the soldiers she had

already assigned to bring out the weapons for the fighters.

"This is gladiatorial combat," Winter shouted. "One-on-one, no holds barred, to the death. You have the opportunity to return to your homes and families with honor, or die in glory on a battlefield. My warriors will oversee each combat. This opportunity will be granted to all who wish it."

The prisoners grinned, almost all of them eager to take Winter up on her offer. She nodded to the group of Rangers she had designated to oversee these fights.

Her Rangers paired off and administered weapons to the prisoners—less than a dozen of the four hundred refused the challenge—and then Winter motioned for the combat to begin.

The first scream rose up only seconds into the fighting, and soon men and women were falling left and right, while others raised their weapons in triumph.

Winter's army watched the gladiatorial matches with varying degrees of interest, some engrossed, many with caution, and a few—many of her original Rangers—with some disgust.

In just a few moments, the first round was complete, and corpses littered the grass.

"Next round!" Winter shouted. More prisoners stepped forward, weapons at the ready. Winter motioned for the combat to begin once more, but this time, as she did so, she rode out again into the gap between her army and the fighting prisoners.

"Rangers!" she shouted. "See the meaning in the combat before you. Each of these prisoners must conquer, or die. That is exactly the situation each of us faces this day."

She pointed across the river, at the Khalic army. "Khale sends us a regiment of their best soldiers. The army we face represents the people who have persecuted, enslaved, and oppressed us for centuries. They have come to quell our movement, to stop the

Druids, and we as their Rangers, from becoming what we were meant to become.

"We will not allow that. Just as these prisoners must conquer their foes or die, so must we. Today we must find victory, or face death."

The second round of combat ended with a final scream, and Winter motioned for the third to begin.

"Should we find victory today, this will only be the beginning," she promised. "We have not been thrown together without reason. We are tiellans, and we were once glorious. We can find that glory again. But first, we must fight."

Winter drew her sword. "Victory or death!"

The tiellan army raised their weapons. "Victory or death!" they echoed.

"Victory or death!" Winter screamed, as loud as she could.

"Victory or death!" her army responded. "Victory or death!" They shouted it over and over again, through the last round of prisoner combat, and still as the victors were given their weapons, armor, and horses, and sent home, and still as they turned to face their enemy across the river, beginning to advance.

Kyfer gave the order, and the Steel Regiment began crossing the river.

"Tell me again their numbers," Kyfer demanded. He found comfort in numbers.

"Nearly six hundred infantry," Razzo said. "More than one thousand cavalry."

"Their cavalry outnumber ours."

"Their riders cannot equal our heavy horse, General. Our infantry will crush theirs with sheer numbers, and then turn to help our cavalry finish off their riders."

"Do you know what the fighting was about?" Kyfer asked.

"No, General. But it thinned their ranks a bit, and another two hundred soldiers fled. I think we can count that in our favor."

The sight of men fighting one another in seemingly controlled circumstances, directly before a pitched battle, was an odd one. It had put Kyfer out of sorts. And if it had put him out of sorts, it had put many of his soldiers out of sorts, too, despite his attempt to spin it in their favor during his speech. Tiellans had died across the river before the battle had even begun, with no explanation as to why. In theory, that helped Kyfer's cause, but he could not shake the feeling that it would have the opposite effect.

"Yes," Kyfer said grimly. "I hope we can." They did not need much favor, he reminded himself. They had superior numbers— two thousand infantry, more than three times the tiellan foot soldiers, and almost one thousand cavalry. His infantry moved in one block at the center of his formation, while he split his cavalry to either flank. Standard turret positioning, and more than adequate for this battle.

As the infantry began crossing the river, Kyfer frowned. The water reached the waists of most men, and as they neared the center of the river, their chests. "This is the shallowest point you could find?"

"The river is deep," Razzo said. "There's no bridge. This was the best crossing point."

Kyfer did not respond. It did not matter. All he had to do was get his regiment across the river, and then they would decimate the tiellan excuse for an army.

"Genio."

The psimancer pulled his horse up alongside Kyfer's. "Yes, General."

"You are ready to counter their telenic?"

"Of course, General. No tiellan psimancer could stand against a trained Nazaniin warrior."

Kyfer hoped that was true. He, at least, had never seen anyone best a Nazaniin fighter.

Soon it was the officers' turn to cross, and Kyfer spurred his horse into the water. The moment his legs touched the water, the chill took his breath away. He looked at his men on the other side of the river, soaking, many of them visibly shivering, and experienced doubt for the briefest moment. Perhaps he had made the wrong choice. Perhaps he should have let his men eat, perhaps he should have been more cautious about the terrain.

But none of that mattered now. Victory was close. He would grasp it by the end of the day, he was sure of it.

The tiellans did not stand a chance.

Urstadt watched Winter silently. She had not expected what her mistress had done with the prisoners that morning; Urstadt still wondered whether it might have been better to coerce the Cracked Spear into fighting with them, instead of killing half of them and letting the rest go.

"Should we attack them now?" Winter asked. One hand clenched the hilt of her sword, while the other toyed gently with the pouch that contained her *faltira*.

"Do not let your nerves control you," Urstadt said. "Nerves force you to react, when you must act." She could understand Winter's nervousness, but it was not acceptable. Not when Winter commanded the battlefield.

"It is tempting to deviate from a plan when a potential advantage presents itself," Urstadt said. "Sometimes, this is the correct choice, but only when the advantage is clear, or when the only other option is certain defeat. Right now, we have our strategy. We have our forces hidden in the grove. I believe we should adhere to our plan."

"Yes," Winter said. She visibly calmed herself, taking deep breaths.

Soon, the last of the Regiment emerged from the river, dripping wet. A chill wind gusted by, and Urstadt thanked the gods—or the Goddess, or whoever was up there to listen— that their luck was coalescing this day. The chill of the river and the chill of the wind did not bode well for the Khalic forces.

"Now?" Winter asked.

A momentary thrill rushed through Urstadt. Much of her life had been spent protecting Daval and his household, and she had taken pride in that position. But she was a soldier at heart, always had been and always would be. As a Rodenese native, animosity towards Khale was in her blood, her bones. And here she was, about to do battle with the Khalic general, Publio Kyfer.

"Now," Urstadt said.

Winter signaled to a pennant boy nearby, who raised a flag and waved it frantically back and forth. That same flag soon flew throughout Winter's army. It was the signal for her cavalry to charge.

Urstadt had suggested Winter split her cavalry and place them on her flanks, following the Khalic formation. Ideally, Winter's riders would make quick work of the Khalic cavalry, and then turn inward to flank the infantry bloc.

No sooner had the pennants begun to wave than the horns sounded. The shouts of over a thousand riders filled the air as Winter's cavalry rushed to meet the Khalic horsemen.

"Infantry, forward," Winter said.

"Infantry, forward!" Urstadt shouted. Winter had given her command of the infantry; while Winter would still be fighting, she would also be using psimancy, and had not been confident in her ability to both lead and fight at once. Urstadt understood the feeling. Such confidence came with time.

They were in the very middle of the infantry line, at the front. Urstadt was pleased Winter had made that decision. Many commanders chose to govern their forces from the back, and while this had its advantages, it was not the honorable thing to do, or the most effective in Urstadt's opinion.

In order to lead most effectively, one had to fight. One's forces had to *see* her fight.

I do not control myself, Urstadt began to recite to herself as she walked forward at Winter's side.

I do not hold back, hoping my rage and power spare the deserving.

On the flanks, their riders collided with the Khalic cavalry amidst screams and clashing metal.

I do not weep through eternity, nor do I scrape my knees along the floors of time, atoning.

Urstadt looked to Winter, who slipped a frost crystal into her mouth.

The Khalic infantry broke into a run, rushing towards them.

Because I love what I love, and I love all things.

"Ready!" Urstadt shouted.

I destroy all things, just as I create them.

Urstadt fidgeted with the shaft of her glaive. It was a nervous tic, but there was nothing wrong with that. Her hand always steadied the moment she made contact with the enemy.

"Charge!" Urstadt screamed, and broke into a run. The rest of the infantry sprinted forward with her, and then they clashed with the Steel Regiment.

I could not destroy that which I did not first love.

Urstadt rammed her glaive into the nearest Khalic soldier, impaling him with such force that his body lifted up from the ground. She spun, slipping the weapon from the man's corpse, flipping the butt of it around to ram into the face of another man.

And so the circle spirals onward.

The blood of her ancestors took over, and Urstadt was a whirlwind on the battlefield, reciting "Wild Calamity" to herself over and over again as men perished in a radius of death around her.

Winter's *tendra* burst forth, forty at once, each seeking a hold on the armored Khalic infantry. She lifted them high into the air, almost as far as her *tendra* could extend, and then she released them.

The infantry of the Khalic Legion were infamous throughout the Sfaera. They were well-trained, efficient killers, capable of hitting hard and maneuvering swiftly. Winter's force would not win this battle unless they could rout the Khalic infantry, so she directed all of her focus—psimantic and otherwise—towards that end.

She drew her sword as she sprinted behind Urstadt, and then she met the enemy. Winter cut one soldier down immediately, then moved behind Urstadt to stab another soldier who'd been trying to flank her captain. Urstadt wore every inch of her rose-gold armor, and her glaive blurred around her in deadly arcs.

Winter sent out her *tendra* again as she parried a soldier's sword jab, but as she began to lift another group of soldiers into the air, something sliced through a half-dozen of the *tendra* that held them before they even left the ground. She parried another thrust from the soldier, then took *bu-tine* form and buried her blade between his neck and shoulder.

Another force cut through six more of her *tendra*, and the soldiers she'd been lifting only dropped a few rods or so to the ground. The iron taste of blood filled her mouth.

There was another psimancer at the battle.

Suddenly, Nash's voice echoed in her mind. *You must be in complete control of whatever you grip with your* tendra.

She remembered practicing with Nash, how he would attempt to break the grip her *tendra* had on an object. He had succeeded, at first, until she had learned to strengthen her control. But it had been so long since she had interacted with another psimancer, she had almost forgotten that lesson.

Nothing should interfere with your control. Complete and total mastery.

Winter dropped the remaining men she'd lifted, earlier than she'd anticipated, but she needed to reform her grip if she wanted it to be solid. At the same time, she continued to fight by Urstadt's side, maneuvering around soldiers, dodging and parrying, and thrusting her blade through chainmail and flesh.

She sent out fewer *tendra*, gripping roughly half as many as she'd attempted previously, but this time she focused on control.

Once again, she felt a force—the other telenic's *tendra*—attempt to slice through hers, but her own *tendra* held strong. The other telenic sent another attack, a huge force slamming into Winter's *tendra*, but again she held firm.

Complete and total mastery, Nash had said.

Winter lifted the soldiers high into the air and dropped them into the river.

She took a step back to survey the battle. Despite her *tendra*, the Regiment's infantry pushed her own back, away from the river. On the flanks, however, their riders were routing the Khalic cavalry; on the south side, the Khalic cavalry had already broken formation. On the north, the Khalic formation held, but had been pushed back to the river's edge.

If her cavalry continued to dominate, they could eventually turn inward as planned and give aid to the outnumbered infantry.

But the taste of blood was still strong in Winter's mouth, and suddenly she was aware of something in the distance, near the rear of the Steel Regiment. A prickling sensation, as if someone was just about to touch her, but had not yet done so.

Then, a large rock the size of a man's torso rose up in the distance, and sailed directly towards Winter.

She leapt out of the way just in time, but the rock crashed into the Rangers behind her. Two soldiers of the Steel Regiment advanced on her, swords and shields brandished. They, apparently, were used to fighting with a telenic on their side; they hardly looked twice at the large stone and the carnage it had caused behind Winter.

She parried the first soldier's attack, but the second bashed into her with his shield and Winter nearly lost her balance. She recovered just in time to parry another sword attack, but this time simultaneously reached out with a *tendron* and snatched one of the shields from her attacker's arm, smashing it into the man's helmet. She pummeled the shield into him again and again, the metal band around the wooden shield denting the helmet and smashing it inward as the shield splintered. She countered the other soldier's attack with the *bu-shu* form, moving quickly into *bu-fan* to deliver a killing blow.

She'd lost her place in her infantry when she'd leapt forward to avoid the stone the other telenic had thrown, but there was no time to get back in line. Another stone of equal size rose from the Regiment's rear lines—her enemy's *tendra* would be there, lifting it up.

She slammed her *tendra* into the space beneath the rock, and the boulder fell to the ground.

Winter smiled grimly.

The boulder wobbled up again, but Winter stopped the telenic easily; she didn't even have to look this time, finding that her *tendra* seemed able to sense the other telenic's *tendra* of their own accord.

Her riders on the south had engaged the infantry on their southern flank. On the north, while the Khalic cavalry had been pushed to the river, they still held strong.

Time for her surprise.

"Reinforcements!" Winter called.

One of her standard-bearers lifted a blood-red banner. Within seconds, she heard shouting from the grove of trees where Selldor and Rorie had hidden their forces. Two hundred Rangers charged forward, crashing into the Khalic cavalry's northern flank, sending them further into the river. The northern contingent of Khalic cavalry scattered almost immediately, and Winter's reinforcements fell upon the Khalic infantry. Within moments, the Steel Regiment's horns sounded the retreat, and they fled west, plunging back across the river.

Pride swelled within her as the Khalic Legion was routed. She had done it. The tiellans had found victory.

This is only the beginning.

28

Somewhere in Kirlan

As KNOT TRIED TO sleep on the cold stone floor of his cell, his feet and hands both chained to the wall, he shifted and felt something hard between his hip and the stone floor.

With some maneuvering, he managed to reach a few fingers into the hidden pocket in his trousers, and withdrew a small object, roughly the size of his thumb, polished black with a bold blood-red rune carved on its face.

Astrid's voidstone.

Knot stared at it for a long time, wondering if the thing was even real. He'd been unconscious since the moment they captured him in Kirlan until this, his first night in the cell. They'd taken everything from him: his weapons, his belongings, all of his clothing— except his now filthy trousers. Could they truly have overlooked this?

The thought crossed his mind that this was some trick of the Black Matron's making. But it was Astrid's same voidstone, the rune shaped exactly as Knot recalled. He remembered enough about psimancy to know that only two voidstones ever had the same rune, and when they did, they alternated colors—there would be a voidstone with a matching rune to Astrid's, but it would be blood-red with a black rune. No other voidstone with the same rune would function.

Knot rubbed the stone with his thumb and forefinger. It

could be a trick, but to what end? What purpose could the Black Matron have in directing Knot through Astrid's memories? How could she possibly have known Knot would have it?

Whether here by the Black Matron's design or by chance, there was only one way for Knot to find out. He twisted around, looking at his cell door. A small crack of light leaked from the hallway beyond, but there was no movement or sign of anyone visiting him anytime soon.

He took a breath and extended a miniscule *tendron* into the stone, and immediately was transported into the Void-like space —he wasn't sure whether it was truly the Void or not, but he might as well call it that—and then further inward into Astrid's voidstone, her memories spread all around him like little star-lights.

With one *tendron* still connected to the voidstone itself, he extended another towards a cluster of memories he had not yet explored.

Rain fell in heavy sheets, soaking the ground, the trees, and everything Knot could see.

He was on the outskirts of a town, standing outside a small clifftop manor. Knot could see a fjord far below, twisting out toward the ocean. Gray clouds blanketed the sky, casting a shadow over the house, the town, the fjord, and everything in sight.

Knot reached out, wishing he could feel the rain splash heavy on his hand, feel it soak through his clothes and hair, but he felt nothing. He was not a part of this world; he was only an observer.

A girl walked along the muddy dirt road, head hung low and shoulders sagging. Astrid. But she looked different, somehow.

This was not the girl Knot was used to seeing, neither in life nor in these memories. Something about her seemed more tangible here, more real. As Astrid neared the house, she slipped in the mud and fell with a wet smack into the road.

Wearily, Astrid pushed herself up, covered in dark mud. Goddess, she looked so *weak*. But she finally got back to her feet again, now trudging from the road across the grassy field to the manor by which Knot stood. She pounded on the door, once, twice, and the third time it slid open and she collapsed inside.

Knot was immediately transported inside the house. A sharply dressed man in well-fitting dark trousers and overcoat stood in the entryway, frowning at Astrid.

"What in Oblivion is this?" the man demanded. "Who are..."

The man's voice trailed off as his eyes swept over Astrid, and then he let out a sob.

"Lucia?"

The man rushed to Astrid, heedless of the mud, and embraced her.

Lucia? Knot wondered. Astrid had used that name once or twice in his presence, always as an alias. But, as he watched the man hug her, he began to suspect it was not an alias at all.

"Papa?"

Knot's breath caught in his throat at the sound of that word from Astrid's lips.

"I'm here, Lucia. Goddess, are you all right? What happened to you?" The man turned his head. "Bannabus!" he called. "I need you!"

Astrid looked up at her father. "I... I don't remember..."

Another man rushed into the room. "Lord Tarlen, what is—?" When he saw Astrid in her father's arms, he gasped. "Miss... Miss Tarlen..."

"Don't just stand there, Bannabus," Lord Tarlen snapped, "help me with her!" His tone was not one of cruelty, but necessity. This was a man worried about his daughter, and nothing else.

Bannabus rushed to Astrid's side, and together the two men lifted her from the anteroom into a sitting area, where they laid Astrid on a large cushioned couch. As they did, another figure blustered into the room, a woman wearing a servant's apron.

"What is the meaning of all this ruckus?" she asked. "I hardly think—"

She stopped short when she saw Astrid on the couch, her face going pale.

"Goddess rising," she whispered. "Miss Tarlen has returned?"

"Papa, is that you?" Astrid asked, her voice still painfully weak. Knot's heart swelled again in his chest at the sound of the word.

"Yes, Lucia, yes, it's me. It's me! I'm here. Are you all right? Are you hurt?"

Astrid looked down at herself, covered in mud. "I do not believe so. But... but I feel a bit sick."

A smile was slowly spreading across Tarlen's face. "I'm not surprised. You're filthy and you've been out in that terrible storm." He turned to the serving woman.

"Agerta, fetch warm water and clean clothes. And water to drink. And something to eat." Tarlen laughed then, tears streaming down his face. "My little girl is home! Bring everything, bring it all, anything she needs!"

Agerta laughed, too, the sound bubbling up from her. "Should I wake the little lord? And the baby? Both are sound asleep, my Lord, but they will be so happy to see their elder sister returned home..."

Tarlen smiled through his tears. "No," he said, his voice husky, "no, give me a moment with her. Her younger brother and sister will have all the time in the world with her, just... let me have this moment." He leaned down, embracing Astrid, but the girl groaned.

"Papa, not so tight," she whispered. "I feel... quite awful."

"Of course, dear, I am sorry. I am sorry, and I am so *happy* you have returned home."

"Returned?" Astrid asked, looking around her. "Did I leave?"

Tarlen and Bannabus exchanged a glance. A crease of worry dented Tarlen's forehead.

"Yes," Tarlen said slowly, "my dear, you have been gone for more than a month. Goddess, we thought you were dead. You don't remember being gone?"

Astrid shook her head slowly, her eyes roving the room in which she lay. For the first time, Knot noticed how strange her eyes looked. Not glowing, or their typical daytime green, but rather a sickly yellow color.

Agerta arrived back in the room, somehow managing to carry blankets, a tray of food, and two different pitchers of water all at once. Bannabus rushed to help, and they laid out the supplies on a low table near the couch. Tarlen stood, making room for Agerta to tend to his daughter.

"Papa," Astrid whispered, reaching up to him. "I... I feel so sick..."

Tarlen's crease of worry compounded, but he kept his voice jovial. "You'll be feeling right as sunshine soon, my dear, just let Agerta—"

With a deep retching sound, Astrid sat up sharply and vomited dark red liquid all over herself and Agerta.

Agerta looked down at herself, turning slowly to face

Tarlen. If her face had been pale before, it was as white as snow now, contrasting sharply with the dark blood that splattered her once pristine apron.

"My Lord…" Agerta said, still looking down at herself.

"Goddess," Bannabus whispered. "Is it… is it the blood blight?"

Tarlen frowned sharply at Bannabus. "My daughter does not have the blood blight," he said firmly. He continued speaking, but Knot did not hear the words. He was staring at Astrid, now slowly standing behind Agerta. Her own vomited blood covered her mouth and chin, dripping down to mix with the mud all over her body. The weakness that had weighed her body down only moments ago was gone, as was the sickly yellow color from her eyes. While they did not yet glow, they were the bright green Knot was used to seeing.

"No," Knot whispered, already knowing what would happen, knowing it had *already* happened, and that he could not stop it. Bannabus and Tarlen continued to talk, heedless of Astrid as she reached her hands around Agerta's head, and twisted sharply.

The two men stopped talking when Agerta's body hit the floor. Both looked up at Astrid, eyes wide.

"Lucia," Tarlen said, taking one step slowly forward, hands raised before him, "you are sick. You need help."

Astrid looked down.

"So… *thirsty…*" she rasped.

Then, she leapt onto Agerta, and tore a chunk from the woman's neck with her teeth.

Bannabus turned and spilled his own sick on the floor. All Tarlen could do, however, was stare.

When Bannabus had emptied his stomach, his face was pale.

"This is not Miss Tarlen," he said quietly. "This is a daemon."

Tarlen could only shake his head, his mouth moving without sound.

After a few moments, Astrid looked up, her entire face now dripping with blood.

"*Thirsty*," Astrid whispered.

"Lucia, please," Tarlen said, finally finding his voice. "I know you're in there, you—"

Astrid sprang forward with a screech, colliding with Bannabus. The two fell to the ground as Bannabus screamed and Astrid buried her face in his neck.

"Lucia, no!" Tarlen wrapped his arms around his daughter in an attempt to pull her off Bannabus. But she snapped her head back, smashing the back of her skull into Tarlen's face. She elbowed her father, sending him stumbling backwards, and then resumed feeding on Bannabus.

"Lucia!" Tarlen fell to his knees with a sob. "My daughter," he said, more quietly.

Astrid stood, turning to face her father, her entire body a muddy, bloody mess.

"*I'm so thirsty…*" she said, taking a step forward, "*Papa*."

This time, when Astrid said the word, Knot only felt sick.

The worried crease finally left Tarlen's face, however, and he looked at his daughter with nothing but love in his eyes.

"I love you, Lucia," Tarlen said. "I don't know what has happened to you. I don't know why. But I want you to know I love you. It doesn't matter what you are. It doesn't matter where you've been. All that matters is what we do—"

And then Astrid was upon him.

Just as she finished feeding, Knot heard another sound echo within the manor. The cry of an infant.

Should I wake the little lord? And the baby? Knot remembered Agerta saying. *Both are sound asleep, my Lord, but they will be so happy to see their elder sister returned home.*

"*Thirsty…*" Astrid rasped, and began making her way up the stairs toward the sound.

Knot never thought he would be happy to escape through the Void and back into his cell, but he could not move quickly enough. The people in the memory genuinely seemed to have known and cared for Astrid—Lucia—when she was human. And yet she had killed them? She'd seemed disoriented when she'd arrived at the manor, and if Knot had to guess he'd say she'd recently undergone the transition process. But her lethargy and sickness at the beginning could have all been feigned to lure those she once knew into her grasp.

Knot could not think about it any longer. He never wanted to return to that scene again.

As he made his way through the Void, something flickered in the corner of his eye. Knot turned sharply, his spine tingling, but he saw nothing but Astrid's memories.

"Who's there?" he called out, feeling foolish the moment he said it. This was Astrid's voidstone, not the actual Void. No one else could possibly be here.

Knot left the voidstone and the memory behind, returning to the relative comfort of his bare stone cell.

317

INTERLUDE: BROKEN THINGS

The Red Community, northern Maven Kol,
at the base of the Taimin Mountains

THE FLAMES ROSE IN Alain's mind as the king entered the courtyard of the Red Community. He prayed—to what or to whom he did not know—that they would stay there. He hated to think what the king, what Brother Maddagon and everyone at the community might think of him if he had an episode now. His hands shook at the thought, and he cracked his knuckles one by one to hide the motion.

He focused on the tall sandstone walls surrounding the courtyard. A dull red-brown color, worn and weathered, but comforting in their dullness. The walls had once belonged to an abbey that pre-dated the Denomination itself. Rebuilt decades ago, they now housed the Red Community, one of several locations in Maven Kol that accommodated the sick and afflicted. The courtyard itself was bare, not much more than dust, a few trees, and the dried-up remains of what was once a small brook.

The king's carriage moved along a narrow road that split the courtyard in half, from the main gate to another opening in the east wall. The sun blazed down brightly on Alain; he could feel it on his face, baking through the long, dark overcoat he wore despite the heat. He felt exposed, in danger, if he did not have his overcoat on. He felt that way most of the time, really, but taking the coat off only made it worse.

The carriage rolled to a stop, and the driver descended to open the door closest to Alain and the community monks. Then the king descended, his smooth, chiseled jaw clenched as he looked at Alain. His brown skin, like Alain's, shone with sweat. The king's eyes and hair were almost matching shades of gray, the color of the sky before a storm.

King Gainil Destrinar-Kol smiled.

Alain frowned. He had learned to spot when his father was pretending. His father smiled and stared a man in the eye when he lied. When Alain was young, he'd thought his father was just a cheerful person. Now he knew better.

Alain fidgeted as Gainil stood there, smiling. Alain's breathing grew sharper, more rapid, louder and louder in his ears. He began humming a wordless tune, the notes dissonant and unrelated.

Brother Maddagon rested a hand gently on Alain's shoulder, bringing him some measure of comfort. Alain's breathing slowed. He clenched his fists to keep himself from cracking his knuckles again.

Brother Tam, on Alain's other side, walked forward to greet Gainil. Tam's long white robe flowed out behind him.

"Your Majesty, we thank you for gracing our humble community with your presence. Welcome."

Tam led the Red Community, where Alain had spent the last few months of his life. It was supposedly the best of the four communities, but Alain had his doubts about such claims. Other than his friendship with Brother Maddagon, he would take away nothing positive from this place when his time to depart came.

The king stepped forward and gripped Tam's forearm. They conversed in hushed tones as Alain, Brother Maddagon, and the other monks in the courtyard looked on.

Alain did not care much for what his father and Tam were doing. He craned his neck, popped his knuckles again despite himself, and looked at the carriage, wondering whether his father had brought Taira Seco.

"You're ready for this, Alain," Brother Maddagon said, his hand still on Alain's shoulder.

Alain turned. Where Tam was tall and imposing with long white hair, Brother Maddagon was short and round, nearly bald. Where Tam shouted, Brother Maddagon encouraged. Tam never ceased dispensing advice and counsel, while Maddagon knew when to listen, or just sit quietly next to Alain. There was a strength in Brother Maddagon's eyes that Alain had never found in Tam's.

"We both know how impervious I am to your lessons," Alain said quietly.

"Daresay we do," Maddagon said with a soft chuckle. "We both know how obstinate I am in giving them, anyway."

The corner of Alain's mouth twitched upwards, a brief ray of calm shining in his mind.

Brother Tam turned back to Alain and the ray of calm disappeared. "Good news, my boy. Your father has come to take you home."

A soft groan escaped Alain's lips. A few months had not been enough time.

"I'm not going."

Gainil's face darkened, just for a moment, before his smile returned. "You've at least made some progress here, I see. You may develop a backbone, yet. Fortunately, I prepared for this."

He turned back to the carriage. "Lady Taira," he called, "Brother Tam informs me it is safe for you to see your betrothed."

Alain's heart twisted. Gainil had brought her.

The carriage door opened slowly and Taira stepped down, as regal as Alain had ever seen her. She was tall, nearly to Alain's shoulder, and he towered at least a head over everyone else in the dusty courtyard except his father. Her black hair was pulled back in braids, which made her look older than Alain remembered, but it showed off her high cheekbones and striking blue eyes—an uncommon feature among the people of Maven Kol.

Alain cracked his knuckles again, humming tunelessly as she approached. Then Taira shifted, her face tilting, and Alain saw the scars.

Rough, discolored webs and wrinkles stretched down her right cheek, along her jaw, and into the neckline of her dress. The contrast against the smooth brown of the other side of her face made Alain want to run, and never look back. Not because of how she looked—Taira looked beautiful, scars or no—but because he was the one who had caused them.

I cannot do this. Each breath tore through him, and the flames rose higher in his mind. What must she think of him? She was here to tell him how much she hated him, surely. And Alain deserved her hatred.

With each jagged breath, the flames rose higher. He took a step back, and the moment he did, the mood in the courtyard changed. The other monks and the king's guards shuffled away from him. Brother Tam and a few other monks reached into their robes. In the community, there were two ways of dealing with a convalescent spiraling out of control: if the person was willing, and if there was time, a powerful concoction of poppy milk and ether would send them into a deep, black unconsciousness. If the convalescent lost control completely or threatened the life of anyone else, there was another option, immediately lethal. Every monk in the community carried a blowpipe and darts for these occasions, and they were well trained.

Taira took a step back from him, eyes wide in horror. Even the king flinched, one arm rising to cover his face.

Brother Maddagon, the only person who did not move away or reach into his robe, squeezed Alain's shoulder.

"You can do this," Brother Maddagon said.

The panic did not leave Alain; it bubbled and boiled beneath the surface, threatening to spill over. But the feeling receded, just enough for the flames in his mind to recede along with it.

"Deep breaths, son," Maddagon said quietly.

Alain obeyed. His breathing evened out somewhat, and he unclenched fists he could not remember clenching in the first place.

"You see," Brother Tam said with a smile, one hand still inside his white robe, "we have made incredible progress. I believe he is ready."

Ready? Alain thought. He'd almost lit the community courtyard, and everyone in it, on fire just now. He was far from ready.

Then, Taira was in front of him.

I can't do this, I can't do this, I can't face her, I—

She reached up, touching Alain's cheek, and a chill ran through his entire body.

"Is it really you?" she asked. She sounded more suspicious than hopeful, but after what he had done to her, and her parents, he could hardly believe she would touch him at all.

He was grateful for it.

Just the sight of her overwhelmed him, made it difficult to think. His father's presence, the danger Alain himself presented— everything made it difficult to think. So much could go wrong, and it would take only seconds for him to threaten—or destroy— the lives of every single one of these people.

"It's him, close enough. Aren't you going to introduce us, boy?" asked Brother Maddagon.

Alain blinked, his hands unmoving at his sides. *I can't do this.*

He did it anyway. "Taira, this is Brother Maddagon. He is my mentor. He has been like a..." Alain glanced at his father, unsure of what to say. "He has been a great teacher. Brother Maddagon, this is Lady Taira. She is the heiress of House Seco, and my intended." Saying her family name brought her parents—and what he had done to them—to mind again. He could still smell the burning flesh, feel the panic in the Decision Room. Alain shut his eyes in an attempt to escape his thoughts.

When he opened them again, he saw Brother Maddagon bowing deeply. "It is a great pleasure, my Lady."

Taira smiled, looking from Alain to Brother Maddagon. For a moment Alain feared she might not say anything, that she might not acknowledge the man who had all but saved Alain's life these past few months.

"Well met, Brother," Taira said, and relief rushed through Alain. But the relief was short-lived, as Taira turned her gaze back to Alain.

"Will you come home with us?" she asked him.

I can't do this.

"I..." Alain glanced from Taira to his father, then over his shoulder to Brother Maddagon.

"Might I have a moment with the boy?" Brother Maddagon asked.

"Of course," the king said, nodding.

Brother Maddagon led Alain a few paces away from everyone else.

"I can't go back," Alain said immediately. "Not yet. I'm not ready. I'm still broken."

"We're all broken, Alain. The whole point of living is to accept that."

Alain shifted his weight from one foot to the other. He was broken, there was no denying that, but it was not a condition he could afford to accept. "I must be made whole."

Brother Maddagon sighed. "I suppose your intentions do not matter as much as your methods," he mumbled. Alain was about to ask what that meant when Maddagon continued. "Do you remember what I've told you about making amends?"

"It's about more than making up for what you've done," Alain said immediately. It was something Maddagon had engrained into him. "It's about living a decent life, and helping those around me."

"You have a chance to make amends to Taira, boy," Maddagon said. "You can show her how your life is changing—how *you* are changing. And, Goddess willing, you might be able to help her, too."

Alain rolled his eyes.

Maddagon snorted. "Don't get petulant with me about the Goddess," he said. "Beggars cannot be choosers, boy. You need a power greater than yourself. Be grateful there's one around who cares."

Alain glanced back at Taira. She was looking at him, eyes hooded, waiting patiently.

Broken things were broken things. Worthless, only good for discarding. He needed to be made whole. He needed to be fixed. Perhaps this was the best way to go about that.

I can't do this. I can't.

"I'll go," Alain said.

Maddagon smiled. Brother Tam, the king, and Taira narrowed their eyes at him.

"What was that, son?" the king asked.

Alain cleared his throat. "I said I'll go." Just saying it gave him the slightest ray of hope. It was enough to keep the flames at bay. He prayed—to whoever would listen—that he would be able to remember what he'd learned at the community.

Mavenil

The carriage ride back was awkward. Alain had never been much of a conversationalist. Never cared for small talk, and he certainly had no idea what to say now.

Both Alain and Taira jumped as Gainil slammed his fist against the carriage wall.

"You will stop that humming," Gainil said, glaring at Alain. "I don't want to hear it."

Alain stopped immediately. Another one of his nervous tics. He had not realized he'd been humming at all. Taira must think him a fool.

Alain made every effort not to move, speak, or make any sound at all for the rest of the carriage ride.

Dusk had fallen when they finally arrived in the city. Mavenil, the capital city of Maven Kol, was an anomaly in the desert. The sight of the sandstone buildings, the clay and thatched rooftops, shaded a dark blue in the evening light, made Alain happy. He had missed the city. He'd missed the dust of the streets, the light on the buildings. He'd missed the scarab statues of House Destrinar that now rose high above them. And even at dusk, Mavenil was full of sound. People shouted and argued, animals neighed, bayed, and howled. The noise was a welcome distraction from the silence that weighed heavy between Alain, Taira, and Gainil.

From outside of the carriage, a deafening explosion shattered the silence. One of the scarab statues Alain had been staring at burst into flames, so loud and so hot Alain felt it and heard it all at once, and just like that his own internal fire engulfed his mind. One moment he was looking up at the massive scarab statues, then came a loud crash and a wave of heat, and his thoughts collapsed inward. His mind took him back to a memory of the palace, of screaming and the smell of burning flesh.

Alain fought the panic, fought the feeling that threatened to claw its way out of him. He closed his eyes, using one of the tricks Brother Maddagon had taught him, and began to count. He concentrated on his breathing. Nothing happened at first, but when he got to twenty, the flames in his mind began to diminish. By the time he reached fifty, they were only sparks. At sixty-seven, they were gone.

Alain opened his eyes to see the carriage turned over on its side, engulfed in flames. He lay outside of the carriage, Taira at his side, and flames surrounded them both. Real flames, Alain realized. These were not just in his mind.

Had he caused this?

His head spun. He couldn't remember whether their carriage entered the city through the market gate or the dust gate. The buildings around them didn't look familiar through the flames.

People screamed, and Gainil's guards—the Scarabs—ran back and forth, but Alain could not see his father anywhere. Already safe somewhere, no doubt. He could not stop the bitterness in his thoughts. Gainil was king, after all, and he needed protection first and foremost. But if he weren't king, Alain knew that would not change.

"Alain!" Taira shook him frantically. Alain had no idea how long she had been calling his name.

"My Lord, my Lady, you both must come with me. Now." A Scarab, one of his father's guards, rushed up to them through the smoke. Alain recognized him as Captain Fedrick, only a few years Alain's senior. They'd known one another since they were young.

"We need to get you both to safety," Fedrick said.

Alain and Taira stood, but Alain stumbled, still disoriented. The fire around them was not as bad as the inferno in his mind had made it seem. In addition to knocking the carriage over and raining fire down on the street, the exploding scarab statue had also ignited the buildings behind it. Alain could not discern whether the structures were businesses or apartments or brothels or something else altogether, and even if he could, he was unsure whether he would be able to process it.

Once the three of them made it to a blissfully flameless alley, Taira turned to face Alain. "A Trigger did this," she said.

"I'm sorry," Alain said, shaking his head. "I—"

"It wasn't you," Taira said emphatically.

Alain stared at her. How could Taira possibly know what had caused the explosion? He popped his knuckles, fingers fidgeting. "If it wasn't me," he said slowly, "then who was it?"

"I know it was not you, son."

He turned to see his father approaching, surrounded by

a half-dozen Scarabs. The king walked with a slight limp, but otherwise appeared unharmed.

He cannot be sure either. No one can. You caused this as much as anyone.

Gainil walked up to Alain, until they stood facing one another. Alain had not been this close to his father since... since long before the Madness began. "I've feared an attack like this for some time, now. That is part of the reason I brought you back." Gainil looked over his shoulder. "This is not the place for us to discuss this. We must get back to the palace."

"Tell us what's going on," Taira demanded as they entered the Decision Room of the royal palace. Alain was grateful for her in that moment, even if she did not say it for his sake. Taira's life had been threatened just as much as anyone else's, and she had a right to know.

Fedrick stood at the entrance, while Gainil swept around the large square table. "I will, in time," he said. "But first, there are a few introductions to be made."

Alain and Taira turned to see a woman walk into the room. He had never met this woman before, and that made him nervous.

He clenched his fists. He'd felt some form of anxiety and fear every moment of his life, for as long as he could remember. But sometimes it spiked inside of him, bubbling up in his chest. It was a feeling very much like excitement, but imbued with a dark dread. A tight, fluttering feeling in his chest, constricting his heart and his gut. Since the Madness, his anxiety had also been accompanied by rising flames in his mind—flames that threatened to reach out and become reality.

"Alain, this is Lailana," Gainil said. "My wife."

Alain had to physically restrain himself from humming as

hc stared at the woman. Of course. He had received a letter informing him of his father's marriage.

"*Alain.*"

Alain coughed. "I am sorry." He bowed to Lailana, bending at the waist. "I am grateful to meet you." Now she thought him a fool, too, and Taira surely even more so.

"Now," Gainil said, "I must tell you why—"

"Did somebody start a party without inviting me?"

A second person Alain had never seen before strode into the Decision Room. A man, handsome and clean-shaven, with pale skin, golden-blonde hair, and a smirk on his face. Anxiety spiked within him again, the dark feeling tightening around his insides, threatening to obstruct his breath. It was immediately relieved, just in the slightest, when he saw the annoyed look on his father's face. The king was not used to being interrupted.

Anyone who got under his father's skin couldn't be that bad.

"My apologies, your grace," Fedrick said. "I told our guest to wait outside, but he insisted on being part of this meeting."

"Not a problem," Gainil said, though the way his mouth turned down said otherwise. "He probably should be here, after all. This concerns him."

This man approached Alain and Taira. He bowed, though he bent only at the neck. "Prince Alain Destrinar-Kol, I presume. The pleasure is all mine."

Alain cracked his knuckles, and shook the man's hand. His grip was strong.

"Code Fehrway. I assume your father has told you why I'm here?"

"I was just getting to that," Gainil said.

Code grinned. "I arrived just in time, then." He turned to

Taira and bowed. "My Lady. I'm happy to see you again."

"And I you," Taira said with a genuine smile. A smile Alain wished she might give him.

"Very well then," Code said, straightening. He strode to the square table at the front of the room, sat himself down at one of the chairs, and kicked his feet up on the table.

Alain's breathing quickened just watching the man. His appreciation for Code would clearly be short-lived; his father would never stand for such behavior. Not from anyone other than himself.

But Gainil only cleared his throat. "Alain, Code is a representative of the Citadel."

Code's smile widened. "His Majesty is being coy. I'm a Nazaniin agent, Alain. I've come to investigate these reports of Madness, as you all like to call it." He met Alain's eyes apologetically. "I am sorry to hear of your own suffering, Your Highness. You have my sympathy."

Something inside Alain told him he didn't. While people rarely referred to the Nazaniin publicly, all nobles knew of their existence. And "agents" was not the name generally used for people of that particular order. The Nazaniin were assassins. What business their organization could possibly have in Maven Kol, Alain could not guess.

"I assume you are aware of events in Roden?" Code asked, looking at the king.

"The empire is clearly a waning power," Gainil said. "Two dead emperors in the space of a year, and religious and civil unrest among its people."

Code snorted. "Unrest. Accurate enough, but there are some details that have not been revealed to the… the general public, shall we say?"

Gainil's brow furrowed. "Such as?"

Again, Alain felt a thrill of satisfaction at his father's discomfort.

Code's smile returned, and he spread his arms wide. "The Rising of the Nine Daemons, of course."

Taira gasped. Lailana, who had moved to stand next to Gainil, looked strangely calm, but Gainil laughed.

Alain's elation died immediately with Code's words, and flames rose in his mind. A clamp of terror squeezed his entire abdomen. The Nine Daemons. Impossibly powerful monsters of legend, returning to the Sfaera. Such silly Cantic lore could not be true. And yet, Alain could manipulate fire with his own Madness. Who was to say what was true anymore?

Alain hummed tunelessly, and began to count.

"You expect us to believe such nonsense?" Lailana said.

Code shrugged. "Believe me or not, I don't care. You asked why I'm here, and I'm telling you."

"No one believes tales of the Nine anymore. They are stories told to children to scare them into going to bed."

"'Anymore' might be the key word you just uttered," Code said. "Just because no one believes the stories doesn't mean they aren't true."

Alain only had to count to twenty-seven this time before the flames receded.

"What do the Daemons have to do with us?" Gainil asked.

Alain's eyes latched onto his father. The man's eyebrows were knitted together. *He is afraid to order this man around*, Alain realized. He had never seen such a thing.

"Have you heard of Nadir?" Code asked. "The Daemon of Insanity?"

"Who?" Gainil asked.

"You didn't pay attention much at the Citadel when you were a student there, did you? Each of the Nine Daemons has an accompanying vice. Azael, the chief Daemon, feeds upon fear. Mefiston on wrath, Iblin on greed, Bazlamit on deception, and so on. Nadir feeds on insanity."

Gainil scoffed. "You can't possibly believe that is what's happening here."

Code's feet swung down from the table, and he leaned forward, glaring at Gainil. For the first time since Alain had met the man, he seemed deadly earnest.

"I just came from an island where the dead rose to consume the living, and it was all because of one of the Nine. So, quite honestly, I don't care what you believe. But I'm here to investigate Nadir, and her involvement in this Madness. You can help me or not. I don't much care."

Silence reigned in the Decision Room.

Alain shifted his weight. He wanted to say something. He cracked his knuckles. "You still haven't told me what caused that explosion, Father."

Gainil glared at Code a moment longer, then met Alain's eyes.

"Of course. It will be good for the Nazaniin to hear this, too. It concerns the strange phenomena occurring lately within our borders."

Gainil walked up to the map, which portrayed the city of Mavenil. "You remember the Denizens?" he asked, looking at Alain.

"A group of commoners who conspired to bring about political change in Maven Kol." They'd started stirring up trouble a few months before the Madness began.

"Political change?" Code asked.

"They want to emulate Khale's republic," Alain said.

"Ah." Code nodded. "They want to get rid of you monarchs."

"More or less," Gainil said. "Their influence has increased. They've even won some of the lesser houses over to their cause."

Taira gripped Alain's hand. "They've done some terrible things, Alain. They don't care who they hurt in their attacks."

Alain's breathing picked up the moment Taira touched him. She seemed to recognize it, and let go of his hand slowly.

"What does this have to do with me?" Alain asked, tearing his attention away from Taira. "Why did I need to come back now?"

"They've recruited some Triggers to their cause," Gainil said. "And, as you saw earlier this evening, they are willing to use them as weapons."

"They've broken the treaty," Alain said quietly.

"Hold on a minute," Code said. He sat back in the chair, and once again placed his feet upon the table. Gainil's face darkened.

"You're going to need to go through some of this with me," Code continued. "Triggers? Treaty? What are you talking about?"

"Triggers are what we call those who have been touched by the Madness," Taira said. "Alain is a Trigger."

"And what makes him a Trigger, exactly? He's a bit crazy, I get that. Anything else?"

Alain flexed his fingers, then cracked each knuckle.

"When the Madness touched him, it had a certain... a certain side effect," Taira said. Her hand touched the scars on her neck. "This manifests differently in every Trigger, but Alain can... he could... he *does*—"

"I can manipulate fire," Alain said quickly. He could not bear to hear Taira stumble over it any longer. "The more out of control I feel, the more powerful the flames become."

"You can manipulate fire," Code repeated, eyes narrowed at Alain. He folded his hands behind his head, leaning back even further into the chair. He glanced at Taira. "That seems a powerful ability."

"It is powerful," Alain said, "but not effective or useful. The more powerful I become, the less in control of myself and my powers I really am."

Code grunted. "I might understand a thing or two about that," he said, turning back to Taira. "You mentioned other effects? What are they?"

"The magic involved is elemental," Taira responded. "Some can manipulate the wind, others water or earth. And, of course, fire, but only those four. At least that's what we've observed so far."

"And the treaty you mentioned?"

"A treaty signed by every noble family, and many other people of import in the kingdom as well, to refrain from using Triggers as weapons. They are too unstable. Everyone agreed to sign."

"*Everyone?*" Code asked. "In the whole kingdom?"

"I'll rephrase that," Gainil said. "Everyone of any *import* agreed to sign."

"But now someone is breaking that treaty."

"Yes," Gainil said. "Our spies tell us it is the Denizens, and the small houses who've joined them. They grow more powerful, and threaten our very way of life. They want to destroy the high nobility and all we represent."

Would that be such a bad thing? Alain wondered. His father was a shrewd leader, but he would never put the needs of the people before his own.

Lailana stepped forward, locking eyes with Alain. "That is why we have brought you back, Alain. We want you to help us in our fight against the Denizens."

"Help how? By breaking the treaty?"

"The treaty is already broken, Alain. You are the only hope we have to defend ourselves."

Alain looked to his father. "Is this true? This is why you brought me back?" *Not because you care for me. Not because you think I'm ready.*

Because you need a weapon?

He could say none of that, however. His father would outspeak him anyway, embarrass him in front of all these people.

"I need your help, son," Gainil said.

Tentatively, carefully, Taira reached out and grasped Alain's hand once more. "*We* need your help." Then, more quietly, she whispered, "If you will not do it for him, do it for me, Alain. Please."

Alain met Taira's eyes.

Making amends is about living a decent life, and helping those around me.

"I'll help," Alain said. But he said it to Taira, not his father.

As Alain left the Decision Room, he worried about the choice he had just made. The first task his father had given him was to infiltrate the lower noble houses that had aligned themselves with the Denizens—to gain their trust. Alain had agreed to attend a noble ball the night after next to do just that. The strain in Gainil and Alain's relationship was not unknown to the nobility, and his status as a Trigger would make him a valuable asset to the movement.

A small part of Alain wanted to laugh. His father clearly did not know him well enough if he thought Alain would be remotely effective at "infiltrating" and "ingratiating" himself into anything. But fear overcame a much larger part of him. He'd barely turned the corner in the hallway when he had to stop and put both hands on the wall to steady himself.

Flames rose higher and higher in his head.

Alain swore. He hated the stupid counting tactic, but it was one of the few that worked for him, as long as he caught himself early enough.

Alain had gotten as high as fifty-four, and the flames were just beginning to recede, when someone said his name.

He opened his eyes to see Code standing next to him.

"You all right, mate?"

Alain blinked.

"I'll be fine," he said, somewhat caught off guard by Code's informality. Caught off guard, but strangely calmed by it, as well. It felt good to not be called "Your Highness" for once.

"Can't say I blame you. I wouldn't be too happy if I were in your place. You got the short end of the stick in more ways than one."

"Maybe," Alain said, "but I have amends to make."

Code raised one eyebrow. "Amends? What manner of amends?"

"I caused great harm when I first fell to the Madness. I've got to do something about that."

"Were you normal before?" Code asked. "Before the Madness, I mean."

Normal? A crack of fear opened in his chest. He hated talking about his problems.

"I've always been nervous, if that's what you mean," Alain

said. "But it got worse after the Madness. The whole thing with the fire didn't help."

"No, I can't imagine it did," Code said. "I'm sorry, mate."

Alain didn't say anything. He didn't want to make an ass of himself in front of this man.

"You aren't one for words, I see that. I do have a few questions for you, though, if you don't mind."

Alain wanted to leave this man without another word. He actually liked Code, but between his hasty departure from the community, the Trigger attack in the city, and navigating his treacherous relationship with his father, Alain wanted more than anything to be alone and to find some semblance of peace. But he did not dare refuse the request of a Nazaniin. Not unless there was a profoundly good reason to do so.

"Go ahead," Alain said. "Talk." He turned to lean his back against the wall, pressing the back of his head into the stone.

"I might know how to stop the Madness from spreading," Code said.

Alain opened his eyes. "There's a cure?"

"Not a cure. But if what is happening here is anything like what happened on Arro, then the Madness has a source. In Alizia, there was a source. Once we removed that, the nightmare stopped. I'm hoping the same will be true here as well. More or less."

Not a cure, but an end of sorts. Perhaps the nightmare could be stopped here, as well. If he could help bring an end to the Madness that plagued Maven Kol, perhaps Taira would look at him with a genuine smile on her face. Perhaps his father would respect him.

And, in his heart of hearts, Alain hoped he might finally be rid of the anxiety that had crippled him his entire life.

"What kind of source?" Alain whispered.

"In Alizia, it was a man. The avatar of the Daemon Hade. It must be the same here. Nadir has found herself an avatar. The Madness must be spreading from there."

"There are thousands of people in Mavenil; millions in Maven Kol. How are we to find the avatar?"

"That's where I could use your help," Code said.

Why does everyone suddenly need my help? Alain wondered. It was all too much; most convalescents worked up to their re-entry into society gradually, taking things one step at a time. Alain, in contrast, felt he was being thrown headfirst down a long flight of stairs.

But if he could stop the nightmare, wouldn't it be worth it?

"You haven't had any… any sort of strange communication lately, have you?" Code asked.

Alain blinked. *All* his communication was strange. "What do you mean?"

"I mean something like voices in your head. Voices that talk to you, try to get you to do things."

"Are you really asking a madman whether or not he hears voices in his head?"

That, at least, got a chuckle out of Code. "Guess I am. I didn't think you were the type to hear voices, though. Was I wrong about that?"

"You weren't wrong."

"Didn't think so."

"Then why did you ask?"

Code's smile faded. "Because some voices are real," he said.

"You mean this Daemon, Nadir, might try to talk to me?"

"It's a possibility. Based on what I've seen, that's how it works."

"You said you'd seen the dead rise. Where was this? When?"

Code took a deep breath and leaned his back against the wall, alongside Alain. "A few months ago. On Arro Isle."

"Arro Isle," Alain murmured. A small resort island, part of Alizia. "You were victorious?"

Code's eyes darted away, just for a moment. "Don't know whether or not you can call it a 'victory.' But we stopped the nightmare, like I said."

Alain didn't say anything to that.

"I'd like you to help me," Code said after a moment.

"Help you how?"

"You're affected by all this. By Nadir's influence. More so than anyone I've yet had contact with."

"So you want me to tell you what it's like?"

Code looked surprised. "No," he said. "I want you to help me find the bitch. Kill her, too, if we can."

"I'm already helping my father," he said. *I'm already helping Taira.*

"You can do both. Wouldn't surprise me if they intertwined a bit, and if they don't... Oblivion, your father can have priority, that's fine. I'd just like a bit of help now and again. You spoke about making amends before. No better way to go about it than this."

Amends. It all seemed to come back to amends, recently. Whether the term would actually ever have any meaning to him, Alain didn't know.

But if he could stop the nightmare, maybe he could do more than make amends. Maybe he could finally be made whole, and live a normal life.

"I'll help you," he said.

Code smiled. "Wonderful."

* * *

Leave it to Alain's father to hold a ball the day after an attempt on his own life. There was a reason for it, of course—Alain needed to make contact with the Denizens—but the ostentatious gesture was typical of his father.

Nevertheless, Alain could not help but look up in awe at the Great Hall of the royal palace. Long stained-glass windows depicting feats of strength and heroics of House Destrinar lined the east wall, almost reaching from floor to ceiling. Tall granite arches rose up over each window, supporting the massive rafters above. Tapestries covered the west wall, huge woven depictions of the history of Maven Kol, and particularly the Destrinar role—both glorious and profound, according to the tapestry.

Knowing his father, Alain could not help but suspect that the tapestries exaggerated more than a few things.

In the middle of the hall a fountain rose from the marble. Crystal-clear water cascaded down three tiers of circular wells, each reflecting light from the windows. The three wells represented the three tiers of Maven Kol: the top well was the royal family. Alain's family. The middle well represented the nobility, serving as vassals to the royal house and intermediaries to the last tier, the commoners.

Alain walked past the fountain, past lords and ladies in formal suits and extravagant gowns, past the king near his throne, silver crown high on his head, and straight to a group near the large entrance to the Great Hall. A group he would never have associated with normally, but one he needed to contact nonetheless.

His reminiscing had allowed him a brief escape, but now that he approached the entire reason his father had held this ball in the first place, he popped his knuckles. Sweat dripped down his spine, cold and indifferent. Inescapable fear trailed his every step; a dozen scenarios raced through his mind, each one demonstrating how this mission his father had given him could go wrong.

"Alain."

He turned to see Taira approaching him, a smile on her face. She wore a sleek, flowing yellow dress, draped perfectly over her body. The neck was open, showing more of her scars than Alain had yet seen. A flash of shame flooded through him, and once again he wanted to run.

I can't do this, he thought to himself. *I cannot be around her.*

"Hello," he said instead, popping knuckles. Goddess rising, he wished he did not have to do that. Such stupid tics must be obvious to everyone around him.

"I am glad you came," she said. She stopped in front of him, close but without contact. She raised a hand, perhaps to take his, but froze before they touched.

"Is it... is it all right if I take your hand?" she asked.

Alain stared at her, surprised. No one had ever considered him enough to ask something like that before. The flames in his mind receded just a touch.

"I... I suppose it is," he stammered.

As her fingers entwined with his own, his heart hammered within his chest. Part of that was good, it had to be. But so much of it was his own inadequacy, his own fear and worry that something could go wrong, that this was all some elaborate joke or scheme, that Taira actually did not like him at all. The thoughts threatened to overwhelm him.

"Let me introduce you to some people," she said, and led him to a group that stood near the fountain. Away from the lesser nobles that Alain was here to infiltrate. At least here, Taira could help him, but Alain's mind still screamed in protest. He had a task to accomplish; he had to do as his father ordered, for her sake. He wished he could express his thoughts to Taira properly, but forming them in his mind and throat was as impossible as pouring the desert sands into a glass.

"Alain, this is Kairin Traxus, Erain Gilbern, and Hannail Koln. They've become good friends of mine over the past year or so—"

"I've met them before," Alain said, glancing at Taira. "I've met each of you before. Before the Madness, I mean."

Taira gave a quick laugh. "Of course you did. Silly of me to forget."

"Your Highness," Kairin said—a petite woman, with a wide, inviting smile. "I am happy to see you again. I trust the past few months have treated you well?"

"Well enough, thank you."

"You look well, Your Highness," Hannail said.

Alain bowed his head in gratitude. "Thank you," he said.

"I trust your time away was... helpful?" Erain asked.

Alain smiled, but said nothing to that. What did one say, after all? Alain expected his time at the Red Community—and the reasons behind it—to be more or less common knowledge among the nobility. *Congratulations on knowing my business*, Alain wanted to say. Of course he didn't. Instead, he cracked his knuckles until Taira placed her hand over his, giving him an awkward smile. Alain's cheeks grew hot.

A few moments of uncomfortable silence trudged past, and Alain felt his control begin to slip.

He could not have an anxiety attack here. Not now.

"There was a time where you could host balls and no one went crazy and no one burst into flames," Alain said with a forced chuckle.

The others stared at one another.

Immediately he berated himself. How could he say something like that in front of Taira? Humor had never been his strong point, but this was hopeless. How did his father expect him to accomplish anything worthwhile tonight?

Taira, however, did not seem to mind. A small frown creased her face, but she squeezed his hand anyway, calming the raging fears inside him.

"Did someone... have an incident tonight?" Hannail asked, finally breaking the awkward silence.

Alain's eyes widened. "No! No, er... it was just a..." Alain trailed off, completely lost.

Taira grabbed him by the arm. "Good seeing you all," she said. "There's someone Alain should meet."

She led Alain away before their goodbyes dissipated.

Alain cleared his throat. "Taira, I'm so sorry," he said. He was supposed to be making amends, not jokes. He should have known better than to speak up.

"How is your assignment going?" Taira asked. Clearly, she did not want to talk about what had just happened. Alain did not blame her. The tight, fluttering feeling was back, clamping around his insides.

"I was just about to introduce myself when you found me."

Taira stopped, releasing his hand. "You haven't spoken with them yet?"

"I..." Alain could not form the words to respond. The darkness constricted further around his chest and stomach.

"You should have told me. I wouldn't have wasted your time." Taira looked around, then leaned in close to whisper, "Do your duty before the Denizens leave. Otherwise we'll have to wait until the next event on the social calendar to make another attempt."

Alain's breathing picked up, his heart racing. He had to get away. He would not lose control again, not in public.

"I'll get it done," he choked out, then walked away without a backward glance at Taira. He would not put her in danger, not again.

Alain struggled to maintain even breaths as he stumbled to the edge of the Great Hall. Between a few of the stained-glass windows, doors opened onto balconies that overlooked the city. He managed to make his way to one of these, leaving the cacophony of the ball behind him, and leaned heavily on the stone railing. The flames were high in his mind, but that wasn't the worst of it. The air began to spark around him.

He started to count.

Alain lived his entire life in varying states of terror, worry, and anxiety, but when a full-blown attack occurred, those feelings magnified a thousandfold. He feared everything— what had gone wrong in the past, what occurred in any given moment, and of course what could happen in the future—but most of all, he was afraid of the fear itself. He was constantly treading water, and the only thing between himself and sheer hysteria was his own willpower.

Right now, his willpower was drowning quickly.

"I'm here if you need me."

Alain spun around, backing up against the balcony, and a flash of orange flame ignited in front of him. The brightness, in contrast to the dark city, blinded him for a moment, and he blinked through the pain to see Taira standing there, at the balcony entrance.

No, not Taira, Alain realized as his vision stabilized.

"I can't... I can't breathe," Alain gasped. He was at two hundred and sixty-four in his head now, but the numbers did not seem to matter when he could not even draw breath.

"I know how you feel," the woman said. She took a step forward.

She did not flinch. The thought passed through Alain's mind like a lark through the palace gardens in the early morning. *She did not flinch, despite the flame I ignited directly in front of her.*

Somehow, that was a small comfort.

"I'll wait here with you until it's over," she said. "If you like. This will pass, like all things."

Alain slumped down against the railing. He could not speak.

At seven hundred and eighty-nine, the flames had finally died down.

Alain looked up. The woman was still there, a few paces away, looking down at him. Dark hair, and dark brown eyes to match. A violet dress, though it seemed slightly too big on her small frame.

"I told you it would pass," the woman said. She was young, perhaps of an age with Alain himself. In her nineteenth, maybe twentieth year.

Alain flushed with embarrassment. "I am sorry you had to see that."

The woman snorted. "I've seen a lot worse." She looked at him, expressionless, but there was a sadness in her eyes Alain could not escape. He wished, immediately, that there was something he could do to help this woman, but knew the thought was ridiculous the moment it entered his head.

Alain wanted to ask how, why, where she had seen worse, but he'd only just gotten himself under control. He could not risk losing that again.

"You're pretty," the woman said. "If I weren't betrothed, I'd think about courting you myself."

Alain stared. He'd never been spoken to in that way, let alone in public.

The woman stepped up to him, touching him on the cheek. Taira had touched him that way, at the community. And yet there was something different between that and this.

Alain stood quickly, and sidestepped away. She was beautiful, that much was easy to admit, but he could do nothing of the sort with her. He was tied to Taira, and owed her his fidelity along with a great deal more.

The woman's eyes turned down the moment Alain stepped away.

"Fine," she said. "I'll see you in Oblivion."

She turned on her heel and stalked back into the Great Hall.

Alain stood there, blinking. One moment the woman had been perfectly kind, comforting him, and the next...

What in Oblivion just happened?

Alain blinked. Music from inside the Great Hall drifted out to him.

He rushed back inside, looking for the group of nobles he needed to contact. Panic threatened to rise in him again when he saw they no longer occupied the space by the entrance to the Great Hall, but after searching the room he saw them, lingering by the three-tiered fountain.

Alain took a deep breath.

This is for Taira, he told himself. *I must make amends.* He would do it for her, without question.

"Good evening," Alain said as he approached. Flames licked the edge of his vision, but he did his best to ignore them. He had to, if it meant doing what he could for Taira.

A tall man with dark hair, almost as tall as Alain, responded first.

"Evening, Your Highness," he said, eyeing Alain warily. The others—three other young men—bowed, but said nothing.

"My name is Alain Destrinar-Kol," Alain said, too late realizing the man had already called him "Highness." Of course they knew his name, who he was. Stupid of him to assume they didn't. The humiliation of such a silly mistake at the very beginning of the conversation almost made him turn and walk away; the flames licking the edges of his mind certainly bid him do as much. It was all he could do to remain where he was.

"I am Sev Sarrton," the man said, bowing once more. House Sarrton was small, but growing more powerful, especially with their connections to the Denizens.

The other three men introduced themselves. Alain had heard of them, but they mattered little. Sev was the man he needed to speak with tonight, if he could find the presence of mind to speak at all.

"What brings you to our circle?" Sev asked.

Alain cleared his throat, about to make his argument, when someone else joined the conversation. A young woman, about Alain's age. Brown hair, brown eyes. Violet dress.

The woman from the balcony.

"Your Highness, this is Morayne Wastrider," Sev said. "She and I are betrothed."

Morayne bowed. "The prince and I have met, Sev," she said.

Sev's eyebrows rose. "Have you? I was unaware."

Alain's cheeks flushed. Surely she wouldn't—

"I told him if I wasn't betrothed, I'd think about courting him myself," Morayne said, her face betraying nothing. Alain was suddenly very aware that he regarded Morayne with the same expression with which people usually looked at him. Alain popped his knuckles, and then had to clasp both hands together to keep himself from wringing them.

"And that he was pretty," Morayne added.

While Sev did not seem happy about Morayne's honesty, he did not seem surprised by it, either. "Goddess rising, Morayne," he said quietly. "We've talked about this. And this is the *prince*, for Canta's sake..."

Alain cleared his throat, and then cleared it again because he couldn't stop himself. "I'm glad we have been properly introduced," he said, and shook Morayne's hand.

"Don't lie to me," Morayne said. "You're shaking hands with a Trigger. You must be scared out of your wits. But, then again—"

"Can we help you, Your Highness?" Sev interrupted.

Alain's gaze lingered on Morayne, then he turned back to Sev. "You can." Alain looked over his shoulder for good measure. They needed to believe every word he was about to say. He hushed his voice to a whisper. "I'm interested in the Denizens."

Sev looked puzzled. "The Denizens? Your Highness, why in the Sfaera would you want to learn more about such a deplorable lot?"

"I'm not looking to learn," Alain said. "I'm looking to join them."

There it was. Alain hoped his bluntness would get through to them; if it didn't, he had no other cards to play.

"Your Highness, such words are dangerous. Some would say treasonous, even for you." While Sev's face remained unreadable, two of the other noblemen with him exchanged a glance.

Alain's breathing picked up. This might actually work. Or burn to the ground around him, but there was no turning back now.

"If you knew my father the way I do, you'd understand why

I'd take such a risk." The ease with which the words came to his mouth surprised Alain. Perhaps, he realized, because they were true. If he had not already committed to do this to help Taira, he might actually consider doing exactly what he was saying.

"Enlighten me, Your Highness," Sev said, his eyes locked on Alain's. "What has your father done that would make you want to take such a drastic step?"

Alain could have responded with any number of evidences in that moment. But his skin was hot, the flames burning bright and dangerous in his mind, and the only thing that escaped his lips were quick, shallow breaths.

After a moment, an eternal moment in which the other members of the group did nothing but stare expectantly at Alain, Sev shrugged. "I'm sorry, Your Highness. I should never have asked such a question. The answer would not matter anyway—I could not possibly offer the information you seek. My own house has been attacked by the Denizens recently, and I'm as interested in their downfall as anyone."

No. Alain smiled, but his heart plummeted. He'd had control of the situation; it had been going in his favor only seconds ago. And now, because of his anxiety, because of his own madness, it crumbled around him.

"I did not mean to offend—"

"You did not offend, Your Highness," Sev said quickly. "I am the one who should apologize." He bowed. "The hour grows late. I bid you a good evening."

Sev, Morayne, and the others with them walked away.

Alain had failed.

Alain spent the rest of the evening avoiding everyone he could—especially Taira and his father—as shame built inside him. How could he face them having already let them down? But as the ball ended and nobles filed out of the Great Hall, one of them bumped into Alain, and dropped something into his hand. Alain looked down to see a piece of folded parchment in his palm. He raised his eyes, trying to catch whoever had given it to him, but they were already lost in the crowd. Looking more closely, Alain saw inscribed on one side of the paper a blocky, simple "D."

The Denizens.

He had not seen the face of the person who'd bumped into him, and by now they were long gone. Instead, Alain made his way out of the Great Hall, and into one of the more obscure hallways of the palace. Once he was sure he was alone, Alain opened the parchment. Inside was a note, addressed simply to "A":

If you mean what you say, you will meet us in the Winter's Dream tavern at midnight. Come alone. We will see where your loyalty truly lies.

There was no name or initial at the end of the parchment.

But it was enough. Alain could not help but grin, despite the warring emotions within him. He was elated that his plan had not failed completely. But now he had to go alone to meet whoever had sent him the note, and he was terrified.

At least it was a start.

The tavern was all but empty when Alain walked in. The barkeeper looked up, narrowing his eyes at Alain, then turned his attention back to wiping down the bar.

Alain wore a large cloak over borrowed armor, and a wide-brimmed hat pulled down over his face. Fedrick had secured him the armor—unmarked, with nary a Scarab insignia to be seen. Alain already missed his long overcoat. While the armor and cloak did help, they were not the same as his coat. In any case, he hoped he looked like an off-duty guard, putting his feet up at the local tavern. Fedrick seemed to think the uniform would work well enough. Alain had always avoided the public eye when he could, but he was the crown prince, after all. An astute citizen might recognize him; a noble almost certainly would. The cloak and hat were less a disguise than a deterrent.

Other than the barkeeper, two other people were in the room with Alain. A man, big and burly, glowered in the corner over a mug of ale, and an older woman snored lightly in her chair. Alain had hoped to see Sev, or at least one of the men in his clique at the ball, but the barkeeper and other two were altogether unfamiliar.

Alain walked up to the barkeeper. He felt surprisingly in control of himself. The ever-present panic still simmered in his chest, but was dormant for now.

"What'll you have?" the man grunted.

Alain cleared his throat. "A *sotola*."

"Be a minute," the barkeeper said.

Alain wanted to ask about the Denizens, or say something that might at least drop a hint as to what he was looking for, but he refrained. The note had said they would test his loyalty; best not blab about the Denizens at every opportunity. There was always the chance that this could be a trap; the note could have been a ploy to get him alone to kidnap him, even kill him. Alain's powers had to be attractive to the Denizens, but that wasn't the only use they might have for the crown prince. Gainil, of course, had been willing to take the risk.

Alain hoped his potential utility as a turncoat would

outweigh what he could offer as a hostage. Whatever the risk, whatever his father thought, it was a gamble he'd decided he needed to make, if it meant doing right by Taira.

The barkeeper slid the tiny glass of liquor to Alain, and Alain downed it in one gulp. Such was the way with *sotola*. The drink burned all the way down, but it was a comfort to Alain. While he'd never liked alcohol in large amounts, a little every so often calmed his nerves.

Alain remained at the bar, occasionally looking around to see if anyone new had entered the tavern, but no one did. Not surprising—it was late. Far past the time Alain preferred to be in bed; he'd always been an early riser, and never enjoyed late nights.

After a while, Alain's impatience—and his weariness—got the better of him. He stood up, paced a bit, then walked up to the burly man, nursing another mug of ale.

"I'm looking for someone," Alain said.

"I'll throw you a party when you find him," the man said, his speech slurred.

The panic that had simmered, dormant, for the past hour or so, surged. Alain took a step back, trying to keep control of his breathing.

The man grunted. Then, slowly, he stood, and Alain realized "burly" was not remotely accurate for the man. He was a *giant*, towering head and shoulders above Alain, and twice as thick, knotted with muscle.

"Say," the man said slowly, "you look familiar. I know you from somewhere?"

"No," Alain said, fighting the relentless anxiety inside of him. "I'm sorry. My mistake." He backed away, moving back towards the bar.

The man kept his eyes on Alain for a moment, then slouched down at his table. "Damn right it's your mistake," he mumbled.

Alain felt a sharp prick in his back.

"You're comin' with me," a gravelly female voice whispered in his ear.

Alain clenched his fists to keep himself from cracking his knuckles and inadvertently triggering whoever it was that had a blade at his back. His throat tightened, and his skin grew hot.

Alain half-turned his head to see the older woman behind him. He put his hands up. "Very well," he said. "Lead the way." Either this was his contact with the Denizens, or something much more sinister was about to play out. He might as well find out which it was.

The woman pushed him toward a door at the back of the tavern. On their way, she stopped at the table where the burly man sat. Alain looked over his shoulder, and out of the corner of his eye watched the old woman lift the man's mug of ale to her lips and take a long draught, her other hand still pressing a blade into Alain's back.

"Hey," the man said, but only frowned in dismay. Alain couldn't tell whether the big man was too drunk to care, or genuinely frightened of the woman.

"Good choice, that," the woman said. "Best brew in the city." She nudged Alain forward, and they walked through the back door and up a narrow staircase, leaving the burly man slack-jawed in their wake.

Alain tried to crane his head around to get another look at the woman, but the blade pressed more firmly into his back.

"No peeking," she said. Her voice didn't sound threatening this time. If Alain didn't know better, he'd say she was being playful.

When they reached the top of the stairs, the woman spoke again.

"Nineteen knocks."

Alain raised his hand to knock, but then hesitated. "Did you say—"

"*Nineteen.* Do it, or you get a dagger in your kidney."

You've got to be kidding me. Alain would have laughed if he hadn't been terrified out of his mind. He immediately did as ordered, knocking solidly on the door nineteen times. A few moments after his last knock, the muffled sound of a latch being undone permeated from the other side, and then the door swung open.

It was Sev.

Alain immediately felt a rush of relief. Sev looked him up and down, then motioned for him to come in.

"Only nineteen this time, Morayne?" Sev asked over his shoulder.

Morayne? Alain looked around, but saw no one in the room besides himself, Sev, and the woman behind—

Alain watched in shock as the woman lifted a black frizzed wig to reveal dark brown hair in a tight bun underneath. With one hand, she removed some sort of adhesive that made her lips more full, and another that gave the illusion of the long scar on her cheek. The crow's feet and age lines that remained on her face were penciled in, Alain realized, as he got a closer look.

Morayne now stood before him.

"I... wasn't expecting that," Alain whispered.

Morayne raised an eyebrow at Alain, then swept past him through the doorway. The room was bare, with just a few chairs and a table against one wall. No other people, no other furniture.

"Your disguise is a lot better than mine," Alain grumbled. He was impressed; he hadn't the slightest clue that the woman downstairs had been closer to his age than his father's.

Morayne shrugged, then walked up to Sev and, on tiptoes, kissed him on the cheek.

If I weren't betrothed, Alain remembered her saying earlier that night.

For a moment the fire rose in Alain's mind—but these flames were different, somehow. He quieted them anyway, and this time they obeyed.

"I have to admit," Sev said, as Morayne sat down on one of the chairs near him, "I did not think you would come. And, now that you're here, I'm sincerely curious." He folded his arms. "Why are you here, Your Highness?"

And there it was. The golden question. Alain had thought about how to answer this many different ways. The best, he had finally decided, was the truth. Or a shadow of it, at least.

"My father is an arrogant, paranoid, selfish bastard that doesn't deserve to rule our family, let alone our kingdom."

"And this is, what, your form of revenge?"

"This is me taking a stand I should have taken a long time ago," Alain said. He found, as he said the words, that he wished they were true. "But, yes, revenge is part of it."

"Are you a Trigger?" Sev asked.

Alain nodded. "I take it you've heard of what happened in the palace, months ago?"

"I have," Sev said. "I don't suppose you'd be able to prove it to me?"

"Not unless you want to risk me blowing up this entire building." Alain could probably summon proof of some kind, if he really thought about it, but it wasn't remotely worth the risk.

"He's a Trigger," Morayne said. "I saw it, Sev."

Sev stared at him for a moment, but something changed in his eyes.

"Very well," Sev said, nodding. He moved towards the door. "I'll present your case to the Chain. They will have the ultimate decision on what to do with you. Wait here."

"The Chain?"

"The leadership of the Denizens. That is all I can tell you, for now."

"Thank you," Alain said, holding in his surprise.

"Don't thank me yet. It'll be their decision, not mine."

Then, Sev was gone, and Alain and Morayne were alone.

Alain felt the woman's eyes on him, her face expressionless. He cracked his knuckles, still standing in the middle of the room. Should he go sit with her at the table? Lean against the wall? Either option seemed awkward, but so did standing there in the middle of the room fiddling with his own knuckles. He had no idea how to act around this woman, especially given her drastic change of attitude since he'd seen her earlier that night. He knew such changes were possible in some people who suffered the Madness, had even witnessed them himself at the community, but seeing them publicly was very different.

"I'm sorry," Morayne said.

Alain coughed. "Ah… about what?"

"Earlier tonight," she said. She slouched in the chair, arms crossed. "I didn't mean what I said, and I'm sorry if it made you uncomfortable."

"You… of course. I mean, not that it made me uncomfortable," *it did*, "but of course you didn't mean what you said, is what I'm intending to… say…"

"Sometimes I treat people in ways I don't want to treat

them. I say or do things I know I don't want to say and do, but... they happen anyway. It's part of me, part of my own madness."

Perhaps it was meeting a new person who could understand, or perhaps it was the way she'd seemed so melancholy at the ball but now seemed more or less pleasant. For whatever reason, Alain decided to actually voice his thoughts.

"Sounds like we have the opposite problem," he said. "I rarely say what I want to say, because I'm terrified of messing it up. Of looking stupid. Of hurting myself or others."

Morayne shrugged. "That's our lot, I guess."

Alain shrugged in return.

"So... you *are* a Trigger, then?" she said after a moment.

Alain's eyebrows rose. "You seemed pretty confident affirming as much to Sev."

Morayne shrugged again. "Doesn't hurt to be sure."

"Well, I am," Alain said. "You are, too?"

"That's what they tell me."

"What's your element?" Alain asked. The question was a popular one at the Red Community. He did not expect her to—

"Earth," Morayne said. She looked at him, and snorted. "I wouldn't be caught dead manipulating fire."

Alain laughed.

"I do wish I could manipulate air, though," Morayne said. "Seems... freeing."

Alain cleared his throat. "We represent the worst of the Madness in a way, I suppose."

For a brief moment, Morayne's face darkened. But, as quickly as it changed, it returned to her normal, expressionless self. Her eyes, however, seemed brighter than he remembered at the ball. "You're just like the rest of them. You don't respect what you can do. What you have might be a gift."

Alain scoffed. "A gift? A gift that nearly made me kill the woman I love? A gift that makes my father want to use me as a weapon? That's no gift."

"You don't understand," she said. Then she stood and walked over to Alain, looking him in the eyes.

"You went to a community?" she asked.

Alain nodded.

"Which one?"

"Red." Alain was conscious of how close she stood to him, but he didn't know what to do about it. He was betrothed, obviously. So was she. He certainly did not want to be any closer.

But he wasn't sure he wanted to be further away, either.

Morayne clicked her tongue as she nodded.

Alain shifted uncomfortably. "What is it?"

"Did you know Brother Maddagon?" she asked.

Alain smiled at that. "He was my mentor."

"I take it he's the one that told you about that stupid counting meditation exercise?"

"That counting exercise actually works for me."

Morayne rolled her eyes. "It's a temporary fix. If you want real peace, you'll need to look deeper."

"You sound just like Brother Maddagon."

Morayne shrugged. "He knows a thing or two."

"Did he teach you about breathing?" Alain asked, curiosity piqued.

Morayne nodded. "The breathing, yes. Worked for me for a while, but less so, lately. What about the stretches?"

Alain cocked his head. Brother Maddagon had never taught him any stretches.

"Goddess rising! The stretches were ridiculous!" Morayne said, her eyes shining.

Who is this girl? Alain wondered to himself.

She proceeded to demonstrate some of Brother Maddagon's stretches. She still wore the clothing she had when disguised as the old woman—dark breeches, and a loose white shirt only partly tucked in. She bent low into one knee, keeping the other leg out straight to the side, then lifted both arms high into the air.

"Root-and-branch pose," she announced.

Alain raised one eyebrow. "I suppose I can see that. Your legs are the roots, and your arms the branches. Sure."

Morayne had already moved on to another stretch. "Graceful swan," she announced, standing on one leg, the other parallel to the ground behind her, one arm straight in front, also parallel to the ground, and the other straight up opposite her standing leg.

Alain nodded appreciatively. Morayne, for all her jesting, was actually good at these. Her limbs were limber enough to remain straight and poised, and strong enough to maintain the position without shaking or visible strain. "Can't see how this one is supposed to be a swan, though," he said.

She showed him two or three other poses, stretching arms behind her back, craning her neck, and lifting one leg high in front of her.

Suddenly an image came into Alain's mind, and he couldn't shake it. He began to laugh.

Morayne dropped her hands, which had been raised above her head again, and looked at Alain.

"What?"

Alain laughed harder, unable to speak. He leaned against the table for support.

"What are you laughing at?"

Alain could tell he'd struck a nerve. Her beautiful brown eyes glared at him.

"Brother Maddagon," Alain managed between gasps, "taught you these poses?"

"Yes," Morayne said. "What's so funny about that?"

"Brother Maddagon is the most uncoordinated person I've ever met," Alain said, calming down. "The thought of him doing any of these…"

And then Alain was laughing again, tears in his eyes.

This time, Morayne laughed, too. It was the first time Alain had seen her smile since they met. "I guess it was pretty funny," she said, her eyes bright once more. "He attempted them, but could never quite make it. No wonder he didn't teach them to you."

Alain breathed deeply, letting the laughter flow out of him. It felt good. He couldn't remember the last time he'd laughed like this. In the Red Community, maybe, once or twice, but he couldn't remember anything specific.

Morayne placed her hand on his arm. Alain looked down, unsure what to do.

"I'm betrothed," he said, blurting it out.

This only made Morayne laugh harder. "So am I," she managed.

Then she took her arm away, leaving Alain's skin with the slightest tingle.

"Thank you," he said, before he knew he was saying it.

She met his eyes, the spark still in hers. "For what?"

"For making me laugh. It has been too long."

"Life is better when you laugh," she said. "That's something I've come to understand all too well."

Alain nodded. The Madness affected everyone differently—usually amplifying symptoms that were already there. For Alain, it was his anxiety. Based on what he'd seen of Morayne, and from what he knew of some of his fellow convalescents at the community, he suspected she was one of those who suffered constant melancholy, interrupted by brief frenzied episodes. He would not wish his own condition on anyone, but from what he had seen from those at the community, hers might be worse.

He had not experienced what she felt. But based on how his own fear magnified when he caught the Madness, when he lost control, he dreaded to think of it.

Footsteps sounded on the stairs, just as flames of anxiety rose again in Alain's mind. Their return made him realize their absence throughout his conversation with Morayne. She actually put him at ease. The flames in his mind and the constricting darkness in his chest had hardly been noticeable.

But now they were back, just as Sev walked through the door and rejoined them.

Sev did not waste any time. "They're cautious about you," he said. "They want a demonstration of your loyalty. And your powers."

"But he's in?" Morayne asked.

"Tentatively," Sev said with a nod.

"Delightful," Morayne said, although all sense of humor had evaporated from her face, and Alain couldn't tell whether she was being sarcastic or not.

"We'll contact you with further instruction about what to do from here," Sev said. "We'll start slowly. In the beginning it will have something to do with feeding us intelligence on Gainil's plans and strategy. Is that something you can do?"

"I can," Alain said. He could certainly broker exactly what information to convey with his father and the others. And, perhaps, he'd feed the Denizens a bit more than that, too.

"Watch for word from us."

"Very well." Alain gripped Sev's hand, exchanged a glance with Morayne, and then walked down the stairs, out of the tavern, and into the night.

Alain walked through the alleyway alone, cloak wrapped around him. The night was chilly. Mavenil was usually warm this time of year, but tonight was an exception.

"Evening, mate."

Alain turned sharply, gripping the sword at his hip. Being the son of a king earned him a fair amount of training when it came to swordplay, but he was no master. It was all he could do to keep his hand on his hilt instead of cracking his knuckles.

Code, the Nazaniin assassin, inclined his head. "Good to see you."

"What are you doing here?"

Code smiled, opening his palms to Alain. "Just checking in with you. How goes your assignment?"

"Well enough." Alain started walking. If Code wanted to accompany him, he could keep up.

"Good to hear. You made some progress tonight, I take it?"

"I might have," Alain said. As much as he'd taken a liking to Code, he couldn't exactly trust this man yet. They hardly knew one another. "Best wait until I report to my father for the details."

Code shrugged. "Suit yourself, mate."

They walked together for a moment, moving from alleyway to alleyway toward the palace. Alain was about to demand what in the Sfaera the man wanted from him when Code spoke again.

"Any insight on Nadir?" Code asked.

Alain considered before responding. The hectic evening had caused him to completely forget Code's request for help.

"I don't think so," Alain said. "I still have no idea who Nadir's avatar could be."

"No voices, yet?"

Alain shook his head. *Just flames.*

Code grunted. "While I'm somewhat disappointed, I suppose that's a good thing on your end."

"What about you?" Alain asked.

"What about me?"

"Any leads?"

Code took a deep breath. "Potentially. Nothing solid yet. But give me another day or so, and I might have something."

Alain was about to ask the nature of these leads, when Code stopped him with a hand on his chest.

"Someone's coming."

Fedrick, the Scarab captain, turned the corner. When he saw them, he bowed slightly.

Alain's internal flames ignited, but not so much with fear this time. He was angry. "I made it explicitly clear that I was not to be followed."

Fedrick looked over his shoulder, then at Alain. "My apologies, Your Highness. His Majesty has new orders for you, and he bid me relay them to you immediately."

Alain sighed, popping his knuckles. For Taira's sake, he had to play along.

"A Scarab contingent awaits us nearby. We are to meet them, and participate in an assault on the Denizen headquarters."

"The Denizen... How do you know where the Denizen

headquarters are?" Alain demanded. His father had told him they had no idea where the faction was based; that was why they'd sent Alain to...

Code let out a long breath. "Looks like they had you followed after all, mate."

"No," Alain said. "Not me. They followed Sev."

"What matters," Fedrick said, "is that we can strike at them now. Come with me."

Flames rose in Alain's mind along with a tumult of emotions. Anger at his father for deceiving him. Anger at himself for allowing it. Fear for what might happen to Sev and Morayne. Fear of what Taira might think of him.

"No," Alain said, vaguely aware he'd begun humming.

Fedrick's face remained emotionless. "Your Highness, you must. The king orders it."

"This was not part of my agreement with the king."

"All due respect, Your Highness, you must obey your father's orders."

Alain wanted to end this puppetry, but his fear of the consequences he might face thundered through him. "If I don't?"

Fedrick locked eyes with Alain and drew a long, slow breath. "If you do not accompany us, His Majesty has ordered me to take retaliatory measures."

Code scoffed. "Retaliatory measures? Goddess rising, man, give us some specifics."

"The Lady Taira."

Heat radiated from Alain. The air shifted and crackled. Panic rose inside him, but it was spiked with rage. He wasn't sure he *wanted* to control himself this time.

"If you refuse, it'll be you who's hurting her," Fedrick said, stepping back. Spontaneous sparks burst in the air around them.

It's about living a decent life, and helping those around me.

How could he live a decent life when there were no decent options?

Alain took a deep breath, in and out. He counted, concentrating on his breathing for a moment, and the sparks in the air around him subsided. He did not want to hurt anyone.

But above all, he owed Taira a debt. No more harm could come to her because of what Alain did, or did not do.

Alain clenched his jaw. "Lead the way."

The Scarab force was not far. Once they'd regrouped, they trotted through the dark streets together, Fedrick leading them. The Scarabs had shed any Destrinar insignia that might identify them; any witnesses would not recognize them as acting for any specific house. Black leathers, black hoods, and black masks covered everything except their eyes. They'd passed similar garb to Code and Alain, who had changed quickly in an alleyway moments before.

Fedrick led them to an unassuming building in the market district. Sandstone and wood, dark purple in the moonlight. Three stories rose above them, lights still burning on the third floor.

A Scarab soldier approached Fedrick. "They're still there, sir. No one has left yet."

Has anyone else arrived? Alain wanted to ask. *A strange girl and a young man with her?* Morayne and Sev could have returned here after their meeting at the tavern. Just the thought of it made Alain's gut heavy with worry.

"Good," Fedrick said, though there was no joy in his voice. He turned to Alain. "You can make this easier on all of us," he said. "Use your powers. Ignite a fire on the third floor; that's where they're meeting. You do that, and we'll do the rest."

Alain swallowed hard. His internal flames already towered high. Sweat dripped down his face, despite the night chill, and he unclenched and clenched his fists over and over again, fingernails digging into palms. "And if I don't?" He knew the response, but he had to ask. He had to be sure.

"We'll kill them anyway," Fedrick said. "Some of us will likely die. And Taira will suffer for it."

Alain's breaths moved quickly, raggedly, in and out of his body.

"If I have a panic attack while I'm using my powers," Alain said, "I'll lose control. You'll all be at risk."

Fedrick slipped something from beneath his armor. A blowpipe. "We are prepared for that, Your Highness," he said. "Get the job done, and I'll make sure you're unconscious before things get out of control."

Alain swore. How could he do this? How could he kill these people, people he did not even know, for rebelling against his father? An act he considered himself? He looked up at the lights, burning in the third-story windows, and gritted his teeth.

"*I can't.*"

Fedrick scowled. "You must, Your Highness. If you care about Taira at all, you must."

Why? Alain asked, to the night sky and the stars and the sparks in the air around him and to no one in particular. *Why is this my choice?*

"Sir, there's movement on the third floor. They might be preparing to leave."

It was Fedrick's turn to curse. "Do it now, Alain. Do it now, or we'll have to do it ourselves."

Alain's lungs tightened. He looked up at the third floor

again, then back at Fedrick. His breaths wheezed in and out of him, barely transferring any air. He reached out a hand to a nearby wall, or perhaps a shoulder, to steady himself, a low groan forming in his gut.

No matter what he did, people would get hurt. No matter what he did, things would burn.

Better he make the choice himself than leave it to chance.

So Alain concentrated on the third floor with his last remaining willpower, panic rising like a mountain in his chest, and he let it burn.

Alain opened his eyes to see Code standing against the doorframe to his chambers in the royal palace.

"You're finally awake. Better get moving. You're wanted in the Decision Room."

Alain groaned. His eyes focused. He was lying in bed, wearing the same black clothing he'd been given before the attack on the Denizen Chain. His entire body felt raw. At the community, there had been periods of time blessedly absent of terror and panic. Since he'd left, he'd barely had a moment's rest.

"What happened?" he asked, fighting the fear humming through him. His body vibrated with it, every particle quaking. He bolted upright. "Where is Taira?"

Code raised his hands, palms forward. "I don't know. But they tell me she's safe, for now."

Alain shut his eyes tightly, trying to dispel the aching pain behind his forehead while simultaneously wondering where his father could have hidden Taira. He needed to find her. He could not allow her to be held captive like this, used as leverage against him.

"As far as what happened," Code continued, "well… you did what they asked you to do. And then you lost control. That Fedrick bloke had to put you under. The other Scarabs carried you back to the palace."

"If I did what they asked me to do…"

"The Denizen Chain is gone. You cut off their head, and your father and his wife don't think they'll threaten you any longer."

Alain rubbed his temples with both hands. "I lost control?"

Code sucked in a breath. "You incinerated the entire building. Burned a number of Scarabs as well, before the toxin took effect."

Alain sat there, unmoving. "Are they… are they dead?" *Was Morayne among them? Sev?*

"Like I said, the Denizen Chain is gone. One of the Scarabs will die soon from his wounds, if he hasn't already. A few more wounded. You've… you've never killed anyone before?" Code sounded surprised.

"I have," Alain whispered. "Taira's parents, the day the Madness took me."

"Shit. Sorry, mate. I was about to say it gets easier, but… I like you. And I like to be honest with people I like. And honestly, it might never get easier."

Alain felt no panic, no rising flames inside of him. Instead, he felt only emptiness. Unexpectedly, the emptiness frightened him more than anything ever had.

"What are you doing here?" he asked, looking up at Code. He didn't know what to do with his hands. Rest them on the bed? Fold them on his lap? Nothing felt right.

"I've got an update for you," Code said. "Figured I'd share it with you before anyone else. Despite your… issues… you seem to be one of the only sane people around here."

"If that's what you think, you're as crazy as I am."

Code laughed out loud at that. "That might be true, mate. That might be true." Code sighed. "I had a hunch that Nadir's avatar was a part of the Denizens. But their leadership is mostly dead, and… and I've received a tip, you could say. The avatar is in the palace."

"It isn't me, Code. I've already told you."

"I believe you. But that means it's somebody else, and we have no idea who. Think of this as a warning. I'd prefer it if you didn't die, all things considered." Code turned to leave the room. "Someone else is here to see you," he said over his shoulder. "Better make it quick, though. Your father's been asking for you."

When Code left, Brother Maddagon walked into the room.

A tumult of emotion disturbed the terrifying stillness within Alain. Shame and anger over the people he'd killed and the people he'd hurt. Horror at what he'd done. But despite that, he needed to see someone who understood him, who knew him the way this man knew him.

Brother Maddagon smiled. "Well, it's good to see you haven't fried yourself yet."

Alain wanted to say something clever in response, but he had nothing except the tears in his eyes. He pushed himself out of bed and embraced his mentor.

Maddagon grunted.

"Good to see you too, son."

Alain told Maddagon everything that had happened: about his father, about the Denizens, about Taira and Morayne— Maddagon smiled at the mention of her name—and about the people he'd killed the previous night. When he was finished,

Maddagon put a hand on Alain's shoulder.

"I am so sorry you've had to go through all of this, son. You've made decisions no one should have to make."

"What about Taira?" Alain asked. "This whole time, I've been trying to help her. Make amends, as you said. It has only made things worse."

Maddagon took a deep breath. "Amends are a strange thing, Alain. Only rarely do they work out the way we expect. But we must never cause further harm. If the path of making amends leads to harm, rethink your actions. We make amends to help ourselves, and to help others if possible. Hurting others has no role in it at all."

Alain's chest felt hollow, as if there were nothing left inside him. "Then the people I killed… I chose wrong."

"It may have been wrong, yes. But you were also under extreme duress. Truth is, I cannot defend or decry your actions, son. You made your choices last night—but you can make more today. You are still alive. There is still time."

Still time. Why did Alain feel like he had already run out of it?

"I want to share something with you," Brother Maddagon said. "It may help with this. May not, I don't know. It's something I wish I could have told you at the community, but… well, the reason I've come here is to tell you in person, where the rules of the community don't apply."

Alain cocked his head. What could Maddagon possibly want to say to him that would have necessitated a journey to Mavenil itself?

They sat down across from one another at the table in Alain's chambers.

Maddagon scoffed. "I'm not even sure why I've come, to be

honest. You've always been impervious to my lessons."

Alain laughed, the sound a welcome ease from the tension in his gut. "But you insist on giving them, anyway."

Maddagon sighed. "That I do."

"You were always different than the other monks," Alain said. "That's why I liked you so much."

"That's part of why I've come to speak with you. You did not trust anyone at the community, especially the monks. Why was that?"

Because they were idiots, Alain thought to himself. Not the truest reason, but a reason nonetheless. "Because they didn't know anything about what it was like to suffer the way I did. The way all of the convalescents did at the community. They did not understand the first thing about the Madness."

Brother Maddagon nodded. "Indeed. Why, then, did you trust me?"

Alain thought about the question for a moment, but eventually shrugged. "I suppose you... you always seemed to understand, even if you weren't mad along with us. You listened instead of taught, maybe."

"I have something to tell you, Alain, and it concerns the Madness."

Alain could not stop his eyes from widening, but Brother Maddagon shook his head.

"Before you start comparing us, I want to be clear that I don't suffer from the Madness, not in the way you do. I know how incredible it is to find someone who understands you in a very specific way, and I'm afraid I cannot offer that to you in the way you expect. But I can give you some measure of it. I used to drink, you see. A great deal. More than any man should."

Alain's eyebrows knitted together. "Drink? You mean you

used to drink spirits? Alcohol? I thought that was forbidden by the Order."

"It is, but I was not always a monk, if you can believe that. I once had a very different life. A family. A different occupation. I was a different man.

"The details do not matter. What does matter is this: I drank a lot, and then I drank too much, and then drinking was all I did. It became the most important thing to me, and that is a form of madness, son. I drank when I should have worked, I drank when I should have loved my wife and children, and I drank when I should have done anything else on this Sfaera."

Maddagon paused, clearing his throat. "I lost my family. It was my fault. I suffered for many years because of that loss, but eventually—I know you don't like to talk about the Goddess, but it was only by a series of miracles—I found the Order. Their teachings do not help everyone, I'd be the first to admit it—for Canta's sake, their teachings hardly help their own Order most of the time—but they helped me."

Alain sat there, blinking. "Why didn't you share this, at the community?"

"The community does not encourage monks to share personal details about themselves," Maddagon said. "That is a serious error in judgment, in my opinion, one that obfuscates and damages progress in many cases, but a rule nonetheless. Here, outside of the community, I feel confident enough to forget the rules and say what I need to say to you."

Alain processed what Brother Maddagon had said. "You... you think your obsession, your addiction to drink, is like my Madness?"

"I think there are similarities. I understand what it's like to feel helpless, to feel completely out of control."

"But you don't drink anymore?" Alain asked.

"No," Brother Maddagon said. "Not anymore."

"How did you do it?" Alain asked, eager. "How did you regain control?"

Brother Maddagon laughed. "You really are impervious to my lessons, aren't you? I've told you time and time again, son, this is not about regaining control. It's about giving it up."

Alain frowned. "I know. And I've told you time and time again, *I don't care about this Goddess of yours.*" Maddagon had spoken of "giving up" before, always in the context of giving up one's life and will to Canta. It sounded too much like becoming a monk to Alain, and while he respected Maddagon for that choice, it was not one he would ever make.

Maddagon shrugged. "That doesn't matter. Who we give control up to does not matter. It only matters that we give it up. The more I tried to control my life when I drank, the more out of control it became. These things aren't intuitive. In the physical world, if something is about to slip out of my grasp, I tighten my hold on it. That doesn't work with things of the soul. The way up is down, son. I needed to let go, to admit I had no power, no chance whatsoever at control. Only then was I able to bring order to my life." While Alain's emotions had calmed since first seeing Brother Maddagon, the familiar, ever-present panic still simmered. He could never escape his own fear. "How can you do such a thing?" he asked. "How can you give up control entirely, to a being"—he refused to refer to the Goddess-damned Goddess—"that you don't even know exists?"

"It is a terrifying thing," Maddagon admitted. "And excruciating, especially at first. But it became easier for me the more I practiced it. And it didn't matter to whom or what I gave control—I just had to give it away to someone, something more powerful than myself. That is the first thing I've learned in my life, son. Trust in a higher power, trust enough to give up your own right to control."

"The first?"

"Yes, the first." Maddagon smiled, and reached across the table to grip Alain's arm. "The second is to share my experience with others."

"Like you're doing right now with me?"

"Like I'm doing right now with you, yes, but also as I've done the entire time I've known you. The Order does not allow me to refer to my past, but I can still share my experience through anecdote and principle. You remember about making amends?"

Of course he remembered. It was what had gotten him into this bloody mess in the first place. "Living a decent life, and helping other people."

"Helping other people," Maddagon said. "Between that, and trust, there is nothing more I need from life."

Alain could not imagine himself ever saying that. If he could live without fear for just a moment, that would be a miracle. He certainly wanted that. For the first time, Alain realized, what Brother Maddagon said sounded appealing.

"Can you teach me how to do this?" Alain asked.

Maddagon smiled. "Of course I can."

A rapid knock sounded on Alain's chamber door.

It was Fedrick.

"Your Highness, His Majesty the king demands your presence. Immediately."

"Very well," Alain said. "Tell my father I am on my way."

"I've been ordered to escort you, Your Highness."

Flames scoured Alain's mind, both of fear and anger. Was he a prisoner, now?

"You cannot control your father," Brother Maddagon said quietly across the table, "only whether you trust in something greater than yourself, or not."

Alain took a deep breath. Bloody bones, this was going to be painful.

He stood. "I'll accompany you," he told Fedrick, "but only if Brother Maddagon comes along."

Fedrick shrugged. "His Majesty requires Brother Maddagon's presence as well."

Alain narrowed his eyes, and began to walk. Time to see what this was all about.

The king and his wife waited at the head of the map table in the Decision Room. Code was there too, leaning against a wall.

"Alain," Gainil said. "It is about time."

Alain popped his knuckles as he walked in. The emptiness he'd felt earlier was gone, as was the peace of speaking with Brother Maddagon. Now, the familiar beginnings of panic burned inside him, flames rising high, intense pressure building up with every heartbeat.

Code had told him Nadir's avatar was in the palace. Looking from Fedrick to Lailana to Gainil, Alain realized it could be any one of them—and he would have no idea.

It could even be Taira. Taira, who was not here.

"What have you done with her, Father?"

Gainil grunted. "Don't worry, son. Taira is safe. She'll remain safe, as long as you cooperate."

Safe. He could not trust anything his father said.

"You did well last night, boy."

"What I did was wrong."

Gainil shrugged. "So what if it was? You burned a building to the ground, murdered a dozen people with it. You're the prince. Such is your right."

"No," Alain said. "If that's what you think, Father, you're less fit to be king than I thought."

Gainil's face darkened. "Easy to say when you've never ruled. Keep that attitude up, boy, and you might not see your chance."

Silence reigned in the Decision Room for a few moments. All eyes remained fixed on Gainil and Alain. Then, Lailana leaned over and whispered something in the king's ear.

Gainil smiled. "Fear not, son. You have much to do for me, yet. Your usefulness will not expire for some time."

Alain began to count. A part of him wanted to let go, here, in this room. Only Brother Maddagon's presence stopped him.

No further harm.

"I won't kill anyone else for you," Alain said, between counts.

Gainil laughed. "I'm afraid you'll have to, son. You don't have any other choice."

Then, Alain exploded. Just briefly, just for a moment, but enough to project a column of flame toward his father. The king dodged behind the table, narrowly escaping. Alain sensed movement behind him, and turned to see Fedrick reaching into his tunic, surely for his blowpipe. Alain reached out a hand to the Scarab captain.

"Don't do it, Fedrick. I could do a lot worse to you." Probably. Alain had rarely attempted to direct his power; it was too easy to lose control completely. But the emptiness called to him. He was beginning to not care whether he had control or not.

Slowly, Fedrick took his hands out of his tunic, raising them both in the air.

Beneath them all, the ground began to shake.

"What in Oblivion is that?" Code asked, steadying himself against the wall.

Alain tried to control his breathing. Earthquakes never happened in Mavenil. Never had before, anyway. Not until the Madness.

Not until people like Morayne.

"That's someone getting revenge," Alain said. The Denizens were retaliating. He didn't dare hope that it was Morayne among them, but he could not help the blossom of anticipation in his chest.

The tremors got worse, and for a moment Alain wondered whether the Decision Room might collapse on them all. A loud crack echoed in the distance, as if a mountain had just broken in two.

Goddess, I hope Taira is safe, wherever she is.

The tremors ceased.

Code reached into a pouch at his belt, and took out a small crystal. He placed it in his mouth.

Alain looked at him. "What was that?"

"A bit of courage. I'll tell you about it later. Right now, we need to find whoever is doing this."

Alain's father stood, leading the way out of the Decision Room. "Finally, someone talking sense. We're under attack, and we're bloody going to crush whoever it is."

Alain hesitated before he followed. He wasn't sure he'd be obeying anything his father said, ever again.

A complement of Scarabs awaited them in the courtyard,

but the other figure with them surprised Alain. Relief rushed through him.

"Taira," he said.

"Hello, Alain." She kept her distance. He could not blame her.

"Are you all right? I heard they—"

"They held me hostage, for a time. But I'm all right." She glanced at his father. "We need to find out what is going on."

"Of course," Alain said. "Stay with me. We'll be all right." He held out his hand to her, surprised at his own boldness. She would be safest with him; he didn't trust anyone else in their group, with the exception of Brother Maddagon. And the monk wouldn't be much use in a fight.

Instead of taking his hand, Taira walked right past him to stand beside Gainil and Lailana.

Alain lowered his arm slowly, staring after Taira in shock. How could she trust his father over him? The man who had taken her captive?

There was no time to think. A new party entered the courtyard. A group of armed men and women, among them two people he recognized: Sev and Morayne.

"That one's the Denizen we followed to find the Chain," Fedrick said, nodding at Sev. He turned to bellow at the newcomers. "Stop in the name of the king! You've attacked the Crown, and are subject to His Majesty's judgment."

"We will not let attacks like the one last night go unpunished," Sev said, ignoring Fedrick and looking directly at Gainil. "The *king* broke the treaty. He started all of this, but we will end it."

The king? Gainil had told Alain that the Denizens had broken the treaty.

"I do not need to defend myself to you," Gainil spat, glaring at Sev. "You've attacked the royal palace, and you're subject to my judgment."

Sev raised his sword. "We won't accept your judgment any longer. You orchestrated the attack on your own carriage, risking the lives of innocent civilians, just to prove a point. You then ordered the destruction of an entire building last night, once again without regard for innocent life. You must be stopped."

Alain turned to face his father.

"That was *you?*" he demanded. "You arranged the attack on the carriage? You've been behind everything?"

Gainil looked right at Alain. "What they say doesn't matter," he growled. "They've been foolish enough to deliver themselves into my hands. Do your job, Alain. Kill them all."

Alain looked from his father to Morayne, who glared in return, eyes hooded. He'd led the Scarabs to Sev, who in turn led them to the Denizen Chain. And then Alain had massacred them. He'd destroyed everything she stood for.

No longer. He was through being his father's puppet.

Despite the crushing anxiety in his chest and the flames rising in his mind, Alain met Gainil's eyes. "I won't do it. Find someone else to be your weapon."

The king's eyes bulged, and then he grabbed Taira, drawing a dagger and holding it to her neck.

"If you don't do it," the king said, "I'll kill your betrothed."

Alain was about to protest, when something made him hesitate. He looked at Taira, held captive by his father, but there was no fear in her face. Instead, she returned Alain's gaze. She *glared* at him.

"He won't buy this," Taira said, tearing free from the king's grasp. "He isn't *that* stupid."

Alain looked from Taira to his father, everything coming together in his mind. Taira had never been in danger, she was here to make Alain do what the king wanted him to do.

Sparks burst in the air around him. He'd gotten it wrong. He hadn't been his father's puppet—he'd been hers. Hot shame burned his face, and the dark fear tightened further around his chest. He wanted to begin counting, *knew* he needed to begin to count, but he did not have it in him. Fear battled anger inside of him, and he did not know which he wanted to win.

Alain took a step towards Taira. "How could you?" he asked. "We're betrothed."

"I'm not betrothed to you any longer, Alain. I haven't been since you killed my parents. Don't act surprised; you should have known."

"Taira… I'm sorry."

Taira laughed mirthlessly. "Your apology means nothing to me unless you do as your father says."

Alain met Taira's eyes, then looked to Brother Maddagon. The man didn't say anything, but Alain remembered what he had said only a short while ago.

Amends should never cause further harm.

He would spend the rest of his life paying for what he had done to Taira's parents, but that did not mean he had to submit to his father, to real evil, to make up for it. Taira could not use him like this.

"I won't, Taira," Alain said. "I'm sorry." This time, he would do what he thought was right.

Gainil growled in rage. In one smooth motion, he sheathed his dagger, drew his sword with the other hand, and stepped toward Brother Maddagon. Before Alain could react, he shoved the sword into Maddagon's chest.

"*No!*" Alain shouted. He rushed to Brother Maddagon as he fell to the ground. Gently, Alain cradled Maddagon's head in his arms.

"You'll be all right," Alain said quietly, knowing the moment he said it how untrue it was. "You'll be all right," he said again, with a sob that racked him, that moved in time with the flames and the fear writhing together inside him.

"They cannot hurt me," Maddagon whispered. "You were my life's work, son." Then, his gaze shifted, and Alain followed it to Morayne. "You both are. You can do so much together…"

Maddagon gasped, and Alain felt blood leaking onto his fingers, arms, soaking through the knees of his trousers.

"Two things," Maddagon said. "Share what you learn with others. And… remember… to trust…"

Maddagon stopped. Alain held an empty shell.

With the inevitability of a sunset, Alain's sanity drowned in the boiling panic, and an inferno raged within him. The fear, the anger, the powerlessness he'd buried for months erupted to the surface. His breaths came so quickly he hardly had time to notice them, and hot talons of dread gripped his chest.

A ring of fire flashed outward. Everyone in the courtyard was knocked to the ground by the force of it.

A roaring ball of flames formed in front of Alain. The flames obeyed his every command; they were completely under his control—and he was under theirs. People cried, shouting out, as the fireball grew before him. Someone shouted his name, but he did not care. He was the fire, and the fire was him.

The burning orb grew. He knew where this one would go. Straight to his father.

Someone touched his arm.

He looked down in anger, in helpless thrall to the flames,

and was about to drop the giant orb of flame on whoever it was that had disturbed him.

"Alain, don't," Morayne shouted. The roar of the flames building in the giant ball of fire was so loud he could hardly hear her. She must have crawled to him; everyone around him was still lying prone on the ground.

"He killed Brother Maddagon," Alain said through the flames, through the tears in his eyes and the terror in his throat. He still cradled his former mentor's head in his arms. "He deserves to die!"

"If you don't stop, you'll take all of us with him!"

Alain looked at the scorched devastation around him. Making amends to Taira had kept him going for so long, had kept him sane. Now, he did not even have that. He had nothing, and was completely powerless to the fear, hysteria, and rage that relentlessly shadowed him. He was about to let everything around him burn, when he remembered something Brother Maddagon had said. He did not know where the words came from; it was not his own voice. But someone, or something, spoke in his mind.

That doesn't work with things of the soul. The way up is down, son. I needed to let go, to admit I had no power, no chance whatsoever at control. Only then was I able to order my life.

Alain stopped. He was about to kill Morayne—perhaps the only person left on the Sfaera who remotely understood him.

You are my life's work, son. You both are.

He was about to kill Sev, and Fedrick, and dozens of others, innocent and guilty.

You two can do much together.

His father had nothing to gain from killing Brother Maddagon; he had done it in anger. Alain was about to kill his father for the same reason.

"I need help," Alain said. He said it out loud, but he did not say it to anyone there. He said it to nature, to the Sfaera, to its people, to any power out there that might listen.

"I cannot do this alone," he said, tears streaming down his face.

The ball in front of him began to fade, just like the flames in his mind. He looked down at Morayne, and reached for her hand. She reached back. She placed her other hand, softly, on Maddagon's forehead.

"I'm sorry," Alain said. "I was wrong, I—"

"You'd damn well better be, you almost ashed me," she said, but then she hugged him, and he hugged her back, and bloody Oblivion if it didn't feel more right than anything he'd ever felt. Together, they rested Brother Maddagon gently on the ground, and then they stood.

Immediately, Alain knew something was wrong.

He looked around at everyone, still on the ground, laid flat by his burst of fire. Smoke rose into the air, some of it from bodies. Some of them were probably dead. Everyone was still down, other than Morayne and himself. Everyone except for one person.

Lailana.

She stood, unburnt, glaring at Alain through fire and smoke.

Nearby, Code also struggled to his feet, singed but still in one piece.

"I told you there was a way to recognize who Nadir's avatar was." Code nodded at Lailana. "What she's doing, that whole not-catching-fire thing? That's one way."

Lailana smiled. No, it wasn't a smile, Alain realized. Her mouth widened into what looked like a grin, but he got the distinct impression she was baring her teeth.

"About time someone figured it out," she rasped, and her voice had changed, somehow. "Of course it had to be the man from Alizia."

She looked at Code, and Alain could swear her eyes burned a bright orange. "Hade told me about you," she said. Her teeth elongated.

Goddess, what was happening?

"He told me how you and that woman ruined his fun on the island. He told me to watch out for you. Well, I have. And I'm prepared, Nazaniin."

Lailana reached toward Code.

"No," Code said, and that was the last coherent thing Alain heard from him. Code began to scream, clutching his head.

"What are you doing?" Alain shouted.

"I'm driving him mad," Lailana said, as her smile grew ever wider. She changed more, now, transformed from the beautiful woman she'd been into something else. Something different, and darker.

Alain reeled. Lailana was Nadir's avatar. She had caused all the death, Madness, and destruction.

This was all because of her.

Another ball of flame formed before Alain, but this time it was different. This time, Alain had purpose. This time, Alain was trying to trust.

"Release Code," Alain told her. "Let him go."

"*No*," she said.

Alain launched the ball of fire, but Lailana didn't move. The fire passed through her, singeing away her hair, clothing, skin. Only a burnt reminder of what was once human remained. Blackened muscles, with cracked, burnt bone beneath. Orange iridescent smoke rose lazily from her glowing eyes, boring into Alain from a dark skull. Her grin widened, teeth sharp and pointed.

"I hold the power of a Daemon," Lailana rasped. "You cannot defeat me."

"Don't we all?" Morayne stepped forward, raising her arms. The earth began to vibrate, rumbling underfoot. An arm of rock jutted up from the ground next to Lailana, and slammed down on her. She screeched, and another arm of earth jutted up on the other side, burying her underneath it. Another arm, and another arm, until piles and piles of rock and rubble and dirt had slammed down onto the space where Lailana once stood.

Alain stared at the heap of rubble. Morayne took ragged, slow breaths behind him. Code had stopped screaming, and struggled to his feet.

Morayne turned to Alain, exhausted. She smiled. The second time Alain had seen her smile since they met. It was beautiful, and he smiled back.

"Remind me never to—"

The pile of rubble exploded, and a black streak zipped towards them. Everything happened slowly. Alain reached out to Morayne, screaming for her to run. Morayne turned, looking over her shoulder. She was there, in front of Alain, in one moment. In the next, she was gone.

A hideous crash behind Alain made him turn to see Lailana, levitating, reaching down to lift Morayne up by her neck from the ground.

"This one was mad enough to think she could defeat me," Lailana said, her voice a burning cackle. "I like that."

The earth rumbled. Morayne was still alive, still conscious. She was fighting. A stone pillar reached up from the ground, but Lailana saw it first. She whipped out her other hand, and the pillar shattered.

Lailana laughed. "Your attempts are valiant, girl. But I'm going to kill you now."

Code reached Alain's side. "We need to work together. It's the only way we stand a chance."

"How can we kill her?" Alain asked. "You saw what my fire did." *Or didn't do.*

"She can die, just like any human. It just takes more. A lot more."

Alain hesitated. The panic still simmered inside of him. He was afraid. He'd surrendered himself, his control, once to Something out there. It had worked. But fear plagued him now, its claws rooting inside him, stopping his breath.

Could he do it again? Could he overcome his fear?

Could he do it when there was a blackened, burning Daemon avatar about to kill someone he cared about?

Immediately, Alain knew the answer. He had been afraid his entire life. Every day, every moment terrified him, for any reason and all reasons and for none at all. He would never escape that fear, he realized; it would always be there. But dealing with fear day in and day out for his entire life had done at least one thing for him. Now, in the midst of sheer terror, Alain could handle fear.

He just had to do something about it.

Another pillar jutted up, and this time Alain reached out to the flames, beckoning them. He did not attempt to exert dominance anymore. Instead, he invited the flames to join him. To aid him, in his time of need.

The flames answered.

At the same time, weapons, discarded by Scarabs and Denizens alike, rose into the air and sped towards Lailana. Code was using telesis.

Lailana deflected them easily, still holding Morayne with one hand, her movements so fast they blurred into the night.

"Don't hurt Morayne," Alain shouted through gritted teeth.

The earth rumbled again, and another pillar rose up.

Alain redirected all his flames from Lailana into the pillar. It glowed an angry orange-red.

Lailana, distracted by Code's constant bombardment, looked about her in frustration. If she noticed the blazing pillar, she wasn't able to do anything about it.

Alain ran towards Lailana and Morayne, still sending heat and fire into the pillar. The earth continued to shake, and another pillar jutted up from the ground. Alain let that one serve as another distraction, and continued to concentrate his effort onto the first.

"Code!" Alain shouted. "Can you take Morayne?"

"Think so," he responded. "Do your thing, mate."

Alain, courting the flames, sent every ounce of heat and fire he could muster into the blazing pillar. It burned from red to orange to a yellow so bright it was almost white, molten, losing its shape.

Exactly what Alain wanted.

Suddenly, he heard Brother Maddagon's voice again.

The way up is down. I needed to let go. Only then was I able to order my life.

Find your serenity, son.

Don't lose yourself in the fire. Find yourself in it.

With his last remaining effort, Alain reached into the pillar, greeting the heat, the molten rock, appropriating it into himself. It recognized him, and it aided him. He sent the burning pillar of earth onto Lailana, just as Code lifted Morayne away, directly into Alain's arms.

The molten rock poured onto Nadir's avatar, and she screamed.

"You have her, mate?" Code shouted.

Alain lowered Morayne gently to the ground. Her eyes were open, but she didn't look at him. She did not respond. Dark, burned bruises enveloped her neck where Lailana had held her.

The earth had stopped shaking.

Alain's vision blurred as he looked back at Code. "I have her."

Code ran forward, sword drawn.

The hideous, burning pile of already-cooling molten rock twisted and churned as Lailana struggled beneath it. An arm reached up, followed by a burning, blackened skull.

Code severed both, and each fell to the ground in a burst of sparks and ash.

It was over.

Morayne did not move.

"Your Majesty," someone said. Alain's jaw clenched. His father. He felt the anger rise within him, the flames in his skull.

He took a breath. He could not support that anger any longer. He let it go, completely and wholly, to something greater.

"Your Majesty," someone said again.

Alain felt no anger this time.

"*Your Majesty. Alain.*"

Only then did Alain realize that the words were addressed to him.

He looked up, vision still blurred, eyes stinging from smoke and ash and horror, to see Fedrick.

"Your father is dead," Fedrick said. "I am deeply sorry for

your loss, Your Majesty." Fedrick bowed his head. Then, he bent the knee.

Alain looked over his shoulder at where his father had been the last time he saw the man. Gainil wasn't there. He must have fled, and been killed as he ran. A death as meaningless as his life.

"I lost a father today," Alain said, his eyes resting on Brother Maddagon's body, "but he was not the king."

Alain looked down at Morayne, and took her again in his arms. She still didn't move; neither did the earth.

Alain bowed his head, and allowed himself to cry.

PART III

WE DIE WITH THE DYING

29

Four months after the battle of the Setso, Triah

RICCAN CARRIERI WOKE TO the sound of incessant pounding on his apartment door. He checked the waterclock by his desk. Still a few hours from midnight. He must have fallen asleep in his armchair. He placed the book he'd been reading—Cetro's *Early Poems*—and stood, picking up a sheathed dagger as he walked to the door. The bloody thing was about to be knocked off its hinges.

"All right, all right," he said loudly.

He opened the door, dagger hidden but at the ready.

Kosarin Lothgarde, Sirana Aqilla, and Karina Vestri stood at his door, grim looks on their faces.

Carrieri muttered a string of curses. Then, "Come in."

The Consular, Venerato, and Authoritar followed him into his chambers, closing the door behind them. Carrieri turned to face them.

"What happened?" He was irritated, but less for the interruption and more because of the reason that must be behind it. They would not personally call on him at this hour unless it was dire.

"The reinforcements we sent to General Kyfer were attacked this morning," Karina said. "Where are your maps?"

Carrieri frowned, but led them to the long table next to his desk. A large map of Khale stretched across the surface.

Karina pointed to the southwest section of the Eastmaw Mountains. "The reinforcements entered the valley between the mountains and Lake Dravian," she said. "But they—"

She looked up at Carrieri. "I need a smaller-scale map, Riccan. One of Lake Dravian."

He opened a large drawer in the table, and flipped through a series of maps. Finally, he found one of the more localized area of the Eastmaw Mountains and Lake Dravian. He pulled it out, placing it over the map of Khale.

"Thank you," Karina said, continuing. "The tiellan forces—"

"You are sure it was the tiellans?" Carrieri asked. "The mountain villages have been giving us trouble, lately. That's why Kyfer was there in the first place."

"They had the psimancer with them," Lothgarde said.

"Goddess, I'll get to her later," Karina said. "We tasked Captain Graggius to lead our troops to Kyfer's position."

After Kyfer's inconceivable loss at the battle of the Setso, Carrieri and the Parliament had sent Captain Ginan Graggius, with an entire regiment of twenty-five hundred legionaries, to reinforce the Steel Regiment and take care of this tiellan problem once and for all.

"Graggius led his troops the shortest way around the lake." Karina traced her finger along the northwestern edge of the lake, between the water and the mountains. "The tiellan forces ambushed them. They'd hidden themselves away in the foothills, and when Graggius's forces spread out far enough, they attacked."

"Shit," Carrieri whispered. Had it been him, he would never have led his forces on that side of the lake. Certainly not without scouting first. Graggius was a strong fighter, but not nearly as strong a tactician. His orders had been to join his forces with Kyfer's and fall under the general's command, and he'd set about doing that in a characteristically straightforward manner.

Carrieri should have seen the blunder coming.

"What were our losses?" Carrieri asked.

"Our forces were crushed." Karina's voice was bordering on hysterical. "Almost one thousand killed in battle. Another hundred drowned or went missing after trying to escape."

Carrieri could not stop his eyes from bulging. *Almost half of the reinforcements we sent.*

"And the Nazaniin *cotirs?*" Carrieri asked. They had sent two full *cotirs*—almost a quarter of the entire Nazaniin force in Triah—to help after the disaster at the Setso. He looked to Lothgarde, but the man's face had turned red. Instead, Aqilla spoke.

"She killed a full *cotir*, and the second telenic as well."

Carrieri took a step back, and sat back into his chair. He let out a long breath.

"You are sure she was the only psimancer?"

"Our… sources conflict, but the general consensus is that yes, she was the only one."

"One woman did all of this," Carrieri said quietly. He would very much like to meet this woman, if he did not kill her first.

"Our sources conflict on the tiellan numbers as well," Aqilla continued, "but most agree they could not have attacked with more than two thousand fighters. Kyfer thinks that might be just over half their full fighting force. Their losses were… minimal."

Two thousand tiellan troops was not a surprise. Kyfer's scouts had informed them that the tiellan force had been increasing in size. A seemingly constant stream of tiellans gathered to the so-called Druids, many joining the fighting branch, who apparently called themselves Rangers.

"They say the lake is red with the blood of the fallen," Karina said. "And that the River Setso flows crimson as well."

Carrieri rubbed the bridge of his nose.

"You must ride to meet her," Karina said.

Carrieri took a deep breath. A part of him wanted to do just that. "Roden continues to prepare for war. If they discover I've left Triah, that might be the catalyst they need to mount an offensive."

"Goddess," Karina said, "I was afraid you would say that."

"I'll send an entire division," Carrieri said. "Fifteen thousand legionaries. Four thousand of them cavalry. I'll order them to ride at first light."

Karina swore. "You would wait in Triah for a threat that may or may not appear, while these tiellan Rangers wreak havoc in our nation?"

"There is more to it than that," Lothgarde said, looking at Carrieri over his spectacles. "Isn't there, Riccan?"

Carrieri glared at Lothgarde. If that man was using psimancy to get this out of him…

Canta's bloody bones, what if he is? What could you do about it?

"Lothgarde, Aqilla, leave us," Karina said.

Carrieri blinked. Karina, as Consular, technically had authority over the Citadel and its leaders, but she knew as well as Carrieri the power these two people wielded. They were not worth alienating under any circumstance.

"Madam Consular," Lothgarde began, but whatever he was about to say Karina did not let him finish.

"*Leave us,*" she said, turning her full frame—which was almost a head shorter than Lothgarde and Aqilla both—to face them.

Lothgarde bowed his head. "As you say, Madam Consular." He left the room, Aqilla following closely behind.

When they were alone, Karina looked up at Carrieri.

"Let us speak frankly," she said. "Tell me what is on your mind."

Immediately, Carrieri began to pace back and forth before the map table. His thoughts always seemed clearest when he was in motion.

"My objective, first and foremost," Carrieri said, "has always been the well-being of Khale."

"So ride out to meet this woman," Karina said. "Do your Goddess-damned job!"

"She is a Khalic citizen, is she not? And her people, they are Khalic as well, is that correct?"

"They may have been at one point," Karina said, her eyes following Carrieri as he walked back and forth, "but they've all but renounced their citizenship. They've killed *thousands* of Khalic soldiers—"

"*And our soldiers killed their people first,*" Carrieri said, slamming his fist on the map table as he stopped pacing and faced Karina. "We forget that too easily. In Cineste, and then that idiot Kyfer," he said, pointing his finger at Karina, "who *your* Parliament appointed, Madam Consular, against my counsel, slaughtered over one hundred tiellan *civilians.* Unprovoked. No wonder they're out for our blood. Canta knows, we've shed enough of theirs over the past few months, let alone the past few centuries."

Carrieri lowered his accusing finger and took a deep breath before he continued. "I will protect Khale at all costs," he said, "from whatever enemies we face. Even these tiellans. Even if I think, in my heart of hearts, that it is *wrong* of me to do so.

I have sworn an oath, and I will uphold it. You needn't worry about that."

Karina's eyes closed, and she shook her head slowly. When she opened them again, the look she gave Carrieri was far too familiar. He wished he'd never seen that side of her, so that when he saw it now, it didn't hurt so badly.

"When we assume these positions of service—and, let's not fool ourselves, of *power*—we accept the responsibility to make the decisions that no one else will make. I don't like this situation any more than you do, Riccan. But even I am subject to the senators, and the majority of them are terrified of this tiellan force. I understand why you stay behind, but know that I'm not afraid to use the power of the Parliament to order you to go if it becomes necessary."

"If it becomes necessary," Carrieri said quietly, "you won't have to ask."

Karina laughed quietly, looking down at the ground. "We've gotten ourselves into a fine mess here, haven't we?"

Carrieri scoffed. He wanted to say it wasn't their fault, that the foolish senators and magistrates and generals were the ones making the mistakes. But those were excuses, and Carrieri had no use for them. These people were under their authority, and thus they shared responsibility.

"A fine mess indeed," Carrieri said. He wanted to reach out to her in that moment, to touch her shoulder, her hand, run his fingers along her cheek, *anything* to remember what their lives had once been like together.

But he didn't.

30

Adimora

SWEAT POURED DOWN WINTER'S face as she finished another round of sparring with Urstadt in the late summer sun. The volume of cheers that rose at the end of their session jarred her—she could remember a few people stopping to watch in passing, months ago, but now there were dozens at least, gathered around the tip of the great *rihnemin* where Winter and Urstadt were training. She did not mind that the cheers had been for her defeat—the fight had *almost* been close, after all. And the tiellans had actually taken a liking to Urstadt, despite her being the only human among the Druids. Dozens of tiellans now dispersed as Winter took a deep draught of water from a skin near her belongings.

The majority of Winter's Rangers remained in the Eastmaw Valley. They had set up a strong supply line from Adimora to the Ranger camp, extending through the Underway beneath the Undritch Mountains. For now, their position was strong. She spent most of her time in the Ranger camp with her soldiers, but on occasion returned to Adimora to report to Ghian, the elders and matriarchs, and the Cracked Spear. She enjoyed her time in Adimora; she was growing attached to the strange underground city, the great *rihnemin*, and her people there.

But Winter was growing restless.

Urstadt approached her, her glaive resting on her shoulders, both arms crooked over it, hands hanging limply. Her chest heaved up and down, too, and her tunic was soaked through. "You faltered in *bu-haka*," she said. "And that flawed the rest of your form set."

Winter nodded. She'd been aware of the mistake. She still had trouble balancing during *bu-haka*. The form required her to parry as she balanced on one leg, crouching like a coiled spring that then struck forward in the *bu-hado, bu-lor,* and then *bu-hakan* forms.

"Practice your balance," Urstadt said, "and you might have a chance at besting me one of these days."

Winter laughed, the sound strangely familiar in her throat. The past few months, she realized, had been more or less happy. She practiced with Urstadt for hours each day, and she loved the way her body felt afterward. The sweat and the soreness made her feel cleaner than any bath could. She had plenty of *faltira*, too—she'd been able to keep herself to less than one crystal a day, lately, and still had supply enough to last her another four or five months at that rate. She would need to figure out how to get more eventually, but for now she had enough.

She had led the tiellans in another decisive battle against the Khalic forces, this time against a large group of reinforcements en route to bolster the Steel Regiment. The River Setso ran red with the blood of Khalic soldiers for days afterwards.

After arriving in Adimora, the Druids had sent small emissary groups to the cities with the most prominent tiellan populations, and hundreds of tiellans had come to join their cause.

The Cracked Spear prisoners she had sent home after fighting their brothers before the battle of the Setso had told the rest of the tiellans in Adimora what had happened. Afterwards, the rest of the Cracked Spear chieftains had united with Ghian under the Druid title. They had pledged their fighters to Winter, and Winter had undisputed command of the Rangers on the field. She had made sure that was clear. In Adimora, however, the power dynamic was complicated—more complicated than Winter thought it needed to be. The chieftains each still had jurisdiction over their own clans, but Ghian was a figure of power in the city now, too. She respected the way he united the tiellan clans; where she intimidated, Ghian soothed, and where she divided, Ghian connected. His leadership was a valuable complement to hers, providing something she could not, and Winter was grateful for his presence.

And now, with the addition of the final Cracked Spear clans, and the influx of female Rangers and other tiellan refugees willing to fight, Winter could field almost nine thousand Rangers—more than half of which were cavalry.

Word of their victories had spread throughout Khale, and tiellans from all over the nation flocked to the Eastmaw Valley, and eventually to Adimora. Between Urstadt, Selldor, Rorie, Eranda, Darrin, and Gord, Winter could even say she had friends, again. Old and new.

And yet, despite all the good, Winter could not shake the feeling that she was an outsider. She experienced it while walking through the depths of Adimora, surrounded by a crowd of her own people, her kin—and yet felt no connection with any of them. Or she experienced it at night, alone, when no one else was around, when she wondered what in Oblivion she was actually doing, leading tiellan forces into battle against her own government.

But, for the most part, she was not unhappy. And that made her cautious.

"I don't know whether I will ever be able to best you," Winter said honestly.

"I do," Urstadt smiled, "and you will not."

Winter laughed again, but was interrupted by someone running up behind her.

"Commander."

Winter turned to see Selldor walking quickly towards her. She tensed. The recent defeat of the Khalic reinforcements at Lake Dravian would not go unanswered. The Legion would come at her in full force, now. She just hoped it was later rather than sooner.

"What is it, Selldor?" Winter asked, wiping sweat from her brow. As she did, she caught scent of herself. Goddess, she smelled worse than she did after an entire day of fish-gutting in Pranna.

Then, behind Selldor, she noticed a group of tiellans walking towards her. They wore traditional tiellan clothing: long dresses and *siaras* for the women, long-sleeved shirts, trousers, and *araifs* for the men.

Tiellans were not, as a general rule, overweight. Winter suspected this had more to do with the fact that food, and ways to pay for food, were more difficult to come by for them than anything else. But the old woman who led the group walking towards her was immense, and Winter had seen her before.

This was Mazille—the tiellan woman who had sold her *faltira* in Navone, and the only other tiellan psimancer Winter had ever met.

An uneasy weight settled into Winter's gut.

"I suspected it was you," Mazille said, her eyes bright beneath a head of long silver hair. Despite her girth and age, she moved easily across the grass towards Winter. "From the moment I saw you, I sensed you were something special."

"Do you know these people?" Urstadt asked.

"She and I are acquaintances," Winter said, nodding at Mazille. "The others..."

She remembered rushing through the alley in Navone, fleeing other psimancers. She remembered feeling herself being lifted off the ground by another's *tendron*.

Deep in her belly, the uneasy feeling grew.

"What brings you to Adimora?"Winter asked. She still held a sword; the sheathed tip rested on the ground with her hand wrapped around the pommel. She was suddenly very aware of her appearance: sweaty, smelly, and disheveled.

Why do you care what these people think of you? Winter wondered to herself. *They are just like all of the other tiellans.*

And yet they were not. They were like her.

"What brings *any* tiellan to Adimora?" Mazille asked with a smile. She stopped a few paces away from Winter, and her companions—five others, male and female tiellans, representing a wide age range—stopped with her. "The draw to our cause," Mazille said, answering her own question. "The cause of the Druids. And, of course, rumors of a tiellan warrior who can't be beaten in battle."

Winter gripped the pommel of her sword. She had a frost crystal in the pouch at her belt, as she always did, but she did not want to take one in front of this woman and her companions. She could use acumency, of course, but that was always risky. Half of the time when Winter used acumency, she ended up in the Void, her body going dormant in the Sfaera. She could not risk that now.

But, for all she knew, these psimancers had their *tendra* at the ready, and could attack her at any moment.

Then, Mazille knelt before Winter, and her companions followed suit.

"'Tis our pleasure to present ourselves at your service, Winter Cordier," Mazille said, her head bowed.

Winter stared at the people kneeling before her. Then she glanced around, suddenly very self-conscious.

"Rise," Winter said quickly, regaining her senses. "Who are your companions, Mazille?" Despite their show of fealty, Winter still did not trust them.

"Ah, you *do* remember me," the woman said, smiling. "Wasn't sure that'd be the case."

"You are the only other tiellan psimancer I've ever met," Winter said. "I'm not likely to forget you."

"Of course, my dear. Forgive my rudeness; I'll introduce my companions. This one is Opal," Mazille said, indicating another older woman, to her right. "She's been with me the longest." Opal was tall for a tiellan woman, and bone-thin, in stark contrast to Mazille.

Mazille pointed to an older man standing to her left. His pointed ears protruded from long locks of straight silver hair, despite his wrinkled skin and stooped stature. "Phares has been with me for almost as long. Orsolya and Astasios are siblings." She indicated a man and woman, both a few years Winter's senior. Both had long brown hair, and light brown, almost golden, eyes.

Finally, Mazille looked at the last of her group, a young lad, perhaps in his fifteenth year. Blonde hair. Light eyes. Serious expression. The lad reminded Winter very much of Lian. "Vlak's our newest. He came to us shortly after you and I met, in fact."

"Are they all psimancers?" Winter asked.

Mazille smiled nervously, her face turning red. "Ain't

typical for us to talk about such things in public, though—"

"I don't care what you usually do and do not do," Winter said. "I asked you a question."

The color in Mazille's face deepened. "Of course. We're all psimancers, as you put it, yes."

"Telenics? Acumens?"

Mazille frowned, and behind her Phares coughed. Winter was making them uncomfortable. Good. She was glad of it. They had to know they had the same effect on her, coming to see her here.

"I really think it'd be better to discuss this in private, Winter—"

"I think we're discussing it quite effectively here and now."

Mazille threw up her arms. "Well then. I'm a telenic, as you've likely noticed, as are Orsolya and Astasios. Opal and Phares are both acumens."

"And Vlak?"

"Vlak is a voyant," Mazille said.

A voyant. Winter had not met one face to face before. She stared at the young man without hiding her curiosity.

"Which one of you attacked me in the alleyway?" Winter asked. And then, suddenly, the reason the worrying weight had settled in her stomach was clear to her. If these people were psimancers, at least some of them were variants—they required the use of frost to access their power. There was a point where Winter would have done anything to secure more frost for herself. She was not sure she was beyond that point now, in fact.

There was no telling what these people might do.

There was a moment's hesitation, and then Astasios stepped forward. "That was me, madam," he said, bowing his head.

"He only did what I ordered him to do," Mazille inserted.

"The amount of *faltira* you bought from us was valuable. Can't blame us for attempting to get it back."

Winter snorted. She hadn't stolen the *faltira*; she'd paid for it, and at an exorbitant price nonetheless.

"Forgive me, Winter, but we've traveled a great distance. We're hungry. Let us get a meal. Let us rest our feet. Then, we'll tell you all you want to know."

Reluctantly, Winter nodded. She could use a bath, anyway.

That night, after cleaning herself up, Winter sat at one of the large campfires in upper Adimora. Mazille and her group had been billeted with the Druids in the upper city, near the massive *rihnemin*, and now sat around the fire with Winter. Urstadt had accompanied her at her request—for protection, and because Winter found there was very little the woman didn't know about her. What she was afraid to tell Eranda or Gord, Urstadt already knew.

"I assume you have something to discuss with me," Winter said, when Mazille remained silent across the fire from her.

"I do, Winter, but…" Mazille glanced at Urstadt. "I don't understand why you brought a humans here."

"Urstadt is close to me. I trust her more than anyone else on the Sfaera."

"Never been comfortable around humans," Mazille grumbled. "Ain't sure I can—"

"You'll either tell me what you have to tell me, in their presence, or you will not," Winter said. She did not have time for such discomforts. There had been a time when she could hardly look a human in the eye. Things were different for her, now.

Mazille cleared her throat. "Very well, Winter. We will do

as you ask." She paused, looking closely at Winter. "You have taken *faltira* recently, have you not?"

Winter forced her face to remain expressionless. She had taken a frost crystal when she'd seen Mazille and the others approaching. How had Mazille discerned this? "I have," she said. No use hiding it.

"You have learned how to create it yourself, then? Is that how you perpetuate your supply?"

"I can provide for my needs well enough," Winter said cautiously, although speaking of the topic brought the heavy suspicion back into her gut.

"But you have not learned how to make it yourself?" Mazille asked, her head cocking to one side.

"Not yet," Winter said. She hoped the woman might offer to teach her, but no such offer came. It had been so long since she had spoken to someone who could help her learn more about psimancy. Kali had not approached her since their falling out in the Void, and that was fine with Winter. She had never trusted Kali.

She did not trust Mazille, either, but Mazille was here, and Winter might as well take advantage of that. Frost burned within her, and she was ready for anything Mazille might try.

"Do you know of the Nazaniin?" Winter asked.

Mazille nodded. "We have little to do with them."

"They are psimancers too," Winter said. "You could learn from them."

"There is nothing of any importance we could learn from them," Mazille spat. "They are abominations. They have inherited something that is not theirs."

Winter narrowed her eyes. "They seem to understand psimancy far better than you do," she said. "And unless you've hidden groups of psimancers throughout the Sfaera, there seem to be far more of them, too." Winter realized how likely what she had just said might actually be. That was the Nazaniin's tactic, after all—plant their *cotirs* in as many major cities as possible, gathering information.

But Mazille's face told Winter all she needed to know. Her features fell as she shook her head. "Psimantic ability in tiellans is rare. Far more rare than in humans. The only surviving tiellan psimancers I've encountered are here, at this campfire."

"And did the power manifest itself in tiellans only recently, as it has in humans?"

"That, my dear, is a long story. And it is why we have sought you out." Mazille's gaze flickered to Urstadt.

Winter said nothing. She would not dignify Mazille's implied question with an answer. Winter had already given hers. Instead she met Mazille's eyes, unblinking.

Mazille sighed deeply. "Very well. I must first go back, far, far into the ages…"

In the Beginning, there was Light and Dark. Light had no end, and thus had no beginning, and likewise Dark had no beginning, and thus no end. And Light was stronger than Dark. And yet Light understood that, without Dark, she had no beauty; without Dark, she had no definition, and no purpose. Without Dark there was nothing to illuminate; without Dark there was nothing to change. And likewise Dark, the weaker of the two, acknowledged that without Light, what use was he? For Dark meant nothing without Light to define him; Dark had no purpose with no source of conflict.

And so the two existed together, Light and Dark, in harmony, and both were happy. Thus they played for countless millennia, moving their forms around and through one another, until one day they lay in such a way that both experienced the greatest pleasure that has ever been known. The two moved together in a moment of such ecstasy, that suddenly they could not discern what was Dark and what was Light. The two became one, for a moment of hazed pleasure, and then both collapsed in content exhaustion. As the breath of Light and the breath of Dark merged together, the stars in the sky were born.

Light and Dark looked on what they had created, and smiled. The stars were beautiful to behold, and countless. But soon they saw that the stars were lonely. They were countless, yes, but they were all so far apart; they had no way to communicate with one another, no way to love one another the way Light loved Dark. Light shared her worries with Dark, and the two agreed to create a place for the stars to live, a place they could be born and exist and die, and meet. Thus, Light and Dark formed the Sfaera, with great waters to house fish and whales of the deep, and high mountains to reach the sky, and rolling forests to beautify and sustain the land. Light and Dark looked on the Sfaera with pride, and began to send the stars down to the Sfaera, to live, to die, and then to live again.

Light created the form for the first stars, and that form was created after the likeness in her own mind. She created the form, and the stars inhabited the form, and thus the tiellans were born.

Dark, too, created a form for yet other stars, and that form was created after the likeness in his own mind. He created the form, and the stars inhabited the form, and thus the humans were born.

And the humans and tiellans lived together in harmony, with love and affection toward one another. And thus the stars, the countless children of Light and Dark, found happiness, life, and love on the Sfaera.

Light and Dark looked on the Sfaera with happiness, and were content.

"My father told me that story," Winter interrupted. "He said my mother used to tell it to him. I thought she had made it up."

"She did not make it up," Mazille said, quietly.

"Then it is real? Dark and Light were real, and we... we are their children?"

"It is as real as any other creation story you have heard. As real as Canta's," Mazille said. "But this story is only the beginning. I have more to tell you. We do not know what happened to Light and Dark..."

Perhaps they grew bored of their creations and left for new horizons. Perhaps they have finally grown old and passed away into Oblivion, as all things must. Perhaps they are still there, waiting, watching.

But what matters is that, other than in their most basic forms, they no longer show themselves. We no longer interact with the great Beings that formed this world, and formed us.

And then came the First Age. By all accounts, that First Age was a paradise. Tiellans and humans lived in harmony, if you can believe such a thing. We hunted the beasts of the Sfaera, we gathered plants and other forms of food, and soon began to grow crops. There was only one monarch, and she ruled with a loving, benevolent hand.

"The Chaos Queen," Winter said.

Mazille glared at her, annoyance plain on her face.

"Some call her by that name," she said. "We called her the Great Matriarch. She loved her people, both human and tiellan, and she treated them fairly."

"The monarchs of the First Age ruled benevolently," Winter said, "until the last one went mad, and broke her kingdom. Bedtime tales. A human once told me there was only one monarch," she added, thinking of Galce. "But she did go mad. She did as Chaos directed."

"Your human friend was only partly right," Mazille said. "There *was* only one monarch, throughout the entire First Age. She was endowed with long life, somehow, but at the end of her life, her mind failed her. She destroyed society as people knew it then, and we fell into the Starless Age…"

In the Starless Age the Sfaera fell into a terrible cycle.

The Mad Queen continued to degenerate, until she was finally overthrown by another being of great power. But that being, in order to keep the Sfaera together, to keep the Outsiders from invading, and because of Soren's Folly, had to take over the Mad Queen's role, and became the Mad Queen herself.

This cycle became known as the Annulus.

The Starless Age lasted longer than all of the other ages combined. Over ten thousand years, and the Sfaera existed as if in stasis, going through the same motions, the same cycle, every thousand years. Until finally, a new queen, the woman Khale, after whom this nation was named, sacrificed herself, and sealed the opening into the Outside, and saved us all from destruction.

This ushered in the Age of Marvels, and this is the age where psimancy truly began. You may have been told that it was a recent thing, and for humans that may be so. But not for tiellans.

Psimancy was a new art, then, though it was not the same as it is now. There was no such thing as *faltira* in those days; all psimancers were actuals, and they were all tiellans. The histories teach that tiellans were one with nature, could control the elements. Tiellans were psimantic masters, and the greatest warriors of the Age of Marvels—Rana Dalther, Kels Erie, Kuote, and Merle of the Lin clan—were all psimancers.

Tiellans rose to power through psimancy. They were respected, honored for their ability not only to fight but to engineer great machines and use their arts to help those around them. There were psimancer Druids, and psimancer Rangers.

But, as all ages must, the Age of Marvels came to an end. The Great War between the humans and tiellans began when the humans became jealous of tiellan psimantic power. Tiellans prevailed at first, because humans could not compete with the very power they coveted. The children of Light fought the children of Dark, and beat them back.

Then, a new weapon was introduced.

No one knows where the ability came from. But one day, the human king brought with him a dagger, and his dagger broke the world.

The dagger, imbued with the blood of a Scorned God, had the power to quell a psimancer's power in an instant. Any psimancer near the dagger lost all power. And as the psimancers fell powerless around him, the king slew them with the dagger, drenching it in their blood, and the more psimancers he killed, the greater the dagger's power became, until he all but wiped out the most powerful warriors.

When the dust cleared, and the blood ceased to flow, the humans found themselves victorious. They enslaved the surviving tiellans for thousands of years.

But the tiellans, while defeated, did not lose hope. They created *rihnemin*, the great monuments of our people, to stand as witness to their fallen brothers and sisters, and to house the power that they would one day reclaim. Psimancy was passed down through tiellan bloodlines, but only a precious few were chosen each generation. Often their power was latent, or simply weak, just a shadow of what was once possible. Tiellans bore their psimantic ability with sacred pride, and soon not even other tiellans knew of this birthright, save for the families who carried the blood themselves.

Mazille said, motioning around the fire, "We few are the inheritors of the true power of the tiellans. Our powers are much stronger than those who came before us. Together, we could move mountains, and crumble nations."

Winter stared, blinking, into the fire. So many questions rushed through her mind, but one above all.

"My mother must have been a psimancer," Winter said softly.

"I saw the resemblance the moment you came to my shop," Mazille said. "You have her hair, and her eyes. You two are very much alike."

"You *knew* my mother?" Winter asked. Her mother had died when she was too young to remember her. Beyond the stories her father had told her, all she had were the horrifying visions she had seen of her in Azael's presence. Visions Winter could only hope were not real.

"Effara was one of us, for a time. Opal, Phares, and I all knew her."

Winter shivered. She had not heard her mother's name since before her father was killed.

"What happened to her?" she asked.

"She left us," Mazille said. "We did not know why at the time. But I suppose now it is clear. She lost interest in our order. She intended to start a family."

Emotions tumbled within her, fighting for breath. She desperately wanted to know more, but another part of her was cautious, distrusting of anything Mazille had to say. Still another part of her fostered the tiniest grain of hope. Perhaps, after all of this time, this was why she had never felt she belonged.

Perhaps, more than the tiellans, more than the Druids and the Rangers, more than even her father and her kin in Pranna, *this* was where she belonged.

"We thought she had gone south," Mazille said. "We searched for her for a time, but in the end it seemed a lost cause."

"She made her intentions clear," Phares said. His voice was deep and quiet, and Winter realized it was the first time she had heard him speak. "She wanted nothing more to do with us. We could not force her to stay, as much as we tried. As much as we wanted to."

"Why did she not want anything to do with you?" Winter asked. She could not imagine leaving the group of people that were more like her than any other in the Sfaera, for any reason.

"She lost her belief in our cause," Mazille said. "She no longer believed our story, everything I just told you. She thought it was something our ancestors had made up, to make us feel special."

"But she could use psimancy?" Winter asked. "She saw the evidence."

"She could," Phares said slowly, "but psimancy alone was not evidence enough. Especially when the humans began to manifest the power as well."

Winter shook her head. "If you knew I was Effara's daughter, why didn't you tell me all of this in Navone, before I left? Why did you come after me, try to kill me?"

"I had not been ordered to kill you," Astasios said. "Just to reclaim the *faltira* you had bought from us, and bring you back. We were going to tell you everything that very night."

"But you were too strong, too quick, even for us," Mazille said. "With each generation we get stronger, but… but you seem far stronger than any of us. How many *tendra* can you wield?"

Winter hesitated. Sharing such a detail seemed dangerous, somehow. She did not want Mazille to use it against her.

And yet, the truth did not seem all that harmful.

"I don't know," Winter said.

"You don't know?" Mazille asked, frowning. "Have you not tried to access your full power?"

"I… I can use more than a dozen," Winter said after a moment. "I think I might be able to wield a few more, if I really tried." That was technically not a lie, but she wasn't disclosing how *many* more than a dozen she could wield. Typically, maybe two score, and that was without testing her limits. She could not remember clearly, but under the dome in Izet, and in the Circle Square in Navone, she thought it was possible she used even more than that.

The other tiellans around the fire stared at her in stunned silence.

"More than a dozen?" Vlak was the first to speak, his eyes wide.

"Are… are you sure?" Mazille asked after a moment.

Winter shrugged. "Not exactly, but I do think I've used at least a dozen." She met Mazille's eyes. "Why? How many can you access?"

Mazille blinked, then her eyes shifted to the fire. "Six," she said. "On a good day, with the purest *faltira*. Vlak can match that, and we are the most powerful tiellan psimancers to exist in memory."

Vlak? So a voyant uses tendra? It made sense, if acumens and telenics both used them as well.

That, however, was the least of her questions. "I want to know more. About the *rihnemin*, and this blood dagger." The strange tale had reminded her of the monks she had faced in Roden—and Daval himself—who had been able to block her telenic ability. "And more about my mother," she added, unable to stop herself.

"Of course," Mazille said, nodding. "We will be happy to share with you all we know."

Winter nodded. "Good," she said. She had other duties, of course—her Rangers, the campaign against the Khalic Legion, and her training sessions with Urstadt—but this was important. She needed to make time for it.

She might, after all, have finally found a home.

31

Odenite camp, outside Kirlan

CINZIA WAITED FOR ASTRID at the edge of the Odenite camp as the last rays of the sun began to vanish. She shifted her weight from one foot to the other. She could hardly contain her nervousness. It had been four months since Knot had been taken—four *months*, and Jane's promised advance to Triah seemed as far away as ever—but Astrid's last check-in had been hopeful. One week ago, the girl said she would soon find Knot, and to look for her by sunset at the end of the week. That was today, the sun was setting, and Cinzia waited.

Soon, Cinzia heard rustling in the forest ahead, and her heart began to thump rapidly in her chest. She could not believe how much she had taken her relationship with Knot for granted—and even her relationship with Astrid. Without Knot, and with Astrid only here on occasion, the Odenite camp had been driving Cinzia mad. She had not realized how much she had been relying on them both to retain her sanity. Once the three of them were together again, Cinzia would never let them go.

Sure enough, Astrid walked out of the forest, her eyes just beginning to glow a soft green.

The girl was alone.

Cinzia looked behind Astrid for any signs of another person, listened for any other sounds. She neither saw nor heard anything. Her heart continued to pound in her chest, so loud she could hear each beat.

"He could not keep up with you, is that it?" Cinzia called, laughing nervously. Knot had to be with her. Astrid insisted she had all but found him.

But as Astrid approached, Cinzia saw the look on the girl's face. It told her all she needed to know.

Cinzia fell to her knees, unable to stop the cry that escaped her lips.

Astrid said nothing, instead moving directly to Cinzia and wrapping her in an embrace.

"Is he—"

"I don't think so," Astrid said quickly. "I didn't... I didn't find *anyone*, Cinzia. No Knot. No one from the Cult. Nothing."

Cinzia stayed in Astrid's arms, grateful for the girl's embrace. When she pulled away, she saw Astrid had fully transformed, her eyes glowing bright green, teeth and claws elongated and sharp. A fleeting thought struck Cinzia that it was peculiar she didn't mind the qualities that once horrified and terrified her in equal measure. It was impossible not to see the differences the girl manifested at night, but Cinzia realized she loved Astrid not just in spite of those differences, but because of them.

But Knot was still gone. Cinzia choked back the lump in her throat, refusing to shed the hot tears that formed in her eyes. "You said you were close."

"I thought I was," Astrid said, her voice unusually earnest. "The trail I was following was a Goddess-damned wild goose chase. The Black Matron planted every informant I've found. In the Ministry, in the City Watch, in the Sons—every single one of them. She led me on an idiotic pursuit through the city, and then out into the forest to a cabin. An empty, stupid cabin. Knot wasn't there, and there was no sign of him, or anyone from the Cult."

"You must have found something. Anything. You mentioned a cabin. What was in it, Astrid?"

"A message," Astrid said. "A single chair in the middle of an empty cabin in the woods. A place only I would recognize."

A chair in an empty cabin. "No," Cinzia said, shaking her head. "The past four months cannot have been for nothing. You had to have found *something*."

"I'm sorry, Cinzia," Astrid said, and even through the green glow Cinzia saw the pain in the girl's eyes. "I thought I could find him, but I was wrong. I'm so sorry."

Inside Cinzia, something broke. She did not know what it was, or what it meant, but she felt a visceral *snap* inside of her.

"This is not your fault," Cinzia said, looking Astrid in the eyes. She meant it, and she hoped the girl understood that, but she did not have time to convince her. Cinzia embraced her again, then stood up and walked towards the forest, ignoring Astrid's calls.

Anger boiled inside of Cinzia as she stalked through the forest. Anger at the Black Matron for doing this to her, to Knot, and to Astrid. Anger at her sister for doing nothing to help Knot, when he had done so much for the Odenites. Most of all, anger at herself. Her sense of helplessness the past four months had nearly driven her mad; the only thing that had kept her sane was knowing that Astrid was out there, looking for Knot.

She should never have put so much responsibility on Astrid. Astrid was at least as distraught as she at Knot's capture. She should have taken some of the burden on herself. Instead, Cinzia and Jane had continued translating the Nine Scriptures faithfully, but no concrete help had come of it. Cinzia could not point at anything over the past four months that had been worth her time.

But now, she was willing to try a last resort.

It was completely dark by the time Cinzia was deep enough in the forest to be sure she was alone. She made careful note of the direction in which she walked, and her surroundings. A huge, wide, gnarly tree here, as big around as a wagon. A small clearing there, to the south. Fireflies winked on and off around her. In Navone and Tinska, Cinzia had grown used to not having them around. They never appeared that far north, even in the summer. But here, in Kirlan, they were plentiful, and gave the forest around her an otherworldly, fantastical feel. Very different from how Cinzia felt inside.

"I am here," Cinzia said out loud. "I am ready to speak with you."

She heard crickets around her, chirping merrily. She did not *want* to feel the ominous sense of horror that weighed heavily on her; the crickets, the fireflies, the moonlight streaming through the trees above, made the forest feel warm, inviting. But she could not avoid the fear that clawed inside of her, and the suffocating guilt that accompanied it.

"*I am here*," Cinzia said again, more emphatically. "I am ready to talk. If you do not take me up on this offer now, I will not attempt to contact you again."

Nothing but the sounds of the forest at night responded to her.

Cinzia rejected the impulse to stamp her foot, to scream, to demand to be heard. Instead, she took a deep breath, calming herself.

"I—"

Then, silence.

The world expanded around her, and Cinzia felt a rush.

This was what she asked for. This was what she wanted.

She had better make it count.

Cinzia once again found herself in the blue-gray forest, without sound and without life. The trees, the grass and other foliage, even the night sky itself emitted a wispy blue light.

"What is it you want?"

Cinzia recognized Luceraf's voice, low and calm, echoing just slightly in the space they now occupied. A slit of blue light slowly took form, growing into the shape of a beautiful young woman.

"I want to speak with you," Cinzia said, raising her chin high.

"Clearly," Luceraf said, moving towards her. Cinzia realized the woman—the Daemon—did not have feet, or at least not that Cinzia could see. Below her knees, the woman's form grew nebulous, blending in with the iridescent blue mist that blanketed the ground. Luceraf did not walk, but levitated forward, hovering.

"What is it you wish to speak about, Cinzia?" Luceraf said. "I thought you wanted nothing to do with me."

"I never said that," Cinzia said. Though it was true, Cinzia no longer had a choice. "I have come to ask you about Knot."

"And what is Knot?" Luceraf asked.

"You know who he is," Cinzia said. "The Black Matron has him. Tell me where, and what they are going to do with him."

Luceraf sniffed. "The Black Matron has always been Azael's creature. And Bazlamit's, on occasion. I've always preferred more... colorful methods."

"But surely you communicate," Cinzia said. "Surely you can find out."

Luceraf laughed, the sound echoing in the muted forest.

It reverberated until it seemed there were a hundred women laughing instead of just one.

"You really think I would tell you? I may not like Bazlamit. I may have my issues with Azael. But my lot has been thrown in with theirs. I have learned not to pretend otherwise."

Did that mean Luceraf *had* pretended otherwise at some point? Did that mean there might be some divide among the Daemons that she could exploit?

If it did, it was a revelation for another time.

"You want someone to be your avatar, do you not?" Cinzia asked.

Luceraf frowned. It might, Cinzia realized, have been the first time she actually saw a look of displeasure from the Daemon. "Where did you hear this?"

"And the avatar must be willing," Cinzia continued. "I... I could do this for you, if you share information with me."

Cinzia swallowed. She could not believe what she was proposing, and yet... it was *Knot*. She had to do something to help him.

And, perhaps in becoming Luceraf's avatar, she could find a weakness within the Nine.

"You would become my avatar?" Luceraf asked, the surprise clear in her voice.

"If you tell me about Knot," Cinzia said.

Cinzia met the Daemon's eyes, and she resisted the chill that crept up her spine. Luceraf's eyes sparkled blue, glowing in the dusk-like space around them.

"Very well," Luceraf said. The Daemon nodded, as if confirming to herself. "I do know something of the Black Matron's plan for Knot. They have spent the last few months attempting to break him in Kirlan."

Knot is still in Kirlan. She tried not to think what Luceraf meant by the Black Matron trying to "break" Knot.

"You'll be happy to know they have not succeeded. Now, they intend to take him to Triah."

"Triah?" Cinzia asked, panic rising within her. "When will they leave?"

"I cannot say for certain," Luceraf said with a shrug, "but within the week, I'd imagine."

"Within the week," Cinzia whispered. "Will she take the Sons of Canta with her?" she asked.

"Of course not," Luceraf said. "The Sons are not hers. The Sons are here for you, and your sister."

"You need to be more specific than that," Cinzia said. "Tell me where they will be, and when."

"I already told you, I cannot say for certain—"

"*Then figure it out, and tell me.*"

Silence descended on the ethereal forest as Cinzia realized what she had just done.

Luceraf smiled. "I like you, Cinzia. You have fire. Very well. Get yourself south of the city. When you reach that point, you will know."

"How will I know?"

"I'll whisper it in your ear, darling."

Cinzia met the Daemon eye to eye, wishing she could trust what Luceraf said, but knowing she would never have that assurance.

"What will they do to him if they break him?" Cinzia asked. She needed to know.

"They have great plans for Knot," Luceraf said with a smile. "He, too, will become an avatar."

"Knot would never willingly become the avatar to a

Daemon," Cinzia spat, although as she said the words, she wondered whether they were true. She would just as vehemently have said them about herself a few months ago. There was no telling what circumstances might cause a person to act in a way they never thought they would.

"Knot might never choose such a thing," Luceraf said, "but Lathe might."

Cinzia's eyes widened. "Lathe is gone," she said. "He was contained by Knot when Wyle helped him—"

"Do you think they did anything a Daemon could not undo?" Luceraf asked sharply. "Do not underestimate our power. We have existed in the Void for millennia. If Knot will not turn, we will find someone within him who will."

"Why Knot?" Cinzia asked, shaking her head. "Why does it matter who you choose as an avatar?"

Luceraf pursed her lips. "You haven't figured that out yet?"

"We could stop them," Cinzia said quietly. "We could still help him."

Luceraf's laughter again rang through the eerie grove. "I do not think so, my dear Cinzia. If I'd thought you could still help him, I would not have told you anything at all."

Cinzia closed her eyes tightly, trying to shut out the sharp sting of tears.

"Our deal does not count if there is nothing I can do," Cinzia said. "I will never be your avatar."

Luceraf had been standing—or floating, rather—a few rods away from Cinzia. But in a fragment of a second, the Daemon had covered the distance between them, and suddenly their faces were only a few fingers' width apart.

"You cannot go back on what you have promised," Luceraf hissed, and for the first time Cinzia caught a hint of something...

something different inside the Daemon. Something inhuman. Her mouth elongated just for a moment, ending in a fiercely pointed beak. "I will come calling on you when it is time to make the bond between us."

The suffocating guilt expanded in Cinzia's belly, overflowing up through her throat.

"You can go—"

Then, in a flash, Cinzia was back in the forest. Crickets chirped merrily around her. The fireflies' lazy glow illuminated the dark. Her breath came in rapid, short rasps, and it took her a moment before she was sure she wasn't about to faint.

Slowly at first, then picking up speed, Cinzia eventually broke out into a run on her way back to the camp.

She had to find Astrid.

32

Adimora

"So RIHNEMIN ARE THE remnants of tiellan power?" Winter asked.

She and Mazille walked alone around the large *rihnemin* at the center of Adimora's upper level. It was early morning, and the sun had yet to rise. Winter was due for another sparring session with Urstadt in an hour or so, but had asked Mazille to walk with her for a while. There was still so much she wanted to know.

"Not remnants," Mazille said. "Receptacles."

"Receptacles of power," Winter whispered. "Like voidstones?"

"In a way, yes. But how they hold power is altogether very different."

Mazille looked up. Winter followed her gaze to see the countless stars above, barely visible as the sky turned from black to a dark, purplish hue. "All the power that tiellans once had still exists," Mazille said. "Just have to learn how to access it."

"Have you tried?"

Mazille laughed. "Course I've tried, many times. I've sent *tendra* into the stone, and made a rune or two glow briefly on the surface, but only for a moment."

"You've made runes glow? Like the runes beneath the Undritch Mountains?"

"Aye," Mazille said with a smile. "Nowhere near that many, but aye. Seems to be a connection there."

"What kind of connection?"

"If I knew that, I'd tell you."

Winter wished she could trust Mazille, but there was so much she still didn't know about the woman.

"Do you believe the stories you have told me?" Winter asked.

"Course I believe them, child. That's why I'm recounting them to you—"

"My mother did not believe them," Winter said. "Is there any real evidence one way or the other?"

"Our existence ain't evidence enough?"

It was not enough for my mother. "Were the two of you friends?"

"We were... close, for many years," Mazille said. "But we also had our differences."

"What was she like?" Winter asked. Her father had told her, of course, but she could only glean so much from a few stories told over and over again.

"I'd be lying if I said she was a kind woman," Mazille said, after a long pause. "She... she spoke her mind, without regard to how her words might affect others. More often than not, she was right, though. She had a softer side, too. A side reserved only for those closest to her. I suspect your father got the large part of that side of Effara, as much as so many others would have wanted it."

"Would she... would she have made a good mother?" Winter asked.

Mazille barked a laugh, her whole frame shaking. "Effara would have made a wonderful mother, my dear. And, at the same time, she would have been abysmal. No mother is perfect, and yours certainly would not have been. But she would have been good, I believe."

She burned with a desire to know more. And yet, Winter

was not here to talk of her mother. Another confrontation with Khale was imminent; Urstadt thought it might come within the next few weeks. Scouts said nothing of any forces on their way, but Winter felt it in her gut, too. Something was about to happen.

She needed to be prepared for it when it did.

"You mentioned the human king's dagger, from the Age of Marvels," Winter said. "The Blood Dagger. This weapon nullified psimantic ability?"

"So the legend states."

"What do you know of the Ceno Order?" Winter asked.

Mazille frowned. "The ancient Rodenese religion?"

"It is not ancient anymore. The religion has resurfaced."

"Wasn't aware of that," Mazille muttered, her eyes glazing over. Then, quickly, she refocused on Winter. "Roden's the least of our problems, ancient religion resurfacing or no."

"The monks of the Ceno Order can block psimantic ability," Winter said.

Mazille stared at Winter. "You cannot know such a thing."

"I've been to Roden, encountered these monks, and they've blocked *my* power. Is there another way to block psimancy? Other than with the dagger?"

Mazille shook her head. "The stories from the Age of Marvels are not clear by any means. The power may have rested only with the dagger itself, but there may have been a way to extract its power. To share it with others."

Winter stopped walking. They stood at the base of the *rihnemin*, which was taller than any building Winter had seen, save for the imperial palace in Izet. Now that she'd been into the gorge and seen the *real* Adimora, she knew this was only a fraction of its true size.

"Mazille, it occurs to me that you could help me with something." She took a frost crystal out of her pouch, slipping it into her mouth. "Do you have *faltira* on you?"

Mazille eyed Winter's pouch. "You must have a large store to take it so casually."

Winter frowned. "I told you, I have enough for my needs. Do you have one of your own?" She could tell the woman was thinking about how to respond. Mazille's eyes did not move from the pouch at Winter's waist.

"I... I have one of my own," Mazille finally said, reaching into a pocket within her dress.

"Take it," Winter said. "I want you to show me what you've attempted with the *rihnemin*."

"No need to be so hasty," Mazille said, shaking her head. "We will have time enough to—"

"Do it," Winter said. "We are going to start now." If she was going to be able to use the power of the *rihnemin*, she wanted to figure out how sooner rather than later.

With a deep breath, Mazille took the crystal she'd pulled out of her dress pocket.

"Now show me," Winter said, the rage of frostfire burning through her.

"Give me a moment," Mazille grumbled, glaring at Winter. "You can't possibly tell me you're already feeling it?"

Winter shut her mouth. She'd forgotten how quickly frost affected her. Nash had told her that others had a significantly slower response rate, but it had been so long since she'd interacted with any other psimancers at all.

When they were ready, Mazille approached the *rihnemin*. "I haven't tried in some time," she muttered. "I don't even know if it will work."

"Try it anyway," Winter said.

Mazille stopped, looking up at the massive stone. "Goddess help me," she whispered.

Thought she didn't believe in the Goddess. Winter would have said as much, but she didn't want to distract her. They had already wasted enough time.

Winter tasted blood. She concentrated, trying to discern Mazille's *tendra*. She could not see them, but slowly she became aware of their presence. Two or three of them, but not more than that. They snaked around the *rihnemin*, searching. Probing.

Above them, a light shone in the pre-dawn dark. Winter looked up. One of the faded runes carved into the massive stone had begun to shine a dull orange color, pulsing gently. Winter looked in awe at the rune, now emblazoned on the stone's surface.

Then, simultaneously, two other runes lit up the early morning. One a faded yellow, blazing up near the first, and the other, by far the brightest of the three, almost directly in front of Winter's face.

Winter stared at the blood-red rune before her, mesmerized. A series of hard, straight slashes were etched in the stone in a circular design. She had no idea what it meant; no one, not even the tiellan elders, could read or speak the ancient runic language anymore.

Slowly, Winter ran her hand along the stone where the red rune shone. She felt nothing; the stone was cool, and no different than if nothing had been burning on it at all.

Then, abruptly, the lights disappeared. Winter looked over her shoulder, and saw Mazille take a step back, breathing heavily.

"That's it?" Winter asked.

"I told you…" Mazille gasped between breaths, "I have not

accomplished much. There's… a reason I stopped trying… so long ago…"

Winter frowned, looking back up at the *rihnemin*.

"Besides, the only crystal I had with me was of poor quality. Perhaps if you'd let me try one of yours…"

Winter ignored Mazille, instead taking a step back herself. Then, she launched a dozen *tendra* towards the great stone. Behind her, Mazille gasped, but Winter paid the woman no mind. She ran her *tendra* along the stone's surface, as she'd sensed Mazille do a moment before. She felt nothing.

Nothing, until suddenly she did. One of her *tendra* moved past a carved rune, but Winter felt pulled back to it, as if by a magnet. Winter retraced her *tendron*, and almost of its own accord it attached itself to the rune.

Immediately, the rune lit up in a blazing bright blue, far brighter than any of the runes Mazille had revealed.

In quick succession, each of Winter's other *tendra*—she restrained herself from sending out more, wanting to keep Mazille ignorant of how many she could actually wield—found other runes, and in moments the dawn sky was ablaze in a rainbow of bright blues, reds, greens, oranges, and purples.

"Goddess rising," Mazille whispered.

The runes blazed, but nothing else happened. Winter's *tendra* certainly felt no more powerful than they had before attaching to the *rihnemin*. She itched to send more *tendra* out, to scour the thing and light up as many runes as she could, but she refrained. Now was not the time.

She withdrew her *tendra*, and the *rihnemin* fell dark once again.

As Winter was on her way to find Urstadt, Selldor stopped her.

"I have news from our scouts, Commander."

"Walk with me and report."

"A massive army is approaching, from Triah. Our scouts estimate at least eleven thousand infantry, and four thousand cavalry. When they join the Steel Regiment, they'll be twenty thousand strong."

Winter tensed, but kept walking. She knew this response would come. They had only fought bits and pieces of the Khalic army so far; this approaching force was a much larger contingent.

"How close?" Winter asked.

"They're nearing the southern edge of the Eastmaw Mountains," Selldor said. "Likely be here in two weeks' time. Three at the most."

"Two weeks," Winter repeated. She shook herself. "Marshal our forces. We will convey this information immediately, and begin preparations for battle. We will ride out to meet them."

"Of course, Commander."

"We will choose our own battleground, just as we did with the Setso," Winter said. "We have defeated the Legion twice, now. We will do it again, twenty thousand soldiers be damned."

Selldor bowed his head. "Yes, Commander."

"Good. I have a sparring session, Selldor. In the meantime, after my session with Urstadt, summon the Ranger captains and the clan chiefs. We'll need to discuss strategy."

"Aye, Commander."

"Gather the Rangers we still have in the city, and as many new recruits as you can round up. Tomorrow morning, we ride for our main camp in Eastmaw Valley."

Winter walked with purpose now. This would be her moment. She thought of the look on Mazille's face. There was nothing she could not do with *faltira*—and that included besting the most powerful armed force on the Sfaera.

Winter was about to demonstrate her value.

Winter walked away from the strategy meeting with adrenaline coursing through her veins. The feeling was almost as good as *faltira*. Not quite, but good enough for now.

Urstadt, however, was cautionary. "The coming weeks will be long and tedious. The weight of the force moving upon us will sink in, and morale may be difficult to maintain."

"Then we will do what we need to do to maintain it," Winter said curtly. She frowned at Urstadt. The woman could not allow them one evening of energy, of strength, without pointing out where they would become weak?

"Of course, Winter."

They walked in silence for a moment, and slowly Winter accepted the truth of Urstadt's claim. "I believe our strategy is sound," she said. "Our discussions this afternoon were productive, were they not?"

"They were," Urstadt said. "And riding to meet them is the strongest option, I am sure of it. Nevertheless, time is the greatest enemy of any force. Everything erodes with time."

In a few moments, they reached Winter's quarters. "Thank you, Urstadt," Winter said. "I will see you in the morning, for our practice session." They intended to meet before sunrise, before they left Adimora for the Ranger camp in Eastmaw Valley.

"Of course. Until then, Winter." Urstadt saluted, then turned and walked away.

Winter took a deep breath, opening the door to her quarters. They were small and practical, but she did not care for much more than that.

She suddenly realized she had not seen Mazille, or any of the other tiellan psimancers, since early that morning. She had been so busy with preparations for the oncoming campaign against Carrieri that she had almost forgotten about them.

Winter had too many questions for them. And, of course, she would require them to join the Rangers. She would need as many psimancers as she could marshal to meet the force that marched against them.

Pouring herself a goblet of water, Winter sat down at the bare wooden table in the middle of her room. She pulled the *faltira* pouch from her waist, checking the contents. Three crystals. She would take one tonight, she had already decided, in celebration of the way she had handled the news about Carrieri and his fifteen thousand legionaries. But she wanted to refill her pouch first; she preferred to keep five or six crystals on her at all times, just in case. Winter moved to the chest she kept beneath her bed, and stopped cold when she saw it.

The chest was open.

Winter tore the box from beneath her bed. Open, and empty.

Winter gasped short, shallow breaths. She looked underneath the bed, but there was nothing else. The majority of her *faltira* stash—upwards of sixty crystals—had been in that chest, and now it was gone.

Winter turned to the cabinet where she kept the rest of it. Her pack, the one she'd carried with her since Izet, was there.

It, too, was empty.

Winter stood, empty pack in hand, breathing fast. Her *faltira*—all but the three crystals she had in her pouch—was gone. And there was only one person she could think of who would've taken it. She bolted from the house, envisioning what she would do to Mazille and the tiellans who had betrayed her. Death would be a mercy for them.

She burst into the tents the tiellan psimancers had occupied, only to find them empty. Mazille and her band were gone, as were all of their belongings. She ran from the tent and grabbed the first person she saw. "Have you seen Mazille? The people in this tent?"

The woman shook her head, eyeing Winter warily.

"Commander?"

Winter whirled to face the Ranger who spoke. "You've seen them?" she asked.

"Aye, saw 'em this morning," he said. "Looked like they were packing up and heading out."

Winter stumbled backwards, the world spinning around her. Mazille would be a day's ride away, now. Winter could send riders out after them, but Mazille and her band were still psimancers. Even if her Rangers found them, they might not come back.

Winter's *faltira* was gone, and that was the cold reality.

When she made it back to her quarters, she did not bother closing the door behind her. She shivered, her skin sticky with dried sweat.

Somehow she found herself with her back against one wall, facing her open door. She slid down to sit on the wood-paneled floor, and stared emptily out into the night. She had three frost crystals left, and a force three times their size was advancing on them.

I can do anything with faltira, Winter thought to herself, unable to stifle a crazed laugh.

Without it... I am nothing.

33

Somewhere in Kirlan

KNOT ONCE AGAIN LURKED in the shadows of Astrid's memories. It had taken him a few days after the first memory he had accessed from his cell to work up the courage to go back inside Astrid's past. But as horrific as the last memory had been, the more time Knot spent thinking about it, the more he thought there had to be some kind of explanation, *something* behind what he had seen. The girl he had seen murder her own family was not the girl he knew.

Knot had been back time and time again since that memory, seeking some explanation, but he'd yet to find it. He'd seen all sorts of things—a few variations of that first memory, where Astrid procured groups of children from humans, always taking them back to her "employer." He'd even seen her take children from another group of vampires, killing one brutally in the process. Other memories played out her days with Cabral, all of which made him sick to his stomach in one way or another. He'd witnessed times when she'd spent days, months, *years* absolutely alone. He hated coming across those memories almost as much as he hated the one where he'd watched her kill her father; experiencing her isolation only compounded his own.

The monotony of his captivity was enough to drive Knot mad. He ate the same meal three meals a day—porridge that was too watery, a crust of bread, and, inexplicably, an apple, of all things—at the same time each day, as far as he could tell. The same four Sons of Canta guarded his cell, switching shifts roughly the same times each day. No contact with anyone else, no explanation of why he was here. Considering how much the Black Matron had wanted him in the first place, she seemed to have little idea of what she was actually supposed to *do* with him. He was clearly being treated well, for a prisoner—fed consistently, not tortured, and so forth. That only confused him all the more.

Finding a reason, some purpose behind's Astrid's actions, had become perhaps the only thing that kept Knot sane while in the Black Matron's captivity.

And now, here he was, in yet another memory.

Astrid walked along a curving road in Triah. Knot did not recognize the street; he had no idea *when* this memory was, but based on the businesses and tower-houses he saw along this section of the city, he guessed it fell between the Twenty-fifth and Thirtieth Circles.

The sun was low on the horizon, and Astrid moved quickly. This time, however, Knot noticed she was not alone. Another young girl, roughly of an external age with Astrid, walked next to her. Knot glided along beside them, staying in the shadows. For some reason, he felt more comfortable there than out in the middle of the road.

He looked closely at the new girl, wondering if he might recognize her from another memory, but she did not look familiar at all. The two spoke almost constantly, even laughing and joking. Knot wondered if this girl was another vampire.

They stopped at a large building with just one sign hanging from a horizontal pole out front that said "We Welcome All Children." Astrid and the other girl entered, and Knot was transported with them.

He moved with them through a reception area, and then toward a large common space with a very high ceiling. Stairs led to a loft above that housed almost two dozen bunks, and through a hallway to his right Knot saw a busy kitchen—most of the people working inside of which were children.

A woman with long blonde hair stood near the stairs of the common area holding the ears of two young boys, both squirming. Knot *did* recognize both of the boys, from two separate memories of Astrid gathering children and bringing them back to her "employer."

"The two of you will behave," the woman said sternly, looking down at each of the boys in turn, "or you'll both end up on dishes duty for the next week!"

"Yes, Homemother," the two boys said in unison.

Homemother?

The Homemother looked up, and her face brightened. "Astrid!" she exclaimed. "I am so happy you've returned safely." She smiled at the other girl who'd entered, now hovering shyly behind Astrid. "And who have you brought with you?"

Astrid squirmed out of the way in a gesture that was surprisingly childlike. "Camy, this is the Homemother, the woman I told you about. Homemother, this is Camy, from Cineste."

The Homemother's eyes widened. "Cineste! That is quite the journey. I am happy to see the two of you made it here safely. Welcome to the First Light Orphanage."

An orphanage? Was this where Astrid had been taking all of the children she'd been rounding up?

"Thank you," Camy said, her head bowed.

Astrid laughed. "You'll love it here, Camy."

Camy glanced around the room, strands of messy brown hair falling in front of her eyes.

A loud knock sounded at the front door of the orphanage. The Homemother cleared her throat. "I'll go see who that is. Won't take me long." She bent down to look Camy in the eye. "Astrid and I can show you around later this evening," the Homemother said, "but first, we're all going to have dinner together. The children have helped cook up something special this evening."

Camy smiled, nodding quietly.

The Homemother went to the door while Astrid and Camy began to chat excitedly.

This is what she's been doing this whole time, Knot realized. *Helping children.* He'd been right; there was more to her story, after all.

From down the hallway, Knot heard anxious, whispered voices in a harsh conversation. Then, despite the Homemother's cry of "Wait!" a group of adults entered the room. Knot recognized the red and white livery. A priestess, a Goddessguard, and half a dozen Sons of Canta, two of whom supported a young man between them. The lad had likely not yet seen his twentieth year, and he did not look in good shape, hanging limply between the two Sons.

The priestess, however, drew Knot's eye the most. The subtle slope of her jaw and the way she wore her hair in a tight bun were hints, but what gave it away was the flatness of the woman's eyes; Knot felt that if he were to look on them, he would not see the reflection of any light whatsoever.

This was the Black Matron. The Black Priestess at this point in time—she was at least fifty years younger than the woman Knot knew—but it was certainly her all the same.

"My dear Homemother, thank you for inviting us in. I was so looking forward to seeing your orphanage with my own eyes."

The Homemother bowed, but she seemed confused as

well. "It was the least I could do, Priestess, after your generous donations to our cause."

"More of which are sure to come, my dear," the Black Matron said.

"Might I ask what brings you by so early?" the Homemother asked.

Knot narrowed his eyes. Something about the way the woman spoke felt off to him.

"We found someone," the Black Matron said, indicating the young man her Sons carried. "Someone very ill, that we are going to help care for. He says he knows you, Homemother. He goes by the name of—"

"Jidri," the Homemother said quietly, rushing to him. "Are you all right?"

Knot recognized the name immediately, and as he looked more closely at the young man, realized he truly was looking at an older version of the young boy he had seen in the first memory of Astrid's he'd experienced.

"He needs medical attention," the Black Matron said. "We can provide him with what he needs, but we wanted to stop by here first. He seemed very insistent on seeing you before we treated him."

Slowly, Jidri looked up, taking in his surroundings. "Where... am I?" he asked.

The Homemother hugged him, holding his face. "Please," she said, looking at the Sons, "put him down. Let him rest."

The Black Matron nodded, and the Sons set him down on a large chair near the center of the common area. The Homemother knelt beside him, holding his face in her hands.

"Jidri," she said, "can you hear me?"

The lad looked up, his eyes a sickly yellow.

"Homemother?" he asked.

"You see?" the Black Matron said. "He recognizes you. So touching." Then, over her shoulder, "Bar all the entrances and exits."

The Sons of Canta quickly obeyed. The Goddessguard stayed by the Black Matron's side.

Astrid stared at Jidri, her feet rooted where she stood. "Homemother, what is going on?"

"Astrid?" Jidri asked. He coughed violently. "Is that you?"

The Homemother looked over her shoulder at the Black Matron. "This was not part of the plan," she said, tears in her eyes.

Astrid's eyes never left Jidri. "What plan?" she asked. The sun must have set outside, as Astrid's eyes were beginning to glow, but her voice quavered.

As the Sons had moved to the exits, children had slowly filed into the common area. Knot counted twenty-two in total, including Camy, all watching what was going on.

"It's Astrid, is it?" the Black Matron said, stepping towards her. "I have a gift for you."

The Black Matron tossed a small flowered sprig toward Astrid, and the girl fell to her knees.

"Vampires are a curious race," the Black Matron said. "So powerful, but their weakness is so... *weak*, is it not? Nightsbane. A simple herb, and you're completely incapacitated." She shoved Astrid over with her foot, and the girl toppled to the side, the nightsbane just touching her shoulder.

Knot had attempted to interact with Astrid's memories numerous times to no avail, but never in his life did he want something more than to take the nightsbane from next to the girl and move it far, far away. He tried, but just like every time he attempted to interact with a memory, his hand passed right through the object.

"There's a phenomenon associated with newborn vampires," the Black Matron said, walking over to Jidri and leaning over to look into his eyes. "Once a vampire has completed its transition, it experiences what most vampires call the Bloodlust. An insatiable thirst for human blood. They will tear apart anyone nearby to satisfy that craving. It is completely involuntary, uncontrollable, and truly horrific to watch."

She shrugged. "Or so I've heard. The tradition surrounding that phenomenon," she continued, "interests me even more. Many vampires, while siring another through the transition, lead the sick, disoriented soul right to their family's doorstep just as they are about to complete the process. They leave that soon-to-be daemon, unattended, in the arms of the people they once loved most in life."

A low groan echoed throughout the common area, and Knot thought at first that it came from Jidri. But the boy was still, his head hung limply in front of him.

Out of the corner of his eye, Knot saw Astrid move, one arm slowly dragging across the floor towards the nightsbane. Goddess, the girl was trying to push the herb away from her.

"Pleeeaaaaase," Astrid moaned, barely above a whisper.

The Black Matron raised one eyebrow. "Impressive," she said. "From what I understand, most vampires are hardly coherent when that close to nightsbane, let alone able to move. I think we chose right when we sought you out, my dear."

"*Pleeeeeeaaaaaaaaase…*"

"You know the tradition of which I speak, don't you, girl?" the Black Matron asked, looking down at Astrid. "Someone did it to you, if my information is correct."

"Get up, girl," Knot whispered, his eyes not leaving Astrid. A tear, reflecting green light from her eyes, slid at an angle down one cheek towards the floor. "*Fight*."

"Priestess, what is the meaning of this?" the Homemother said, tears streaming down her face as she turned to face the Black Matron. "Our deal was for you to take the vampire, not to threaten my entire orphanage."

"I didn't just want to *take* the vampire, my dear," the Black Matron said. "I wanted to *own* the vampire. This is how I'm going to do it."

"The deal is off," the Homemother said. "I'm sorry, but I can't do this. I can't watch it happen, and I can't let you risk the lives of my children. You were supposed to donate to us so we could give *more* children better lives, not—"The Homemother's voice broke in a sob. "Not take away the lives of the children I have," she whispered.

The Black Matron pursed her lips. "I'm sorry, dear," she said. "I'll do what I can to get what I want. And this is the surest, most secure way to get that."

Knot sensed movement from the chair in the middle of the room, and turned to see Jidri standing slowly.

Astrid's groan amplified, becoming a strangled, gurgling shout.

"You want to stop this?" the Black Matron asked, crouching down next to Astrid.

The girl nodded her head, almost imperceptibly, but it was there.

"Then swear fealty to me," the Black Matron said. "Swear you will obey me, swear you will do what I say, when I say it."

"*I sweaaaar,*"Astrid whispered.

The Black Matron smiled. "Good." She nodded to her

Goddessguard, who walked right past Jidri, and bent to pick up Astrid, placing the nightsbane gently on her chest as he cradled her.

Astrid groaned, the sound broken and cracked as she struggled weakly in the Goddessguard's arms.

"Let's go," the Black Matron said.

"Wait," the Homemother said, looking up at Jidri as his eyes began to glow red. "You can't leave us alone with this!"

The Black Matron did not respond. The last sound Knot heard was Jidri's croaking voice.

"*So... thirsty...*"

Strangely, Knot didn't return directly to the Void. Every memory he'd experienced so far had been one continuous scene, more or less, occasionally transitioning from one adjacent space to another. This time, however, the memory went black, and then Knot found himself in a plain stone room, not unlike the cell in which he knew his body now rested. Somehow, even though it did not take place sequentially, this must be part of the same memory.

Astrid was chained to a chair in the middle of the room, staring vacantly into nothing. It must have been day, as her eyes no longer glowed, and she did not even bother struggling against the chains.

Thick steel bars split the room in two, and on the other side of them stood the Black Matron.

"I know you said you would serve me," the Black Matron said, "and I want to take you at your word, but I hope you understand why I cannot do that."

Astrid said nothing, did not even move, and Knot wondered whether her mind was really there at all.

"What I can do is offer you something."

The Black Matron placed both hands on the steel bars in front of her, her face almost touching the metal.

"Redemption," she said.

Astrid snarled as she railed against the chains that bound her.

The Black Matron leapt backwards from the bars, eyes wide. She cleared her throat, composing herself. "Well, I thought it was worth a try. The basic idea is there, at least. Why else would you devote your life to helping children after you killed your own younger brother and sister?"

Astrid continued to snarl, struggling against her chains, but her daytime strength simply wasn't enough.

"I have one more thing to offer you," the Black Matron said. "Something I think you might actually consider. You've been through a great deal over the years, my dear. Much of it has been very difficult, I'm sorry to say. I already mentioned you tearing your family to pieces. But then, oh—the first woman you'd begun to trust in decades betrayed you, and all you'd worked to build with her was destroyed. That *cannot* be a good feeling."

Astrid's struggling slowed, and Knot saw the tears forming in her eyes.

"What I'm offering could fix all of that," the Black Matron said. She leaned forward once more. "I can make you forget."

Astrid met the Black Matron's eyes.

"Forget," Astrid said, her voice hoarse and raw.

"Yes," the Black Matron said. "If you promise to serve me, I can make all of those memories go away."

There was a silence that seemed to last a lifetime, until Astrid finally responded, her voice barely above a whisper. She nodded, once.

"*Forget.*"

34

Outskirts of Kirlan

THE ODENITES WERE PACKING up camp.

Astrid stood outside Cinzia's tent, staring at the people taking down tents, wrestling to close packs, and running to and fro.

She'd been out last night, in the city, searching for Knot again. According to Cinzia, he was still in Kirlan, but would not be for long. Very soon, he would be taken to Triah. When Astrid had asked how Cinzia came by this information, she had refused to answer. But Cinzia believed it was valid, and that had been enough for Astrid. She'd checked the Cantic chapel where the Black Matron had held her, multiple times, but found nothing. She'd checked every other Cantic chapel in the city as well, and the apartments where the clergy stayed.

Knot was nowhere to be found.

But they weren't giving up hope. Astrid and Cinzia had elected to sneak into the city that evening and simply wait on the southern side until the Black Matron made her way south. Astrid could gain entry to the city easily, but getting Cinzia in would be much more difficult. They still hadn't figured that out yet, exactly, but they had the entire day to plan for it.

Or thought they had. Now, as Astrid saw the Odenites getting ready to move, she knew their plan would have to change.

"What in Oblivion is going on?"

Astrid turned to see Cinzia emerging from her tent into the morning light. It was a windy morning, despite the sun, and Astrid had drawn her cloak over her face, protecting her from the sunlight. The light shone on Cinzia clearly, and her auburn hair shimmered like copper as it waved in the wind.

"I was about to ask you the same thing," Astrid said.

"Jane held a meeting last night, but I do not know what it was about."

"Apparently it was about leaving."

"Apparently it was," Cinzia said, looking around. "Jane does not seem to have slept in her bed. Have you seen her?"

Astrid shook her head. Jane had always been kind to her, but the woman's decision to abandon Knot had irrevocably changed things between them.

On the other hand, her relationship with Cinzia had never been better.

"We must find her," Cinzia said, standing on tiptoe to see over the heads of the people around them. "We cannot go through with our plan if the Odenite movement might cause conflict."

The entire group of Odenites really was packing up. The Odenite following had continued to grow, receiving dozens of new people every day, and now numbered nearly two thousand. The group had completely filled Lord Derard's huge field north of Kirlan. How such a large group survived—and even thrived—was beyond Astrid's comprehension. Jane referred to it as a miracle, as Canta providing for them all. Astrid didn't know about that, but she acknowledged that while Derard's holdings were bountiful, they were not so bountiful as to sustain thousands of people for months. Astrid wondered if the

Odenites knew how fortunate they were to not be dealing with disease and starvation at every turn.

Finally, they found Jane, helping a tiellan family take down their tent.

"Sister," Cinzia said, approaching Jane with a smile, "can I have a word?"

Jane looked up, wiping sweat from her brow. "Of course," she said with a smile. "As soon as I help the Ganir family pack their belongings. Give us a hand, and we'll get it done faster."

Astrid snorted. A shameless attempt at recruiting help. She wasn't going to fall for such a—

"We would love to help," Cinzia said, rolling up the sleeves of her dress.

Astrid grumbled, but followed suit. She supposed it was fine if it helped them speak with Jane more quickly.

When the tent and belongings were all packed onto a handcart, Jane turned to them.

"How can I help you?"

Cinzia spread her arms wide. "Jane… what is going on?"

Jane's eyes widened, and she touched Cinzia's arm. "Of course! I am so sorry, I'd completely forgotten that you were not at the assembly last night. Or at the council meeting yesterday morning." Jane cocked her head to one side. "I suppose you've been a bit absent lately, haven't you?"

Cinzia held Jane's gaze. "I suppose I have been, but someone has had to do something about Knot," she said.

"Someone is."

Astrid growled. If Jane said, "He's in Canta's hands," one more time, she would rip out the Prophetess's throat.

"Just tell me what is going on, Jane."

"I do not mean to be obstinate."

"Could have bloody fooled me," Astrid muttered. That earned her a surprised glance from Jane—was the woman really surprised? After how she had treated Knot?—but she continued nonetheless.

"I have received new direction from Canta. We are to continue south, to Triah."

Astrid rolled her eyes.

Cinzia was equally skeptical. "That has been the understanding for months, now. Why is it different? Are the Sons of Canta gone?"

"No," Jane said, "the Sons still guard the gate. But the immediacy has changed. Canta needs us to move *now*."

"So, what, the Goddess is just going to fight the Sons for us?" Astrid asked.

"She will provide a way."

Astrid scoffed. "You can't be serious. At best, the Odenites will walk up to the wall, and simply have to turn around and walk back when nothing happens. At worst, there will be a conflict with the Sons. Odenites will *die*, Jane."

"That is in Canta's hands, now."

"Have you told the Odenites all of this?" Cinzia asked. "Are they aware what they are walking towards?"

"They are aware," Jane said, "and they have faith. That faith will carry us south to Triah."

Astrid suddenly had a vision of the entire Odenite following—nearly two thousand people—being lifted up on a massive cloud and flown through the air directly to Triah. She laughed out loud.

Jane looked at her, clearly not understanding her humor. Astrid just laughed harder.

"When is this movement happening?" asked Cinzia.

"Midday. As soon as we have everything packed up and ready."

"Bloody Oblivion," Cinzia muttered.

Astrid turned to face Cinzia, eyebrows raised. But who was she to judge?

At midday, Astrid and Cinzia stood together in front of the Odenite crowd, at Jane's left hand. On her right stood the other three disciples: Ocrestia, Elessa, and Baetrissa. The wind whipped at Astrid's hair and clothing, threatening to tear her hood away.

"You really think anything will come of this?" Astrid asked Cinzia, pulling her hood down tighter over her face.

Cinzia shrugged. "Jane has made some ridiculous claims in the past, but..."

"But she isn't often wrong," Astrid finished.

"No," Cinzia said, "she isn't. Although she has not quite been right, either."

Astrid snorted. That was true enough.

She had expected Jane to give another speech before they began this ridiculous march—two thousand unarmed civilians marching on a walled city reinforced by a contingent of the Sons of Canta—but instead, Jane simply walked forward, away from the crowd and toward the city.

Cinzia said nothing, and began to slowly walk forward with her sister.

The entire Odenite following moved forward as one, and Astrid felt a strange kinship with everyone around her. Despite the disconnect between them—despite the fact that she was a bloody *vampire*, and these people had nothing to do with her— she felt a *part* of them.

The gates ahead were closed and barred. On top of the wall, Astrid could see the Sons, armed with bows and crossbows, waiting for them.

When Jane, Astrid, and the disciples reached a distance at which they could communicate, they stopped, and Jane shouted up at the Sons, "Good day to you." Her voice sounded calm, as if she were not shouting at all, but her voice somehow projected far enough that all in the area could hear.

The Sons looked at one another, then back down at Jane. "What do you want?" one of them shouted.

"Safe passage through Kirlan, and onward to Triah. Nothing more."

The Sons' laughter drifted down from the wall. Astrid didn't blame them.

"We've given you our answer," the same Son shouted back down. "None of you are getting through this gate."

Jane squinted in the sun. "I will ask you one more time. We seek safe passage through Kirlan, and onward to Triah."

"And we'll respond the same way," the Son shouted in return. "That will not happen."

"Very well," Jane said, though only loud enough this time for her voice to be heard by those around her. "We walk forward," she said to her followers, "one foot in front of the other, and have faith in Canta's power. That is all we ever need do."

She took Cinzia's hand on one side, and Ocrestia's on the other. Cinzia seemed surprised at the gesture, but then reluctantly held out her other hand to Astrid.

"Don't think so," Astrid said.

"Just do it," Cinzia whispered. "Play along, for now. Do it for Knot, if nothing else."

Astrid sighed heavily, pulling the cloak further down

over her head. Then, she took Cinzia's hand, while almost simultaneously the person next to her—a woman Astrid didn't even *know*—took her other hand. She barely restrained the growl that began in her throat.

She glanced over her shoulder. Every Odenite on foot that Astrid could see had followed suit, holding hands. And behind them came the wagons, handcarts, people on horseback. Jane had eschewed her own horse, and insisted the disciples do the same, while they first approached the wall.

"Forward," Jane said, so quietly that Astrid was not sure anyone besides the few around her could actually hear. "One front in front of the other. Have faith."

As one, the Odenites began to walk forward. But what would they do when they reached the wall? Astrid wondered. The gates were barred—there was nowhere to go. Even so, the Sons seemed worried.

"Stop right there!" the Son called from the walltop, only his head and chest visible above the parapet. "Do not go any farther! In the name of the Essera, the Denomination, and Holy Canta Herself, I command you to stop!"

The Odenites paid the man no heed.

On the wall, Sons chattered among themselves in obvious confusion. Some were raising crossbows, others nocking arrows to their bows, but still more cast their eyes about, unsure of what to do. The Sons would retaliate somehow, very soon, if something did not happen. Jane was expecting a miracle. She would need one to get the Odenites out of this mess.

"One foot in front of the other," Jane repeated. "Have faith."

Astrid tensed. If it came to violence, she would only be able to do so much. The sun was high in a cloudless sky, and there were a lot of Sons on that wall. She looked up at Cinzia; the woman was staring straight ahead, eyes wide.

"This had better bloody—"

A low rumble interrupted Astrid's words. The wind picked up, whipping her cloak around her. Beneath her feet, the earth began to quake. People shouted in panic, both the Odenites around her and Sons from the wall. Astrid gripped Cinzia's hand more tightly, and felt Cinzia do the same.

The city wall began to crumble.

The merlons collapsed first, the stones breaking and fragmenting again and again as they fell. The rest of the parapet followed, the Sons now standing awkwardly atop the wall, in full view without anything to protect them. They did not stand there long; with a tremendous rumble, the entire wall buckled, then collapsed. Sons screamed as they lost their footing and then fell. The crumbling stones, however, never touched the ground. They disintegrated completely as they collapsed, and the strong wind carried the dust away, eastward, over the forest. The earth continued to shake beneath Astrid's feet, but soon all that remained where Kirlan's wall once stood were the Sons of Canta, injured and moaning on the bare ground.

Astrid stood only a few rods away from the wall itself, but, looking down at herself, she was surprised to see she was untouched by dust or debris.

"What the shit," Astrid whispered. She looked up at Cinzia.

Tears were streaming down Cinzia's face. She opened her mouth, but whether she meant to say anything or not, Astrid could not tell. No sound came from her.

"One foot in front of the other," Jane said, and she motioned for their horses. "Have faith."

They mounted, and began weaving their way through the Sons.

The Sons allowed the Odenites to move right past them. Many Sons cared for those who'd been wounded in the fall from the wall, but to Astrid's surprise, none of the injuries seemed grievous. Perhaps a few broken bones here and there, at the worst.

The rest of the Sons just stared at the passing Odenites in confusion, concern, and awe.

Jane led the Odenites through the city streets of Kirlan. Citizens stared at where their wall used to be, and then at the Odenites, bewilderment etched on their faces.

No one said a word to them as they passed through the city. As they walked, it became clear the *entire* wall had fallen, not just the section to the north. Soon Jane, Astrid, and the disciples had led the Odenites through Kirlan and over the disintegrated stump of the wall on the southern side of the city. The Coastal Road, leading south toward Triah, was open before them.

Astrid and Cinzia rode their horses a short distance away from the main group.

"What now? We wait?" Astrid asked.

Cinzia opened her mouth to respond, but then her eyes glazed over as she cocked her head to one side. Before Astrid could ask her what in Oblivion was going on, Cinzia's eyes widened, focusing once again on Astrid.

"We need to ride south. Now," she said.

Astrid narrowed her eyes at Cinzia. "What just happened, Cinzia?"

"Trust me, Astrid. If we want to catch Knot, we need to leave immediately."

"You're going to need to tell me sooner or later."

"*Please*, Astrid. If we want to save Knot—"

"All right, all right," Astrid said. Cinzia was a grown woman.

She knew what she was doing.

And Canta rising, Astrid bloody wanted to find Knot.

Eward rode up beside them. "You are going after Knot?" he asked.

"We are," Cinzia said.

Apparently we're not keeping it much of a secret.

"I will come with you," Eward said.

Immediately Cinzia shook her head. "We need you here, Eward. With Knot *and* Astrid gone, you and the Prelates are the last line of defense for the Odenites."

"I'll only take a few of my Prelates," Eward said, "and I'll leave the rest with Jane. Horas can lead them while I am gone; he is capable."

Cinzia looked down at Astrid, lips pursed.

Astrid shrugged. "The Black Matron will have Sons with her, and probably a Goddessguard or two. Might be good to have extra swords to handle them." Astrid had taken the Black Matron's nightsbane, but that had been four months ago. She could have procured more. Even if she hadn't, the Black Matron had made it abundantly clear that she did not need nightsbane to handle Astrid.

"Very well," Cinzia said. "Come with us. Bring half a dozen of your best soldiers."

"We don't need to run this by Jane, first?" Astrid asked.

"No," Cinzia said. "We don't."

Astrid smiled. *That's my girl.*

It was time to settle things with the Black Matron once and for all.

35

Canaian Fields, central Khale

Winter shivered despite the late summer heat, wiping sweat from her brow.

"These are the Canaian Fields?" she asked. She stood with Urstadt, Selldor, Ghian, Rorie, and Nardo in the flatlands. Not far to the west, a small river ran southwards. To the north and to the east, the outlines of the Eastmaw and Undritch Mountains, respectively, jutted above the horizon.

"Aye, Commander," Rorie said. The Canaian Fields were just more plains, really, extending from the Eastmaw Mountains southward, where they eventually met with Canai's lake, one of three huge lakes in Central Khale. Both the lake and the fields took their name from King Canai Mazen—the King Who Gave Up His Crown one hundred and seventy-two years ago. The act had abolished the monarchy that had ruled Khale for millennia, establishing the Parliament, and emancipated the tiellan race from slavery.

They had all agreed it seemed an ideal place to pitch the battle.

"Don't we want to position ourselves somewhere where it ain't so flat?" Nardo asked. The chieftain had become Winter's main liaison with the Cracked Spear. "The Khalic force is three times the size of our own. Don't we want the high ground?"

"Don't you want to shut your Goddess-damned mouth?"

Winter snapped. "Last I checked, you haven't won two battles, outnumbered, against the Khalic army." *Canta's bloody bones.* Nardo was supposed to be a chieftain.

Winter felt Urstadt's hand on her shoulder, and she took a deep breath.

"We have our strategy," Winter said, keeping her voice even only with great effort. "We will move forward with it as long as it proves successful."

"Commander, you are still sick," Selldor said. "We should get you back to a fire."

Winter waved her hand angrily at her lieutenant. "I don't need a fire, it's warm enough as it is." She was conscious of the fact that she shivered as she said it. She wasn't sick, though. She had felt this way once before, in the dungeons of Izet, after overdosing on Knot's frost crystals. For the first few months of her imprisonment, Daval had not given her frost, and this was what her body had done to her. She had not cared so much then, because she'd had nothing to live for at the time.

But now Winter's *faltira* was gone, and tomorrow she was going to fight a battle larger than any she could possibly imagine. The stakes were just a bit higher this time.

The sweating, the chills, the vomiting, were all part of this process. She suspected her withdrawal from frost might have something to do with her irritability, too, but that didn't matter. She had taken two of her crystals, spaced out over the past week and a half, when the symptoms had become too much for her, when her defenses had completely crumbled. Now, she had one left, and she prayed with every ounce of her strength to any god or goddess that would listen that she'd be able to abstain from taking it before the battle.

"I'm fine," Winter said, but she wasn't. A rest next to a

fire might not help her much, but it would help her more than wandering around this Goddess-damned field.

The woman shivers in her cot, vomiting intermittently. She has given her last *faltira* crystal to Urstadt for safekeeping; she does not trust herself with it tonight.

Tomorrow, when the battle begins, she will be able to take the frost crystal. Tomorrow, she will feel better. But tonight, she is alone with her nightmares.

Instead of facing them, the woman turns to the Void.

In the Void, while her pain is still present, she at least finds herself removed from it, like an echo, or a memory. It is still there, and it will return in full force whenever she leaves the Void, but for now, it is in the background. It is part of her, but in the Void, at least, *it is not her*. When she returns to the Sfaera, she will become the pain, the pain will be her, and there will be no separation between the two.

But, for now, the woman drifts.

She drifts, and she hears voices, although she cannot decide whether they are real or not. She thinks she hears Kali, and for a moment she is happy; she has not spoken to Kali since Izet, but despite how much she distrusts the woman, she realizes she would appreciate the contact. She hears other voices, too, but the one that cuts through them all is a deep, rumbling bass wreathed in crackling fire. Is Azael truly here, with her? Or is she imagining it in her fevered state? She may not be in the Void at all. All of this, the blinking star-lights around her, the voices, the distance from the pain, might not be real, might all simply be the product of her fevered, writhing, pathetic state.

Without frost, I am nothing. With it, I can do anything.

She remembers the visions she had in Izet, when Azael

threatened her. The Void stars expanding and contracting. Knot and Astrid. A great battle, around a *rihnemin*. Panic cracks inside her; should she have found a *rihnemin* around which to stage the battle with the Khalic army? Or was that a different battle altogether? She remembers the other visions, too. A stone giant, falling on flowers. A pillar of light defending a city from Daemons. Other things, some she knows to be true and real, and others she knows are not.

I wish I understood the nature of these visions, because if I did, I might be able to do something about them.

She sees something new, now. A different world? It is the Sfaera, but it is not. She lives there, but she does not. Knot and Winter have a child in this world, but they do not.

None of this makes any sense.

She sees another battle, this time without a *rihnemin*—has her vision changed, or is this something different? She sees herself, in the middle of this battle, and takes *faltira* at the beginning, before the armies engage. She seeks out the enemy psimancers through the Void, and kills all of them. Seven psimancers.

And then the battle begins, and the Khalic Legion pushes her army back...

The woman blinks, her form drifting in the Void, and then blinks again, and she comes crashing back down to her form on her cot in her tent, shivering.

Winter leaned over her cot, grabbing the pot that had been placed there, and vomited until she felt she had nothing left inside of her.

36

"They've put their weakest in the middle, on the front lines," Razzo said.

Kyfer glowered at the tiellan force in position ahead of him, but said nothing.

"Our heavy infantry will crush them," Razzo added. The fifteen thousand soldiers Carrieri had sent had joined Kyfer's Steel Regiment a few days ago, and together they had advanced to the tiellan position on the Canaian Fields. More than twenty thousand legionaries in total.

Kyfer thought the tiellans' choice of battlefield shameless. The Canaian Fields, for Canta's sake. He snorted to himself. A human may have freed the tiellans years ago, but a human would end them now.

"Our infantry may crush theirs," Kyfer said, "but their cavalry outnumbers ours." The tiellans fielded over five thousand riders; their cavalry, in fact, was the majority of their force. Their infantry did not exceed four thousand. "In the previous battles they've relied on their riders to make quick work of our cavalry, and then turned on our footmen." Kyfer had underestimated the tiellans severely at the battle of the Setso. He would not do so again.

"It'd be a fool's errand to repeat what happened on the Setso," Razzo said.

"Would it?" Kyfer asked, raising an eyebrow. "It worked quite well the first time."

"It did," Razzo admitted, glaring at the tiellans assembled across the field. "But it will not work again."

Kyfer didn't respond. The Khalic Legion had assembled more than double the number of tiellan fighters on the field, but that was no comfort to him. The way the tiellans had routed the Steel Regiment on the Setso still stung.

"Goddess, look at them," Razzo muttered. "I've never seen a force so disorganized. No sense of unity whatsoever."

Kyfer glanced sideways at Razzo. His second was acting much more brash than usual. Kyfer hated to admit it when a defeat humbled him, but he at least was willing to do so. The battle of the Setso seemed to have had the opposite effect on Razzo, if anything.

But Razzo was not wrong. The tiellan force wore armor taken from the Cinestean City Watch, the Steel Regiment, and the Legion forces they'd defeated in battle. Tiellans were slightly smaller than humans, which explained the piecemeal appearance. The Rangers must have pilfered whatever random pieces actually fit them. The brown dusted leather of the tiellan clans was also visible. Contrasted with the Legion, completely uniform from the plate mail of their heavy cavalry down to the tabards and chainmail of their light infantry, the difference was clear.

"Let's not criticize an enemy that has already bested us in battle," Kyfer said. As much as he wanted to, he knew it was less than useless. Carrieri, he imagined, would say something about never criticizing an enemy at all. The man didn't have a bone of humor in his body.

"Of course, General," Razzo said. "But I feel the Goddess strengthening us today. I think they will break after one charge. We will annihilate them with the main body of our heavy infantry, and the tiellan threat will be gone."

The Khalic infantry, both heavy and light, had formed in a massive block, hundreds of men deep. A battering ram with which they would crush the relatively thin ranks of the tiellan forces ahead of them.

And yet, despite all their advantages, Kyfer felt an overwhelming sense of unease.

He looked over his shoulder. Behind him were the seven remaining psimancers under Kyfer's command—two full *cotirs*, and one more acumen.

"You will wait for the tiellan psimancer to reveal herself," Kyfer said to them, "and then you will *stop* her. At any cost." He was reiterating earlier orders, but they bore repeating. One more lesson he'd learned from the Setso. He could not risk his psimancers tiring themselves out while contributing to the offensive only to then reveal their positions, opening them up to the tiellan woman's power.

"Of course, General."

For battles, Kyfer preferred to have only telenics—their utility was unrivaled. While an acumen could cause a significant amount of damage as well, they did not have the widespread psychological effect of a telenic lobbing massive stones and whatever else they could find at the enemy. And most voyants were less than useless—the Nazaniin kept the only one with any power locked away in the Heart of the Void. Kyfer had yet to meet a single voyant who could predict an enemy's troop movements, or tell him accurately the outcome of a battle.

On the front line, tiellan and human troops alike taunted one another, even engaging in small skirmishes before pulling back to their respective forces. Such was the nature of a battle of this size.

"Form up the charge," Kyfer finally said. "Time to destroy this threat once and for all."

Razzo grinned. "As you say, General."

He rode his horse a few paces forward, and shouted out over the Khalic Legion. "Sound the charge!"

Dozens of horns groaned over the fields, and the Khalic infantry rumbled forward to the steady beat of marching drums.

The battle had begun.

"Ready!" Winter shouted, her Rangers raising shields and weapons around her. Urstadt braced herself on one side of her, while Gord and Eranda stood on the other. Winter hated that this was the first battle for both of the tiellans from Pranna, and that they were fighting with her at the center of their line. At least here, she could try to protect them, but there were no guarantees in a battle.

"Ready?" Winter asked, looking from Gord to Eranda. Her head pounded, but she tried not to let it show, especially not to these two. And, soon, she would find relief. Her remaining frost crystal was practically burning a hole in the palm of one hand.

"Aye," Gord said, eyeing the human force. Anger radiated from him, and he clashed his spear and shield together.

Eranda nodded, but said nothing, and Winter's heart went out to the woman. She was surely too nervous to speak. Winter could relate. If she didn't have to speak before every battle, she certainly wouldn't.

The Khalic soldiers surged forward, and Winter lifted a shaking hand to her mouth. She placed the *faltira* lightly on her tongue, and the crystal immediately began to dissolve.

Finally, *finally*, Winter was complete. She was whole. Fire burned through her, chilled her skin. She recalled, just for a moment, the first time she had taken *faltira*, the immense, ineffable pleasure that had coursed through her. It was not so much pleasure she felt anymore, as it was simply the absence of pain.

Then, Winter becomes the woman, and the woman zones in on a group of Khalic officers on horseback towards the back of the massive Khalic Legion block, sending her consciousness into them, and the first she finds is…

Razzo Vaile, who wonders whether the Grand Marshal knows Kyfer's secret, and whether Kyfer himself…

The woman passes to the next, knowing she must move quickly, but the next is Kyfer, and the one after that…

I need to wait until the telenic shows herself, Genio Hule thinks to himself, but he itches to access his own *tendra*. He feels naked in a battle without them.

The woman smiles. She has found her prey.

Kyfer glared at the tiellan forces, satisfaction filling him as he watched the great hammer of Khalic infantry smash into the meager line of tiellans.

"She's here—"

Kyfer turned to look at the psimancers riding behind him. Three of them—the three acumens—were on the verge of panic, eyes wide.

"She can sense us," Ila said, her voice quavering. "She… she's an *acumen*."

Kyfer glared at her, his voice hard. "I thought you told me she was a telenic."

"We thought she *was* a telenic," another psimancer said quickly. "We had no evidence to suspect otherwise—"

A series of *thuds* silenced him. One by one, the psimancers toppled from their horses, long, thin metal shafts embedded in skulls, faces, and necks.

The psimancers were all dead.

"Shit," Razzo said.

Immediately, Kyfer slid from his horse.

"Get *down*, you fool," Kyfer hissed at Razzo. "If she could kill the psimancers that easily, she can kill us as well."

Razzo immediately dismounted, rushing forward with Kyfer. Their aides and lieutenants followed suit.

"We make our way to the left cavalry flank," Kyfer said. "We'll mount up again there, and hope she doesn't notice. If she does, nothing can save us."

He looked up, but saw the infantry had already begun to push the tiellan forces back. They did not need psimancers. They would overwhelm this woman, whoever she was, with sheer numbers, and make sure she paid the price for her betrayal.

Urstadt rammed her glaive into a Khalic man's chest just as he was about to attack the Ranger next to her.

In the distance, a few dozen Khalic soldiers flew into the air. If Winter was already focusing on the infantry, that meant she had found the enemy psimancers with little problem.

Urstadt fought, but she slowly gave ground, per Winter's instructions, and the rest of the front line gave ground with her. They had placed their greenest Rangers in the center line, and informed them at the last moment of their intention to give ground to the Khalic infantry.

"Let them think they are pushing us back," Winter had told them, "but do not fear. Urstadt, Selldor, and I will all fight among you. You will not be forgotten. You are not fodder to be lost; the center line will be the most important part of this battle, but in order for our plan to work, you need to slowly give ground."

In reality, there was no chance the Khalic infantry would *not* push them back, but by ordering the Rangers to do it anyway, she had given them the illusion of control. And, if the rest of Winter's plan succeeded—as insane as it sounded—then they might actually stand a chance of winning, even though Winter's only remaining *faltira* crystal would surely run out soon. When Urstadt had learned that Mazille had stolen Winter's *faltira* supply, she'd been half worried Winter would run off after them on her own to get it back. Thankfully, she'd had the presence of mind to stay—a decision which actually made Urstadt proud.

So Urstadt fought on, but she gave ground, and the line gave ground with her. Their position slowly shifted from bowed outward, to flat, to bowing slightly inward, as the more hardened troops on the infantry flanks held their ground as instructed.

Urstadt rammed the butt of her weapon into the face of an oncoming Khalic soldier, then spun to slice the arm off another, blood spurting onto her armor.

Winter's frost ran out more quickly than she'd anticipated, and soon she was left cold, without her power. In the heat of the battle she had lost track of Kyfer, otherwise she would have attempted to assassinate him as well, perhaps ending this whole conflict.

Having just taken frost, she'd warded off the inevitable crash. It would come soon, but for the next few hours, maybe the next day, she would feel normal. Or as close to normal as was possible for her. She had one hope, however: if she could find the psimancer corpses after the battle, she could take any *faltira* they'd been carrying with them. She had no idea whether they were actuals or variants, but Kali and Nash, both actuals, had carried *faltira* with them so they could test any potential psimancers they encountered in the field as quickly as possible.

She hoped that was the case with at least a few of the psimancers she'd killed.

The Khalic infantry pushed them back faster than Winter would have liked, but her soldiers managed the tactical retreat well. Winter kept a close eye on Gord and Eranda, and had ordered Urstadt to do the same. She'd be damned if she'd let either of them die here today.

The more experienced Rangers on the flanks held their own. They had been pushed back slightly, but fared much better than the middle of her formation. And the tiellan riders were routing the Khalic cavalry, as she'd hoped. No one could stand against her mounted Rangers.

Without *faltira*, Winter had only one option. She drew her sword and ran to Eranda's side, swinging her blade into the neck of an oncoming legionary, pressing her foot against the man's chest to lever it back out again. She turned and attacked the nearest soldier bearing down on Eranda. He danced around her first attack, but Urstadt's glaive took him in the side.

In a surge, the Khalic troops pressed forward. The sheer weight of the number of soldiers propelled them into Winter's infantry. A Khalic soldier stumbled into Winter, but the woman took too long to bring her sword up; Winter kneed her in the gut, then brought the pommel of her sword down hard on the woman's head.

But the Khalic push had broken her line, effectively splitting her force. Some tiellan soldiers were already fleeing. Winter saw Eranda backing away from the break in the line, fear in her eyes.

Canta's bloody bones. This was not part of her plan.

Winter grabbed Eranda's shoulder. "Stay with me!" she shouted. "This isn't over yet." She raised her sword and shouted, "Rangers! Rally to me!"

She glanced at Urstadt, and together the two of them attacked the Khalic soldiers that had broken through. Winter hacked and stabbed, parried and danced around attacks, and was about to stab a Khalic soldier Urstadt had thrown to the ground when something slammed into the side of her head. Winter felt the force of it before the pain, throwing her off balance, but the moment her knees hit the ground pain ruptured in her skull, focused in a tight node between her ear and temple. Winter blinked rapidly as darkness leaked from the edges of her vision.

Her eyes refocused just in time to see a Khalic soldier, armor glinting, thrust his sword into her chest. Two things happened at once to save her: Winter twisted clumsily, knowing it wouldn't be enough, but simultaneously a bloody glaive cleaved into the base of the man's neck from behind. Urstadt's blow disrupted the soldier's attack just enough to deflect it into Winter's shoulder instead of her heart.

Goddess, it had been stupid of her and Urstadt to charge into the breach alone.

Searing pain flashed down Winter's arm, but she didn't have time to check the wound. Another pair of Khalic soldiers attacked, and Winter ducked under the swing of a battleaxe just in time, rolling to her feet. She kicked one of them straight onto a Ranger's blade, and sliced the heel tendon of the other. He fell to the ground screaming.

Winter stumbled back, reorienting herself and catching her breath. Her Rangers had finally rallied to her, Eranda and Gord and a dozen others fighting at her side. Together they reformed the line against the Khalic infantry, meeting their opponents sword to sword. Urstadt took the lead, apparently unscathed, her glaive a blur around her.

Winter let out a sob of relief. She looked down at the wound on her shoulder. It didn't look bad. Blood was leaking onto her black leather armor, but it came slowly. Gord and Eranda still lived. There was hope for this battle yet.

Selldor approached her, covered in gore from head to toe, bloody sword in one hand. "Commander," he gasped, nodding at her shoulder, "let me escort you back. You need a healer."

Winter looked back at the battle, her head pounding. "No," she said, her voice hoarse. Now that they'd reformed the line, she needed to make her move before it broke again. "It is time." She signaled to her standard-bearer. The lad waved a red flag frantically.

"*Turn!*" she shouted, with as much energy as she could gather.

"Commander, your wounds need tending," Selldor said, stepping closer to her.

Winter raised her sword, and Selldor immediately stepped back. She hadn't meant it to be intimidating, but she didn't mind. These wounds wouldn't kill her. Not yet, anyway.

She whispered one word to Selldor, and the moment she said it, he nodded, and about-faced to charge back into battle.

"Turn."

All around her, Rangers echoed the signal word, their shouts rising in the air.

Turn.

Winter climbed atop a small pile of corpses, human and tiellan both, to get a better view of the battlefield. Her heavy infantry on the flanks had received the signal, and now turned inward. The Khalic force had pushed Winter's center so far back that they were now hemmed into a pocket of Winter's soldiers, all but surrounded on three sides. Winter's cavalry on the far left, led by Nardo, had routed the opposing Khalic horse and currently pursued them off to the south. Her riders on the right, led by Rorie, had all but scattered the Khalic cavalry on her side as well. Rorie had already regrouped her riders, leading them behind the massive block of Khalic infantry. For a moment, Winter worried Nardo was too distracted to bring his riders around as well, but when he turned to see the battlefield, he rallied his cavalry with a shout.

Nardo's riders joined Rorie's, and together they hedged in the rear of the Khalic infantry, closing the circle of tiellan fighters.

Winter had successfully surrounded the massive block of Khalic infantry.

"We have them!" she screamed, jumping down and sprinting towards the front line. She, along with her Rangers, fought their way inwards, crushing the Khalic force together.

Urstadt had once cautioned her to never attempt to surround an enemy that outnumbered her. But seeing the terrain, the way the Khalic army had formed against them, she knew she had to try. Without frost, it was the only way she could think of that might defeat such a force.

And, Goddess rising, it had worked.

Her elation quickly faded at the realization of the work that lay before her. The Khalic army still outnumbered them by a great deal, and surrender was nowhere in sight. The Khalic soldiers were packed so tightly together she wondered whether they could even lift their arms. She could not imagine how terrifying it must be for them, to watch their fellows dying around them, and to be completely helpless to do anything about it—and to know that they were likely next.

The battle had turned into butchery. The tiellans took numerous breaks, regaining their strength, while the Khalic force obstinately refused to surrender. Then her forces would simply attack again, continuing the work of murdering Khalic humans, one by one.

Finally, after hours of this, the Khalic force seemed to recognize its fate, and the soldiers who remained in the middle of the tiellan ring laid down their weapons, kneeling.

Blood soaked the grass and collected in small pools everywhere on the field; soldiers slipped on red mud all around her.

Everything was red.

Winter suddenly doubled over and vomited into the red grass. Her shoulder burned with pain, and the side of her head throbbed. She wondered how long she had been running on adrenaline alone. The sudden rush of pain, combined with the sight of the red beneath her and her own sick, only made her want to vomit more.

Goddess, she had to get away, she had to get clean.

When she had emptied her stomach, she turned and began walking quickly away from the battlefield, from the massive red stain on the landscape. Before she got far, Selldor found her.

"Commander," he said, saluting.

Winter let out a ragged breath. She returned his salute with all the energy she could muster. "What is it, Selldor?"

"First, I've brought healers for you." Two older tiellan men rushed up to her, inspecting her shoulder.

Winter nodded, and almost collapsed with gratitude. The healers immediately grabbed her arms, supporting her and leading her to a large rock on which she could sit. Goddess rising, she hadn't realized how exhausted she was.

Her gratitude immediately turned to anger as one of the healers poured a liquid on her shoulder wound that burned like a Goddess-damned furnace.

"What in Oblivion—"

"Sorry 'bout that, Commander," one of the healers said. Neither met her eyes; they were both focused on her shoulder.

Winter's eyes bored holes in the man, but he didn't seem to notice.

"I am ready to report, Commander." One of Selldor's duties consisted of gathering as much information as possible after each battle, and relaying it to Winter. She almost did not want to know what he had to say.

Winter growled in pain as one of the healers scraped a small metal tool against—no, she realized as she looked down, *inside*—her wound. Winter brought her other arm around and punched the man in the side of the head.

The healer stumbled backwards, but when he regained his balance came right back to Winter, the small tool held ready. "Sorry again, Commander," he said, finally looking her in the eyes. "This ain't going to heal properly without pain first. The pain's good. Means the wound's gettin' clean."

Winter clenched her jaw, then nodded curtly.

"Go ahead," Winter said, both to Selldor and the healer, the words heavy on her tongue.

"We took heavy losses," Selldor said, his face grim. "Thirteen hundred casualties from our infantry. Almost half of them dead."

Winter sucked in a sharp breath, both from the Goddess-damned healers and from the numbers Selldor reported. "Nearly a third," she whispered. They had begun the battle with just over four thousand infantry. "Our riders?"

"Fifteen hundred casualties, almost one thousand dead."

By far the heaviest losses the tiellans had experienced on a battlefield—and not just because it was the largest army Winter had ever fielded; previously, her casualties had been closer to six or seven percent. Today it had been over thirty.

Winter growled at the scraping pain in her shoulder, and was about to punch the idiot healer again when he removed the tool, hands raised.

"All finished, Commander. All that's left now is to dress the wound. The worst is over."

Winter eyed the healer warily, then turned back to Selldor. "The Khalic Legion?" Winter asked.

Selldor swallowed hard. "We… we are still counting the dead, Commander. Most of the Khalic cavalry fled after they were routed, so we have no accurate estimate of their horse. But their infantry… we estimate they lost at least twelve thousand soldiers."

Winter's eyes widened. "Twelve thousand casualties?"

"Twelve thousand dead, Commander."

The last few hours of the battle had been a slaughter, nothing but butchery. But *twelve thousand dead*. Maybe more. At her command.

Murderer.

Slowly, Selldor sat down beside her.

"Is Kyfer among them?" Winter asked. "Or the psimancers?"

"We have not found them yet," Selldor said.

Winter stared at the ground, blinking. Twelve thousand dead. The shock of it was almost enough to make her forget about her pounding head, or the pain in her shoulder, or even about the fact that, if they didn't find the psimancer bodies, she would have no more *faltira*.

"We have taken the prisoners, Commander. What are your wishes for them?"

Kill them all, a part of Winter wanted to say.

Their victory was decisive; she could make it even more so,

and horrify their enemies in the process.

But as Urstadt had emphasized time and time again, that was not how warfare was conducted. One day Winter would lose a battle, Urstadt insisted, and her own troops, or she herself, would be taken prisoner. How would she want her own Rangers treated?

And another part of Winter could not bear the thought of more death that day. The Canaian Fields were stained red. So many had died, and many by her own hand. How could she contribute to another?

The dark part of her flared. What did death matter to her? When did Winter start caring about anything on this Sfaera? Everything she had ever loved had been taken from her. If she took that from others, what did it matter?

"Commander? Are you all right?"

Winter's eyes met Selldor's, the whites of them surprisingly bright against his red-stained face.

There was another way, Winter realized. *The only order is chaos.*

Winter closed her eyes, and Chaos waited for her, smooth and the purest white.

"Send word to whoever is in charge of their remaining forces," Winter said. "Kyfer, if he escaped. Inform them that we have prisoners, and are willing to exchange them for ransom."

"Of course, Commander."

"Is that all, Selldor?"

"That is all, Commander."

"Thank you," Winter said. Then, she stood. "Now, please… give me a moment alone."

She did not wait to hear his response, but instead walked away from him, from the massive bloody stain on the landscape, and from everything.

37

Foothills of the Eastmaw Mountains

OVER *TWO-THIRDS* OF THE Khalic force, killed or taken prisoner. Kyfer could not believe the number, despite the evidence.

And it was the fault of the tiellans.

Kyfer stood at the top of a small hill at the base of the Eastmaw Mountains. He could not believe that only months before, he had experienced a victory in these same mountains, and had looked on the tiellans as nothing but a nuisance, a way to expand his power, if anything. He had not known them then for what they were.

Daemons.

Kyfer clenched his fists, looking up at the sky, and let out a shriek, a scream he had pent up inside of himself since barely escaping the Canaian Fields—the killing fields, as his troops now called them. Since he had lost that first battle on the Setso.

The sound echoed against the stars, and finally faded into the night. The rest of his cavalry camped just on the other hill; they would have undoubtedly heard him, but Kyfer no longer cared. His reputation was ruined. All he had worked for, all he had ever wanted, had now been taken from him by the tiellans.

"I sense your anger, my son."

Kyfer turned quickly, looking for the source of the voice. He had been alone on this hilltop, he had made sure of it. And as he looked around, he saw nothing but an empty hilltop still;

except for the stars in the sky, he was alone. Kyfer chuckled to himself. He was likely going mad. Perhaps this whole ordeal would rob him of his sanity.

"Sanity was never my domain," the voice said. It was a man's voice, strong and confident, echoing against the night sky. "Wrath, however, is."

"Who are you?" Kyfer asked, looking around himself. Still, he saw nothing, no one. Just the stars, and...

And one star, a bright red star Kyfer had never seen before. The star glimmered scarlet, and then it *grew*. It elongated into a bright red shaft, and that shaft expanded into a man—a man bigger than any Kyfer had ever seen, standing a head taller than he, and ripped with muscle and sinew.

"I am Mefiston," the man said. The redness had all but faded from him now, although Kyfer could swear he could see the hints of iridescent red tendrils of smoke rising from the man's eyes, his skin.

"I... I do not know you," Kyfer said.

"No, you don't. Would you like to?"

Kyfer stared at the man, unsure of what to say, what to think.

"You are angry," the man repeated. "I can help you channel that anger, if you accept my power. I can help you exact the revenge you seek."

Revenge.

"You will help me kill the tiellans?" Kyfer asked. "You will help me kill the tiellan witch?"

"I will help you do whatever you wish," Mefiston said with a smile. "All you have to do is let me in."

Kyfer hesitated. He did not know who this man was, what this man was. He did not know the nature of this deal the man claimed to offer. It would be foolish to accept.

Or, rather, it would be foolish for the old Kyfer to accept such a thing; the Kyfer who still had a reputation, who still had something to lose.

This Kyfer was willing to do anything.

"Very well—"

Before Kyfer could finish his thought, he began to scream.

Razzo grabbed his sword, looking to the neighboring hilltop where the screams came from.

"Captain," one of his lieutenants said, looking to him, "I can take a few men to investigate..."

"Do it." Razzo had seen Kyfer wander off in that direction as night fell. His general could be having a breakdown, or the tiellans could be up to something. Razzo took a deep breath. He prayed to the Goddess Kyfer was just losing his mind. After the horror of the Canaian Fields, he did not want to see another tiellan ever again. He shook his head, remembering the way he'd spoken before the battle. He'd been a Goddess-damned fool. "Take a hundred light horsemen with you. If it's the tiellans, gather as much information as you can before returning to me so we can form up."

"As you wish, Captain." The soldier gathered a small team of riders. Soon, they were galloping off towards the neighboring hill.

"Captain, where is General Kyfer?"

Razzo turned to see a courier approaching.

"He... he should return soon," Razzo said, hoping the statement was true.

"Someone just arrived to see the general. Should I bring him to you?"

Razzo sighed. He was long past wishing he'd never joined the bloody Legion—he'd passed that point before the battle of the Canaian Fields was halfway over.

He just wanted a rest, for Canta's sake.

With great effort, Razzo nodded his head. "Bring him to me."

Soon the courier returned, two men with him. One was a tall man, in the plate mail and white-and-red tabard of a Goddessguard, helm in the crook of one arm, sword sheathed at his side.

The other was Grand Marshal Carrieri.

Razzo straightened, sheathing his sword before saluting the Grand Marshal.

"Captain Razzo. Where is Kyfer?" Carrieri demanded.

Razzo gulped down the phlegm suddenly coating his throat. "He should return any moment, Grand Marshal."

The Goddessguard coughed expectantly.

"Captain Razzo, this is High Cleric Butarian," Carrieri said. "He has graciously offered his support in our hour of need."

Razzo looked from the High Cleric to Carrieri and back again. A High Cleric was a general of the Sons of Canta. There were only a handful in the entire Denomination. The Sons were a completely separate body from the Khalic Legion; Razzo did not have to salute the man, but he did it anyway. He'd left his pride in the pool of blood on the Canaian Fields.

Butarian returned the salute, though his face was creased with disdain.

Razzo cleared his throat. "How can I be of service?"

Carrieri was pacing back and forth as Razzo and Butarian stood before him when Kyfer finally strode into the tent later that night.

Razzo's normally imposing frame was hunched over, as if he were carrying massive weights in each arm and around his neck. He looked about to collapse, he was so exhausted. Butarian actually looked *bored*. It was Kyfer, however, who filled Carrieri with a rage he had not known in many, many years. Somehow, the general looked fresh as a Goddess-damned spring flower as he entered the tent, stronger and more healthy than Carrieri ever remembered seeing him. It was infuriating.

"General," Razzo said, saluting, "are you well? We heard a scream earlier and I thought it might be where you—"

"I'm fine, clearly," Kyfer said. "I see I have guests. Welcome, Grand Marshal." Kyfer offered his own salute to Carrieri, who reluctantly returned it.

Carrieri glared at Kyfer. "Twelve thousand…"

He couldn't continue, and just kept pacing until he calmed down enough to speak again. Such rage was not common for Carrieri, but these circumstances were far from common.

Finally, when he felt ready, he stopped in front of Kyfer.

"You realize," he said, doing his best to keep his breathing even and his teeth from grating, "that no army has suffered such a defeat in the history of Khale. No army has suffered such a defeat in the *history of the Sfaera*."

"It was the last victory the tiellans will see," Kyfer said. He didn't smile, but, Canta rising, it looked like he *wanted* to. There was no twitch at the corners of Kyfer's mouth, no creasing around the man's eyes, but Kyfer might as well be grinning ear to ear as far as Carrieri was concerned.

"You'd better hope, for the sake of our nation, that you're right," Carrieri said.

He took a few more deep breaths to compose himself. Despite the circumstances, he could not believe the insatiable anger that boiled inside of him. The mistake of acting out of anger, even in the worst of times, was a lesson Carrieri had learned years and years ago. He refused to do so again now, no matter how foolish Kyfer had been.

"Forgive me, Grand Marshal," Kyfer said, inclining his head, "but you still haven't told me why you've come."

Carrieri resisted the urge to draw his sword and stab the man on the spot. It was a reasonable question. Carrieri would never have believed he would be here, of all places, just a few days ago.

"Shortly after I sent the Legion to reinforce you," *the Legion that has now been crushed under your command*, "Rune came to visit me." Rune was the third member of the Triad, the ruling body of the Nazaniin, along with Kosarin Lothgarde and Sirana Aqilla. He was a voyant—one of the few people on the Sfaera who could use the form of psimancy called clairvoyance to prophesy and discern future events. Carrieri could still see Rune's face when he answered the man's summons, as white as pure snow.

"He told me the Legion would suffer a devastating defeat," Carrieri continued, "and that if I did not ride out to meet what remained of the soldiers under your command, our whole nation would be at risk. I left Triah, against my better judgment, to come to your aid, Kyfer."

Carrieri glanced at Butarian. "I could not afford to take any more of the Legion away from Triah," he said, "not with the threat of Roden growing on the northern horizon. But the Denomination was generous enough to lend me High Cleric Butarian and the soldiers under his command. Five thousand Sons of Canta and five Cantic psimancers ride behind us."

Kyfer shook his head. "Five thousand? That gives us just over ten thousand, total. Even with the psimancers, that will not be enough to make a dent in the tiellan forces, let alone defeat them."

"*You* could not defeat them with twenty thousand soldiers," Carrieri said. "But let me remind you, General, *I* am not *you*."

"Then you mean for us to attack the tiellans again?" Razzo said. The fear in his eyes was palpable.

"We're going to *defeat* them," Carrieri said, "or die trying."

PART IV

IT'S ALWAYS BLOOD

38

The Coastal Road, somewhere between Kirlan and Triah

KNOT TRIED TO SLEEP as best he could, arms chained up above his head to either side of him, feet chained to the floor below, as he sat on the bench of a carriage very much like the one the Black Matron had taken Astrid in—barred, locked, and meant for transporting a prisoner. At least he wasn't in that damn cell anymore.

Outside, he could hear whispering.

The first voice, full of frustration, Knot recognized as that of Harak, one of the Black Matron's Goddessguards.

"I thought he wanted us to wait until we arrived in Triah."

"I do not dictate his will," the Black Matron replied. "I only carry it out. And we need to do it now. Open the Goddess-damned carriage."

Knot squirmed in his chains. Whatever they intended, he didn't like the sound of it. And he *definitely* didn't like the sound of this nameless "he" they referred to.

Harak took a deep breath. "You are sure this is his will?"

"I am sure, Harak. Now *open the carriage.*"

The lock clanked, then clicked, and the door swung open. The Black Matron looked in at him, Harak at her side.

Rage boiled through Knot's veins at the sight of the woman. The last time he'd seen her had been in Astrid's memories. He knew what she'd done to the girl, now. He could not wait for the opportunity to kill her.

"The time has come, my dear," the Black Matron said, a smile spreading across her face.

"Don't suppose you'll tell me which time has come, exactly," Knot said, looking at her flatly. "Supper time, maybe? I'm starving."

The Black Matron's lips formed into a wide, thin line. "Get him out of there," she said to Harak.

Harak was a large man, but as he unlocked the chain that held Knot's right hand to the roof of the carriage, Knot swung at the man's face. His fist connected, but Harak hardly flinched. He glared at Knot, gripping Knot's fist in his own, and squeezed.

Knot cursed. "Can't blame me for trying," he said through gritted teeth. Harak's hand was massive; it almost enveloped Knot's entire fist, and Knot could feel the bones in his hand straining. If Knot hadn't been chained up, he'd have been able to stand against Harak. But just as Knot knew instinctively what to do in a fight, he also knew instinctively when to stop.

"*Harak.* We don't have time for this."

Harak grumbled something, but unlocked Knot's other hand. He yanked Knot out of the carriage, and dragged him across the ground to a wooden chair standing near the small fire. Two other priestesses waited, and a dozen Sons of Canta stood a few rods back. Two more Goddessguards stood with the priestesses.

Harak slammed Knot down onto the chair and chained his arms, then his legs.

"Means a lot that you're willing to lavish all this attention on me," Knot said, looking around at the people staring down at him, "but it really ain't necessary. I do much better without it."

The Black Matron glared at him. "I've only been around you for a few hours and I'm already tired of your commentary.

Thankfully, we'll be free of that soon enough."

"I'm hurt," Knot said, struggling against his chains, trying for weaknesses. "All this time I thought you liked my commentary." He might be able to slam himself down on the chair hard enough to break it, but his feet would still be chained, and he'd have Harak to deal with. Not to mention it would bloody hurt.

That said, the Black Matron was talking in absolutes here, and he wasn't interested in seeing things through.

"Please. You're almost as bad as that ridiculous vampire."

Knot was silent at that. He had nothing to say to this woman about Astrid.

"Don't suppose you'll tell me what you're about to do with me?" Knot asked, changing the subject. If anything, he hoped to keep her talking.

"No," the Black Matron said, "don't suppose I will." She turned to the priestesses. "Anoint him."

The two priestesses approached, each with a dagger in one hand. Simultaneously, they raised their hands above Knot's head, and then he felt warm liquid drip into his hair and down his face.

It's always blood.

The Black Matron placed her hands on his head, and the world around Knot went black.

As quickly as his world went black, it exploded again with lights and color, and Knot found himself once again in the Void. The real Void, not Astrid's voidstone, and this time he wasn't alone.

"Hello, Knot."

The speaker looked very much like he did.

"Shit," Knot murmured. "You're—"

"Lathe. I suppose you could say I'm also you, technically."

Lathe took a step towards Knot. Ripples of color echoed outward as his feet touched the empty blackness. "But I think we can both agree that you have something that belongs to me."

"You're dead," Knot said, stepping back as Lathe advanced on him. But even as he said the words, he knew they could not be completely true. And he had to admit, he did have something of Lathe's—Lathe's own body. And when Knot really thought about it, what right did he have to stop Lathe from taking it back?

"Do you really think that?" Lathe asked.

Knot didn't respond. A shadow flickered at the corner of his eye, and he turned to see what it was. Nothing was there, just like the strange thing he'd seen—or hadn't seen—when using Astrid's voidstone months ago.

"No matter," Lathe said. "They made a deal with me. Said they'd help restore me to my body if I then chose to become the avatar to some Daemon. Doesn't sound like the best deal, I'll admit, but it sounds infinitely better than Oblivion."

"A Daemon," Knot said slowly. The Black Matron wanted his body... so that she could give it to a Daemon? "The Black Matron ain't talking about some little daemon, Lathe. She's talking about one of the Nine."

"I don't care who she's talking about," Lathe said coldly. "I just want my life back."

Lathe charged the last few paces towards Knot, leaping through the Void, and *through* Knot.

Then, Knot was alone in the Void, and Lathe was gone.

39

South of the Eastmaw Mountains

WINTER WOKE WITH A start, sitting up straight in her cot. She was covered in sweat, shivering, with a headache strong enough to split a mountain.

Someone was outside her tent.

She was terrified of the presence, whatever it was, but at the same time she felt drawn towards it. Slowly, she crept out of her cot. Her breath came fast and shallow, but she tried to keep it quiet. She reached down for her sword, and moved to the tent opening. Peeking out the partially open door, she saw nothing outside except the night sky.

Winter slipped out, sword at the ready.

There were no other tents around hers. No campfires. No Rangers, no Khalic prisoners. She was alone in a great field, the night sky above her.

Winter looked down, and saw her legs in a pool of dark blood up to her knees.

The blood crept up her legs, soaking her, staining her a dark, blackish red.

"Hello, Winter."

Winter looked up sharply. She knew that voice. Dark, deep, rolled in flame.

Azael stood before her.

Black cloak, ragged and worn, fading into coils of mist

where it met the ground. Hood drawn low over his face, and nothing inside it but darkness.

"What do you want?" she asked. The blood continued to creep up her body, and with it a panicked, obliviating fear. The higher the blood rose, the more helpless she felt, the more fear consumed her.

"I want you to be my avatar," Azael said. "We can help one another."

The blood had reached her chest, now, and soaked slowly higher. Winter fought the feeling that accompanied it, pushing the panic and terror down deep inside of her.

"I do not need your help."

"Your body cannot sustain itself for long without frost," Azael said. "But I can strengthen you. I can take away this sickness, and make you mighty."

"I... I..."

The blood had reached her neck.

I am *mighty*, Winter wanted to say.

"I am nothing without *faltira*," is what she said instead.

"Then you will join with me?" Azael asked, his voice rising.

"No—" Winter managed, but then the blood reached her mouth, filled it, warm and thick. Winter choked on it, spluttering it up, but it kept coming.

"No matter," Azael said. "There is another."

Winter woke with a start, sitting up straight in her cot. She was covered in sweat, shivering, with a headache strong enough to split a mountain. She was sick and weak as Oblivion.

But at least this time, she was alone.

There is another, Azael had said. Another body he could possess?

"Commander."

Winter coughed violently, rising to her feet. She steadied herself on a tent pole. She had hoped to plunder *faltira* from the slain, but her people had not been able to identify the psimancers among the dead at the Canaian Fields. Their bodies had been there, Winter had been sure of that, but it was not easy to find a half-dozen psimancers among twelve thousand dead. Impossible, in fact. She had sent riders to the nearest cities to procure more *faltira* for her, but they might not return for days, perhaps weeks.

Between her withdrawal from *faltira* and the node of pain that still pulsed between her ear and her temple, her head felt as if it might split open with every sudden movement. Her shoulder was healing, but it still hurt, and she would have limited use of that arm for the next few weeks, the healers told her. Her only consolation was that she'd taken the wound on the shoulder of her non-dominant hand; she could at least still use a sword relatively effectively.

"A moment," she said, between coughs. She dressed quickly—as quickly as her lethargic limbs would allow, anyway—and strapped her sword to her waist. Then, she walked outside. The gray sky above threatened rain. They had made their camp north of the Canaian Fields, near the Eastmaw Mountains. Trees spotted the land here, growing thicker closer to the mountain range. They'd found one grove to serve as their base camp for now, Ranger tents spilling out of the copse and into the plains beyond. There were a surprising number of *rihnemin* in the area. Nothing like the great monolith at Adimora, but a dozen or so great stones roughly the size of horses, and a few as large as a building, dotted the landscape, covered in tiellan runes. Her Rangers took courage at the sight of so many relics of their people, but Winter was more cautious. She had yet to see a *rihnemin* do anything to actually help her people.

Selldor, Urstadt, and Ghian were waiting for her.

"Are you all right, Commander?" Urstadt asked.

She, too, had taken to calling Winter commander since the battle at the Canaian Fields. Winter did not like it; she felt as if she had lost a friend, despite no other discernible change in their relationship.

"Fine," Winter said, coughing again, but she got a hold of herself more quickly this time. Pain branched through her skull with every cough. "Are we ready to make the exchange?"

"We are ready," Selldor said. "The Khalic contingent waits for us just over the hill."

"There is other news," Ghian said.

Everyone looked at the Druid leader. Winter wondered what news Ghian could possibly have that she wouldn't already be privy to.

"Some of our scouts returned early this morning," Ghian said, looking straight at Winter. "They discovered a hidden force not far off."

"A hidden force?" Winter asked. "More Khalic soldiers?"

"Not Khalic," Ghian said. "Cantic."

"The Sons of Canta," Winter said quietly. Whatever business the Sons had here, it surely could not be in her favor. While the Denomination claimed to treat humans and tiellans equally, their actual practice made their opinion quite clear. And Winter's tiellan force now threatened the very existence of the government that sustained the Denomination.

"Goddess, why didn't you tell us this earlier?" Selldor demanded, gaping at Ghian.

"How many?" Winter asked.

"At least five thousand," Ghian said.

"Ghian," Winter said, stepping forward so they stood face to face, "my scouts would never report to you before they did to any of us. How did you come across this information?" Something bothered Winter about the whole exchange. Ghian seemed... different, somehow.

While Winter could not access telesis without *faltira*, she still had acumency. One acumenic *tendron* snaked from her toward Ghian. When it made contact, the *tendron* snapped back to her, and an image flashed in her mind.

A black skull, wreathed in dark flame.

There is another.

Winter grabbed Ghian by the throat and slammed him against a large tree trunk. She immediately regretted the action when pain thundered through her skull. Her shoulder throbbed, too, but it was nothing compared to the pain in her head.

"What have you done?" she demanded.

"Commander—"

Winter's hands wrapped around Ghian's throat, and he began to laugh. The sound was eerie, a choking rasp.

"What is wrong with him?" Selldor asked.

"I have become... something greater than myself," Ghian rasped.

"Commander, what..." Urstadt approached, but did not say anything further. She looked at Ghian intently.

"You need me," Ghian whispered. "You cannot lead the tiellans without me."

"*Why can't you just leave me alone,*" Winter seethed, speaking not to Ghian, but to the thing that had taken him. The Daemon. If this was similar to how it had gone with Daval, Ghian was still in there, probably still largely in control. But he had been imbued with Azael's power, and could become a force for the Daemon at any moment.

She could not allow him to live.

But he was right. Ghian's power was waning, but he still technically commanded the Druids. Winter could attempt a hostile takeover, but the Druids would not respond well if they knew she'd killed Ghian with her own hands. But she couldn't very well let the avatar of the Lord of the Nine Daemons roam around freely.

Winter released him.

"Commander, what is going on?" Selldor asked, glancing at Ghian. The Druid leader rubbed his neck where Winter had gripped him, but the smile did not leave his face.

"Take him into custody," she ordered.

Immediately, Selldor signaled for some nearby Rangers. The men approached, binding Ghian at Selldor's command.

"Be careful, and keep a close eye on him," Winter said. "He will be much stronger than he once was. He could probably break those bonds, if he really tried."

The Rangers tied Ghian up, looking at the man cautiously.

"He is like Daval once was," Urstadt said, realization dawning on her face.

"Yes," Winter said quietly, rubbing the bridge of her nose with one hand as pain drummed in her head. "I am quite sure he is." Goddess, this was the last thing she needed at this moment. She pointed at the Rangers who had secured Ghian between them. "Do not let him out of your sight. I will explain more when I can, but for now, we need to prepare for another battle. The Khalic army clearly is not done with us yet."

* * *

Winter's first objective was dealing with the Khalic prisoners.

"Any hope of exchanging them is gone?" she asked Urstadt.

"I believe so, Commander," Urstadt said. She was staring straight ahead, clearly lost in thought.

"Ghian isn't Daval," Winter said, guessing what occupied Urstadt's mind. "The force that possessed him is the same, but Ghian is still Ghian—only stronger, more powerful, and now in the service of one of the darkest forces on the Sfaera."

Goddess, Winter thought to herself, *if you're trying to make her feel better you're doing a shitty job of it.*

"I know," Urstadt said. Winter had explained what had happened to Daval after they killed him together in Izet—everything about Azael and the Nine Daemons that Winter knew, which admittedly wasn't much. "It was just… I did not expect that presence to be back so soon."

Winter sighed. She rotated her injured arm experimentally. It lanced with pain when she rose her hand above her shoulder, but she at least had some mobility if she needed it. Her head still hurt like Oblivion, but that was a pain she'd already determined to grow used to. It made the pain that ached through her entire body feel like a light massage, which was one advantage of the splitting headache, she supposed. "Neither did I. But now is not the time to discuss Ghian and Azael. Will you be ready to fight, Urstadt?"

Urstadt straightened, her eyes finally focusing on Winter. "Yes, Commander."

Winter nodded, relieved. "Then we must deal with the prisoners first."

"What are your orders, Commander?"

"Do we have a choice?" Winter asked. "We cannot exchange them, not when they'll likely go right back into a battle against us. We can't keep them around. Even unarmed, we couldn't manage that many prisoners during a battle. We have to eliminate them."

"If I may, Commander, there may be a way to get rid of them without immediate bloodshed."

Winter took a deep breath, rubbing the side of her head with one hand. In truth, she'd hoped Urstadt would say something like that. She did not know if she could order her Rangers to kill two thousand prisoners in cold blood, no matter what those prisoners had done or represented.

"We know something the prisoners don't," Urstadt said.

"That we're about to have another battle," Winter said. "But how does that help us?"

"We let them go," Urstadt said. "The Khalic and Cantic armies are amassed to the east. We give the prisoners the option: run south, where we tell them the rest of the Khalic army waits for them, or die by our hand. They'll all choose to run. We leave them weaponless, with the bare minimum to survive."

"They might circle around and make their way back to the Khalic army to the east."

"Unlikely," Urstadt said. "The only intelligence they have is what we give them. They'll eventually rejoin the Khalic Legion, but by then the battle should be long over."

"Then that is what we'll do," Winter said. It wasn't ideal, but it was better than funneling two thousand soldiers directly back into the Khalic war machine.

That afternoon, after they had sent the Khalic prisoners packing southward, Winter rode out with Urstadt, Selldor, and Nardo to meet the Legion's leadership to negotiate. Rain pattered on Winter's leather armor, and the sky above had grown slowly darker throughout the day, though the sun would not set for another few hours. The weather reflected Winter's mood.

So far, Winter had refused to meet with the leaders of the armies she had faced in battle. Her anger over the slaughter of hundreds of tiellans from Cineste still burned brightly. This time, however, she did not have much of a choice. She had to at least attempt to negotiate.

"Our situation is dire," Winter said as they rode. Four men waited near one of the larger *rihnemin* in the area, at the base of a shallow hollow between two hills. On the western hill, the remaining Khalic troops had taken formation, while Winter's Rangers occupied the hill to the east.

She noticed a Goddessguard among the four men waiting for her. They certainly weren't being subtle.

"It has been dire before," Urstadt responded. "We have defeated forces that outnumbered us four times over. We can do it again."

"We could," Winter said, "if I had *faltira*. What if the Cantic troops have psimancers with them?"

If Winter had *faltira*, their outlook on this battle would be very different. But she did not. Not only that, she was weak and disoriented from withdrawal and from her injuries. Her entire body ached, but her head specifically still thrummed with pain.

Urstadt swore. Winter looked at her captain. "You knew I was out of frost—"

"No, Commander," Urstadt said, pointing at the men who waited for them. "One of those men is Riccan Carrieri."

"Canta's bloody bones," Winter muttered. Urstadt had reviewed everything she'd known about the Khalic Legion with Winter at the beginning of their campaign, placing special emphasis on the Grand Marshal of the Khalic forces, Riccan

Carrieri. According to Urstadt, the man was unsurpassed on the battlefield.

"What in Oblivion is he doing here?" Selldor asked.

"I suppose we're about to find out," Winter said.

Winter sat straight in her saddle, head high, determined not to let her infirm state show. Her retinue reached the top of the hill, and they rode forward together to meet with the four humans. Winter recognized General Publio Kyfer, and the tall bearded fellow next to him looked familiar as well. The Goddessguard she'd never seen before. And the fourth human must be Riccan Carrieri.

The man was shorter than Winter would have thought; he was taller than Winter, but that was not saying much for a human. He had handsome features, dark brown hair going gray at the temples, and a long scar on one cheek.

Publio Kyfer glared at Winter. Winter could not blame him. She had routed his forces time and time again on the battlefield. She would be upset, too. But the way he smiled threw her; his eyes were full of wrath, boring holes into her, but his smile was wide, gleeful. Winter shivered.

"Lagerta Urstadt," Carrieri said, when he saw the Rodenese woman. "I did not expect to see you here, of all places. I don't suppose you could tell us what brought you into the tiellan fold?"

Lagerta? Was that Urstadt's given name? Winter realized she had never thought to ask. Urstadt was Urstadt; adding anything to it seemed superfluous.

Winter wondered why Carrieri recognized Urstadt on sight; Urstadt had never given the impression that she knew the Grand Marshal personally. Urstadt, however, said nothing.

"Very well," Carrieri said. His eyes met Winter's. "And you are Danica Winter Cordier, I presume?"

How in Oblivion does he know my name?

"Who's that?" Winter asked, nodding at the Goddessguard.

"That is High Cleric Butarian," Carrieri said.

"He the one in charge of the Sons of Canta you have holed up not far from here?" Winter asked.

Carrieri's eyebrows rose, and he looked from Kyfer to Butarian, and then back to Winter. "Your intelligence is impressive," he said. "The Cantic soldiers are a contingency plan, that's all."

"Is that what they're calling an ambush these days?"

Carrieri shrugged. "Is it any different than what you did to the legionaries you killed at Lake Dravian?"

Yes, Winter thought. *You are doing this to* me.

"We don't have your prisoners anymore," Winter said. "When we heard about the Sons, we figured you wouldn't bother with the ransom."

Carrieri's face darkened. It was the first sign of real emotion he'd shown in the conversation. "If you've murdered prisoners of war—"

"We haven't," Winter said quickly. No sense in provoking them if she could avoid it. "But they won't be joining you any time soon, if that's what you were hoping."

"If you have no prisoners to exchange, then we have nothing to negotiate," Carrieri said.

"If that is the case, I would be happy to take my Rangers and go," Winter said, her voice sincere. "I do not wish to fight you today."

Kyfer laughed quietly, but Carrieri ignored the general.

"I never wish to fight anyone," Carrieri said quietly, his voice barely audible above the rain. "But I have a duty to Khale, and I will fulfill it at any cost."

"You outnumber us," Winter said, "but you have outnumbered us in every battle we've fought. That hasn't mattered. You've seen what I can do."

"I have," Carrieri said, "but your luck was bound to run out at some point, Winter. This is the end of the tiellan movement."

"Somehow I disagree," Winter said.

Carrieri grew somber. "You could surrender. Give yourselves up, turn your army over as prisoners. It would go better for you."

"I'd rather rot in Oblivion."

Carrieri sighed. "I'm afraid we can arrange that. I am sorry it has come to this, Winter."

"We will see what the day has in store for us both."

She turned her horse and rode away, and Urstadt, Selldor, and Nardo followed.

40

The Coastal Road, somewhere between Kirlan and Triah

IT WAS A CLOUDY, foggy morning, especially for a late summer day, and Cinzia did not see the Black Matron's caravan until they almost stumbled upon its rearguard on the road. They had been riding hard, hoping to catch their quarry before they arrived at Triah, but now they caught a warning glimpse of the white-and-red tabards of the Sons ahead and reined in their horses as one. If she narrowed her eyes, Cinzia thought she could just about see a Cantic banner flapping in the distance, but it could be an illusion of the fog.

"Did they see us?" she asked no one in particular. The Sons ahead had already been swallowed up by the fog ahead of her.

"Can't be sure one way or another," Astrid said quietly. She looked up. "You can thank your goddess for these clouds and fog. Not as good as a night sky, but at least I won't have to worry about the sun."

"How should we proceed?" Eward asked. "I counted three Sons, and those were just outriders."

"You've seen me handle worse," Astrid said. "The question is whether they have any nightsbane."

"Astrid, make your approach," Cinzia said. "Take out as many of them as you can while you have surprise on your side. Once they realize it's you, they'll bring out the nightsbane, if they have it, at which point Eward and I will attack. I'm sorry, but it's the only chance we have."

"Better I lead anyway. I want first crack at the bitch."

Before Astrid rode away, Cinzia leaned over and grabbed the girl's arm. "Be careful," she said.

Astrid held Cinzia's gaze for a moment, then nodded. She slipped off her horse and rushed off into the fog to flank the Cantic caravan.

Astrid sprinted through the fog, rushing out into a field on the western side of the road, and then angling back towards where she hoped the caravan was. Soon, she saw the rearguard again. It was a shame she did not have her claws. She unsheathed the short sword and dagger she carried at her waist.

As Astrid approached the Sons, one of the horses spooked, bucking and throwing its rider onto the dirt road. Astrid leapt up onto one of the other horses, jamming her dagger into the Son's neck. The man's life leaked out of him in a sigh, and Astrid threw herself onto the other horse, wrapping her arms around the Son's neck and pulling him to the ground in a crash of armor. She stabbed both her dagger and sword down into the man's chest, and that was that. The fog was so thick she could barely see a few rods ahead of her.

Then, a great looming shape. The carriage. And on top of it stood Knot.

"Hello, Astrid," he said. But his voice was different. This wasn't Knot. And yet... as he spoke, Astrid knew it wasn't Lathe, either. She had met Lathe, briefly, when Knot had one of his episodes at Harmoth, and this was not him. Not entirely.

Astrid was about to ask which Daemon she was speaking with when Knot, or Lathe, or whoever it was leapt down from the carriage, and Astrid froze.

In his hand was a bunch of nightsbane.

Pain blossomed within her as he moved closer.

"I did not expect to see you so soon," the man said. "But this will do." He looked over his shoulder. "Come get her."

Emerging from the fog as she descended the carriage, the Black Matron walked towards her.

"Hello, dear," she said with a smile. "I was *so* hoping I would see you again."

Astrid fell to her knees.

The Void

In the Void, Knot drifted.

He drifted, but not aimlessly. Something drew him towards it, slowly at first. He picked up speed so gradually that he was flying along before he realized it. Soon, in the distance, Knot saw what he figured must be the source of the draw. It seemed to be a star, but unlike any of the other star-lights he'd seen in the Void. This one was black, somehow, despite emitting a glow like all of the other star-lights. And this one had an aura of some kind as well—not like his own sift, which was a star-light around which orbited nine other tiny star-lights, but an aura of greater magnitude, and greater power.

He was being drawn to the strange dark star with such force that he could not stop himself, and suddenly he slipped into the star, and *through* it.

And then, for a brief moment that also seemed to last an eternity, he was no longer in the Void, but in the Sfaera. He was still his incorporeal self, but the Sfaera was as clear around him as he had ever seen it. Knot looked around at the people fighting, the cavalry clashing, the people dying, and realized he was in a battle.

Or, rather, above a battle. Knot levitated a few rods above the earth, looking down at the people fighting below.

A large, cubical *rihnemin* roughly the size of a small home protruded from the base of a shallow valley where the two armies clashed. The tide of the battle was clearly swinging toward the combined Khalic-Cantic force; they had broken through their opposition's front line, outflanked their enemy on both sides, and outnumbered them almost two to one.

The other side of the battle, Knot realized, consisted entirely of tiellans. Many wore helms, but he saw the pointed ears on those who didn't, and their stature, the way they moved, the way they fought, was more familiar to Knot than he could have imagined.

And there, in the middle of the tiellan force, Winter fought fiercely, covered in sweat and mud and blood, sword in hand, hair streaked across her face.

She looked so different from the Winter he remembered in Pranna—in traditional tiellan clothing, a loose dress and *siara* wrapped around her neck, taciturn but with an inner fire that drew him to her—and far more similar to the woman he had known after Navone and in their brief journey into Roden, wearing tight leather clothing and sporting a chip on her shoulder that had nearly torn them apart.

And yet she was different still, as he watched her. She fought with confidence and skill, despite her soldiers losing ground around her. She was wounded, Knot could tell—she favored her right shoulder—but fought on with grace and skill. And she was *leading* them, that much was clear. Standard-bearers obeyed her beck and call.

What in Oblivion was he seeing?

Winter was dead, and yet here she was. It was certainly her: her black eyes, raven-dark hair, high cheekbones and pointed nose; her compact, now tightly-muscled frame. She was different, but the same. This was the woman who had married him.

Just like that, Knot snapped back into the Void, in darkness, with the star-lights around him. And there, most prominent of all, the dark star. Knot stared at the strange image, his mind racing.

"That is her, if you're wondering."

Knot whirled to see a woman standing behind him. Knot blinked. One moment she was blonde, the next brunette. One moment tall, the next short. Her visage shifted constantly, never quite settling on a face or body, though it seemed to cycle through the same four or five appearances.

Two of which Knot recognized. One was tall, with short brown hair and sky-blue eyes. The other shorter, younger, and blonde.

As strange as it was to see this woman, Knot had just experienced something stranger. He looked back at the dark star. "That," he said, his eyes almost unable to focus on the shifting phenomenon, "is Winter?"

"It is her sift, more accurately," Kali said.

"If that's her sift, then..."

"Then what you just saw was real. Yes, Knot. Winter is alive."

Winter was *alive*.

And, Knot realized, so was this woman.

"Kali," Knot said. "Didn't I kill you?"

"You tried," she said, "but it didn't quite stick."

Knot's gaze drew back to the dark star. *Seems to be a trend.*

Goddess, could it be true? Winter was *alive.*

"How long have you known?" Knot turned back to Kali.

"I've known she was alive for months, now. You, for slightly less time. That was more of a happy accident."

"Why wouldn't I be alive?"

"Winter thinks you are dead, too. The feeling was mutual, you could say, until now."

With a growl, Knot launched himself at Kali. He quickly realized the futility of the attack when his ethereal form passed straight through Kali's image.

Kali clicked her tongue, shaking her head. "Can't say I didn't expect that kind of response, but it's still disappointingly pathetic. I can't believe you actually *killed* me."

"Thought you said it didn't stick."

"Well, it did and it didn't. Why don't we settle on that."

Realization dawned on Knot. "You're the shadow I've been seein' around."

"Guilty," Kali said. "I admit I've been monitoring you. I'm trapped here, you see, and I've been looking for a way out. I think you might be my ticket."

Knot had so many questions. How was Winter alive? How had this woman monitored him in Astrid's voidstone? How was any of this possible?

But questions would only take time. He had very little of that.

Knot hesitated. What difference did it make if Winter was alive? His body was still not his own to reclaim. As much as it was his, it belonged to Lathe first.

Knot could choose to stay for Winter, but somehow that seemed just as much a mistake. Then, he remembered something from one of Astrid's memories. Her father, just before she had killed him, had looked at Astrid calmly.

It doesn't matter what you are, he had said, *it doesn't matter where you've been. All that matters is what you do.*

All that matters is what you do.

Lathe was an assassin, a killer. Lathe was willing to unleash a Daemon on the Sfaera.

Knot had his flaws, his own inner daemons. But at least he wasn't interested in contributing to the end of the Sfaera.

All that matters is what you do.

"I need to get back," Knot said calmly. "Not just for Winter, but for me, and for the Sfaera." He would take his body back, somehow. And he would make sure he did something that mattered with it.

Kali smiled, the expression remaining while the faces that held it shifted and changed.

"And for me, incidentally," Kali said. "I'll help you reclaim your body, but I'll need something from you in return…"

The Coastal Road, somewhere between Kirlan and Triah

"They have nightsbane," Cinzia said quietly to Eward and the other Prelates.

They had slowly edged forward until they could make out the three Sons in the rear of the formation, and then witnessed Astrid take each one of them out.

And then, just as she did, Knot had leapt from the carriage, nightsbane in hand.

"Go around," Cinzia said. "Flank them. I will approach them head-on, and hopefully distract them long enough for you to rush in. The priority should be getting the nightsbane away from Astrid."

Eward hesitated. "I do not want to leave you alone."

Cinzia nudged her horse closer and gave him a hug. "I will be fine. Do as I say."

Eward signaled to the Prelates. Half of them curved off to the west, the other half went with Eward to the east.

Then Cinzia dismounted, and slowly led her horse forward.

Astrid's prone form, and Knot's, standing tall, became more clear through the fog as she approached. She noticed a third figure, in matron's robes, emerge through the fog, and then more Sons and Goddessguards began to appear.

"And who might this be?" Knot asked as Cinzia walked forward.

"Knot?" Cinzia asked. "Are you all right?"

Knot laughed. "Knot is gone," he said. "I am something completely different, now."

Cinzia had suspected as much when she had seen Knot leap from the carriage, seemingly free, with nightsbane in hand. He would never do such a thing to Astrid.

The man narrowed his eyes. "You are Luceraf's plaything," he said. "What are you doing here?"

Cinzia frowned. "What do you know of Luceraf?" she asked.

"She is a... colleague of my master," the man said. "And..." the man stopped, squinting. "And I know you from somewhere else, too. That fever dream of that country manor. You were there. With the vampire."

"Lathe," Cinzia breathed.

"One and the same," the man said, with a bow. "Although... not exactly the same. I am different, now. As you soon will be. Very soon, in fact. Luceraf comes to claim her bounty."

"You are Cinzia," the Black Matron said. "The former priestess."

Cinzia raised an eyebrow. "You have heard of me?" Hopefully, she could buy enough time for Eward and his Prelates to attack.

"Of course I have," she said. "Everyone in the Denomination knows of Cinzia the Heretic."

"Somehow I cannot help but wonder why heresy means anything to you," Cinzia said, meeting the woman's eyes. "Given your line of work."

Then, out of the fog, Eward attacked. Cinzia heard the shouts, heard the screams, the clanging of metal.

And then, suddenly, she heard nothing. All sound deflated around her, and her vision expanded. When it contracted, she found herself once again in the ethereal, wispy place of blue light.

"Goddess," Cinzia pleaded, "not now."

"Hello, daughter."

"Luceraf," Cinzia said, "I cannot speak now. You must take me back."

Luceraf's laughter filled the space around them, echoing between the blue-gray trees.

"We will go back soon enough," the Daemon said with a smile. "But first, you must give me what you promised."

41

South of the Eastmaw Mountains

CARRIERI NODDED TO HIS standard-bearer, who took a soaked black flag from his bundle and began waving it in the downpour.

Despite the unfavorable weather, the battle was going well. One of the tiellan cavalry flanks had already broken and fled. The other held strong, but soon the tiellan center would fall. The new psimancers the Denomination had brought continued to rain chaos down on the tiellan ranks. The Cantic psimancers were not nearly as effective as Nazaniin agents, but they got the job done. Winter's abilities, on the other hand, were nowhere to be seen. Carrieri suspected she had run out of frost, but there was always the possibility the woman was saving her powers for something specific.

His feelings were mixed as he watched his combined force chip away at the remaining tiellans. Relief was foremost. Given time, given their current trajectory, if the tiellans had not been stopped, they could have eventually threatened the very foundations of the Circle City itself. Triah had not fallen to an enemy army in Ages, but this tiellan woman presented the first real threat to the Khalic republic Carrieri could remember. Skirmishes with Roden were one thing, but there had not been a significant conflict with Roden in centuries. Who would have known the greatest enemy of the republic would come from within its own borders?

He felt a certain sadness. He had met Urstadt once, at a formal dinner in Roden when the two nations were on slightly better terms, and she had been as taciturn then as she was now. He still itched to know why she had fallen in with the tiellans, and why in Oblivion they had *let* her.

His forces pressed inward, and soon the tiellans would either surrender and be taken prisoner, or die by the sword. Carrieri sincerely hoped it would be the former—while he mourned for the slaughter of the Canaian Fields, he was not fond of bloodshed in any form, even from his enemies. A victory was a victory, after all, and the fewer deaths the better.

He turned to face Kyfer, who looked out over the battlefield with a strange expression on his face. Carrieri could not tell whether the man was angry—his eyes certainly seemed to indicate as much, turned downward and so full of wrathful energy that they almost seemed to glow—or delighted at the destruction of the tiellan force, as his wide smile seemed to indicate.

"This should have happened months ago," Carrieri said, frowning at his general. "You should have heeded my counsel, and never engaged them on the Setso."

Kyfer turned, that exaggerated smile almost unmoving on his face.

"If I had not lost to them at the Setso," he said, "you would not have been able to defeat them here."

Carrieri snorted. "That is a foolish thing to say. Better to learn your lesson than to justify the deaths of so many with hindsight."

"Forgive me, Grand Marshal." Kyfer lowered his head.

Carrieri should have been pleased at the general's show of humility, but something about the man was completely off.

When the man looked up, his eyes no longer had the illusion of glowing—they *were* glowing, a bright, shining red. The voice that emanated from his lips was not of anything in the Sfaera.

"I believe my time for lessons has come to an end."

Instinctively, Carrieri nudged his horse further away. "Kyfer!" Carrieri called. "What is this?"

"I have done what any desperate man would do in my position," Kyfer said, a low rumble somehow accompanying his speech. "I have given in to wrath, and wrath... now... becomes me..."

Kyfer threw back his head and *roared*, the sound so loud that it split through the cacophony of battle, the rain, and the thunder above. Tiellans and humans alike stopped fighting and turned to see what had made the sound.

As Kyfer roared, his mouth opened wider and wider, until it was no longer a human mouth at all. His limbs elongated, and he fell from his horse, writhing on the ground. The horse galloped away, mad with panic. Carrieri was of a mind to do the same thing, but could not tear his eyes away from the scene before him.

As Kyfer writhed and roared on the ground, beams of scarlet light broke through his skin, bursting from his eyes, his fingers, his chest.

Carrieri turned his head away, shielding his eyes from a burst of red light that bathed the entire battlefield. He blinked, blinded for a moment, as his eyes and ears readjusted. When his sight cleared, he saw standing before him a massive beast, twice the height of a man, with russet-red skin, the color of blood that had not quite dried. It stood on two massive, muscular legs. Huge claws protruded from its toes and feet, and a long tail swung lazily back and forth.

"Kyfer!" Carrieri called again. A devastating fear burst inside of his chest, and an overwhelming anger—at Kyfer for... for doing whatever it was he had done to become this beast, and at himself for not knowing what in Oblivion to do about it.

The Daemon looked down at him, eyes glowing scarlet red. Tendrils of luminous red smoke drifted sluggishly up from its eyes, its skin, everywhere on the monster. The largest muscles Carrieri had ever seen bulged and strained. Massive jaws, split with rows of fangs, moved as it spoke.

"Kyfer is no more," the Daemon rumbled. "The last of us has claimed an avatar." The thing stretched its arms out, looking at itself. "I can now take my true form," it said, although Carrieri could swear he heard a hint of surprise in its voice.

Razzo, who had been mounted nearby, rode up to Carrieri. "What in Oblivion is going on, Grand Marshal? What *is* that?"

"I haven't the slightest idea," Carrieri murmured.

High Cleric Butarian reined his horse up beside them.

"That," Butarian said, "is one of the Nine Daemons."

"Grand Marshal…" Razzo's eyes were glowing red.

"Razzo," Carrieri said, "not you, too."

Razzo drew his sword. His burning eyes turned to Carrieri through the drenching rain. Then, he spurred his horse forward and attacked.

Carrieri directed his horse to sidestep as Razzo rode past him, parrying the man's insane blows.

"Razzo!" Carrieri shouted. "I order you to stop, as your commander-in-chief!"

Razzo only turned his horse and charged again, screaming. Carrieri parried blow after blow. Razzo used his sword like a club, smashing it at Carrieri again and again. Carrieri spurred his horse around Razzo, deflecting as much as he could. Razzo had a reputation as a renowned swordsman, particularly for his strength, but this was beyond any human capacity. And Razzo showed no finesse or discipline now—only brawn and muscle.

Carrieri soon found an opening, and disarmed his lieutenant with a flick of his sword.

"Stand down, Razzo," Carrieri said, sword held ready to strike. "It's over."

Razzo glared at Carrieri, his eyes burning within his skull. Weaponless, he lunged at Carrieri from his saddle with a roar.

Carrieri struck, his sword plunging into Razzo's chest, but Razzo did not stop. Instead, he slid forward on Carrieri's sword, arms reaching forward.

Carrieri pulled his saddle dagger and rammed it into Razzo's neck once, twice, then a third time, blood spurting out of each wound. Slowly, Razzo slumped forward, still impaled on Carrieri's sword.

Carrieri withdrew the blade, breathing heavily. He was about to berate the soldiers around him for not jumping in to help their Grand Marshal, but he looked up to see the battlefield had completely changed.

It was chaos.

Whatever had affected Razzo had also affected hundreds of soldiers, from both sides—tiellans and humans, eyes burning red, attacked with berserk strength, heedless of who once might have fought by their side.

Nearby, the Daemon that had begun it all, the thing that had once been Kyfer, rumbled a low, rolling chuckle.

"Bloodlust," the thing growled.

Carrieri spurred his horse away from the Daemon. He needed to regroup his men—the ones still in control of themselves—to rally them against this horrifying beast. Whatever it was, it was clearly an enemy to both the Khalic forces and the tiellans.

Above his head, black mist began to form.

42

Coastal Road, somewhere between Kirlan and Triah

CINZIA KNEW SHE WAS back in the Sfaera when Knot— –Lathe—looked at her, smiling. His eyes glowed silver. She had not noticed that before.

That is Bazlamit, a voice said inside of her. *She is a tricky one.*

You, Cinzia hissed. *I don't want this, get out of my head.*

I've infested more than your head, my dear. You cannot get rid of me now.

Cinzia frowned. No matter. She would help Astrid, free Knot, and then deal with the bloody Daemon inside of her.

I'm not sure you'll have time for that, Cinzia. We all have avatars, now. Mefiston has already taken his true form. Samann will be next, and I will soon follow. You will not last long enough to save your friends.

Around her, Eward and his Prelates fought the Sons of Canta and the Goddessguards. A few Sons had fallen, but so had two Prelates. The Black Matron knelt by Astrid, while Lathe, eyes glowing silver, walked towards her.

You never told me that becoming your avatar would mean I would have to die, Cinzia thought.

You never asked, darling.

"Knot!" Cinzia shouted, looking at the man who had once been her Goddessguard. "You must be in there somewhere. I know you can hear me!"

She heard Luceraf's echoing laugh inside her head, while

513

Lathe laughed along with her. "I'm sorry, Cinzia. Knot is gone. He really can't hear you."

"Let me speak to him," Cinzia said, meeting Lathe's eyes—although such a thing was impossible, with the strange effect his eyes had.

Do my eyes glow now, too? Cinzia wondered.

They do, Luceraf replied, *but only Lathe can see it now. Only another avatar can see the glow behind your eyes, the essence of your power, until I am able to take my true form through you.*

You said I have power. That you've enhanced me. You mean I am strong?

Cinzia could feel the pride emanating from Luceraf within her. *Stronger than you know, darling.*

Good, Cinzia thought. Then, she rushed forward, kicking the Black Matron in the face with all her might. The woman's head snapped back as she flew into the air, then slid along the dirt road.

Cinzia grabbed the nightsbane and sprinted away, tossing it as far as she could. She sprinted back—faster than any human could—in time to see Astrid stir.

"You shouldn't have done that," Lathe said with a frown.

"You should have stopped me," Cinzia said, glaring at him.

Then, Lathe rushed at her.

As Astrid slowly regained awareness, she saw Cinzia trying to defend herself against Knot. Or Lathe, perhaps, or whatever Goddess-damned daemon had taken over his body.

Bloody Oblivion, this shit got confusing.

In the distance, Eward and his remaining Prelates battled the Sons, but she could not help them, now. Knot was more important.

Astrid stumbled to her feet. Cinzia rushed at Lathe, but he kicked her, hard, in the chest. Cinzia stumbled back, gasping. A kick of that power should have cracked a few of her ribs, but the woman seemed to be all right.

"Knot, I know you can hear me!" Cinzia shouted. But her voice was different. Malice and pride underlay every syllable.

There are daemons even daemons fear.

A shiver swept through Astrid's bones. "Cinzia, what have you done?"

"What I had to do," Cinzia replied, her voice nearly a growl. "*Now bloody help me.*"

"I... I don't think I can help you anymore," Astrid whispered.

"You can, you stupid girl."

Lathe attacked Cinzia again, and the woman dodged with more speed than she should've been able to muster, then punched Lathe in the gut. Lathe recoiled, but retaliated quickly, shoving Cinzia to the ground.

"I'm still *me*," Cinzia said, looking at her. "*That*," she said, pointing at Lathe, "is no longer Knot. We can still save him."

Instead of advancing on Cinzia, Lathe took a step back. Behind him, Eward and his Prelates had gained the upper hand against the Sons. But then Lathe rushed to Eward, grabbing him from behind, and dragged him towards Cinzia.

"I can't kill you now," Lathe seethed, "Bazlamit will not let me. But I can kill this one. Your brother, isn't he?"

"No," Cinzia said, tears in her eyes.

Astrid looked back and forth between them, Cinzia lying on the ground, Lathe standing tall, holding Eward in front of him.

Then, Cinzia's eyes began to glow a bright, bold blue.

Lathe laughed. "Or perhaps I won't have to. It seems it is Luceraf's turn, after all."

Astrid watched in horror as Cinzia's head snapped back, and her friend's high-pitched scream entwined with another voice, monstrous and menacing. The fog around Cinzia was blown back, as if by a swift wind that originated within her. Blue light leaked from Cinzia's body, from her eyes and mouth, as bright blue smoke seethed from her.

"No," Astrid whispered. There was nothing she could do. Cinzia was far beyond her help, now.

43

South of the Eastmaw Mountains

WINTER FELT THE ROAR almost before it began. She looked for the source, and quickly found it near the *rihnemin*, where the Khalic officers were now stationed after pushing the tiellan forces back.

One of the officers, Winter could not tell who, had thrown his head back to make the sound. The man's eyes glowed red, sending twin beams of crimson light up into the dark, stormy sky. The battle around her paused for a moment, while all faces turned to see what was happening.

Then, the Daemon appeared. Winter knew instinctively that it was a Daemon; she suddenly worried for the Rangers she had ordered to guard Ghian, but there was nothing she could do for them now. She glanced around quickly for Ghian, but he was nowhere in sight.

With a guttural howl, a soldier charged Winter, axe swinging.

The soldier wasn't Khalic or Cantic, however. He was a tiellan, eyes glowing deep red.

Winter brought her sword up, sliding one hand onto the blade to block the axe strike, but the force of the blow sent vibrations of pain through her body, amplifying the throbbing in her skull. Her injured shoulder screamed in agony at the strain.

The tiellan man raised the axe to strike again, and Winter

rolled out of the way just in time. She leapt to her feet and stabbed the man in the back. She withdrew her sword as the man turned with a growl, eyes still glowing. With a cry, Winter swung her blade deep into the man's neck, and he fell.

Breathing heavily, she looked around to see the red-eyed bloodlust spreading around her. Tiellans and humans alike turned on their allies. This battle was no longer about the tiellan movement. It was not about the Khalic government. It was suddenly, and only, about survival.

Winter and Urstadt rallied as many of their tiellan forces as they could. They had to keep together if they wanted to survive. She couldn't see Gord or Eranda. She had lost track of them in the initial charge.

They were all right. They had to be.

"What is this madness?" Urstadt panted, knocking out a red-eyed tiellan with her sword hilt as he plunged a dagger uselessly towards her. "Why have our fighters turned on us?"

"That Daemon is the cause. We must fight our way to Carrieri!" Winter shouted back. "We have to ally with him to defeat the creature."

The Rangers who were not affected pulled closer as she spoke. Her heart leapt to see Selldor, Gord, and Eranda were in the small band. They charged toward the *rihnemin* as one. The Khalic soldiers in front of them were half-distracted by their own berserkers, and Winter's organized group smashed into them. Just as they were about to break through, a group of human soldiers, some red-eyed, some not, struck their flank. One man set his glowing red eyes on Winter and charged at her. Winter dodged the first swing of the man's axe, and parried the next as best she could, but he was *strong*. Another berserker came at her from the side. She could only dodge and parry as the two maddened, red-eyed men attacked her at once. Her small force was likely to be overwhelmed.

The exhaustion that had been tugging at the back of Winter's mind since the battle began set in deep. Her limbs burned as she maneuvered for her life, barely escaping one man's axe, only to parry the other's sword with a glancing blow that set her hands, arms, and entire body vibrating. She could not keep this up much longer. Sooner or later—

Winter slipped, one leg giving out beneath her. She fell to one knee, and the berserker with the sword swung down. Winter lifted her own to parry, but she was not quick enough. She deflected the blow from her face and torso, but the sword cut deep into her arm. Winter dropped to the ground, avoiding the berserker's kick, only to find herself looking straight up at an axe coming towards her.

With a scream, someone blurred into the axe-wielding berserker just in time, sending him off balance. Winter thought it was Urstadt at first, but as she struggled to her feet, she saw it was Eranda.

Before Winter could even scream, the man with the sword turned and swung with such force that his blade buried itself between Eranda's neck and shoulder, biting deep into her back. He kicked Eranda, freeing his sword. She fell to the ground, and both berserkers turned to face Winter.

Urstadt swept in between Winter and the berserkers. In all her training, in all Winter's time with Urstadt on the battlefield, she had never seen the warrior move so quickly. Her glaive cut, slashed, and stabbed, until both berserkers bled out onto the rain-soaked muddy ground.

Winter ran to Eranda's body. Her oldest remaining friend lay still and face down in the mud.

Urstadt grabbed her shoulder roughly.

"I have to—"

"Do not let your emotions control you," Urstadt growled. Above them, lightning split the sky, and thunder rolled.

"*Let go of me!*"

"You know what we must do, Winter."

Winter stared at Eranda's body. Urstadt was right. Eranda was gone. The Daemon was here.

And, she realized, a strange glimmer catching her eye, something else was here too. Shimmering shapes in the sky above her.

Winter's heart sank. She had seen those shapes before, in the imperial palace in Izet. She knew what came from them. Without frost, none of them stood a chance.

Her gaze lingered on Eranda for a moment longer, then she turned and stalked the rest of the way to Carrieri, the Daemon, and the end of this conflict, as Outsiders began to drop to the ground around her.

44

The Void

KNOT RUSHED BACK THROUGH the Void, finally finding the place where he'd first entered it. He recognized it easily enough; Winter was not the only one with an anomalous appearance in the Void. As he was pulled away from the Coastal Road, he'd noticed two great spheres of translucent color in the Void—one blue, the other a shining silver. The two bubbles were impossible to miss, and he navigated his way easily back to them. They'd almost merged, their outlines barely discernible.

"You see Lathe?" Kali asked. She had traveled with Knot, gliding by his side back to the Coastal Road.

"Aye," Knot said. At the center of the two spheres, Knot saw Lathe's sift. Without Knot's multiple sifts, it was a simple star-light, blueish in hue.

"Yes," Kali said, approaching the sift with him. "That one is definitely Lathe. Without his sift, you won't have your psimantic abilities, but I'll tell you something very few people know. Everyone…"

Kali trailed off as Knot tentatively reached out his *tendra*—two of them, each hardly more than a trickle—towards Lathe's sift.

"How did you know to do that?" Kali asked.

"A psimancer named Wyle," Knot said. "He told me all beings technically have *tendra* in the Void, if they somehow find their way into this plane of existence."

Kali huffed. "Wyle. I should've known. He's the one that stabilized your sift, I take it?"

"He is," Knot said. He stopped his *tendra* just before they made contact with Lathe's sift. "Ain't sure what to do here. Any suggestions?"

"You'll need to make contact with him first," Kali said. "After that—"

When Knot's *tendra* made contact with Lathe's sift, a burst of light radiated outward.

Then, Knot felt himself propelled forward through the Void, *inward*, into Lathe's sift. Everything magnified around him, and then was still.

Knot stood within what appeared to be a huge ball of blue light, facing Lathe. It was like looking in a mirror: shaggy brown hair, brown eyes, sinewy bodies, nondescript features. Beneath that, they could not be any more different.

"How did you get in here?" Lathe asked. His voice echoed in the blue haze. It was flat, without emotion, without pretense.

"Long story," Knot mumbled.

"Your priestess is about to be taken over by a Daemon," Lathe remarked.

"We must…" Knot hesitated. "Cinzia is about to be taken over by a Daemon?" *What in Oblivion is he talking about?*

"I can't let you back in," Lathe said, shaking his head. "Even if I wanted to, I… she would not allow it. It appears I've gotten in a bit over my head this time."

"What happened to Cinzia?" Knot demanded.

"She will be destroyed, and only the Daemon will exist. I didn't know until just now—Goddess, of *course* she didn't tell me—but the same thing will happen to me. It's already happened to Mefiston's avatar." Lathe's eyes slid away from Knot, his voice still eerily flat and emotionless. "I thought I wanted to live. I suppose I still do. But this… this wasn't what I had in mind."

"Then *let me back in*. We can fix this."

"No," Lathe said. "I don't control that anymore. She will not let me."

Knot swore. He hated not having a physical body. He needed to *hit* something.

Then, a third presence joined them in Lathe's sift. While both Knot and Lathe were almost solid, the third presence had a fuzzy, transparent quality to it. At first Knot worried it was Bazlamit, but the form's ever-shifting face gave her away.

Lathe stared at the new projection, eyes wide. "*Kali?*"

"Hello, Lathe," Kali said. "It's been a while."

"What in Oblivion are you doing here?"

"I wish I had time to explain that," Kali said, "but I don't. I think I can help you. *Both* of you. I think I can distract Bazlamit long enough for her to relax her guard. Then you can let Knot back in to take over your body, Lathe."

"I'll die," Lathe said. "Or I'll be as good as dead, anyway."

Kali shrugged. "You'll die either way. At least if you let me help, you won't be responsible for allowing a Daemon to take its true form on the Sfaera."

Lathe met Knot's eyes, and again Knot had the strange sensation he was looking into a mirror.

"Shit. Let's do it." Then, Lathe actually chuckled. It was the first sign of emotion Knot had seen from him throughout the conversation. "Knot… take care of myself, if you know what I mean. And, Kali, it was good seeing you. Give my love to Sirana, if you can."

Lathe's form flickered, then faded, as did the blue light all around them.

Knot and Kali were back in the Void.

"Even if I could, I doubt that would happen," Kali muttered to herself.

"Don't you have a job to do?" Knot asked.

Kali smiled at him. "On it."

Almost two dozen multicolored *tendra* exploded outward from Kali's shifting form, jutting out in all directions. The *tendra* extended outward an impossible distance, until finally each one made contact with the very edge of the silver bubble around Lathe's sift.

The moment they made contact, the hazy exterior of the silver bubble shifted, and it suddenly became solid.

"What—"

"Send your *tendra* into Lathe's sift again," Kali said through gritted teeth. "*Do it now.*"

Knot obeyed without hesitation. As his own *tendra* made contact with Lathe's sift, the same flash of light pierced his vision.

When Knot opened his eyes, he found he actually had eyes to open.

He was in his own body, and it was a foggy morning on the Coastal Road. He was holding Eward, as if threatening him. He immediately released the man. Cinzia writhed before him on the dirt road, blue light bursting forth from her as she screamed.

What… what are you *doing here?* a voice inside of himself asked.

Throwing you out, Knot thought. *I do not want you here. I did not give you permission. Get out.*

You cannot—

Then, the voice was gone, and Knot was himself again. The light crackling from Cinzia's body faded, and she slumped backwards into the road.

Knot looked around. Eward was with him, and five Prelates. The bodies of the Sons and Goddessguard lay behind him.

And there, at his side, was Astrid.

"Knot?" she asked.

Not trusting himself to speak, Knot knelt down and held her as if he would never let go.

"Uh... nomad? I know it's been a long time and everything, but isn't this a bit much?"

Never.

And, for all her talk, Astrid was not the first to pull away.

When they separated, Knot reached into the secret pocket in his trousers, pulling out Astrid's voidstone, the blood-red rune glinting. He held it out to her.

"I've had a lot of free time over the last few months," he said.

Astrid stared at the voidstone. Then she turned away. "I don't think I can hear it. Whatever it is, I don't think I can—"

"It ain't what you think," Knot said. He pressed the voidstone into her hand. "You've been responsible for a lot of shitty things on this Sfaera, darlin', there's no getting around that. But that ain't all there is. The Black Matron, she made you forget all the terrible things, but she made you forget all the good things you've done, too. And you did a lot of good, Astrid. The Black Matron made you think your only redemption was through her, but the truth is, you've been working at it your whole life."

Astrid buried her face in his shoulder. "I don't... I don't know what to say."

"You don't have to say anything," Knot said. "We can talk about it as much as you want later. Or as little. It's completely up to you. I just wanted to… to thank you, for lettin' me in."

Astrid pulled away, wiping her face. "Enough with the hugs, nomad. Eward's going to think we aren't fit to lead him into battle any longer."

Knot laughed, as did Eward behind them. Astrid had almost forgotten the lad was there.

"I'm glad you're back," Astrid said, looking up at him.

Knot smiled. "Me too." He glanced over at Cinzia. "We'd better help her…"

"She's out cold." Astrid grabbed Knot's hand and led him a few rods down the road. "Come here, I want to show you something."

There, lying on the damp dirt road, mangled and filthy, was the Black Matron. The woman's eyes were open wide, staring up at the clouded sky, but she did not move. Her head was bent back and twisted unnaturally. Dust caked her robes, staining the once bright white and red fabric.

"The bitch is dead," Knot said.

"Damn right she is."

The Black Matron was dead, and Astrid could do nothing but stare at the woman's mangled body. She was vaguely aware of Cinzia regaining consciousness behind her, of Knot moving away to help her to her feet, and of Eward and the remaining Prelates gathering the scattered horses and preparing to leave. The entire time, Astrid could not tear herself away. How one person could have caused her so much grief, Astrid could not comprehend.

She flinched as a hand gently touched her shoulder. She

turned to see Knot standing behind her.

"Eward and the Prelates will take care of the bodies," Knot said.

Of course they would. They could not very well leave the bodies of a Cantic matron, priestesses, Goddessguards, and Sons in the middle of the road.

She looked back at the Black Matron's body.

"You all right?" Knot asked.

Astrid took a deep breath, felt the dampness of the fog around her, the comforting cover of the clouds in the sky. Then, she turned away, and did not look back.

"I will be."

45

South of the Eastmaw Mountains

THUNDER RUMBLED ABOVE WINTER as she cut her way through frenzied men and women, tiellans and humans, their eyes glowing red beneath the dark gray clouds above.

People screamed all around her. Outsiders roared, the eerie, multitonal screech taking Winter back to a time where she had lost two men she cared a great deal about, and much more besides.

Some of the red-eyed berserkers attacked the Outsiders as well as any soldiers around them—apparently the rage within them truly was no respecter of persons. If anything, the berserkers seemed more effective against the monsters, considering how heedless they were to damage and harm. They died quickly, but caused significant damage to some of the Outsiders in the process.

Finding Carrieri was not difficult; Winter directed herself towards the great red beast that had started all of this in the first place. The monster laughed, twice the height of a man, as tall as the Outsiders that had dropped from the sky.

Then, up ahead, in a crack of lightning, Winter glimpsed Carrieri. She shouted his name, and somehow, through the cacophony, Carrieri heard her.

Immediately, the Khalic soldiers around Carrieri formed up, facing Winter's squad. Carrieri had a few dozen horsemen around him, along with some infantry, though they were scattered, fighting berserkers and Outsiders.

Winter's own forces readied their weapons, eyeing the Khalic soldiers. Rain continued to pour down from above, pattering on helmets and plate mail, soaking through Winter's leather armor and clothing.

"Did you do this?" Carrieri shouted over the troops that separated them.

"No! That is a Daemon, Carrieri," Winter called back. "We won't escape unless we work together!"

A Goddessguard approached Carrieri, speaking into the man's ear. Carrieri nodded, slowly.

"What do you suggest?"

"Where are your psimancers?" Winter shouted above the chaos. "Do they have any *faltira*?"

Carrieri turned his head as another person spoke to him, then looked back at Winter. "They do."

"Give it to me!" Winter shouted. She wanted to sob with joy at the news. She wanted to sob with joy, and sink into herself and die, because she felt such elation despite the horrors around her, despite Eranda's death. "I can stop them!"

Mefiston laughed. "You cannot stop us now. We are taking our true forms, one by one."

The Daemon moved, more quickly than Winter could anticipate, crashing towards them. Selldor ran forward to meet him, but Mefiston swung one hand casually at the tiellan Ranger and sent him flying across the battlefield.

In a rage, Winter ran towards the Daemon, now advancing on Carrieri.

"You work so hard to resist your anger, Carrieri," the Daemon growled. "I cannot tolerate such behavior."

"Leave him be!" Winter shouted.

Mefiston turned, a smile on his face. "And you," he growled. "You…"

Mefiston stopped, cocking his head to the side.

"*No*," he growled.

"Bazlamit! *No*."

With a roar, Mefiston burst into a thousand rays of red light. Winter shielded her eyes, the light blinding her for a few moments. When she looked back up, Mefiston was gone. Winter blinked. She could not believe it. Had he died? Winter could not be sure, except that he was no longer here.

That was a good thing, she had to believe. At least for now.

"The other daemons!" one of her tiellan soldiers shouted.

Winter turned to look out at the battlefield. In the intermittent lightning flashes, Winter sighted *dozens* of Outsiders slaughtering humans and tiellans alike. Mefiston may have been destroyed, but what he had wrought remained.

"Give me the *faltira*," Winter said.

"Do it," Carrieri ordered.

One of the human psimancers protested, but Carrieri spoke over the woman. "*Do it*."

The woman rushed forward, a frost crystal in her hand.

Winter snatched the crystal, the rough, light feel of the thing filling her with longing. "How many more do you have?"

The woman glanced at Winter. "Just one," she said.

Winter swore. Two crystals would never give her enough power.

"Your colleagues don't have any more?"

"They're dead," the woman said. She did not attempt to hide the bitterness in her voice.

Winter frowned. Of course they were dead—she had killed them.

"Give me the last crystal," Winter demanded, holding out her hand.

Just as the psimancer handed Winter her final frost crystal, she heard Carrieri's shout above the storm.

"Retreat!" he shouted. "Khalic forces, retreat!"

Winter turned in horror. "What are you doing?"

"We are leaving you to deal with this," Carrieri shouted, looking her in the eye. "I am sorry to do it this way, but we came here to defeat the tiellan forces. I will not leave without that victory."

"But the Outsiders are more of an enemy than we will ever be!" Winter shouted above the rain, screams, and violence. She could not believe he was doing this. She had thought, just for a moment, that they might work together, to the benefit of both tiellan and human ends.

She could not have been more wrong.

"We can regroup and deal with them," Carrieri said. "But we cannot allow you to continue carving your path through Khale. I am sorry, Winter." Then, he turned and rode off, taking his forces with him.

Throughout the battlefield, the Khalic horn of retreat sounded, and Carrieri's army—with the exception of those still affected by Mefiston's wrath, who still fought anything in sight blindly and wildly—disengaged, running or riding away for their lives, following Carrieri down the hill and away. Some of the humans didn't make it, either killed by Outsiders, too far away to hear the call to retreat, or too deep into the melee to be able to find their way out, but thousands of human soldiers fled the battlefield.

Only the tiellans remained to face the Outsiders.

Winter looked down at the two frost crystals in her hand.

With faltira, *I can do anything*.

She immediately swallowed one of the crystals, and the rush filled her, engulfed her. She was whole again.

She turned to the Outsiders and released her *tendra*, snatching up weapons from corpses' hands. She focused a dozen or so *tendra* on each Outsider at once, taking on seven Outsiders at a time. Almost a hundred different weapons cut through the air, and then through Outsider flesh and armor and bone. The Outsiders roared, unable to fight the invisible foes.

Suddenly, Winter remembered the dome in Izet. She remembered how the Outsiders seemed to sense her, to recognize her power. They clearly could do so now. As one, the Outsiders turned to her, their blank, black eyes staring through the storm, and they began to fight their way to her.

One Outsider took a flying leap across the battlefield, shaking the soil beneath Winter's feet as it landed just a few rods from her. Winter dove out of the way, dozens of her *tendra* still fighting other Outsiders, as Urstadt and the tiellans who had accompanied them moved to defend her.

"Protect Winter!" Urstadt shouted. Rangers responded, advancing on the beast.

Swords, spears, javelins, shields, axes, and any other blades she could get her *tendra* on flew wildly in the rain-soaked sky, piercing and slashing and impaling Outsiders who seemed to take hundreds of wounds before they showed signs of weakening. Rainwater and blood and mud were everywhere, and lightning split the sky every few seconds. Thunder cracked and rumbled almost as continuously as the Outsiders roared and screamed. Beneath it all, if Winter listened with intent, she could hear the groans of the wounded and screams of the fighting and dying.

Winter had taken down two, now three Outsiders, but she couldn't work fast enough. Although the portals had closed off when Mefiston perished, at least fifty or sixty of the beasts still remained.

Canta bloody rising. Fifty Outsiders. They had faced half a dozen in Izet, and only Winter had survived. Winter could not possibly kill them all, and at the rate she was using psimancy, her power would run out soon.

Tiellan men and women were still trying to fight the Outsiders, but they were no defense. Each of the Outsiders slowly cut a path towards her, circling inward. Winter had cut down another half-dozen Outsiders, but so many still remained. Berserkers still roamed the battlefield, but their numbers dwindled. Very few with the glowing red eyes remained that Winter could see.

And then, abruptly, her power faded. She had run out of *faltira*.

Immediately, she raised the other crystal the human psimancer had given her. She hesitated, looking at the thing. This was their last hope. If she could not do something with this, they were lost.

She took the crystal, and the power continued to surge through her. Suddenly another Outsider leapt through the air, almost landing on top of her.

"Winter!"

A force slammed into her, pushing her aside and out of the Outsider's path just in time.

Winter, dazed from the crash, moaned as she stood up. Urstadt rolled to her feet, armor dented and covered in blood.

"You all right?" Urstadt grunted.

"Fine," Winter gasped, "for now." Her *tendra* exploded outward in a new burst of power. In the meantime, the other Outsiders had already advanced a terrifying distance towards her.

The Outsider that had nearly leapt onto her rose to its feet, growling. Urstadt rallied more tiellan troops and they attacked the beast, though the Outsider seemed to keep its eyes focused on Winter the entire time.

Winter stumbled backwards, trying to get some distance between herself and the beast, and backed right into the *rihnemin*.

Winter turned to look at the stone, standing tall over her. A flash of lightning illuminated the fading runes on its surface.

Thunder broke the sky above her, and Winter retracted her *tendra*, dropping her weapons, and turned to face the *rihnemin*. She could not defeat all of the remaining Outsiders, not with the few tiellan Rangers that remained and a single frost crystal.

But Mazille had told her the *rihnemin* housed ancient tiellan power. She had a choice, now. She could either die fighting the Outsiders with her *tendra*, or die trying to access the power of the *rihnemin*.

She sent every single *tendron* she could muster searching over the *rihnemin*'s surface, until each found that strange, magnetic draw point. Dozens of *tendra,* then more. Sixty. Seventy. Before Winter knew what she was doing she had sent nearly one hundred telenic *tendra* into the *rihnemin*. Every rune on the stone burned into the dark, storming sky. Colors of every shade, purple and yellow and green and red and orange and blue, burned brightly, their light reflecting on the pouring rain.

Winter wiped her eyes. *What else do I need to do?* she pleaded. She stepped towards the stone, placing her hands on it.

Then, her world changed.

The woman is suddenly aware of all of the minds around her, thousands of tiellan minds that fight and die on the battlefield. She senses the thoughts and intents of the fleeing Khalic soldiers, leaving their enemies to die. She even feels the unconscious rage of the berserkers, their only desire to kill. The whispers and screams and moans threaten to overwhelm her, but she pushes past them. Her sudden awareness does nothing for her, nothing against the Outsiders that threaten her, her tiellan friends and family, and everything that remains on the Sfaera.

Show me what else I need to do, the woman pleads. *I plead again for someone, anyone, a goddess or a daemon or anything in between to show me the way, to show me how to save what is left of what I love.*

And then, suddenly, I am back in the imperial palace of Izet, fighting the Outsiders, smashing the massive stone pillars of the dome into the huge Outsider that has been let loose in my world.

I'm with Knot, striking his face in an inn in Tir, beating his chest, pushing him against the wall, kissing him.

I'm sitting on a makeshift throne in a royal tent and Knot approaches me, a frown on his face. It is the first time I have seen him since he died, the first time he has seen me, and he cannot help but be disappointed in me.

I am commanding an army of Outsiders, and cannot comprehend why.

A voice calls me murderer, and another one calls me queen, and a third calls me mother.

Then I am back at the *rihnemin* by the Eastmaw Mountains, surrounded by dying tiellans and snarling Outsiders. The *rihnemin* glows brightly at my touch.

Use blood to access the firestone, an inner voice says.

I cut open my palm with my dagger, and press the wound against the *rihnemin*.

The woman's blood, on the *rihnemin*.

Winter's blood, on the firestone.

The multicolored runes on the *rihnemin* suddenly grew brighter, so bright they lit up the darkest storm clouds Winter had ever seen in a rainbow of color. The lights faded, almost to nothing, and then lit up once more, this time in unison in color and hue—bright blue. A beam, or a river, or some monstrous limb of blue liquid fire poured forth from the top of the *rihnemin* and connected directly with the Outsider that had just tried to leap onto Winter. Blue fire, burning so hot Winter could feel the heat against her back, singeing her hair and clothes. Somehow the *rihnemin*, the runes, and the blue fire itself were her eyes.

The Outsider drowned in the fire, its skin and bones smoking and burning as it screamed, melting into a puddle of putrid destruction. The blue beam immediately jumped from the immolated Outsider into the nearest of its kin, a few poles away, dripping blue flames through the rain and onto the ground as it traveled, melting the next Outsider. Then the blue river of fire split into two, falling onto two more Outsiders, and then six, and then more than Winter could count, and soon arcs of blue flowing fire curled over the entire battlefield. Bits of liquid flame poured down with the rain, hissing and sizzling and falling on tiellans, on Winter's soldiers, injuring the living and singeing the dead.

Every last remaining Outsider burned a blue death. Then, the arcs of fire withdrew, retracting all the way back to the *rihnemin,* where Winter stood still, bloody palm on the stone, as the liquid azure flame disappeared, and the runes faded.

Winter took her hands from the *rihnemin* and turned, falling to her knees. The stench of burning flesh permeated the field, despite the heavy rain. Another flash of lightning lit the dark sky, followed by a crack of thunder that made Winter flinch.

Then Urstadt was at her side.

"Are you all right?" she asked.

Winter could not respond. Corpses of all kinds littered the battlefield; charred Outsiders, flesh still smoking and sizzling in the rain. Mutilated soldiers, both human and tiellan, that had been regurgitated, mauled, clawed, and crushed by the Outsiders. Other dead soldiers, fallen in battle. And, of course, the moans of the wounded and dying, rising over the sound of the rain, between crashes of thunder.

Hands gripped Winter's arms, lifting her to her feet.

"I am done," Winter said, shaking her head. "This is over. We've lost, Urstadt."

"We took heavy losses, Commander," Urstadt said, "there is no denying that. But ours is the only side that has not retreated or been wiped out. That makes us the victors. Look at what your Rangers have to say."

Winter's remaining soldiers—perhaps three thousand, at most—slowly made their way through the corpses on the battlefield, towards the hilltop where Winter stood. She felt frozen. What could she possibly say to them?

But, as the first tiellan approached her, walking close

enough to her that Winter thought he might strike her, the man stopped abruptly. Then, he fell to his knees.

"My queen," he said.

Winter stared at the man for what seemed an eternity. All she could think of in that moment was Eranda. When Winter finally found her voice, she shook her head. "I am not—"

Urstadt touched her arm. "Listen, first."

The second tiellan, a woman, approached her. She, too, knelt in the pouring rain. "You saved us, my queen. I am forever in your debt."

Eranda told me I should be queen.

Another knelt. "My queen."

And another. "Thank you, my queen."

And another. "You are the leader we have waited for. You have my fealty, my queen."

Eranda did not live to see it.

Soon, the entire remaining population knelt before her, thousands of tiellan men and women, their knees soaked in blood and rain.

"Long live the queen!" someone shouted.

"Long live the queen!" another repeated.

The entire crowd took up the cry.

"Long live the queen! Long live the queen! Long live the queen!"

Winter closed her eyes, willing all thoughts of Eranda out of her mind. She could grieve later, if she had anything left in her that could grieve. As the tiellans shouted around her, Winter stood a little taller. She wiped the rain and blood and tears from her face, and looked out over her people.

Someone needed to lead the tiellans out of this disaster. She had gotten them into it, after all. She would get them out, and restore to them what was rightfully theirs.

Humans had taken everything from them—their heritage, their dignity, their souls. Humans would pay for this.

Beginning with Riccan bloody Carrieri.

Urstadt turned to face her, and bowed her head.

"Long live the queen."

46

*Two weeks later, Coastal Road,
approaching the outskirts of Triah*

EVEN THOUGH CINZIA HAD spent seven years of her life in Triah, she still found the Circle City to be a breathtaking sight. The Coastal Road ran along the Cliffs of Litori north of the city, and provided a spectacular view of the Sinefin River's delta in which the city nestled, and of the Great Western Gulf.

The high cliffs took a sharp, tapered turn east and gradually descended to sea level. The Coastal Road curved along with the cliffs, and then curved back west towards the Triahn city walls. Soon they would reach their destination.

Cinzia, Knot, and Astrid, along with Eward and his handful of Prelates, had waited on the Coastal Road for Jane and the Odenites to catch up with them. Now, they once again all travelled together. From the Cliffs of Litori on which Cinzia, Knot, Astrid, Jane, and the entire Odenite following now stood, Cinzia could make out the major landmarks of the city. The Center Circle stood out, of course, with Canta's Fane, the Citadel, and the House of Aldermen forming the three points of the triangle. Above the entire city towered God's Eye, the ancient weapon rumored to channel the power of the sun itself, planted on the northern river bank. No building on the Sfaera held a candle to God's Eye; the tower was almost fifty floors high. Cinzia doubted God's Eye had ever been used, but it was an incredible sight to behold.

A road encircled that central Trinacrya, wrapping around its circumference and bridging over the Sinefin—the only road on the seaward side of the Center Circle to bridge the river. Another road encircled that one, and another road encircled that one, on and on until the very outskirts of the city. Three major roads, each starting from a point of the Trinacrya, led outward, intersecting each of the concentric roads, while other, smaller roads joined the concentric circles in other places. The fifty-fourth circle formed Triah's great city wall, but beyond that wall were many other concentric circles spilling out into the countryside, as if a giant had thrown an incredibly large stone that landed at the Center Circle, and each of the concentric roads were ripples waving outward. This design was what gave Triah its nickname: the Circle City. It was the largest city on the Sfaera, the largest city in history, and it was Cinzia's second home.

Or at least it had been, once. Now, she returned as a heretic to the Denomination, the religion to which she had sworn herself, and then betrayed. This was no more her home than Navone was, now.

Cinzia would never be ready to face the Denomination. She was more unsure of Jane now than she ever was. She knew there was some power out there that loved her, could help her, but Cinzia did not know what to do with that power, how to relate to it.

Inside her head, Luceraf chuckled.

Are you sure there is a power out there that loves you? the Daemon asked. *In my experience, the only power worth obeying exists solely to destroy.*

I do not have to explain myself to you, Cinzia thought. *I know what I know, and you will not change that.*

I've always enjoyed a challenge.

"How does it feel to come home?"

Cinzia turned to see that Knot was beside her, gazing out over the cliffs at Triah.

"Excitement, fear, trepidation, joy. All of that, and more. I love this city, Knot. I am worried it does not love me back."

"If it doesn't," Knot said, "it ain't worth your time."

Cinzia could not help but smile at that.

They stood in silence for a moment and Cinzia's gaze eventually shifted and found Astrid. She was discussing something with a man Cinzia had never seen before. It was difficult to see his features—the man wore a long hood that covered his face—but Cinzia did glimpse an eyepatch over one eye. An odd man, indeed. Cinzia would have to ask the girl about him when she had the chance.

"You and Astrid have reconciled, then?" Cinzia asked.

"Seems that way," Knot said.

"I am glad. I do not like it when the two of you do not get along."

"Ain't the only one," Knot muttered, "believe me."

Cinzia took a deep breath, then turned to face Knot. "And... the two of us," Cinzia said. "Where do we stand?"

Knot looked at her. "What d'you mean?"

"You agreed to be my Goddessguard once. Does that agreement still stand?" She had been afraid to ask the question since the moment she and Astrid had found him on the Coastal Road, but something in the way he addressed her just now gave her the courage.

"We forged a bond," Knot said. "Ain't gonna break that anytime soon."

"Even though you... you think Winter is alive, and part

of this tiellan rebellion?" Word of the tiellan movement had reached them—of Druids, Rangers, and battles the tiellans had actually won against the Khalic Legion itself. They sounded like fables, and Cinzia would have dismissed them as such if they had not been so prevalent. Everywhere they went, people spoke of the tiellan rebellion, and the tiellan witch who led them.

The tiellan witch who Knot believed was Winter. His wife.

"Can't be sure about any of that," Knot said. "I had a vision, and I did see something, but… for now, yes. I am with you."

One corner of Cinzia's mouth tweaked.

You like him, Luceraf said.

Cinzia frowned. *Of course I like him.*

You like him more than that. The day will come when you'll admit that to yourself. Unless I possess you first, that is.

"Still think what you did is problematic, darlin', don't get me wrong," Knot said after a moment. "That voice I'm sure you're hearing in your head… we're going to have to do something about that."

Luceraf snorted. *I'd like to see him try.*

I daresay you will get that chance. She had not told anyone about her new relationship with Luceraf except Knot—and Astrid, who had already intuited what Cinzia had done. Knot was the only person she trusted with such information.

"I know," Cinzia said out loud.

"I'll… I'll do what I can to help you," Knot said. "I've been there, after all, even if it was just for a few moments. Can't imagine what it's like having a Daemon in your head all day, every day."

"You simply willed her out of your head." They had danced around this conversation more than once over the past couple of weeks.

Knot shrugged. "She'd never had my permission to be there in the first place. When I reclaimed my body, I think the bond she'd made with Lathe was invalidated."

I've told you, dear. You gave me permission. You cannot rescind that invitation. Knot is fortunate that free will still matters with us.

"Nomad," Astrid said, approaching them. She turned to Cinzia. "Daemon-shack."

"Hush," Cinzia hissed, glaring at the girl.

Astrid snorted. "Jane still doesn't know, then? Why am I not surprised?"

"Jane left Knot to die," Cinzia responded. "There's no shame in doubting her judgment."

"You're going to have to tell her eventually," Astrid said.

That isn't necessarily true.

For once we agree on something, Cinzia thought.

Eward was calling Knot's name. Knot nodded to both of them and walked away, leaving Cinzia and Astrid alone.

"We have to talk about what happened," Astrid said, her face serious.

"What is there to talk about?"

"What you did... who you are, now. You are a liability, Cinzia. If Jane's movement is important to you, you'll tell her."

Are you a liability? Luceraf asked. *Or are you an asset?*

"I can gain unique knowledge of the Nine Daemons," Cinzia said. "I may be able to help."

Astrid scoffed. "If you think that, you're further gone than I thought."

The two stood in silence for a moment, both staring down at the city. Then, Astrid looked up at Cinzia.

"Remember what you told me?" she said.

Cinzia did not respond.

What did you tell her? Luceraf asked.

"You said family is not about what we remember, or where we are. It's about how we feel."

"So—"

"Do you really feel part of a family right now?" Astrid asked.

Cinzia had nothing to say to that. She did not belong with the Denomination. She did not belong with Jane and the disciples, not in her current state. She wanted to say she belonged with Knot, but even that was a stretch.

"Someone once told me," Astrid continued, "that it doesn't matter what we are, or where we've been. All that matters is what we do." She paused for a moment, until Cinzia met her eyes.

Do you believe that? Luceraf asked.

When Cinzia didn't reply, Luceraf laughed. The sound echoed cruelly in her head for so long, Cinzia feared it would never leave her.

47

Adimora

WINTER KNOCKED QUIETLY ON the door of Darrin and Eranda's home. It was after dark, and she hoped the children were already asleep. Facing Darrin would be difficult enough; she could not look at Sena, Lelanda, and Tohn, and tell them their mother was dead.

Fortunately, some of her riders had finally procured *faltira* for her, one of them going all the way back to Cineste to get it. Her withdrawal symptoms had all but faded now that she was taking the drug semi-regularly again. Her shoulder wound was well on its way to full recovery, and even the node of pain in her head from the blow she'd taken at the battle of the Canaian Fields was fading.

Nevertheless, she needed as much courage as she could get right now. She took a crystal, and the fire began to burn in her veins.

Darrin opened the door, bleary-eyed, his hair unkempt and his clothes disheveled. His eyes met Winter's, and his weary, vacant stare did not change in the slightest.

He already knows, Winter realized.

"What d'you want?" Darrin asked.

"I... I wanted to speak with you," Winter whispered.

Darrin's eyes slid over Winter's shoulder, staring off into the night. For a moment Winter thought Darrin might not say anything at all, but finally he turned, walked back inside, and looked over his shoulder.

"Come in," he said.

Winter walked into the hut, out of the autumn chill. Darrin walked directly to a wooden chair in a corner of the room and sat down. Winter stayed standing, unable to bring herself to do anything else.

"I have something to tell you," Winter said.

"Gord already did."

Winter stood still. She should have told Gord not to say anything so she could tell Darrin herself. And yet, that would have accomplished nothing but delaying Darrin's suffering by a day, maybe two.

"Ain't you got some coronation tomorrow?" Darrin's voice was raw and gravelly.

"That… that doesn't matter," Winter said. The Druid elders, along with the Cracked Spear leaders, had agreed to crown Winter queen of the tiellan people the next morning. Agreed, perhaps, was a strong word, but both groups of leadership could not go against the will of the people. More than that, they could not go against their fear of Winter.

"Ain't that the *only* thing that matters?" Darrin asked. "You've done nothin' but order people around since the moment you came back."

Winter shifted her weight, unsure what to say. Anger did not surprise her. She could remember feeling that way herself, in her cell in Izet, after realizing Knot was dead.

She straightened. Best say what she came here to say. "Darrin, I am sorry for what happened to Eranda. She was a good woman, and deserved better than she got."

Darrin snorted. "We agree on that," he said. Then, he looked up at Winter. "Did she die because of you?"

Winter's breath caught in her throat. "I… Eranda died a courageous death in battle," Winter said after a moment, "fighting for the tiellan cause."

"I hear she died protecting you," Darrin said. "Sounds a lot like she died protecting *your* cause, whatever in Oblivion that is."

Winter said nothing in response—what could she possibly say that would help?

"You're the one that allowed tiellan women to join the Rangers in the first place," Darrin said quietly. "Way I see it, ain't nobody more responsible for my wife's death than you."

Winter could not deny what Darrin said, and his words pierced through the apathetic shell she'd made for herself.

"You're right," Winter whispered. "I am sorry, Darrin."

Darrin was silent for a moment, and then he stood. "Your sorry ain't worth shit to me." He did not show her out, but walked into the room he and Eranda had shared without another word.

Winter's breaths came quick and shallow. She feared if she breathed any deeper she might break down, and she did not want that. Not here. She moved to the door, and then heard Darrin's voice behind her.

"She'd want you to have this."

Winter turned to see Darrin holding out the white swaddling cloth Eranda had kept for her. It was folded neatly into a long, thick rectangle.

"I…" Winter reached out, but stopped before her fingers touched the cloth.

"*Bloody take it*," Darrin said, voice broken, in the first show of emotion Winter had seen from him since she came to his doorstep.

Winter willed herself to grasp the white cloth, and then turned and rushed out the door.

* * *

Hours later, Winter sobbed on the floor of her own hut in Adimora, the white swaddling cloth clutched tightly to her chest.

She cried for Darrin and his children, for the pain they felt now but especially for the pain they would feel in years to come, as Darrin watched his children become tall, as Sena became more and more like her mother, as little Tohn's last memories of Eranda would inevitably fade.

She cried for the many thousands lost, for the many families without a mother or father, for the orphaned tiellan children.

She cried for her people, defeated and dwindling, and foolishly thinking that making her their queen would solve any of their problems. They did not know what they were doing.

And yet, she thought with bitterness, *you will not refuse them.*

She cried for herself, for the illusion of her own indifference. After Knot's death, she thought she would never feel again. She thought she was immune to such things. But being back with her people, and being irrevocably responsible for Eranda's death among thousands more—holding the white cloth she'd received as a gift at her Doting on the day of her wedding—she realized the lie she'd been telling herself.

The pain had always been there. Only now had it grown too powerful to push down, bury, or ignore.

As Winter's denial turned to acceptance, her sobs faded, and as her sobs faded, acceptance became anger. Winter had her own part in all that had happened, but there were others at fault, too. Riccan Carrieri. The Khalic Legions. The people of Khale themselves, and every human on the Sfaera, save Urstadt and Galce, as far as Winter was concerned.

And, lest she forget, Mazille and her psimancers.

Winter's vengeance would find them all.

EPILOGUE

South of the Eastmaw Mountains

As RICCAN CARRIERI CRESTED the hill and looked down at the weeks-old carnage below, his breath caught in his chest.

"Canta rising," he whispered.

"I told you, sir. The tiellans are gone, and they left nothing but destruction in their wake." Ambria, the telenic who had accompanied him at what his troops were now calling the battle of the Rihnemin just over two weeks ago, stood next to him. They had tied their horses to trees in a thicket at the other side of the hill on which they now stood, overlooking the battlefield.

"May I ask why you wanted to come here, Grand Marshal?"

Carrieri frowned, taking deep breaths through his mouth. The stench had hit them both before they'd even dismounted, and death was strong in the air, now. "I needed to see for myself."

Rotting corpses, tiellan and human, littered the field. But the most striking landmarks were the dozens of Outsider bodies, blackened and deformed.

"The Outsiders were… were burned?" Carrieri asked.

"Melted, more like," Ambria said. "No idea how it happened. Closest thing I can think of are some rumors we've heard from Maven Kol about people who've learned to manipulate fire, but there's been nothing of that sort north of the Taimin Mountains. Not that we've heard of, anyway."

"It seems now you have," Carrieri said.

Something still did not seem right to him, however. He had left the tiellans to die with the intent of returning with a larger force later to defeat what remained of the Outsiders, but quickly his spies had told him what had happened. The Outsiders had all been killed; somehow, the tiellans had been victorious against them, and lived to fight another day. He did not know how they had done it—whether Winter had performed some psimantic trick, or something else altogether—but the aftermath was clear.

"How many tiellan survivors?" Carrieri asked.

"No way to be sure, Grand Marshal," Ambria said, "but we estimate a few thousand at most."

"A few thousand," Carrieri repeated. A few thousand could not possibly stand against the might of Khale's army—even what remained of it. But he had not thought they could stand against the Outsiders, either, and he had been woefully mistaken on that particular point. Riccan Carrieri was beginning to see why the tiellans had given Publio Kyfer such trouble.

"Keep gathering intelligence," Carrieri said. "We need to know the tiellan position, their numbers, and, if possible, what they are capable of at all times."

"And what of our forces?" Ambria asked.

Carrieri raised an eyebrow at the woman's use of "our." She was a Cantic psimancer, after all. Not technically part of the Legion.

But, truthfully, he shared the sentiment. To face what was coming—whether tiellan, daemonic, or otherwise—Carrieri could not shake the feeling that they needed to band together as many people as possible.

"We outnumber the tiellans, that much is sure. But I do not think we can risk meeting them in open battle anymore.

Better we let time do our work for us." Some would call him cowardly. Others would berate him for letting the tiellans run free throughout Khale, but they had not seen what he had seen.

The last thing the Khalic Legion wanted to do now was engage the tiellans in open battle, and Carrieri would be sure to affirm that it never happened again.

Not until he was ready.

Imperial palace, Izet

Empress Cova Amok sat on the throne in the council chamber, contemplating all of the information now before her.

"Your Grace," Andia said quietly, "the Council awaits your decision."

"Give me a moment, Andia," Cova said. This was not a decision she wanted to make lightly. But the chance to exact revenge on the nation that had oppressed them for decades was too clear.

Then, Cova Amok stood. The members of the Ruling Council turned to face her, as did every other eye in the overflowing council chamber. Cova counted three empty chairs. Word of the happenings in Khale had spread quickly.

"In light of recent events," Cova began, "I have come to a decision. The tiellan rebellion in Khale has changed things. While I do not necessarily agree with the logic, I know many of you would say that this was why our ancestors exiled the race from our empire completely. Whatever you believe, one thing is clear. The tiellans have provided us with an opportunity."

"What of the tiellans themselves?" Arstan Dagnatar, Roden's merchant leader, asked. "Would they not present as much an obstacle for us as they do for Khale? We are the ones that murdered and banished their kind, after all. One would think their rage against Roden would be greater."

"The tiellans' focus is upon their own home; they will direct their wrath at Triah. We must attack while our enemy is divided, and fighting itself. The tiellans will be crushed by Khale eventually, and Khale, weakened from the fight, will fall to us."

"And the tiellan commander?" the high priestess asked. "Is that... is that the tiellan woman that your father held in custody here?"

You mean to ask whether, by releasing her, I caused this tiellan rebellion.

"I imagine we will soon find out. We have discussed a campaign against Khale for many years, now, but the time has never been right. Now, the tiellans have made the time right for us.

"We will rally our banners; we will call upon Andrinar and the Island Coalition to add their might to ours.

"We will take our ships, and sail to Triah itself. We will strike at the heart of the Khalic nation, and do what so many of our ancestors wished they could have done.

"We will conquer the greatest nation, and the greatest city, on the Sfaera."

Baetrissa's Cathedral, Mavenil

Funerals are always a bleak business, Alain thought. *Especially when it's the funeral of someone close to you. Someone you thought, one day, you might love. Someone you thought might love you back.*

He stood in the back of Baetrissa's Cathedral, despite his misgivings. The coffin was simple, dark wood. The pews were filled to overflowing. Outside the chapel, more people crowded around and back into the streets of Mavenil. Alain suspected this was one of the largest funerals in the history of Maven Kol.

The Cantic high priestess lit a candle at the shrine, then took her place at the pulpit, throwing back the hood of her robe.

"We gather here together," she said, her voice low and carrying, "to mourn the passing of a soul who knew the meaning of sacrifice. We mourn our great king, Gainil Destrinar-Kol, and celebrate his life and reign."

Alain smiled, turned, and walked out of the cathedral. He did not need to be here for this. He'd made his peace with Gainil.

Heedless of the stares and judging looks, he wove through the crowd on the street, pushing his way back and, eventually, out of the city.

She was waiting for him outside the city gates.

"Didn't want to stay 'til the end?" Morayne asked. She didn't smile. Her throat still bore the angry red marks of Lailana's grip, the pain of it etched clearly on her face. Recovery would be a long time coming.

"I've never liked endings. You gave my letter to Sev?"

She nodded, lifting a pack at her feet and handing it to him. "I did. You've officially resigned the kingship and given power to the Denizens. You are now the second king in history to give up his crown."

Alain took his pack, hefting it by the straps. Heavy, and solid. He liked the feel of it.

"It won't be easy for the Denizens, at first. It may never be easy for them. Many nobles will resist. Some of the commoners won't want the responsibility. Blood will still be shed."

"It will," Morayne said. "But it's the right thing to do."

Alain was about to slip the pack over his shoulders when Morayne stopped him. "We have a long journey ahead of us," she said. "And a lot of work to do."

"True," Alain said. He looked into her eyes. "We'll probably never finish. We can seek all the Triggers we want, but we'll never find them all. And the ones we do… who knows whether we can even help them?" It would be as impossible as pouring the desert sands into a glass. And yet, this time, Alain embraced the impossibility of it.

"We can start, one person at a time," Morayne said. "Brother Maddagon's work will go beyond him, and then beyond us."

Take what you've learned, what you are, and share that with others.

Alain had a thought. "I'm broken," he said quietly.

Morayne snorted. "Tell me about it."

"I'm broken," Alain repeated, "and that's all right."

This time she met his eyes. "I know. So am I. And that's all right."

Alain smiled. Bloody bones, it felt good to say that out loud.

He tried to slip his pack on again, but once more, she stopped him.

"What?" he asked.

"We have a long journey ahead of us," she repeated. "We should probably stretch before we begin."

That brought a smile to Alain's lips, and joy to his heart.

Alain leaned down and kissed her. She wrapped her arms around him, and they stood there for a moment, fitting together perfectly.

"Now we can go," she said, picking up her own pack.

Alain finally slipped his over his shoulders, the weight heavy but bearable, the smile still on his face.

The flames were still there, in the back of his mind. Panic still simmered in his gut. But he did not worry about them anymore. He still could not handle them; he'd never been able to do that. But there was something greater out there that could.

Morayne still did not return his smile. Not yet. But, he'd decided, that was his life's mission. To see that third smile. And the fourth. And the fifth and sixth, and so on, into the rest of their lives.

ABOUT THE AUTHOR

CHRISTOPHER HUSBERG GREW UP in Eagle River, Alaska. He now lives in Utah, and spends his time writing, reading, hiking, and playing video games, but mostly hanging out with his wife, Rachel, and daughter, Buffy. He received an MFA in creative writing from Brigham Young University, and an honorary PhD in *Buffy the Vampire Slayer* from himself. The first novel in the Chaos Queen Quintet, *Duskfall,* was published in 2016.

www.christopherhusberg.com
@usbergo

ACKNOWLEDGMENTS

FIRST OF ALL, I owe a big thank you to Sam Matthews for going through the editorial process with me on this book. She did phenomenal work, and this book would not be what it is without her. Thank you as well to the whole team at Titan for putting together these books.

As always, thank you to Sam Morgan for being the agent I deserve, not the agent I want. (Just kidding, Sam! I love you and I want you and don't ever leave meeeeeeee!) Seriously, though, you're the best agent I could imagine. You're like… the platonic ideal of an agent. What, now I'm laying it on too thick? Fine. Look, Sam, you're an amazing agent and a great friend. I'm grateful to know you. That's truth.

Thanks to my writing group, "Accidental Erotica" (it's a thing, we have T-shirts), for being awesome and for offering incredible feedback. I'm so grateful to have a space where I can get together with writers and talk about writing and I get to do that with you all and I love that. And, of course, a HUGE thank you to Janci Patterson for her feedback and input with this book. Janci, you're a brilliant writer and I'm grateful to be your friend.

I must also thank Dave Butler, a man touched by the genius of Edward M. Kovel himself, for tag-teaming it with me across the western states, hosting an awesome writing retreat, writing good books, and being a fantastic friend. (Are you noticing a trend of good friends, here? I'm a fortunate guy.)

A quick throwback shoutout: thank you to Steve and Kristi—may your basement forever be known as the place in which Duskfall became a book! I love you both.

Thank you to my amazingly supportive family and friends. A special thank you to Camille for being an incredible nanny to my daughter, Buffy.

Speaking of whom, thank you, Buffy, for being you. I love every moment watching you (and, on occasion, helping you) grow up. You are a bright light in my life.

And, always, thank you to Rachel for being an incredible support, my love, my life, my best friend. We're awesome, aren't we?

DUSKFALL

THE CHAOS QUEEN QUINTET

Christopher Husberg

Pulled from a frozen sea, pierced by arrows and close to death, Knot has no memory of who he was. But his dreams are dark, filled with violence and unknown faces. Winter, a tiellan woman whose people have long been oppressed by humans, is married to and abandoned by Knot on the same day. In her search for him, she will discover her control of magic, but risk losing herself utterly. And Cinzia, priestess and true believer, returns home to discover her family at the heart of a heretical rebellion. A rebellion that only the Inquisition can crush…

Their fates and those of others will intertwine, in a land where magic and daemons are believed dead, but dark forces still vie for power.

"A delicious mix of Jason Bourne, dark fantasy, and horror. The kind of debut that has me thrilled for the future of fantasy."
Steve Diamond, author of *Residue*

"A fascinating mystery that slowly unfolds, and cultures and religions in conflict. Enjoy."
Melinda Snodgrass, author of *The Edge of Reason*

TITANBOOKS.COM